GLASBY'S

FORTUNE

Glasby's Fortune

James H. Drescher

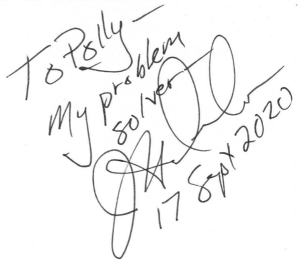

To Polly —
My problem
solver

17 Sept 2020

DEADEYE

Glasby's Fortune
Copyright© 2017 James H. Drescher

www.facebook.com/glasbysfortune
www.jaydrescherlaw.com

Published by Deadeye Press
8112 Isabella Lane, Suite 103
Brentwood, Tennessee 37027

Editions
Paperback: ISBN: 978-0-9989369-1-8
eBook: ISBN: 978-0-9989369-0-1

Cover Design: Mario Lampic

International English Language Version

Dedicated to a great writer and
a great friend, Mark K. Gilroy.

Author's Note

PIRATES—THE WORD CONJURES UP familiar images of swashbuckling adventurers rebelling against authority and convention.

Given their mythical status, it is perplexing that Bartholomew Roberts dwells in relative obscurity. Roberts seized more than 400 prizes which arguably makes him the most successful captain to sail the Caribbean. One might argue his success was enhanced by the navigator he kidnapped in 1720; Harry Glasby. In addition to Roberts, Glasby encountered other real men like pirate Valentine Ashplant, Royal Navy Captain Chaloner Ogle and his kind surgeon, John Atkins.

The collision of their lives inspired this story.

You will encounter various seagoing vessels, most of which existed. You will not have to wrestle with jargon-filled descriptions of their sailing characteristics. You will need to know port from starboard and you've likely seen a deadeye, made of elm or ash, in the rigging of a ship. Deadeyes will become familiar to you soon enough.

As for dates, most are historically correct as are the events that coincide. The brooding Cape Coast Castle still stands on the coast of Africa and the manicured gardens outside its thick walls were real.

Because *Glasby's Fortune* strives to honor the historical record and avoid distracting stereotypes, there are no parrots, eye-patches or peg-legs. I even struggled with use of the word 'booty'. I used it, but sparingly.

Embellishments aside, the real world of pirates was populated with complex and violent men. While Harry Glasby would agree, it was a world he struggled to escape but a world, nonetheless, populated with rogues and outcasts who continue to fascinate us with their exploits and depredations.

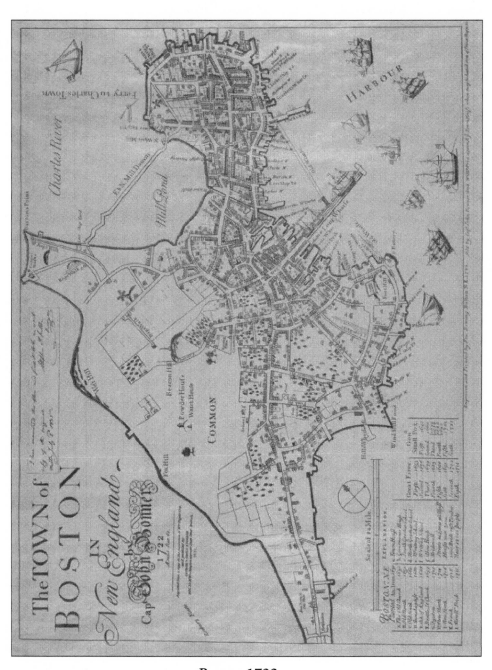

Boston 1722

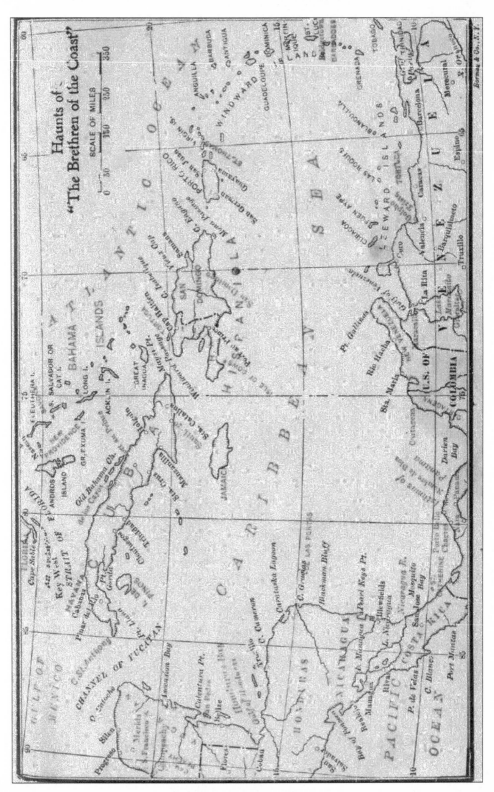

The Caribbean Sea

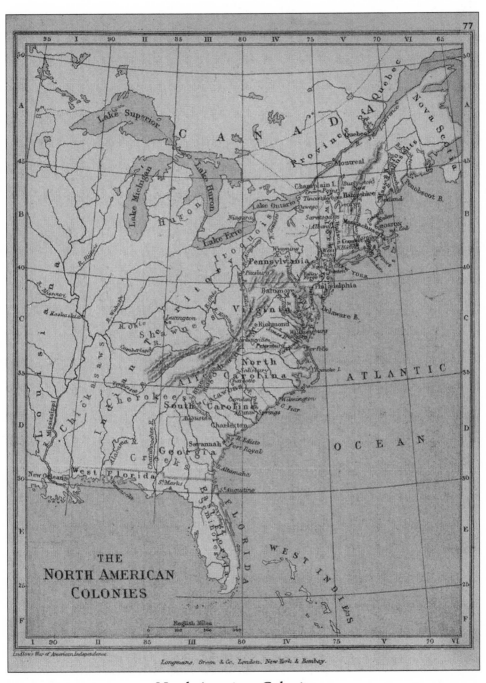

North American Colonies

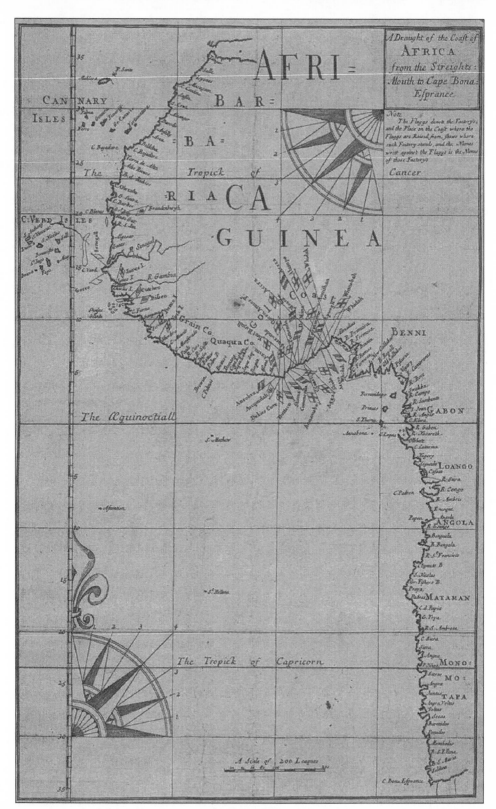

Western Africa

Glasby's Fortune

"Fortune brings in some boats that are not steer'd"

William Shakespeare (Cymbeline)

Chapter 1
July 13, 1720

SOME HAVE SAID THE IMPACT pirates would have on my life was foretold the day I was born. If there was such a sign, it would have taken a seer to divine its significance although it was not long before pirates struck their first blow.

Five years after my birth, condemned pirates in the Boston jail cut my father's throat. Two days later, my mother clutched my hand as we watched ropes looped around the necks of the bad men. I heard them drop and watched them kick. If you've seen a man hang, I'll wager much you haven't forgotten and take it from me, you won't. My ears rang with the screams and jeers of a tumultuous mob thirsting for revenge and entertainment, but mostly entertainment. After all, I reasoned, did any of those pirates kill your father?

The death of an unremarkable jailer gained these brigands nothing but I would later know men who kill merely for the pleasure of seeing other men die. Not all such men become pirates and not all pirates kill for sport, but since a man can only be executed once, the murder cost these pirates nothing.

It cost my mother everything, because once my father was dead, all she had left was me.

After seven painful years, my mother died from grief. The alcohol she believed would ease her suffering hastened her demise and I buried her next to my father.

I went to sea on a merchantman as orphans often do. I had to become a man before I was thirteen. My grief was short-lived and the freedom and adventure of being on my own filled me with such joy I felt guilty. I blame the Puritans for that. Landsmen said I had nowhere else to go but the sea proved to be my refuge and my home, sailors my family. The vast and endless sea seemed to accept this arrangement and she was good to me. I learned about men, I learned about ships and I learned the ways of the sea, but I never lost my immense respect for her limitless power. The secret to lifelong love is mutual respect. As for me and the sea, even though I abandoned her decades ago, I love her still.

On a pleasant day in July, 1720, pirates led by the infamous Bartholomew Roberts made me their prisoner, forcing me to be their navigator. My kidnapping was days after my twenty-first birthday. During my captivity, I bore witness to the brutal hanging of an innocent man, shootings, men drowning, beheadings, stabbings, and scenes of bloody torture. I watched scores of terrified men burned alive. The men I saw die due to sickness is beyond counting.

When the pirate captain who kidnapped me perished, I stood over him as he writhed on the deck of the *Royal Fortune*. Bartholomew Roberts bled from a round hole in his neck as loyal men he had long commanded watched the life flow out of him. When he breathed his last, his earthly remains were sent to the bottom of the sea, as he had ordained.

Captain Roberts escaped the noose yet it was his death, at long last, that finally set me free.

Life is about choices and I tell you true, I've done wicked things, things I have struggled, in vain, to forget. Fate says we don't always have the liberty of charting our own course. With due regard to Fate, who never fails to play her hand, it was because of the choices I made that I've been able to live a long and prosperous life.

This is my tale.

We were sailing the sloop *Samuel* back to Scarlett's Wharf in Boston Harbor under the imminently capable Captain Samuel Cary. It had been my first journey to London and I'd been promoted to sailing master a year before. There were nine good men who made up our crew and we carried a dozen passengers. During four rainy days in London, at the docks in Wapping, we were occupied unloading and loading the sloop and had little time for frolic. On our return, we carried forty-five barrels of gunpowder, ironware and assorted English goods packed in trunks and bales. We were armed with ten guns but only six were mounted on carriages.

"We're forty miles off the banks of Newfoundland. If this weather holds we should make Boston late tomorrow," I said.

Cary was distracted. He raised his glass to look off the port bow. I followed his gaze but saw nothing.

"Two ships approaching," he said.

"Aye, sir. Can you see their colors?"

"No, but they're heading right at us so it won't be long. We're too low in the water to distance ourselves from them. They're closing." His suggestion that we would want to distance ourselves from the approaching ships made my heart skip a beat.

I was tempted to borrow Cary's expensive brass spyglass but thought better of it. As the ships came into view, I saw worry in the captain's eyes. The passengers and crew gathered on the rail, straining to see what was coming at us, and why.

The larger vessel was double-masted and looked to be over two hundred tons. "God save us," Captain Cary whispered. An enormous black flag was being hoisted on the topmast. The white skull removed any doubt as to their intentions. The bigger vessel was near enough for us to count the open gun ports and see movement on the deck. The second vessel was also a sloop, about eighty tons.

Reynolds, a member of our crew called out, "sir, that's Bartholomew Roberts."

"Steady. Steady please. Stay calm," Cary responded. To his credit, our helmsman took the order literally and said nothing. I, on the other hand, was anything but calm.

"What now?"

"We're at their mercy Harry. There's a hundred men on each of those ships, twenty to one."

Captain Cary surveyed the thin group of men anxiously watching the pirates approach. "Pass the word, best to keep weapons out of sight." While I relayed the order the big ship fired her heavy guns and two explosions erupted from her port side. I was already tense and the boom startled me and made me grind my teeth. When I hurried back to the captain he gave me a pat on the back which reassured me, but not much. He had always been kind and I felt a twinge of shame for worrying only about my own well-being. Captain Cary would have to deal with these marauders and if something went wrong, who knew what they might do to him.

Pirates could be unspeakably cruel and all of us knew gory tales of murder and torture meted out by pirates to defiant sea captains who refused to offer immediate surrender and complete cooperation. In light of the notoriety of certain blood-soaked captains, of whom

Bartholomew Roberts was without equal, no sane man would resist a pirate attack unless success was guaranteed.

After the report of the cannon blasts an unearthly and altogether different noise emanated from the approaching vessels, growing louder with each passing second. Men were blaring trumpets and horns, hulking black men pounded drums and capering houtboys made an infernal racket on oboes. This cacophony was designed to assault a man's mind by passing through his ears, making it impossible to conjure up rational thoughts. It was not music. Adding to the tumult, pirates chanted and called out vile and profane threats. There was a method to this tribal display and it had a name—'vaporing'.

Vaporing was meant to terrify and it was working.

Someone with a speaking trumpet called from the bow of the larger ship, "captain, hoist out your boat and come aboard."

Having no choice our captain did as he was told. I watched his smallish form in the launch, bravely and resolutely riding across the choppy waves. He maintained his dignity as he struggled to climb aboard the larger ship while two of our men remained in the boat, loosely tied to the side. We had one pirate ship on our port and the other off to starboard. I gawked at blackened faces of men on their decks bearing long muskets, gleaming cutlasses and axes. Their vaporing was so loud I wondered how the pirates could bear the discomfort.

As if on some invisible signal or secret command, with a roaring, guttural cheer, a seething mass of demons poured over our rails and attacked our hatches with swords and axes. They dragged bales and trunks and wooden crates up from our hold. Berserk men smashed our trade goods, ripping and tearing rope, canvas, and wood, scattering the contents across the deck. They were laughing and cursing and bickering and awkwardly tripping over the debris created by their frenzy.

Their bloodshot eyes were bulging with an unnatural love of mayhem. Fear, pure and absolute, inundated and enveloped our helpless crew and our mortified passengers. Pistol shots cracked amidst a stream of threats spewing from sweating maniacs who bore a startling resemblance to a horde of savage beasts.

Pandemonium wormed its way into my bowels, turning my innards to brackish water. Would I be burned, hanged, skinned alive, or, if I was fortunate, would they just cut my throat? With our captain gone and no one to turn to, I completely lost my composure, I was without a rudder. Convinced I was about to soil myself, I fled the maelstrom to preserve what little sanity and whatever dignity remained.

Groping my way down the dark companionway, I was shocked at not being molested. Arriving below decks, I found an empty storage cupboard on the port side amidships. I squeezed inside, barely, drawing my shaking knees to my chin and gingerly reached out to pull the door shut, expecting to have my hand hacked off at the wrist. I sat trembling, trying in vain to quiet my breathing which seemed as loud as mid-winter breakers crashing on the rocks of the Block Island lighthouse.

The shouting and thudding overhead merged with the clanging of pots, kettles and pans being kicked down the passageway. Glass shattered and one of the heavy copper pots clanged to a stop immediately in front of my hiding place. I felt a man thundering down the passage. Judging by the way the planking shook he was huge and his outburst of crude oaths echoed against the bulkheads. He gave the pot a resounding kick, which must have hurt because he yelled, "Jesus Christ, damn that fuckin' pot." The pot landed with a clang, bounced and bounded in the direction of the galley.

The terror affected others. One or two men were sobbing in the midst of the incessant shouting. As was later reported in the August 1720 *Boston News Letter,* witnesses reported that Bartholomew Roberts threatened any who refused to hand over their valuables with instant death. It was also reported, accurately I might add, that swarms of pirates ripped open the hatches 'like a parcel of furies', breaking open everything they could lay their hands on. What they did not want they threw over the side. From my dark hiding place, every time I heard a splash I cringed, believing my friends were being murdered and their bodies dumped over the side.

A boot shattered the thin cupboard door, peppering me with splinters as I clamped my eyes shut. "Come out you cowardly shit." Whoever was after me, it was not the pirate who had angrily kicked kettles. My burly antagonist dropped to his knees and shot his filthy hand at me, clawing at my face to get purchase and growling in frustration. I sought unsuccessfully to make myself smaller and put my hands over my eyes. He finally succeeded in getting a grip on my wrist and jerked so hard I thought he pulled my shoulder out of its socket. "Captain wants you, you sniveling sack of snot."

Half dragged and half stumbling, I found myself blinking in the glare of the afternoon sun, face to face with the Devil Roberts. He spoke confidently and in a firm manner, like a man accustomed to being in charge and the undisputed master of anyone within earshot.

"I see you've learned a farthing cannot be hidden on a ship scoured by scores of pirates." He seemed unimpressed by what he saw and picked at his teeth with an elegantly pointed dagger, the hilt of which was decorated with faceted red rubies. He leaned closer and I could smell his foul breath and see the black powder burns in the pitted pores of his sun browned cheeks. As I drew away he smiled sardonically, "they tell me you are chief mate. Is this so? Answer me or I'll put this dagger in your eye."

If you have ever been threatened by an insouciant madman laden with pistols and cutlasses, with splotches of dried blood festooning his person, then you will know why I looked at Captain Roberts and without the slightest hesitation replied, "yes my Lord, I am the chief mate of the *Samuel.*"

"Wrong you are," he said. His response frightened me for I had answered directly and with candor. I had no desire to antagonize these murderers and I was not, by nature, defiant. He gazed past me, stepping sideways and pointing in the direction of some damaged crates about to be hoisted onto the larger of the two ships, ordering his men, "take those to the galley and be quick about it."

Turning his attention back to me, he doffed his grand and weathered hat by one of its three corners and bent forward to wave it with his out-stretched arm, announcing with a hint of pomposity, "the name is Bartholomew Roberts, captain to you."

"Glasby, Harry Glasby of Boston in the Massachusetts Bay colony".

Returning his tricorn hat to this head he brought his hand down on my sore shoulder, "Harry Glasby of Boston eh? Well, Glasby, you are no longer 'of Boston' nor are you of the Massachusetts Bay colony. You are henceforth Chief Mate Glasby of the *Good Fortune* and I have the honor and privilege of being your new captain." I was too shaken to respond, protest, quibble, or ask any of the thousand and one questions vying for priority on the tip of my uncooperative tongue. Had he dubbed me King George, I would have obliged the man and offered to make him a knight of the realm.

Roberts beckoned for Captain Cary who came back aboard the *Samuel.* Illogically perhaps, seeing Cary alive and unharmed made me believe I might survive this nascent ordeal. I was, of course, unable to comprehend the full scope of what was happening, futilely wishing that all the discord was the product of a particularly vivid nightmare.

"Ajax, Seahorse. Take their large sails and that rigging. Take two of the mounted cannons, the two that are easiest to move, leave the rest. Make sure the powder is safe and dry. Time is precious, sails have been spotted to the northeast and we have no time to tarry." The pirates obeyed and seemed to operate with heightened efficiency.

Two members of our crew sullenly slouched near the *Samuel's* stern. I recognized one as an Irishman who had signed on in London two days after our arrival. The other, a seaman from Salem, was holding his arm at an awkward angle.

Roberts was lecturing Captain Cary, "and please tell the fine people of Boston we will never accept the King's pardon. We are free men. In the unlikely event we are captured we will set fire to the powder with a pistol and all go merrily to hell."

Captain Roberts was alluding to the controversial decision taken by King George I to offer a full and unconditional pardon to any man who had engaged in piracy. The King's approach embodied elements of the carrot and the stick. The September 1717 proclamation commanded ". . . Admirals, Captains and other Officers at Sea, and all our Governors and Commanders of any forts or castles to seize and take such of the Pirates . . ." A reward of one hundred pounds was offered for the capture of a captain, forty pounds for an officer, to wit; lieutenant, boatswain, carpenter, gunner, or master; and for every seaman, twenty pounds. These were substantial sums but who in their right mind would seek to confront the sort of men I watched demolishing the *Samuel?*

Men possessing the skills of a carpenter, surgeon, navigator, cooper or gunner were known, collectively and admiringly, as artists. Because of their expertise, I had heard of artists being forced to serve pirate crews but never had I envisioned such a fate, tending to believe as all men do that unpleasant things, like being kidnapped by pirates, inevitably involves others. The more unpleasant or unusual the event in question, the stronger the belief that such things befall other men.

Piracy was on the rise and its impact on the flow of commerce in and around the West Indies and the colonies was enormous. I was shocked that pirates were operating this far north. The King's pardon was part of a pantheon of tactics being tried in a vain effort to rid the seas of desperate and brutal men who knew no law but force and violence. Rumor said some had accepted a pardon but many of those, unable to feed themselves or, perhaps, missing the life, returned to marauding despite the ever present risk of disease, deprivation and for many, the necklace of hemp.

Roberts defied the King's offer with contempt and disdain and threatened to blow himself to Kingdom Come if captured. His haughty demeanor suggested he found the prospect of capture unlikely. Nonetheless, for me and my shipmates, capture would be our salvation, our rescue.

I grimly admitted there would be no rescue and no miracle from man or angel on this day. This was not a dream. As I stood on the deck of the *Samuel*, there was a sliver of hope that dared believe Fortune might provide me with a chance to escape, maybe soon enough to make landfall before harvest season. Hope is not always rational.

Knowing that Fortune has a will of her own, I resolved in the meantime to do all I could to preserve my life. Whatever resolve I could muster was not the result of bravado or some reserve of inner strength, nor was it a product of fortitude or defiant determination.

It was the only choice I had.

Chapter 2
The Articles

"I'M SEAHORSE, THE BOSUN. Captain said to get you aboard. Your things?" The bosun had thick lips, flaring nostrils, high cheekbones and tightly curled hair the color of coal. He wore a blue and white shirt with horizontal stripes. I recognized it as a shirt acquired in London just a few days ago by one of my shipmates. The pirate was compact and muscular and had a smooth, light brown complexion, suggesting he was not all of one race. I stammered, "things? Yes, my things are below." He followed me to my cabin and I picked up my sea bag which had been emptied on the deck.

"It's probably gone," Seahorse said. He'd watched me run my hand across the smooth boards where I slept and under which I'd wedged a brown leather purse in a crevice. The purse held a ring and my coins, including two gold sovereigns. I met his steady gaze and shrugged my shoulders, "you're right, it's gone." He watched me jam what was left of my clothing and three books in my canvas sea bag.

Arching an eyebrow, he asked "you read eh? Those books yours?"

"I read."

A tall man joined us and told Seahorse in a French accent, "get his charts and instruments,oui?" The tall man had brown hair bound with silk ribbons, a single braid hung down the middle of his back. He held my small leather purse in his clenched fist. When he caught me looking at it he slid his hand behind his back. "Your maps monsieur?"

"Follow me," I said, annoyed he had stolen my valuables and made a pretense of trying to hide the deed.

While I gathered the charts and maps I needed to navigate, a conglomeration called a 'waggoner', Seahorse absentmindedly fingered a flintlock pistol stuck in his tooled black leather belt. The pistol was beautifully decorated with ornate brass filigree.

"You going to shoot me?" I asked.

The Frenchman answered, "captain says you are to join us. He would not much like to have you shot. Lucky for you." He was jovial and that annoyed me too.

"Yes, I feel very lucky. Why does your captain need me to be his sailing master?" There were more maps and charts than I remembered.

"Our sailing master, rest his soul. He died. Of the flux. So they said. He was often sick. Do you have everything, we must be away." The Frenchman took my seabag and motioned toward the hatch, his braid swinging behind him.

"Away", he repeated.

"When did he die?"

Seahorse made a noise like someone gagging, "like Jacques said, our chief mate was often sick. Alas we have a young and healthy sailing master now. You." He smiled and pointed at my chest.

The *Samuel's* great cabin had been torn asunder but I salvaged what I needed, to include all my instruments. "Are you taking me to the *Good Fortune?*"

Seahorse looked at me like I suffered from a serious mental deficiency, "where else would we be taking you? The rest of your crew is going to the *Sea King*. All but three." I was not the only man being taken, as if that would make me feel better about my predicament.

"The *Sea King*? They are not killing anyone." A chill ran down my spine. "Is that sloop the *Sea King*?"

"We must go. Your captain has enough men. One man had his arm broken while trying to hide. He still has one arm in working order. Captain Roberts said there was no reason to kill them. We were going to burn the *Samuel* but he said no to that too. Move." Seahorse gave me a shove.

We got to the deck and I spotted Captain Cary. He waved and mouthed the words "good luck". Responding in kind, I mouthed "thank you". I was grateful for all he had done, figuring I would never see him again, but I was relieved to know his life would be spared and he was being allowed to go unharmed.

The deck of the pirate vessel, the *Good Fortune,* was crowded with barrels and rigging and canvas hauled over from the *Samuel*. As soon as I was on board a gap appeared between our hulls and we were soon underway. The familiar sounds of the canvas sails snapping in the wind gave me some comfort and I felt the brigantine ease forward. Every ship has its own unique sailing characteristics when it comes to fair winds, foul weather and stormy seas. A sailing master must learn these quirks in addition to possessing the refined skills of a navigator. The *Good Fortune* was a more complicated vessel than our familiar and forlorn sloop, receding and growing smaller in the distance.

"Seahorse, you said men were left to aid Captain Cary. Not the one with the broken arm. Who else?"

"An Irishman and a cook."

"Rafferty Moran. Why him?"

"Glasby, you have much to learn. Captain Roberts hates the Irish. Your Moran was left because Irish are never to be trusted." He relayed his explanation as if I was a child, as if he had been telling me that the moon caused the tides. I murmured, "aye, luck o' the Irish," admitting it was part of being an Englishman to loath the Irish. How a Welshman like Bartholomew Roberts fit into that never ending feud was a mystery but I had to concede, there was something not quite right about Moran.

Seahorse guided me past all the staring and curious faces to my new berthing area. At least they weren't looking at me with hostility.

There is never enough room for everyone and everything on a sailing vessel. Everyone knows what a sailing ship looks like on the outside, cutting majestically through the waves, billowing sails, foam and scud flying. What completes a ship are the things and men inside it. A pirate vessel in particular is a hive of activity with men crowded like ants; colliding, conversing, cursing, laughing, eating, sleeping and all the things men do. To feed these men, the decks and the hold are crowded with live cattle, hogs, goats, chickens and more often than not, an array of dogs and cats. Captain Cary was not far off when it came to his estimate of the size of the crew, if anything, he was on the lean side. Then there are spare parts, rigging, equipment, weapons, and foodstuffs stacked from the deck to the overhead and lashed in place to avoid injury and mishap.

I was directed to a hammock on the starboard side of the ship near the forecastle. I dropped my bag and was escorted to the captain's cabin to stow the maps, charts and instruments from the *Samuel*.

The captain's cabin, or the great cabin, is a refuge from the crowded, damp and aromatic parts of the vessel and as I would soon learn, any may enter with or without a reason, according to the rules of life as a pirate. Even so, sailors respect the sanctity of the captain's space, which serves as a formal dining room, office and bedchamber.

"Beg pardon sir," Seahorse said. Captain Roberts had his back to us, facing the large array of glass windows in the stern. The sashes were open which made the cabin seem larger. His crimson coat was tossed over a table along with his tricorn hat and a black silk sash. I recognized the jeweled dagger he had used to pick his teeth. We were sailing east southeast and the sun was going from burnt orange to a deep red. The sea was rolling gently with long slashes of white as the shallow waves gently broke.

"Thank you Seahorse, please invite the quartermaster and Mr. Sharp to join us." Seahorse left us and Captain Roberts looked over his shoulder and shot me a cursory glance.

"Take a seat Mr. Glasby." I surveyed various unmatched chairs scattered around a long and battered oak table, choosing the one farthest from the stern, farthest from the captain. "Our quartermaster is an important fellow. Wales, like the country, not the sea creature." Roberts' frame was silhouetted by the setting sun but he did deign to turn his head to give me another quick inspection. He seemed content to let me sit in silence.

Roberts had a swarthy complexion, even darker than Seahorse. He had thick black hair, crudely parted in the middle and hanging in ringlets to his shoulders. Several days of stubble made him appear even darker and he bore two white scars, one extending from his lower lip on the left, downward across his chin to the jaw line and the other bisected his right eyebrow. He had the intelligent eyes of a curious man and long eyelashes that curved gently but were in no way effeminate. Roberts was a man women would consider handsome inasmuch as his features were somewhat unremarkable when taken individually but in relation to one another there was something striking about their proportions. It also occurred to me that Roberts was the type most men would not want to fight. He had to be close to forty but had the easy gait and energy of a younger man.

His intimidating presence was undeniable, but beyond that, he projected an aura of quiet determination. He seemed entirely comfortable wielding unquestioned authority over men who cared little for discipline. My initial impressions about his character and the ease with which he exercised command would prove to be remarkably accurate.

He knew I was sizing him up.

Earlier that day I had money, a fine captain, a solid knowledge of seafaring and every reason to believe I would soon be lying in a featherbed with the smell of fresh baked bread in my nostrils. Now I was nervously sitting in the cabin of a notorious pirate who had the gall to seize me as his new sailing master because some other murdering thief picked this week to get sick and die.

Bartholomew Roberts was one among dozens of lawless men who prowled the sea lanes to rape, plunder and murder. Their depredations were known wherever civilized men lived in the Americas and throughout France, Holland, England, Spain and Portugal. At one time or another these countries issued letters of marque to privateers authorizing the bearer to prey on ships flying certain foreign flags. The enemy of my enemy or some such nonsense. Pirates sometimes claimed to be privateers lacking the proper papers. To me, papers or not, they were common thieves, loosely descended from highwaymen who darted on horseback from the forest, pistols primed, and demanded the loot of rich people cowering in their enameled carriages. Europe was plagued by one war after another so it was hard to distinguish between friend and foe, privateer or pirate. Every time your queen or your king gained a new ally, the right to plunder might be rescinded but the lure of piracy, like strong drink, is a habit easy to acquire and hard to break. My honor was not to be forfeited or stolen and it certainly was not for sale.

I found my predicament and the silence oppressive, damn this arrogant man.

"Sir, I'm sure Captain Cary told you I am Irish, " my words sounded flat even to me. Captain Roberts lowered his folded arms and turned, leaning on the far end of the oak table, gazing at me with a bemused expression.

"Glasby." He enunciated my name. "You have heard that your new captain is not so fond of the Irish. Is anyone? Has anyone told you how I feel about liars? Your Captain Cary is a man of honor. He said he had one Irishman in his crew and none who were passengers. I do not recall that the sailor was called Glasby. He did tell me that you were a fine sailing master and that your skills were far beyond your years. Your friend offered to pay a ransom to keep you behind. Of course, he had to offer in the form of a promise to pay—my men are known for being very diligent when it comes to finding money and valuables on a ship. They left nothing behind. They even found your poorly hidden purse. Fate or the Devil, take your pick, took my sailing master and I found you. Fortune has a way, sometimes, of smiling on the undeserving. Your misfortune, my lucky day. Odd that, very odd. I strive to make my own good fortune. My sailing master was adequate but he was ill, often as not. Your captain put a high value on you, a very high value, a sum I was obliged by circumstances to decline. I need you more than I needed Captain Cary's promissory note. To make matters better for me I daresay, you look like the picture of health."

"So I'm your prisoner and if I don't do your bidding your men will abuse me or kill me depending on Fortune's whim. Slave sounds like a better word. Sir."

"I know the stories you hear Harry. I do. You may have been a slave before but you, in all likelihood, will never be as free as you are at this moment. We needed more men to sail the *Pink Rover,* our consort, and I needed a sailing master. I also need a surgeon and we are forever in need of gunners and good musicians. Bad musicians, not so much. Your friends who are now on the *Rover* are needed too or we would not have taken them. Unless they sign The Articles, no one will make them go over the side in a fight nor will they be made to search and question passengers and crew. We have plenty who relish that. Some relish it too much. But your friends will perform the duties of a seaman and maintain the ship when we do not sail. And you will guide us. I know men. I assure you that we will provide your needs and I assure you that no one on this ship will harm you without reason. Ah, what reason you ask. Should you attack one of us, steal from us, or betray us in some way, you will find yourself in danger. You are not special Harry Glasby but none of us are. We're all the same here and we have rules, as you shall see." Roberts sat in a high-backed chair which was missing a spindle or two, tossing his crossed feet up on the table with a thud, leaning back on the rear legs like a pampered schoolboy.

Seahorse rapped twice on the hatch then stuck his head in, "captain, a thousand pardons. I had a time finding Mr. Sharp, he and Wales are on their way. Would you and Glasby like a cup of tea? I can have some sent in rightly." I looked at Seahorse to see if he was joking. He appeared to be serious.

Roberts asked me politely, "Mr. Glasby, do you like tea? Or, I can offer you rum, grog, and thanks to the *Samuel* I think ale is among your choices. Seahorse, do we have ale?"

"Yes sir. Uh, I think so. I can check." He waited for instructions.

My host added as an afterthought, "we have coffee I believe. It is the color of soot and tastes much the same. I've tried it once or twice."

I declined the rum, grog and ale but tea was tempting. I had tried coffee in one of the newest and most popular coffee houses in London and agreed it was an acquired taste.

"Bring us a pot of tea." Roberts said, "and plenty of sugar, I've run out again."

"Aye sir." Seahorse touched his forelock and turned to go while the quartermaster and Sharp made their apologies for being hard to locate and took seats on either side of the table. Roberts took his feet down so we could do whatever it was that needed doing.

The quartermaster offered me his hand and I took it. "I'm Wales, like the country not the sea animal. That embarrassingly ugly man who claims to assist me from time to time, when he is not drunk or asleep, is Mr. Sharp, Mr. Hunter Sharp. All he ever does is drink and sleep." Wales sat to my left. Sharp's eyes were rimmed with red and he had the dizzy look of someone who was lost.

Words cascaded out of Wales with unusual rapidity, his voice mellow like warm molasses. Wales was squarely built, just above my height. Active years at sea had given him strength and his skin was reddened and bronzed by the wind and the sun. His eyes were lively and gave the impression of a man who likes to enjoy himself. I pegged him to be in his early thirties.

"Harry Glasby," I said. "Forgive my manners but I will not claim that it's nice to make your acquaintance."

"Manners are not required aboard the *Good Fortune*. But you may learn that lack of manners in this group of murderers and lunatics carries a degree of risk. Right Hunter?" Wales stared at Hunter Sharp who stared back. "Lunatic," Wales muttered. Mr. Sharp either did not hear or did not care.

Captain Roberts pursed his lips and shook his head in the direction of Mr. Sharp then resumed cleaning his fingernails with the blade of a tiny folding knife.

"So, Mr. Glasby, did our esteemed captain promise you that these cutthroats and imbeciles would not harm you if you refuse to fall in and do your bit?" Wales paused a heartbeat, "Captain Roberts means well, he truly does. But you know how things work at sea. You do what you're told or bad things happen. Bad things Glasby. Bad men. Bad things. Ever been on the account?"

"I am no pirate if that's what you mean."

"Of course Harry. You are no pirate. Some men are born to this, others take to it gradually. Some refuse. Some are forced. That's when we have problems. When a man refuses it can cause problems. My job is to solve problems. Right Hunter?"

I joined Wales in staring at Mr. Sharp who slowly nodded his head, presumably in agreement. Hunter's eyes seemed more open than shut, it was hard to tell. If Wales said I was a wizard, I was certain the very odd Mr. Sharp would have concurred without dissent.

A slender black man came in with a tray, a steaming pot of tea and several matching painted china cups. He set a folded waxed paper packet full of brown sugar crystals and a small silver spoon in front of the captain. Roberts thanked the man, folded his knife, and poured two cups of tea and put sugar in each, stirring to his apparent satisfaction and sliding me a cup while Wales kept talking. The negro, who seemed to be a sort of servant, lit some scattered candles in hurricane lanterns.

The affable quartermaster declared, "I am a proud Welshman and so is your captain. Since the days of Henry Morgan, Wales has birthed many a fine pirate." Roberts raised his blue and white cup to acknowledge his countryman's compliment. "Captain Roberts, much like you Mr. Glasby, did not yearn to be a pirate while a young lad wandering the emerald hills of our beloved Wales. When he went to sea at thirteen, he aspired to be an able seaman. After many arduous years, he became that and more. It was just over a year ago I believe. My, how time passes. He was the third mate on the slave ship *Princess*. You likely never heard of Captain Abraham Plumb. Captain Plumb was a hard man but a fair man. Slaving is unpleasant and dangerous work, as you can appreciate. The *Princess* was anchored at Annamaboa along the Gold Coast and cruising in the vicinity were two other ships, the *Royal Rover* and the *Royal James*. Ever hear of them? " Wales asked, helping himself to a cup of tea.

"I have heard of Annamaboa in West Africa but neither vessel comes to mind," I confessed.

"Prowling then, not cruising. Sorry. They were hunting under the watchful eye of Captain Howell Davis. Ever hear of Davis? He was from Milford Haven in Pembrokeshire. Another great Welshman." Wales waited and I shook my head. I had heard the names of many pirates but not Howell Davis.

Roberts spoke, "Davis was a bold captain, but I didn't see it that way at first. When Davis took our ship, Captain Plumb was asked about the skills of his crew and he informed the pirates that I, your humble servant, was a navigator. Captain Davis forced me and several others to join him. He sought my advice about the ship and the countless problems posed by the men under his command. Before our second week ended, he started sharing information with me that was unknown to his crew. This put me at risk but I demonstrated that I could keep his confidences. I expect it was natural that I came to respect him. I told him I would be his navigator but I would not become a pirate. He accepted that. A few weeks later, we had to abandon the *Royal James* because of worm damage so we sailed into the harbor at the Island of Princes, hoisting the ensign of a British man-of-war to gain entry. Do you know how much I made in the merchant navy?"

"Not much," I answered.

"Less than three pounds a month, so not much. Because I lacked breeding and connections, I could never hope to be a captain. I was not a young man. Davis could force me to navigate and work, any sea captain can do that. Davis was too smart to force me to become a pirate. I was too smart not to seize the opportunity. In honest service there are thin commons, low wages and hard labor. As you can see, I have plenty, I have pleasure and I have ease. I have liberty and I have power."

There was nothing ominous or smug in Roberts' tone.

Captain Roberts gently sipped his tea, "we waited a few days and Captain Davis invited the governor of Princes Island to come aboard for a midday meal. The governor was Portuguese. We do not like governors Glasby. Davis' plan was to seize the governor and hold him for ransom. We are also not fond of the Portuguese, or the Spanish for that matter, but somehow they learned we were pirates. This was unbeknownst to us. Armed with this intelligence, they invited Davis to call at the fortress for a glass of wine. Captain Davis discussed their invitation with me and I urged him to decline, fearing a trap. He argued that to decline would endanger the plan so he ordered me to remain on the ship while he went ashore. On the way to the fort, he and our landing party were ambushed. Davis, may he rest in peace, was shot dead."

Wales raised his eyes skyward, then said, "the crew of the *Royal Rover* was divided into the 'Lords' and the 'Commons'. I am a Lord, naturally, and under our rules, the Lords had the right to go to the crew to propose a replacement for the murdered Davis. Mr. Glasby, in the days ahead, you will meet my fellow Lords, gentlemen of distinction to be sure. The great Slingsby Copplestone, Alexander Wedderburn, Basil Ringrose, and the irrepressible and sometimes irresponsible Skeffington Lutwidge. We are the captain's privy council. The Lords will do all in their power to make your stay as comfortable as possible, as they are wise men, and loyal. We Lords knew, and I believe the crew knew, that Captain Davis had affection for Roberts and more importantly, Davis put great trust in him. We set aside the fact that Roberts had not immediately joined us but Roberts demonstrated he would speak his mind and stand his ground. Captain Roberts, Bartholomew if you will, had only been with us for six weeks,which tells you much about the impression he made. He accepted the honor and told us 'that since he dipped his hands in muddy water and must be a pirate, 'tis better to be a commander than a commoner.'" Wales looked at his captain who was gazing at the darkening indigo sky and absentmindedly drinking his tea. Well, I thought, at least this pirate war lord has a thoughtful streak.

Wales pushed his chair back and stood, prompting Hunter Sharp to sit up straight, as if suddenly awakened. Wales procured a bottle, yanked the cork out with his teeth and poured two glasses of amber liquid. "Rum Glasby?" he offered, handing a glass to his addled partner. "I was afraid Hunter was falling asleep." Wales held the second glass toward me and I waved him off. He shrugged his shoulders and resumed his seat.

"This is good rum if you change your mind. As I was saying, Roberts, our new captain. What do you suppose he did first? Not only a brand new captain but a brand new pirate. We left the island but not before Captain Roberts laid out his plans. The Lords were astounded, I was astounded. You could smell the excitement of the crew as they went about their work. That night, we sailed back to the Island of Princes. Captain Roberts and the bulk of the crew landed on the beach and quietly made their way into the town. We killed every man who tried to stop us and carried away everything we could lay our hands on. We left the town in ruins and having avenged Captain Davis, we went back to sea and soon took a Dutch prize. Two days later, we took the *Experiment*, a British merchant ship out of Portsmouth. We took on provisions and water at Annamaboa. By now the crew was convinced that Captain Roberts was pistol proof. He called us together and put it to a vote, Brazil or the East Indies. We voted Brazil. But I tell you Glasby, the captain could have ordered us to sail to the gates of hell and we would have cheered him all the way. All the way." Wales smiled from ear to ear and drank his glass of rum in one great swallow, slamming the glass down on the table.

Wales fixed me with a look of sublime satisfaction.

"Gentlemen," said I, fighting the urge to sound facetious, "that is some tale. Even for pirates, it is a stirring tale. Captain Roberts, my compliments on all your accomplishments. Why, it's almost as if I'd be following in the master's footsteps. Forced first mate, late blooming pirate, a captain ambushed, the Lords anoint thee and you avenge Davis. In the dead of night no less. I suppose you think you can bring me here and tell me about these grand adventures and lure me into signing up?" I had unintentionally found myself neck deep in sarcasm.

Wales chuckled. Captain Roberts just looked at me paternalistically. Wales poured more rum and said to his captain, "I told you he was a bright one sir, he's got us pegged." Then to me, "I can only speak for me and the captain, Hunter is never all there. Yes, *of course* that's why we brought you here. Captain Roberts is so sick of hearing about how he became our captain I am forced to tell it. How can you not want to sign up after hearing all that?"

"Gentlemen, I will steer your ship but I will *not* become a pirate." I was angry and confused, in part because it was hard not to find something refreshing about Wales. This charming Welshman had the ability to disarm me by being so direct and forthright. Hunter looked at me as I grew adamant, his head moving slowly and deliberately, as if he slept wrong and hurt his neck. Wales was right about one thing, Hunter was not all there. "Rum?" he asked me out of the blue. I suspect that was his answer to every predicament. "None for me Mr. Sharp, no thanks. You may have my share," I told the delusional man. He closed his eyes but one after the other, or crossed them, it was hard to tell, nodded curtly and responded loudly and smartly, "why thank you".

I shook my head in disbelief at Mr. Sharp and their invitation to join the crew. Me, a pirate. The idea was ludicrous.

"I know you can read," Captain Roberts said as he produced a sheaf of papers and one page of parchment, all of which he laid on a silver platter. Next to the documents was a well-oiled pistol.

"You need me to read to you?" I said. He ignored the insult and handed Wales the tray who, in turn, offered it to me. Refusing the papers and the weapon, I demanded, "what, what can you possibly want of me?"

Wales said, somber and serious, "these are The Articles, signed by every member of this crew. To be more precise, signed by every man who is willing to put his life in the hands of his brothers. I've never known a ship flying the black that does not have articles or something akin to them. You'll read these to us, here and now. Whether you sign or not, you can never say you did not know the rules. See? Simple. If you elect not to sign, you'll know what you're giving up. Start with number one." He waited.

I could not believe this.

"So why the pistol?" I kept my hands to myself. Wales took the pistol and set it aside.

"Old pirate tradition. A would-be pirate must sign the Articles or shoot himself. The pistol is a symbol Mr. Glasby. If you do not sign, we will not make you blow your brains out. Every tradition has its exceptions, shall we continue?" Wales nudged the platter toward me, urging me to stop being stubborn. I decided the only way to get this over with was to go along with their ritual and, by now, I was curious about how men who shun rules purport to govern themselves.

"You know I will not sign." I thought it wise to hold my ground as much as I could.

Wales was growing edgy.

"Just read the damn papers," he said.

The Articles were written on yellowing parchment and the penmanship was remarkably good. There were meandering columns of marks and signatures, mostly marks. Some of the marks and names had a long black line written through them, some were names Wales had mentioned, like Alexander Wedderburn and Slingsby Copplestone. I knew what the black lines meant. I stared at the documents in my hands.

"Please proceed Harry," Roberts urged, not unkindly.

I cleared my throat.

"Every man shall have an equal vote in the affairs of moment. He shall have an equal title to provisions or strong liquors at the time seized and shall use them at pleasure unless a scarcity may make it necessary for the common good that retrenchment may be voted." Roberts and Wales knew the Articles but they were watching me intently in order to gauge my reaction. Most people in the world had little say in their lives and certainly not in the workings of governments that told them how to live, even how to worship. I was no man of the world but the last thing a man of influence or power would do is to give all men an 'equal vote in affairs of the moment'.

The same observation could apply to the foreign concept of sharing liquor and food. The rich always had plenty even when the poor starved. This article was too revolutionary to be used in the outside world. "Do you expect me to believe a mere seaman has the same power as you captain? And eats the same food and drinks the same drink? So you and Hunter have equal say?" The last part of my question would expose their ridiculous fraud.

"Hunter, tell Glasby." The captain seemed to be taking an inordinate chance asking for Hunter's view on this or any other subject.

Hunter pointed at his chest with his extended thumb. "We're equals. Him and me." Hunter, in turn, gestured with his thumb toward the captain and paused in what appeared to be an effort to gather his thoughts. "Equals, we are", he said, with a hint more enthusiasm.

Captain Roberts seemed relieved. "Read on Glasby. The Articles talk about the authority of a captain. You'll see. I serve at the pleasure of the crew, not the other way round. I have a debt to the men, an obligation. I daresay, since they had a hand in selecting me to be their captain, their obedience is of a firmer fiber, it being voluntary. Very unlike a peasant's obedience to his king, which can be forced or grudging. I ask you to name any man that can replace his king? It's a form of loyalty but on this vessel that loyalty runs both ways and that makes it stronger. You can accomplish much with loyalty, but you can do little without it."

I was skeptical about this whole scheme but was curious to see what other surprises were in store. "Two. Every man shall be called fairly in turn by the list on board of prizes, because over and above their proper share, they are allowed a shift of clothes. If any man defrauds the company to the value of even one dollar in plate, jewels or money, the man shall be marooned. If any man robs another he shall have his nose and ears slit, and he too be put ashore where he shall be sure to encounter hardships." More sharing and more equality. Every man got his share of the prizes and booty captured and if you were caught stealing from your fellow thieves, you had to suffer the consequences. As if reading my mind, Roberts offered, "many a captain has lost his crew, his ship or his life trying to steal from his men. Do go on." No king or duke or prince would ever agree to such a strange rule.

"So," I said, "if one of your men takes valuables from a prize and hoards them for himself he runs a grave risk?"

"Even ugly pirates," said Wales, as he cast a sideways glance at Mr. Sharp, "don't want their nose and ears slit. No sir. So if a member of the crew were to steal a leather purse with a ring and two gold sovereigns from the crevice of a berth in a cabin on the *Samuel*, no. That would not be tolerated." He waited for me to show surprise. With difficulty I forced myself to keep a straight face and found my place in The Articles.

"Three. None shall game for money either with dice or cards." I felt my jaw drop. "Sailors eh, sailors who become pirates—pirates cannot game for money with dice or cards?" This was too much to swallow.

Wales piped up, explaining, "men on this ship drink. No rule against that. If we let them drink *and* wager they would end up fighting and clubbing and stabbing each other and there would be no work done because few would be able enough to do the work. They can wager on land but not at sea. I will concede, Article Three is not popular."

I was sure the men clubbed and stabbed each other regardless of these rules but now was not the time.

"Four. Lights and candles shall be put out at eight bells, and if any of the crew desire to drink after that hour, they will sit upon the open deck but must do without lights." On a clear night, even tiny flames could be seen for miles at sea. Pirates do not like to be found so keeping the lights out at night was prudent, a matter of survival. Of course being pirates, they added the clause about drinking after lights out.

"Five. Each man shall keep his cutlass and pistols at all times clean and ready for action."

Wales piped up enthusiastically, "exactly. This rule is not mere advice. This rule is strictly enforced. A man was flogged not a month ago for having a dull rusty blade and a pistol that one doubts would even fire." Before I could comment, Wales saw fit to add, "it was not the first time the man in question had been found lax in this respect. And, when we sail, every heavy gun and cannon is loaded and ready to fire."

"I am sure the flogging helped improve his memory," I offered. I had overheard this remark a few weeks ago in London from the small mouth of a pompous and powdered Royal Navy officer. Wales merely nodded and motioned for me to resume.

"Six. No boy or woman shall be allowed on board. If any man shall be found seducing any of the latter sex and carrying her to sea in disguise he shall suffer death." Everyone knew that having a woman on a seagoing vessel was bad luck. There were stories of women pretending to be men so they could finagle their way on a ship and be with their lover. This masquerade was not limited to the merchant navy and I had heard tales of women dressing as men for years before they were discovered, even on warships. Discussing the exploits of female pirates was popular fare on the docks and in seaside taverns.

Wales elaborated, "it's not that we don't like women. We love women and their womanly ways. We spend months at sea and Article Six is strictly enforced. You will also see that some of the men prefer the company of other men. So, if a man wants to lie with another man that is not a punishable offense. We are not bound by convention. A man becomes a pirate to be free from condemnation and endless rules, rules and laws which deny him the right to do as he wants, when he wants and with anyone who strikes his fancy. Men who like men in the Royal Navy are flogged and imprisoned. Some are hanged. Why? Because it's a sin? Most of what we do is a sin according to the laws of God, so what's one more? We are experts at sinning, a few of us qualify as professionals." He smiled at his exposition on the merits of sinning. "If we are going to spend eternity in hell what difference does it make to us where a man finds his solace?"

"A merry life and a short one shall be my motto," said the captain.

Roberts and Wales would not last long or fare well among the Puritans in the Massachusetts Bay Colony, to say nothing of the dozing Mr. Sharp.

"Seven. He that shall desert the ship or his quarters in time of battle shall be punished by death or marooning. Eight. None shall strike another on board the ship, but every man's quarrel shall be ended on shore by pistol or sword. At the word of command from the quartermaster," Wales winked at me.

"Where was I? At the word of command from the quartermaster, each man being placed back to back, shall march five paces, turn and fire. If any man does not, the quartermaster shall knock the piece out of his hand. If any man miss their aim they shall take to their cutlasses and he that draws first blood declared the victor." Dueling was an accepted and arguably honorable custom among gentlemen and while not common in Boston, most colonies had dueling grounds set aside for this purpose. The rules for dueling were full of bothersome, particular and minute details.

"Nine. No man shall talk of breaking up their way of living until each has a share of one thousand pounds. Every man who shall lose a limb in service shall have eight hundred pieces of eight from the common stock and for lesser hurts proportionately." This latter bit was a novel and generous idea. I had seen blind, lame and crippled sailors shaking a tin cup, begging for coins, so they could avoid starvation and with any luck, spend their day in a tavern. Working on a sailing vessel sixty feet above the deck in foul weather was hazardous and being seriously hurt or wounded in a sea battle usually meant death, sooner or later. If a lead ball or oak splinter hit a man squarely in the arm or leg, the standard treatment was to hack it off. Even so, the chances of an injured man surviving the butchery of the surgeon were not good. I heard of a man having his leg taken off by a carpenter who, in the necessity of the moment, reached for his saw, severed the bone hurriedly and promptly burned the stump with a hatchet head heated red hot in a fire.

Surgeons were also notoriously fond of drink which seemed reasonable given their working conditions.

"Ten. The captain and the quartermaster shall receive two shares of a prize, the master gunner, bosun, and chief mate, one and a half, all officers one and a quarter and private gentlemen of fortune, one share each. Shares of a dead man shall go to his family or friends." According to this formula, I would get a share and one half of any booty. The notion of divvying up the loot from a prize and getting more than a share made me turn red and I could feel the warmth. Addressing Wales I said, "do you believe this share and a half is going to bring me across the threshold? This lure of easy money is too good to turn down? If I work my way up to a thousand pounds I can go? That's the theory, isn't it? Only you and the captain earn more. Oh, did I say 'earn'? My humble apologies. You steal. And when you find it convenient, or if it pleases you, you murder so you can steal." My spirited condemnation of their way of life seemed to cause none of these men offense. If they were the slightest bit embarrassed about being rogues, thieves and murderers they kept it hidden.

Sure enough, Captain Roberts ignored my tirade and said, "read eleven and you are done."

"Eleven. Musicians shall have rest on the Sabbath Day only by right, on other days by favor only." Below this signatures and marks began. I had seen these musicians when they seized me from the *Samuel.* "Your musicians must perform on demand but they get to rest on the Sabbath. How remarkable you are. I cannot wait to meet the members of the *Good Fortune* string ensemble."

Wales assured me it would not be long before I had that chance. He praised their talents and the value of the entertainments and delights they provided. "They keep the crew amused and they are, to a man, devilish in a fight. 'Tis a wonder they don't get more than a share when I think on it." I was to learn that the musicians were not as devoted to fighting in close quarters as Wales claimed.

Roberts said, "you read well Mr. Glasby. We need more educated men. The world needs more educated men. I'm afraid of no man but we have men in this crew who frighten me. Does that make sense? Any pirate crew has men who enjoy killing for killing's sake. None of us are afraid to kill *as needed.* Even a man with your temperament and pious upbringing has the capacity to kill under compelling circumstances. As an educated man, do you know what Columbus did on his second voyage to the New World? He brought hounds to hunt Arawaks and Caribs and reduced these inoffensive childlike men to slavery. That is why he brought the dogs. And he murdered. The Spanish took gold, silver, slaves and whatever else they could carry back to their kings and queens. These men called themselves Christians. When the Indians died in the mines they sent to Africa to get better, hardier slaves. Do slaves rest on the Sabbath? What of women and children? They too are forced to toil. I served on a slaver, I know about stealing and I know about killing. All men are thieves Glasby. All men."

I knew better and opened my mouth to say so. Roberts raised his hand to quiet me, he was not finished.

"You will claim that not all men are thieves because you do not consider yourself a thief. Fair enough Harry Glasby of Boston. Consider this, life is really about power. Men crave power over other men. Kings, dukes, bishops, popes, pirate captains, money or wealth, it's about power. Few have greater power than a captain in his Majesty's Royal Navy. Do you suppose they have articles as you just read them? Of course not. They have regulations and laws to preserve power over their crew. Find me a place where there are no slaves? These," he pointed at the Articles in front of me, "recognize the power of the captain, the quartermaster, the officers—but it has limits. We must have rules to have order but we also have freedom. It is not just money we want, it is the power that money brings. And yes Harry, my young friend from Boston, we steal. We take gold from men with power. When we have their gold, we have some of the power that goes with it. Is my meaning clear?"

"A man can earn money," I replied, even though I was surprised that Roberts was taking so much time to explain his demented view of the world. Was he trying to convince me or himself?

"You are educated and you think. Even more impressive, you ask questions. A man can earn money but how much he earns is determined by a more powerful man. As for me, I told you a merry life and a short one shall be my motto. Life is about choices. I have seen black people drown themselves rather than submit to a life of slaving. I have seen men like you, good men, work for a pittance to feed themselves and their family only to have it taken by a prince or a duke or just some greedy unscrupulous man born into power even though that man is a shit. We all make choices. Wales and Hunter and Seahorse signed, each made his choice. You can sign or not. If you were forced it would not be a choice. We," and here he waved his arm in a sweeping gesture, "would not use our power to compel you to be one of us. That is the essence of power. Not using power is just as crucial as using it."

The captain employed a relaxed tone and of his sincerity, I had no doubt.

He rose from his chair and hooked his thumbs in his wide brown belt.

"If you sign you will be one of us, a pirate. If you do not, we will not force you to bear arms or engage in a fight. You will work and in return we will safeguard you from harm and provide you with the necessities of life. But you forego your right to vote and your share of any loot. From this day, I will never ask you again to sign. That is a choice you will make. Captain Davis gave me time to make my choice and I do likewise. I trust you will enjoy the sweet taste of freedom, Harry Glasby. It has been a long day gentlemen. If you will kindly see yourselves out, I bid you adieu until the morrow."

I went to my hammock but try as I might, I found sleep to be elusive.

Chapter 3
Captain Kidd

AWAKENING IN A CONFUSED STATE of mind, I could barely determine if I was still asleep, much less where I was. I thought for a long instant I was in some hidden nook of the *Samuel*. Once I realized it was not the *Samuel*, I still had to look about my unfamiliar surroundings to absorb the horror of my new reality, to confirm where I was and what I was; a prisoner of pirates in the midst of the great Atlantic.

I was ravenously hungry.

I left the forecastle and walked the length of the deck to explore my new home. The brigantine was under full sail, flying French colors. After asking the helmsman a few questions, I made my way to the galley, seeing no sign of Roberts, Wales or Seahorse.

Thick boards bolted in slabs were suspended from lines and pulleys in the overhead, serving as tables. When necessary, the makeshift tables could be removed quickly, in whole or in part, to make room for the rapid movement of men or material. Gathered around most of them were men quietly conversing, eating or drinking tea. Although it was a pirate crew it looked just like any other vessel but because they were pirates, I caught myself avoiding their eyes.

A cook saw me and introduced himself as Pineapple. One look at the shape of his head and the odd marks on his face explained the name. He was amiable enough and without me asking, he handed me a wooden bowl filled with oatmeal and a mug of hot tea. I sprinkled generous amounts of brown sugar in both and looked for an empty table. The gun ports were open to let in air and I chose a table with two men sitting across from each other. I asked if I might join them, one said "sure, mate" and the other pulled up a sea chest so I could sit.

"You the new sailing master, bucko?" The man's forearms and the top of his hands and fingers were mottled blue from tattoos, some exquisitely done, some crude and rough. There was a manly looking mermaid with bounteous breasts, a cracked and grinning skull and a fouled anchor among the designs. He was roughly my age, maybe a year or two older and he spoke cheerfully, with an English accent. "I'm Joseph Hough and this piece of shit is William Spavens." Spavens nodded, his mouth full of food. Hough had a thin black beard, trimmed like a Spaniard, and small hoops of shining silver, one in each ear. Hough's friend was older. Spavens had a week's growth of whiskers on his lean face and there was a gray hair here and there.

A pair of fiddlers were playing on the deck above.

"I'm Harry Glasby."

After the captain and the quartermaster, the chief mate was, arguably, the third in command. While underway, the bosun took charge of the array and adjustment of the sails, a complex task that could be extraordinarily perilous during foul weather. In the hierarchy of pirates, the quartermaster was responsible for the details of the ship's day to day operations. If the Articles were to be believed, our captain and quartermaster could be replaced at any time, for any reason. I feared that to acknowledge Hough's question, asking if I was the new first mate, would imply that I had joined the crew of my own volition. I did not want to foster any misunderstandings or give offense to these men.

"Where are we headed?" I asked.

Hough's dark eyebrows went up, "why Mr. Glasby sir, isn't that your job? You're the sailing master. We're going south, eh Spavens?"

Spavens grunted and I interpreted the sound to represent assent.

Hough continued, "which makes sense after all the havoc we did up north. You ever been to Nova Scotia? Newfoundland way. We were sailing a sloop dubbed the *Adventure Galley*. It was right after that we made the new Articles. You know about the Articles?"

"Yes I do." Was this all these men ever talked about?

"We had to swear to 'em. We swore on the Holy Bible, we did. You probably didn't think pirates carried a Bible." He laughed at his little joke. I had not seen a Bible during last night's session and now that I thought about it, Mr. Hough was right, this was the last place on earth I would expect to find a Bible.

Hough talked while I ate. "You ever hear of Montigny la Palisse? Frenchman. I use the word 'man' with some reservations. He joined us, commanding the *Sea King*. A sloop. Fast vessel that. The bastards in Barbados sent two war ships after us, I think they were the *Summerset* and the *Philipa*. La Palisse abandoned us to fend for ourselves and we had no choice but to fight. The *Adventure Galley* took her punishment and even with the damage we managed to slip away to Dominica. We had near twenty men perish. Some suffered a long while—they died in the days after. Ask me, all Frenchmen are worthless."

I had never heard of this French pirate. If their sloop was fast and capable of sailing away to avoid a fight, the French captain likely did the prudent thing but Hough still had a right to be resentful.

He undoubtedly lost some friends. The realization that I was already starting to think like a pirate gave me pause.

"Then those bastards in Martinique sent two more armed ships after us. Captain Roberts swore vengeance against them too and that's why our flag has the captain standing on two skulls. Under one skull it says 'ABH' and the other 'AMH'. Know what that means?" he asked.

I had a guess, "what?"

"A Barbadian's head and a Martiniquan's head." He spoke with such enthusiasm and conviction it was as if he had been the one to come up with the idea. "ABH and AMH", he said proudly.

"Hough, you claiming you drew up our ensign again?" A thin man with dark but lively eyes joined us, introducing himself as Lintorn Highlett. His hair was close cropped but uneven, giving him the appearance of a mangy unkempt dog or more likely, just a man who preferred to chop off his own hair when it got in his way. Highlett had a prominent Adam's apple that rose up and down when he spoke.

"Here Highlett, I saved you a bowl of nice warm turds," Hough said without rancor. "I was telling Mr. Glasby about the skulls and those worthless French pirates. Anyway, with the situation being so warm we went north. You know what I mean by 'warm' Mr. Glasby?"

"I believe so."

"So Captain Roberts took us north to put some distance between us and our pursuers. As I was saying, about Newfoundland. We found some easy pickings around Cape Breton and the banks. We hit the harbor at Ferryland and took a dozen ships there. By June, Roberts had us in a bigger harbor. What was that grand harbor called Highlett, had a funny name? "

Highlett supplied the name, "Trepassey. We swept in with our black flag and our pennants flying. Hough, you might want to cut down on the rum. Your memory is abnormally weak this mornin', even by my low standards. We burned twenty-two ships, you do remember that?"

"Go to hell Highlett." Hough described the panic stricken men on the merchant ships and the fleet of fishing vessels trapped in the harbor.

I knew people up that way and wanted to know if anyone was hurt.

Hough shook his head, "Captain Roberts says killing costs us money. Mind you sir, he is not afraid to kill. No indeed, Roberts is fearless, but cruelty is not part of his nature as far as I can see. We have a captain who is cunning. When we must fight, which we will do when a fight is needed, we fight like devils. But if we fight, we sometimes lose men and men get hurt. We had those doves in Trepassey at our mercy and never had to fire a gun. Well, we did fire one gun. The captain had us pick clean near twenty-two merchant ships which were floating like fat geese. Every morning, he had a gun fired and made a group of unhappy captains pay him homage on the *Adventure Galley*. The other captains who abandoned their ships were cowards and it made Roberts mad. Never a good thing to make Roberts mad. He told the captains who remained if they missed morning muster he would burn their ships." As Hough relayed all this, I could see how much he admired his captain.

Highlett took over, "that's when we left the *Adventure Galley* and took a brig as our new ship, it was out of Bristol and fitted with sixteen guns. When we sailed, we set the ships on fire anyway but no one had to be killed. Then we came across those French ships."

"Damn the French," Hough said. "Just before we found you Mr. Glasby we took ten French ships and the ship you are now on is one of them. How many guns do we have Highlett?"

"Twenty-six. As you see, we call her the *Good Fortune*. More tea Mr. Glasby?" Highlett started to reach for my mug.

"Thank you, no."

Hough was using an unbreakable leather mug called a blackjack. He pushed it forward and said, "sure, I'll have some."

"Damn you too Hough, lazy ass." Highlett grabbed Hough's blackjack and went for more tea.

Hough described the strengths and weaknesses of this particular French ship. "Speaking of the French, you'll never guess who we saw again. That French bastard La Palisse came back in the *Sea King,* acted as if nothing had happened. Captain Roberts seemed not to carry a grudge and with our more powerful ship and Captain La Palisse and his sloop we took a few more ships, including yours."

There was an embarrassed pause at the reference to the *Samuel* and I noticed Spavens had not uttered a word.

Changing the subject, Hough wanted to know about me.

Before I could speak, Highlett returned and asked what he missed. Hough said I was about to tell them my life's story. The trio looked at me expectantly. Whatever I said would become common knowledge before nightfall, from Captain Roberts on down. The fiddlers above had been joined by a piper.

I shrugged, "well, not much to tell. I'm from Boston;went to sea when I was thirteen." I told them about my first ship and some of the voyages I'd made.

Hough wanted to know about my family.

"My parents are dead. My father was Augustus Glasby and he was in charge of the jail in Boston. At least when he died he was. He started as a jailer, did a good job, moved up over the years. My father called it Stone Prison. I suppose that made sense as the walls were three feet thick." I did not want to elaborate and worried the men would sense my unease.

Hough, in an effort to encourage me, began boasting, "my father was in jail too. But not as a jailer. What of your mum then?"

Sailors invariably claimed their mothers were far more worthy than they really were.

"Her name was Sarah. We lived on Treamount Street. They built a new jail on Prison Lane which became Queen Street. Are any of you familiar with Boston?" My small but attentive audience shook their heads. "The new jail was built when I was eight and that might be when they changed the name of the street." It was taking an effort to keep the more unpleasant memories of my past where they belonged. "My birth, you might say, was somewhat unusual. My father worked at the jail before he married my mother. My mother lost a child before I was born and my father was tending to her when she prepared to deliver me. I was born July 6, 1699, which happens to be the day Governor Bellomont had Captain Kidd arrested in Boston. My father heard of the arrest and left my mother with a midwife so he could hurry over to the jail to see the new prisoner."

"Bellomont's a right shifty bastard, "Hough said, with venom.

Highlett had a far off look in his eyes, "this bit about Kidd explains your destiny," he said with great sincerity, "you were born to be a pirate."

Hough agreed, "Highlett's right for once. You were born to be a pirate, a famous pirate. I can't wait to tell McKenzie. McKenzie's from Greenock. You know Greenock?"

"I know of it but I've never been to Scotland. Kidd spent a year in the Boston jail. Being locked up that long, he nearly went insane." Greenock was Kidd's supposed birthplace. All seafaring men knew the story of Captain Kidd.

Hough claimed to be acquainted with an old sailor who was in Wapping when Captain Kidd was executed. Kidd's trial in the London Admiralty Court was notorious. "Peacock, my friend, Peacock. Ol' Peacock was there, he saw Kidd pass by in the cart. They give the poor prisoner a quart of ale when he was being trudged along in that cart. He was paraded behind the Marshall who carries that damned silver oar. The silver oar is a symbol or such, you know how the Royal Navy loves symbols. The bastards used a short rope on Kidd to make the 'Marshall's Dance' more amusin' to the crowd. Peacock said the first rope, the short one, it broke. They had to rig another to hang him proper. Seems mighty suspicious to me as few people know more 'bout ropes than sailors, eh?"

I knew more about the hanging of pirates then I let on. Hough bemoaned the way they covered Kidd's body in tar and gibbeted it for all to see at Tilbury Point, claiming correctly, "he hung there for three years."

I wanted them to stay interested in Kidd.

Every family has its secrets.

Years before my birth, witch Goody Wildes languished in the Stone Prison waiting to hang. It was rumored my father forced himself on her. As far back as I can remember, children took delight in telling me when Goody was taken to the gallows, she spit in my father's face, promising he would die in the jail. The curse extended to his offspring. Just before her death, my mother told me she lost two babies during childbirth. Knowing about Goody Wildes, it pained me to imagine her grief and the absolute terror that must have accompanied my arrival. When news of Captain Kidd's sudden arrest reached my father, he had the excuse he needed to leave my mother and me to the midwife. My mother never totally forgave him for abandoning her but my survival allowed them to breathe a sigh of relief. The relief was to be temporary.

When I was five, a score of pirates under Captain John Quelch were packed in the dungeon of the jail. My father complained they were being treated like royalty. Quelch and six of his men were sentenced to hang in June, 1704. One of the scoundrels, angry about the complaints, broke a piece of crockery and cut my father's throat. As ordained, my father died in the jail.

Cotton Mather ministered to the condemned pirates but they would not reveal who killed my father. I was there. I watched it all.

The throng near Hudson's Point was unruly but seeing those men hanged satisfied my need for justice, or, perhaps, revenge. My most vivid memory of that day was the piercing scream of a woman which echoed along the waterfront at the precise instant when the pirates dropped. Walking home, my mother gripped my hand so hard it hurt. Sensing it was now my duty to take care of her I put on a brave face.Kind neighbors stopped to express sorrow and offer assistance, one gave my mother a bottle of brandy. When I awoke the next morning, the bottle was empty and my mother was sound asleep.

This became her habit, day in and day out.

Despite her constant drinking, she took care of me and insisted I learn to read but in short order, her mind started to wander. She mumbled about witches and demons and devils and murderers and God and Jesus, admonishing me to beware of her lost babies and Captain Kidd. Toward the end, I worried someone would accuse her of being a witch.

When death finally took her, creditors took our home. She spent nearly all her money on drink. After burying her next to my father, I took what little remained and bought a sea chest. A kind captain took me on as a cabin boy.

The prospect of going to sea was a dream come true. It was also a chance to escape cruel children and bad memories of jail, witches, hangings and most of all, pirates.

In short order, I became a man.

Since then, the sea has been my home but there was someone in Boston who I loved more than my own life.

Highlett and Hough were still arguing about Captain Kidd's lost treasure.

I looked at Spavens who was paying rapt attention to their debate. "Spavens", I said, "is that right? Spavens?" He nodded and looked at me, his mouth shut. "Is there anything you can tell us about Kidd's treasure?" I immediately realized something was amiss.

Hough gave Spavens a friendly shove on the shoulder.Highlett leaned back, grinning.

"Mr. Glasby," Hough announced, "Mr. Spavens was on a slaver in Africa and got mixed up with the natives one night. He woke up in a stupor and them savages, the bloody bastards, they'd cut out his tongue."

Spavens flashed a good-natured smile and rolled his languid eyes. I suddenly felt sheepish but how was I to know?

"Of all the idiots on board, he is the best, by far, at keeping secrets," Highlett proclaimed. He and Hough took great delight in my ignorance. I had little doubt that Spavens had grown used to being the butt of jokes whenever a new man came aboard as he seemed to be as amused as anyone.

Hearing the voice of Seahorse approaching from behind, I turned. He was calling my name,"Mr. Glasby,captain would like you in his cabin when you finish."

"Aye, Seahorse." I shook hands with my new shipmates, left the galley and went forward to the bow to use the head.

The head, consisting of a thick board with three crudely cut holes, was vacant. The pirates called these holes 'seats of easement'. I selected the seat closest to the bow. I retrieved a letter that had survived the pirate onslaught, a letter I had previously kept hidden in a spare pair of shoes.Pirates had stolen my shoes but the letter, to my great relief, was left behind.The shoes were unimportant. Listening for a moment to confirm no one was coming, I unfolded the carefully creased paper and read again;

'My Dearest Harry'....

Not an hour passes that I do not ask myself why it is that we must be apart. Is it not so that happiness is within our reach? You say a girl of sixteen (almost seventeen) is not a woman but your touch tells me that I am. I live only to feel you again and to hear your kind words and endearments. Eliza stares at my belly more and more but alas, she is just a girl. I pray you return soon so we can be married. London will be a marvelous adventure and you will be sure to tell me every detail of what you see, hear, smell and taste. So long as you are not beguiled by the temptations of those who would taste your sweet lips if they could. I could not bear such a thing my love.

When I am with company, I struggle to hear their voices because I start to remember how you touched me (there). The way you ran your fingers through my hair. These are a few of my warm thoughts of you. Mother says you were cursed by a witch. I know she wants us to part because she of all can see in my eyes the pain arising from your absence. I do not abide witches or curses, I believe in my beloved Harry. The sea that seems to hold you so has no hold on me but I would leave Boston today and be at sea forever if it meant we could be together. Patience is not among my virtues (I have given you my virtue so maybe when virtue is lost, patience must not be far behind). O Harry, I cherished your clever letter and my tears fell on it when your ship left Scarlett's Wharf. I read it every day (nearly). When I do, I can hear your voice and I smile. You will find me there each day when your return is imminent and until that joyous time, let my love for you shelter you from harm so you may be delivered swiftly to my bosom. There are no riches I would have to compare to the warmth of your embrace. I want for nothing but you my dear. May the wind fill your sails and hurry you to me. With the whole of my being and my abiding love, I am yours, now and forever, C.

Constance had artfully drawn two matching turtle doves under the 'C'.

I carefully refolded her letter and tucked it back under my shirt.

Constance would do her utmost to be at Scarlett's Wharf today and it was more than likely that the dire news about my fate, as well as others in our crew, would soon arrive with Captain Cary and the *Samuel*. The thought of not being there pained me in ways I find difficult to describe. Escape from these miscreants seemed at once both impossible and imperative.

I imagined Constance's shock when she heard that pirates had taken me prisoner with no hope of parole or ransom. I prayed mightily that the news would not break her heart. I considered a prayer for the well-being of our baby, knowing all too well of such matters, but a heretofore unknown part of me determined such a loss might be for the best. My prayer was for Constance only. This willful and selfish omission served only to emphasize my wickedness and the realization that Constance would be forced to bear the shame of her sin as well as mine filled me with revulsion, revulsion at myself and fury toward the men who had kidnapped me. Never before or since has my moral ambivalence, if not outright depravity, filled me with such crushing guilt and abject self-loathing. The fleeting notion that I might secretly be asking God to take the life of a baby in order to extinguish my guilt was beyond any mortal sin known to me and so unspeakably vile, I dared not seek forgiveness from above.

God had spared me from death but why would He be so merciful toward one so undeserving? If I was not meant to die just yet, then I must cling to life and accept my sin and my sorrow with the hope that the answer might reveal itself in its own time. Maybe this is how believers define the word 'faith'. Leaving the head, I promised myself that the next time I prayed it would be in a more suitable location.

I dried my eyes with my shirt sleeve and reluctantly made my way to the captain's cabin, dreading the realization that this would be my first day as the guide for pirate Captain Bartholomew Roberts, the seaborne murderer and thief who had become my jailer.

Chapter 4
Pedro

WITH LITTLE FANFARE, I CELEBRATED the end of my first full week as sailing master of the *Good Fortune.*

Seeing no harm in becoming better acquainted with the crew, and believing it was inevitable, I unspooled the main threads of my life story as I had with Hough, Highlett and Spavens and found life aboard this particular pirate vessel was becoming tolerable. Seahorse kept the men busy, was fair in the allocation of work and took great pains to maintain the thousands of bits and pieces that when combined, enabled us to sail. He was the glue that kept all things together and we sailed in sole possession of the sea, uneventfully and without mishap.

The *Good Fortune* was a brigantine and larger than the *Samuel* but in relative terms, and this was true for nearly all pirate vessels, we had a far larger crew. A bigger crew means less work per man, although that does not signify that men could lay about all day doing nothing, a state that is not good for a sailing craft and a state that would be disastrous for any crew, much less one where each wields equal power. If nothing else, lack of activity is detrimental to their physical health. Per the Articles, they could not play cards or dice, nor could they fight amongst themselves to pass the time and amuse each other. There was little else to do but commiserate, eat, drink and enjoy the ship's musicians who proved to have an inexhaustible array of tunes as well as a seemingly endless supply of good humor. Some of their raunchy ditties were hilarious.

Roberts and Wales tested me by demanding that I chart our position far more than necessary, something I had anticipated, and because this kept me occupied, I did not resent it. They knew I knew their motives but I did as they asked and did so diligently, knowing that resistance would merely prolong my initiation. If I made a serious error or miscalculation, every man aboard could perish, including me, so a premium was put on attention to detail. Besides, my navigational prowess was a source of pride and gave me the confidence I needed to help preserve my deep seated desire to get back to civilization. As long as I was of value to these men, the chance of me coming to harm, while ever present, was reduced. Earning the respect of the captain, the quartermaster and even the crew could do nothing but help me cope with my vexatious predicament. Before most of these men turned to piracy, they were mariners and good sailors respect a competent navigator.

We made our way south, then southwesterly, and changed course for no apparent reason, two or three times a day. The days grew warmer as a consequence and the smell of tar, damp hemp, bilge water, animal excrement and most of all, the crew in cramped quarters, made being below decks rather unpleasant.

This life, while hard and challenging, was preferable to the harsh conditions on a man o' war. A warship is equally crowded with men and provisions, but we lacked a lurking covey of naval officers whose only purpose is to prowl about looking for reasons to find fault with us, our work, our appearance and anything else that might strike their dull imagination. Good officers quickly become captains and I have known of captains who were my age. Poor and inefficient officers passed over for promotion affix the blame on everyone but themselves and vent their frustrations on seamen forced to accept abuse without protest. This is not to say all naval officers are unworthy but unless you have sound prospects of becoming a captain, the privations, risk of injury or disease and the low pay hardly justify foregoing the ease of a gentleman's life ashore.

As ever, the uncertainties of life in the Royal Navy or on a merchant ship depend primarily on the personality and character of the captain. This truism is ingrained in every sailor from the moment he sets foot on the deck of a vessel and reinforced thereafter every waking moment of each and every day. Sea captains and officers are much like women, the good ones are rare and worth their weight in gold. Bad ones are plentiful and can cause a man to dream of clever ways to commit murder without being found out.

When not engaged in fulfilling my duties, I sat for long hours and talked to the men about their lives and hardships they'd endured, finding that men who strive to be rough often make light of their suffering to mask the pain and anger and fear that dwells in their damaged souls. Pirates are fellows of desperate fortunes, forced to flee from their place of birth on account of their poverty or their misdeeds. Some were undone by drinking, whoring and gaming, others by lawsuits, accusations of treason, murder, theft, poisoning, robbery, coining false money, rape and sodomy. Some were fleeing from their colors, many had been imprisoned or abused by family members or corrupt officials, but all were outcasts. As such, they could not go home for fear of hanging or starving or being locked in a dungeon.

Their hardships were different, as all men are different, but they were also all the same. Many was the night I thought about my murdered father and my grieving mother and came to realize that most of the pirates I met had experienced far worse.

Despite occasional visits from my meandering ghosts of the past, the crew treated me as they treated their shipmates, maybe better, since I spent most of my time with Wales and the captain. It was likely they envied me for not being a man of desperate fortune, an insight arising from my circumstances and a conclusion I found somewhat awkward. To them I was an important man by virtue of the role I played. But I also played the role of a man of virtue, not by artifice mind you and not because I think I am special, but due to the good nature God and my parents instilled in my heart from the days of my youth. Many of the men found it hard to be kind, just as I would have found it impossible to be cruel.

More often than not, I listened to them without condemnation. Listening is an art, an art held in low esteem given the undue emphasis on speeches, lectures, books and long-winded sermons. To gain a man's trust, I've learned, all you have to do is ask questions and let the man answer. Listening patiently to a man tell you about himself is, often times, just as important to that man as food and drink. Trust naturally arises when you listen without judgment. As most pirates are sailors first, all pirates are men first and most men seek the same things. Behaving agreeably toward most of the crew came easily to me and when I found a man who was selfish or conniving or a bully, I did my best to avoid that man, as did my shipmates. It may surprise you, as it did me, to know that such men were in the minority. Most of the men were like the friendly Hough, the knowledgeable Highlett or the mute Mr. Spavens, and that was fine by me.

There were a number of negro pirates and they were assigned most of the menial tasks, which I attribute to the natural tendency of white men to treat dark-skinned people as members of the servant class. Menial tasks included scrubbing the decks, tending to the animals and chickens, cleaning the head and galley and other forms of manual or unpleasant labor that called only for a pair of willing hands and, inevitably, a strong back. As a practical matter, a former slave did not possess the finer skills that months or years at sea provided his white counterpart. However, once a black pirate learned his trade as a sailor, he was treated almost as if he were white. Our bosun, Seahorse, exemplified this and the men obeyed his commands regardless of the color of their skin. I have no doubt there were white men who resented Seahorse but as I had discovered, some of the men were selfish and conniving and such men are to be found in every crew.

Stories of life in His Majesty's Royal Navy typically centered around the shortcomings of officers and particularly captains. The former were inevitably deemed to be lazy, stupid, deceitful and cowardly, especially when it came to standing up to tyrannical captains. The latter were portrayed as sadistic brutes who terrorized the crew on the least provocation. The smallest mistake or insignificant infraction could result in a brutal flogging which at best was horribly painful and sometimes, fatal.

It was well known that Navy pay was often months in arrears. It was common practice to deny sailors the chance to go ashore, thus, they were confined to their ship for years on end. Shore visits caused desertions to spike so sailors were routinely forbidden to disembark and lack of shore visits motivated men to desert, a self-perpetuating problem if ever there was one.

Since desertion was a capital offense, many a man fleeing the Royal Navy turned to piracy. Most of the white crewmen serving under Captain Roberts had experience on a merchant vessel, a Royal Navy ship, or both.

If you heard the tales I heard, the ones about brutality and deprivation, you might have cause to wonder why mutinies were so infrequent. Rebellions were usually impulsive and typically involved a determined and desperate handful of men, in other words, rarely the entire crew. These eruptions were like dropping a match in a powder keg and were characterized by outbursts of extraordinary violence, most often the murder of the captain and some or all of the ship's officers. Since killing the captain or leading a mutiny led to the gallows, one must wonder why, during any mutiny, an offending captain was ever allowed to live. A mutineer who murders suffers the same fate as a mutineer who does not, and a man can only be hanged once, Captain Kidd notwithstanding. Alas, rebellions on naval vessels were doomed from the outset given the size, tenacity and reach of His Majesty's Royal Navy. A captured mutineer would inevitably find himself doing the 'Marshall's Dance'.

During my first few days on the *Good Fortune*, I could point out members of our crew who had served on merchant ships and those who had served on board a warship simply by the cut of their jib.

One of the more colorful members of our crew was a man called 'Deadeye'. A deadeye is a piece of hardwood with three holes bored in the childish pattern of a face, two holes for eyes and one below, resembling an open mouth. It was used in the standing and running of rigging. Deadeye the pirate had been hit squarely in the middle of the forehead by a spent musket ball and after the wound healed, he had the skin inside and around the scar tattooed with black ink. Deadeye claimed he and Captain Roberts were among the exclusive pirate fraternity who were pistol proof. The two had served together since Captain Davis. Deadeye was present when a group of disgruntled pirates attempted to unseat the newly elected Captain Roberts in an aborted mutiny. These mutineers happened to be Irish and they met an inglorious end at the hands of pirates loyal to their duly elected captain, Deadeye being prominent in their number.

As I said, mutinies rarely achieve their ostensible ends.

Should I ever have doubts about our captain, Deadeye urged me to come to him and he would set me straight. Other than his bizarre appearance, he was a loyal and hardworking sailor.

Deadeye's story explained why Roberts refused to trust an Irishman and as far as I could tell, there were none in his crew.

Another pirate whose reputation preceded him worked in the galley and went about his duties in nothing but a pair of white canvas trousers with a patterned silk scarf on his head. Newly made trousers like his cost only six pence and thus, the silk scarf was his sole nod to fashion. He was called Spades. His shipmates, especially those working in the galley and caring for the livestock and chickens, browbeat Spades constantly about his gambling habits. Spades was forever playing at dice, backgammon, cards and finding any odd thing on which to make a wager. He hailed from Yorkshire in England and was forced to dress the way he did because he invariably lost his clothing and his shoes. More than one pirate pulled me aside and warned me never to lend Spades anything of value, telling me I would be better off throwing my money into the sea. Thanking them, I made it clear I had no money, but resolved to protect my property which consisted of my books, my attire and my navigational tools.

One morning I walked into the galley and saw Spades wearing a shirt. I remarked on it and he happily told me he had had an unusual run of good luck. The next day, he was shirtless once more.

Aside from getting to know the ship and the crew, I began to learn something of great import, that being the manner in which the men talked about Roberts when he was not present. Sailors can go without water longer than they can go without complaining but the real test of leadership is how you are talked about behind your back. There were times I believed the crew was going out of their way to convince me that Roberts was intelligent, crafty, brave and bold. Admittedly, I did have his ear, but the crew also grew to accept that I did not repeat their confidences or their grievances to the captain, to Wales, or to anyone else for that matter. To be sure, not all the men looked up to him in equal measure, but as far as I could surmise, the crew obeyed orders willingly and not through fear.

Some in the crew were foolhardy, some were constantly drunk and some took a keen pleasure in making other men suffer. A few were just plain ignorant and I found these men to be among the most difficult. Callousness is often the child of stupidity and small-minded men tended to enjoy inflicting pain for its own sake. There was something primal in their brutishness and I will have you know that such men were not to be found among the negroes.

A woeful lack of formal education is the norm among seafaring men but exceptions exist and I suppose I am such a man. Dispersed among the habitual liars, killers and thieves, I found more than a dozen men who had a depth of insight and mental abilities which would have put them in good stead at Oxford or Cambridge. Finding brutes in a pirate crew was to be expected but finding thoughtful philosophers and creative thinkers came as a great revelation.

From what I saw and heard in those first few impressionable days, the crew was willing to fight under a commander who viewed their interests as his own, a leader who did not risk their lives needlessly and who, genuinely, sought to make them rich. This widely divergent cross section of men could not have been found in the world beyond the sea. They would only have existed in the ports and harbors where men of the sea congregate. My new world, the tiny world of the *Good Fortune,* was a hundred and ten feet long and twenty-five feet wide, at best. It is a small space but sailors get used to such things and give it little or no thought. Some things just are.

Taken as a whole, this crew was successful and well led. This crew was dangerous because the men living shoulder to shoulder aboard this vessel would willingly follow Bartholomew Roberts to certain death. Their willingness to do this arose in part from the fact that there were times when he inspired them and other times when he made them feel good about themselves. Some loved him, most liked him and even those who did neither respected him. Roberts had a firm hold on his crew. It was impressive because it seemed to have been achieved with little or no overt effort and not a shred of fear or force.

Regardless of a man's intellect or lack thereof, all seafaring men are subject to the scourge of incurable afflictions and fatal illnesses. A pirate's precarious life is fraught with danger. The risk of being killed or wounded in a battle or a brawl is ever present. If captured, a pirate can expect a short trial and more often than not, a very public execution. Despite these hazards, disease, by far, is the biggest killer on any sailing vessel.

Even being idle can prove fatal.

Look as long as you desire and you will not find boredom listed in the surgeon's log, despite it being among the most serious maladies we endured. It is a malady that can drive unoccupied men, men who are too long at sea, to behave in the most unexpected ways. This is especially true when drink is involved.

I was tending to some routine tasks on the quarterdeck when a man I knew only as Pedro came ambling toward the stern, drunk as a lord, mumbling and cursing and swinging a cutlass at some imaginary demon. It was during the early evening and the disappearing sun was deep red, like the pips in a pomegranate. Soon enough, it would slip below the distant horizon until we saw nothing but thin purple slivers of reflected light.

Somehow Pedro laboriously managed to drag himself up to the quarterdeck.

He came to an abrupt halt a few steps away and began berating Captain Roberts.

Calmly and firmly the captain interrupted him, "shut your damned mouth Pedro or you'll be keelhauled before that there orb goes behind the earth".

The unsteady Pedro licked his lips and waved his cutlass with menace toward the Captain's breast. He gingerly put his free hand on a bone handled butcher knife he had sheathed by his side. I could see he was a man who took care of his weapons and presumably that knife was as sharp as a whore's razor.

"Pedro," I said with an unmistakeable hint of uncertainty, "you're on the Devil's road and you would be wise to go below." I glanced up into the rigging and saw two brawny black men watching us from a shroud.One raised his hand to shield his eyes so he could see what was happening. There were other men gathered by the bow, a few more lingering near the forecastle and six or seven on the main deck but Captain Roberts and I had been the only two on the quarterdeck, unless you include the helmsman. It was unusually quiet so I assumed the musicians were below. The deck would start to fill with men when the sun was gone, many of them preferring to spend the night in the cool fresh air.

Had I any foreknowledge of what was about to happen, there is no doubt I would have behaved with less composure.

Pedro was so drunk he could barely stand upright or keep his eyes open, much less focused.

"Capitan, you are no Drake, no sir to me, no Sir Drake as was knighted by his queen." Pedro's slurred accent was worse due to drink and he gingerly pulled out his knife as if by stealth and guile we might not notice his threatening gesture.

Captain Roberts thoughtfully scratched his chin and straightened his back, putting both hands on his hips in a position of authority, a pose very comfortable to him.

"Listen to me Pedro. Savvy? I'm in need of no queen and no Act of Grace and no king and I am in need of no advice from the bastard of a Port Royal slut who is not worth the price of the hemp rope it would take to hang him— so the Devil take your folly and get off my quarterdeck this instant." Roberts had put great emphasis on the word 'my' and waved Pedro off as if he were addressing an unruly child.

Pedro's eyes narrowed to dark slits, one eye seemed to look downward, the other eye rolled erratically like a defective compass needle.

Maybe it was because Pedro was the son of a Port Royal whore and resented being reminded of it. Maybe it was because Pedro had lost his money in a card game the night before, drank too much rum and was remembering with unjustified anger that the captain had denied Pedro his share in a lucrative prize because Pedro was passed out when the prize was taken. Anger can fester, especially the unjustified kind. There was no doubt Roberts remembered the prize and he knew Pedro had vowed to get his share or get even.

Rumors on ships travel like lightening and these were rumors I had heard.

I took a step back, closer to the helmsman, awaiting the thunder.

If Pedro could not get his share, he would get his revenge. So said the rumors and so said the deranged look on Pedro's oval face. His head lolled from side to side with the rhythm of the ship as we made a steady eight knots. He seemed to be struggling to think about what to say or what to do next, his mouth opened but I knew there was nothing yet poised to fly out. Maybe the price of revenge was too steep? In my view, it always is, but for too many pirates, revenge is the brutal component of what they perceive as honor, the sort of honor that borders on dementia.

Pedro was teetering on the crumbling edge of a deep abyss, determined to take the plunge. Captain Roberts was right, life is about choices.

Pedro had probably made many bad decisions in his life and he was about to make his last. From the murky depths of his addled brain, Pedro pointed his knife at the captain and stammered, "you.... you...you are a thief and you lick the balls of dogs." Pedro's crooked yellow teeth were on display and his gnarled grimace suggested that he, and he alone, deemed his insult to be particularly witty. He blinked slowly.

The abyss beckoned.

I heard the unmistakable click of a pistol hammer being cocked and the noise gave me a start. Captain Roberts bore no particular expression unless being grim and annoyed qualifies. I had seen that look on men many times and as I thought that fleeting thought Roberts leveled his pistol about six feet from Pedro. The tense silence was shattered by a loud retort as the hammer hit the flint and the powder exploded, sending a one ounce ball of lead into Pedro's face. Blood spatter speckled my face, making me wince. The helmsman, a light-haired pirate named Hill, moved his head like a tortoise, first at Pedro, then at Roberts, then at me. And like a tortoise, he turned his head toward the bow, his hands on the ship's wheel.

I reached up to wipe Pedro's blood out of my eye as Pedro dropped with a thump to the oak deck. The captain lowered his weapon and curling gray smoke drifted off. The two negro crewmen in the rigging remained motionless, transfixed, one assumes, by the sudden, bloody, and noisy death of one of their shipmates.

Every other face on the deck had turned toward us in mute wonder.

The seemingly unfazed Roberts looked away from the dead man in my general direction, then shouted, "I am a gentleman rover which makes me a thief and a good one I am. But I will be damned if I have ever licked the balls of a dog." He shoved his pistol in his belt and ordered the men in the rigging to come down. In the time it takes to brew a cup of tea, Pedro's body was stripped naked and dropped over the side. Thick pools of fresh blood were washed away with wooden buckets filled with seawater.

Pedro made his choice. He was gone forever and now, in a flash, it was as if he had never lived.

This was not the first or the last time I wanted to climb inside a bottle of rum. As word about the captain, the gunshot, and Pedro raced through the ship and as Pedro's body sank into the depths of the sea, Pedro's friend Thomas Jones came thundering across the deck.

Jones had served as a gunner in the Royal Navy and his captain had him flogged for disrespect. The impetuous and garrulous Jones told a snotty fifteen-year-old midshipman to 'go fuck himself' after the self-important junior officer told Jones, in excruciating and condescending detail, how to properly run 'his gun crew'. Following the humiliation of being whipped as his shipmates watched and as soon as he was ashore, Jones deserted in Nassau. In short order he joined a pirate crew, sailing on a leaky schooner that had three captains in less than a week. Young Jones was a capable seaman, a competent gunner and he stood over six feet tall. His Achilles' heel was his inability to submit to authority.

What had happened to Pedro and what was happening now seemed somehow personal but at the heart of it, at the very core of all this, Pedro and Jones were men of the sea and both had to know that every captain is a sailor but not every sailor is a captain. A castle can only have one king and a ship can only have one master.

Thirty men, who also knew this, because they too were sailors, had gathered near the quarterdeck to get a better view of what was happening.

"Roberts?" roared the distraught and enraged Jones.

"I'm right here by God. You will refer to me as captain or I'll know the reason why." Roberts, who should have been distraught, but seemed to be quite in control of himself, still carried a brace of loaded pistols on his person. Instead of pulling a pistol, he hoisted the cutlass that moments ago had been hoisted by Pedro. Opening and closing his fists, Jones looked over at me. Meeting his eyes I slowly shook my head from side to side, knowing Jones would ignore me just as Pedro had mere minutes ago. Roberts pointed the cutlass at Jones and said loudly, "I will tell you what I told your dead friend. I order you below at once, be gone and trouble me no more."

Someone shouted "watch him," although to this day I am not at all sure who the man was trying to warn.

Jones lurched toward the captain. Roberts had a dozen shining flecks of Pedro's bright wet blood on his face and bigger bits and droplets scattered across the embroidered white collar of his silk shirt, to include the sleeves and lace cuffs. Jones growled "you damned bastard" and dived for the Captain's midsection, shoving him back toward the gunwale. As if possessed, Jones bodily heaved the struggling Roberts over a long black cannon barrel and commenced pounding him with his fists. Blood oozed through Jones' faded calico shirt. I assumed Captain Roberts stabbed at Jones with the cutlass just before being tackled.

It took six men to pry Jones off the captain. Roberts had open cuts, gashes really, above his blackened eyes, a bloody nose and blood coming from both corners of his mouth. When they had the sweating, panting Jones subdued, Hill still manned the helm, his feet having never moved an inch from the moment the pistol shot shattered the silence to the hasty burial at sea to the flurry of flailing fists behind the carriage of the heavy gun.

The episode had rendered me nearly insensible, but not Hill. As if sensing my wonder, he turned to me, pursed his closed lips outward, sent his barely discernable blond eyebrows skyward and simultaneously shrugged his shoulders in that universal message roughly translated as "nothing we could do."

Ninety men and one animated and agitated quartermaster had emerged, the latter pushed his way through the crowd and ordered that Jones be put in irons and taken below. A pair of men tended to their battered captain who kept telling them he was 'fine'.

"Alright men, shut up and listen," Wales began, "our captain is going to his cabin. He is not to be disturbed. Even if you think you see half the Royal Navy off the bow, you report to me, not to him. I repeat, the captain is not to be disturbed." Wales eyed the throng to look for signs of resistance or unease. Seeing none, he resumed. "Tomorrow, we'll have a trial. Thomas Jones, as many of you saw, assaulted our captain." A few men murmured and others hissed at them to be quiet. Nothing was going to be settled tonight. Stating the obvious, a glowering Wales told them, "there has been plenty of excitement for one night. This crew shall remain true to the Articles we signed and by which we must abide. I will appoint six men to judge Seaman Jones and per our rules and customs, Jones shall have the right to select six more. There will be no more drinking on board this vessel until after the trial."

The last restriction was greeted by an immediate chorus of moans from virtually all assembled.

"You assholes heard me. No more drinking. Some of you imbeciles will be on my jury and you have to at least look like you are awake and paying attention. You are not English judges, after all, who can sleep through a case." The insult to English judges was met with laughter and warmed Wales to his task. He had a particular way with men during a crisis. "We'll get Jones patched up but he is going to be in irons until I say otherwise. It's for his own good."

There were no more stabbings or shootings, leastways, not that night.

Chapter 5

Pirate Justice

THE FOLLOWING DAY, WITH A scorching white sun directly above the deck, two patched mainsails were braced to provide shade, an operation carried out with haste and skill. A shirtless Spades was skulking about the deck, annoying the riggers and taking wagers on the outcome of the trial. I overheard a man say Spades was offering two pieces of eight to one that Jones would have to accept some form of punishment for what he had done to the captain. It was doubtful Spades would find many takers.

As he deemed one man after another sober enough to sit in judgment, Wales motioned his jurors to find a seat on crates facing the bulk of the 140 men who would constitute the gallery. Lords Lutwidge and Ringrose were jurors and I had precious little doubt how they would view an assault on their hallowed captain.

Jones selected his six and in short order twelve pirates sat awaiting the evidence. The defendant was no longer in shackles and he sat off to one side. The captain sat opposite his attacker, well away and to the far side of the deck, his swollen face more black and blue than I expected. By his dour facial expression, Jones seemed to accept that the captain's cuts and bruises would not endear him to the jury.

Wales, in the role of presiding judge, recited the charges and invited Jones to address the jury first.

Jones stood before the jury, his back to the crew. He justified his attack on Roberts by claiming the captain was wrong to shoot Senor de Mendez, the man I knew as Pedro. I was told that most of the men had been in the crew when Pedro lay unconscious during the taking of a prize. There had been a brief but bloody skirmish with the terrified crew of that particular merchant vessel, the name of which I cannot recall, so having every able-bodied man on deck to board the prize mattered. Pedro was fortunate he had not been charged with cowardice during a fight, an offense that carried the death penalty. When it was mentioned that Jones had not been present during the tense exchange between Pedro and the captain, the tongue-tied Jones had to admit that no one else cared much about the captain shooting Pedro.

The jury had to assess the actions of Jones in attacking and beating the captain, not to judge the captain's decision to shoot Pedro, even though the two events were inseparable.

Jones turned to his claim of self-defense, claiming the captain struck first. He raised his shirt to expose the raw wound where the captain jabbed him with Pedro's cutlass.

It is unlikely there is any group of human beings who have seen more blade wounds than pirates.

The scratch had been cleaned and a thin pink mark barely three inches long remained, a wound devoid of anger. A cut would need to be dramatically more severe to sway these men into believing it was Jones who had been attacked. The injury, if one could call it that, could not have been deep, otherwise Jones would not have been able to throw the captain, no small man himself, over a mounted cannon and viciously pound his face half a dozen times. The jurors were unimpressed and two of them playfully nudged each other in the ribs when Jones raised his shirt. Witnesses contradicted Jones, testifying that the captain stabbed at Jones *after* Jones rushed him, not before. This seemed to settle the secondary question of whether the captain had overreached and struck the first blow. If anyone acted in self-defense, it was Roberts. In light of the number of witnesses to the scuffle between Jones and the captain, Roberts did not need to speak. Thankfully, no one asked me or the silent helmsman, Hill, to testify, even though we saw everything.

If the jury found Jones guilty of assaulting the captain, they still had the more onerous task of assessing suitable punishment.

Friends of Jones, and there were many, gave testimonials about his prowess in battle and his loyalty. His loyalty extended primarily to his friends, not to the captain, for Jones had the reputation of a grumbler, a man who despised orders and those who gave them. These men begrudgingly conceded that the captain stabbed at Jones in self-defense but took the position that shooting a member of the crew in the face for drunken insults was extreme, even if the person being insulted was the captain. As I could confirm, Senor de Mendez menaced Roberts so he would have a pretext to launch an attack. In the violent world of pirates, the captain not only had the option of responding forcefully to such a provocation, it was expected.

The insult "licking the balls of dogs" was said so often that each time it was repeated, the crew made rude remarks and started barking. One wag shouted in perfect French, 'les couilles du chien'. Everyone instinctively understood the remark even if they did not speak French, causing more guffawing and good-natured banter.

"Order, order," shouted Wales, banging the butt of a pistol on an upturned barrel. Despite his admonition and attempts to restore decorum, we could see he saw the humor in the situation by the levity in his eyes. This had a salutary effect on the proceedings, as it lessened the tension between those who sympathized with Jones and those who were on the side of Roberts the man, as well as Roberts the captain.

Wales made it clear when the trial commenced that Roberts would not interfere with the proceedings nor influence the punishment if Jones was found guilty. This was a matter for the men. I had known Roberts a week but his deference to the crew and his recognition of the sanctity of the proceedings was wisely calculated to impress the men with his confidence and his magnanimity. It is unlikely that the Royal Navy, with its hundreds of ships, had one captain with equal foresight and sagacity. If Jones had attacked a Royal Navy captain on one of His Majesty's warships, he would have had a quick court-martial before being dangled from a yardarm. Respect for the authority and person of a sea captain, any captain, was deeply ingrained in all who had served as sailors.

Sailors on this jury, indeed, all sailors on this vessel, carried respect for their captain in the marrow of their bones.

Unfortunately for Jones, trials are notorious for hatching surprises and this proceeding spawned a surprise in the guise of an unexpected witness. The man who asked to speak was not a former sailor, therefore, he was not among the majority who were trained to believe that when it came down to it, a captain's word was law.

The witness was a former slave.

Few could pronounce his tribal name, Halake Lukado Legalgalo, so they called him Cheddar. Cheddar was an Akan speaking member of the Coromantee people of the Gold Coast, people with a ferocious disposition. After the trial I learned that Cheddar was an Ashanti, warriors who epitomized strength, pride and limitless physical courage, traits possessed by males and females alike. It was impossible to know his age but I put him at twenty-five. After hoisting Cheddar from the pestilential stench of a slave ship, he joined the crew. To celebrate taking his first prize, he ate two pounds of cheese and made himself sick. He still loved cheese and sought it out in port and at sea. He was terrifying in a fight, as one would expect of an Ashanti warrior, and reputedly a high-ranking warrior at that. It must have taken a mob or an incapacitating injury to capture such a man.

Cheddar was also one of the crewmen in the rigging the night before so he had seen and heard everything. Cheddar saw Pedro fall and helped throw the remains overboard. He was still present on the deck when Jones rushed up and angrily went after the captain, helping pull Jones off before he could beat Roberts senseless.

"I am Cheddar." He was wearing a tattered gray waistcoat without a shirt and tapped his well-muscled chest. There were uniform rows of ritual scars on his upper arms and the sides of his face.

"Cheddar is the name you gave me. I see Pedro. I see Jones. Captain is my captain. He is captain of all." He swept his arm across the sea of dirty faces and despite his thick accent, he took pains to speak slowly and enunciate each word carefully. "All. Captain order Pedro leave. Captain order Jones. 'Jones leave deck. At one'." Someone yelled "once" and Cheddar sheepishly flashed his perfect white teeth and nodded shyly, "yes, very sorry. Captain say, 'Jones leave deck at once' ".

Stiffening to maintain his composure, Cheddar pointed toward Roberts and solemnly said "this my captain,your captain, all captain. If captain say 'leave deck at once'. We leave deck. At once. No? Is this not how captains make men on ship?" He meant this is how a captain insures that the crew works, functions, and goes forth into battle. Cheddar, despite his background as a landsman, had deftly observed that this was not about Pedro, Seaman Jones or even Bartholomew Roberts. The issue at stake was the supreme authority of a man elected captain to have his orders obeyed,instantly and without question. Without order and discipline, a ship would be in a state of chaos,and a pirate ship without order would be a ship of murdering fools.

No one spoke because there was nothing to add. As Cheddar regained his seat, a man or two gave him a nod of recognition indicating concurrence if not outright respect. The warrior's argument was unassailable. Disrespecting the captain while overcome by drink was one thing but disobeying a direct order was another thing altogether.

Gravity now took the place of levity, the crude jests about dogs forgotten. Cheddar had steered the trial back on course.

The captain of a ship is tantamount to an almighty and powerful god. As I ruminated on this I realized Cheddar did not need years of experience at sea to recognize the importance of obedience to authority. Cheddar had to have grown up paying homage to his gods, his shaman, his father, but of all these, someone in Cheddar's tribal life was his chief, an Ashanti chief no less. To a man like Cheddar, there was no difference between his captain and his chief. A man did not attack his chief or his captain, the idea was rather unthinkable.

It took almost an hour for the jury to announce its decision.

It took this long, in part, because a minority favored Jones and the majority agreed with Cheddar and leaned inexorably toward upholding the inviolate nature of the authority and dignity of the one made captain. Ultimately, good order and discipline triumphed personal loyalty and friendship. However, the reason it took this long was to reach consensus on punishment. Some said there were men on the jury who voted for Jones to suffer death and it took some doing to reach an acceptable compromise which allowed Jones to live.

Wales somberly read the judgment from a torn piece of foolscap, "these jury men, by their mark made below, hereby and do find that

Good Fortune seaman Thomas Jones did disobey the direct order of the captain and he is guilty of said offense. We the jury do find that the captain did use lawful force to make good his order and defend his person and that seaman Jones did then wrongfully and unlawfully assault the captain with the intention of doing the captain serious and grave bodily harm. We hereby sentence seaman Thomas Jones to suffer two lashes from each and every member of the crew."

Wales rolled up the paper and with his stern gaze dared anyone to express displeasure or voice an objection. His challenge was met with respectful silence. Being satisfied he could proceed, Wales went about the grim duty of seeing to it that the sentence was properly carried out. By long-standing custom, Jones was compelled to make his own cat o' nine tails. Captain Roberts, who had the power, declined to reduce or set aside the sentence, which was wholly expected. How could he show leniency to a man who brutally attacked him? The lives of his crew, especially in battle, rested on this immutable law of the sea. A captain's orders are law and his person is inviolate. With a nod to Cheddar, there was a tribal aspect to these events. Failure to honor such ancient laws and customs would be intolerable.

Later that hot afternoon, Jones had his wrists tied to the mainmast and his wide back was whipped raw. Wales dutifully made sure that Jones' friends gave it the required amount of effort but no one was made to lash Jones more than twice. Many on board had been flogged as revealed by the crisscrossing stripes on their backs. In addition to the pain, which was immense, there was a certain amount of shame involved in the ordeal, for the man being flogged and the men who swung the lash. As for me, I would almost rather be whipped then forced to flog another.

After strenuously seeking to avoid the task by virtue of not having signed the Articles, I laid my two strikes on as weak as decorum allowed.

To his credit, Jones bit a piece of oak in half but he never cried out.

A few weeks later we landed in Carriacou, a small island northeast of Grenada and north of the South American coast. The island is small and part of a chain of islands leading to St. Vincent. The *Good Fortune* was in dire need of repairs and overdue for a careening. Jones and four of his most fervent supporters stole a dugout canoe and it was believed they sailed or paddled to Union Island.

Captain Roberts and Wales, despite foreknowledge of the escape, did nothing to intervene.

The day the men went missing, we were ashore under some palm trees and Seahorse was overseeing maintenance on the ship. Wales was hoping to find a pig to roast and Captain Roberts was in a rare mood, professing relief that Jones had taken the law into his own feet. "Having Jones on board was like sailing with a corpse in the cargo. He and John Connelly and that idiot Shane Robinson can be someone else's problem," Captain Roberts told Wales, Sharp, me and a number of others milling about, men vying to avoid work and find some shade.

It was Sharp who added, "sir, beg pardon, they also took Edgar Pigot."

"Pigot?", Roberts said with a hint of mock surprise, "by God no, tell me it's not so. Mr. Pigot was the closest thing we had to a surgeon. I suppose now those duties will fall to Jacob Martin. In the meantime, remind me not to get sick."

I'd talked with the bumbling drunk Jacob Martin and even I laughed, despite wishing with all my might that Jones and his friends had taken me with them.

Chapter 6

We Beard the Lion

DAYS TURNED INTO WEEKS, WEEKS turned into months. The tattered edges of my letter from Constance were as brown as the back of my neck. There was no way to know if she was alive, if she had a baby, if it lived and whether it was a boy or a girl. If she had borne our baby without catastrophe it would be six months old.

To get back to her, or them, I had to ascertain a means of escape. Fleeing on the small and remote islands we visited to take on wood and water would have been tantamount to being marooned. If we visited a port or an island of any size, Wales saw to it that I was never unaccompanied or allowed off the vessel after dark.

We rarely remained in one spot for more than a few days and my navigational skills improved due to our constant movements. We sailed in search of booty or we fled to avoid battle with a patrolling man o' war. Since I was no pirate, it was all the same to me. During the early months of 1721, we sailed 2,300 miles to an island six miles wide, landing without incident. There were few navigators alive who could accomplish this feat. It was one thing to box the compass, another thing to steer a sailing vessel across a vast ocean to an island not much bigger than a medium sized sugar plantation.

Bartholomew Roberts proved himself to be an extraordinarily efficient pirate and nothing does more for the morale of a pirate crew than success. Some prizes were rich, others not so much. Roberts captured over a hundred ships in and around the West Indies, bringing sea borne commerce to a trickle. The planters, merchants, moneymen and sea captains grew increasingly reluctant to risk a sea voyage unless accompanied by a warship. Insurance rates in London climbed steadily upward. Consequently, plunder became harder and harder to find and then the Royal Navy made it worse by deploying more ships to stop the depredations. It would be wrong to say ours was the only pirate ship afloat but few captains could come close to Roberts in terms of the number of ships seized and the value of the cargo stolen.

King George and his fellow monarchs desperately wanted to hang Roberts and various and sundry pirate captains who were roaming about wreaking havoc. There were too many pirates, too many warships, and not enough prizes in the vicinity so the crew decided it was time to make another cross ocean voyage. Roberts put it to a vote and the crew decided to sail east to the coast of West Africa, or, as many called it, the Guinea Coast.

Weeks later, upon our arrival, the slave hunters became the prey.

The trade in human beings, sometimes called black ivory, had been growing rapidly and represented an enormous amount of money and an incalculable amount of suffering. Men, women and children were forced to work from sunrise to sunset in the cane fields and sugar refineries on the sweltering plantations in the disease infested West Indies and in settlements on the edges of the Spanish Main. Sugar plantations had become so profitable selling 'white gold' that their proprietors owned their personal fleet of slave and merchant vessels. It became fashionable for wealthy aristocratic English women to keep little negro boys as pets. When these unfortunate lads were on the edge of manhood, they were sent from the townhomes and manor houses in England back to the West Indies to toil for their overseers and masters.

Slavers frequently carried large quantities of ivory, gold and valuable trade goods. To save their owners and investors money, they made do with small crews and for all intents and purposes, the ships were unarmed. To the pirates who sailed under Roberts, a man who had thoroughly mastered the craft of high seas theft, these ships were vulnerable and profitable.

Whenever we seized a west bound slave ship loaded to overflowing with hundreds of human beings it sickened me, as it did a number of others in our crew. The inhumane conditions in these hellish ships made me despise the cruel men who kidnapped thousands of dark-skinned natives purely for profit. So vile were these slave traders, and the investors who supported them, a group that included kings and queens, I began to resolutely wish Roberts would order a slow death for these traffickers in human misery, ever mindful that Roberts himself had served on such a ship when he was taken prisoner by Captain Howell Davis.

Slavers sat idle for months before leaving port to insure a full hold, the naked bodies of the prisoners chained and packed so closely together they could scarcely breathe. The holds were packed in this manner because it was known that ten to twenty percent of the people would not survive the journey. Once the ship was full, it began the journey west, the lucky souls who died from disease were dumped into the sea, each carcass representing a loss of revenue but allowing room for the miserable survivors to move their shackled limbs. The ships had nets around the gunwales to prevent prisoners from jumping overboard when they were brought on the upper decks for air and a bit of exercise.

To save on food and water, diseased slaves, while barely alive but still breathing, were hurled to the sharks, leaving a trail of blood extending across the Atlantic. It was the barbaric habit of many crewmen to rape captive women and girls during the journey. This outrageous practice may give you some idea of the brutish nature of these so-called sailors.

Slaves spoke dozens of languages and dialects but we found inventive ways to offer some of the fitter men the chance to join our crew. They were permitted to join on the condition that they use any resulting plunder to purchase their freedom. This practice arose because whenever a slave was seized by pirates there were three options; killing, selling and keeping. There were hundreds of men on a slave ship and even if we wanted to keep them all, we lacked the space. As you would expect, in light of these practicalities, Captain Roberts sold most of the seized slaves at a discounted price to slavers waiting in one of the coastal forts. Unscrupulous buyers turned a blind eye to how he obtained his wares because they were eager to fill their holds, set sail, and reap a fortune selling the terrorized humanity making up their cargo.

I would agree that selling people made us no better than the slavers I found so despicable. To his credit, Roberts treated slaves humanely enough, although it came to my attention that some of the women were misused by white members of our crew. To avoid troubles with our negro pirates, the women were given scraps of food or items of clothing as payment for their 'favors'.

With each seized vessel our coffers filled but true to his word, Roberts never pressured me to sign the Articles. As such, I forfeited my share of the growing profits, not that this ever tempted me to change my mind. What I wanted money could not buy. The crew had expanded as well and not just due to the recruitment of negroes. Merchant seamen turned pirate trickled aboard as we seized one ship after another.

Consequently, we had just shy of two hundred men on board the *Good Fortune* and about a third of these were negroes for whom the choice was, in my view, somewhat easy. A black man allowed to join our crew was immediately freed from a degrading life of whippings, misery and unrelenting work.

As we prowled off the African coast, Cheddar became a sort of minor chieftain to our negro contingent. Fortunately for all, his recognition of the captain's authority was genuine and the respect accorded to Cheddar by the captain was reciprocal. Roberts and Cheddar possessed the ephemeral and elusive traits a leader needs to wield power effectively.

When a member of Cheddar's clan or tribe joined the crew, I would listen to Cheddar in his unintelligible sing-song native tongue trying to obtain news about his family and loved ones. Inevitably, when he could learn nothing, he would sulk for days. Who can blame him? I knew how he felt.

Intelligence reached Captain Roberts in September that a forty gun frigate under the auspices of the Royal African Company was patrolling the area in which we operated. We were no match for a warship possessing this much firepower.

An hour after I was made aware of this information Wales summoned the Lords to the captain's cabin to discuss the prospect of sailing west once again, possibly to Brazil. During the meeting, Lord Lutwidge casually sat reading a book, something he did quite often. Lutwidge hailed from Somerset and was filled with bonhomie. I had long ago surmised he was one of Roberts' favorites and as such, he could do no wrong. I also surmised Lutwidge was listening very carefully to the discussion, his book notwithstanding. If he had objections, he would make them known but in his own way and in his own time. He was not devious, just prudent.

"Aye, Brazil, that has its advantages. What do you say Wales?" Roberts asked.

"It might still be too warm in the West Indies. As you know, the men are eager to enjoy the fruits of their labors. We lost Hosea Lewis and Richard Whitbourne to the flux. Even so, with the addition of these Africans, we are woefully short of space, we are short of provisions and storing sufficient water to make it back across the Atlantic would be a challenge. I need not remind you we nearly perished of thirst last May," Wales said.

"Lewis was a good man," Roberts remarked. "Maybe if we could find a damned surgeon we would not lose so many of our experienced men to fevers. You've heard about *HMS Onslow*. The *Onslow* is ferrying soldiers to Sondozowi up to the mouth of the Cess. You know of it Glasby?"

"The Cess? I know of it. If the *Onslow* is sailing toward the Cess, that keeps them from troubling us for at least a week," I said.

Roberts brought some charts back to the table and unrolled them so I could pinpoint our position.

"Glasby, would you please fetch Cheddar," the captain said. He sat back making a tent with his fingers.

Returning with Cheddar, Captain Roberts had us gather round. As Cheddar nodded, Roberts explained his plan in simple terms. Copplestone and Ringrose added their thoughts and suggestions but it was abundantly clear, we were not going to flee.

Instead, we were going to attack the *Onslow.*

Three days later, after sailing north northwest, we changed course for the coast, heading east, ostensibly aiming for the mouth of the Cess. Long after the sun had reached its highest point, the lookout spotted sails off to starboard. Those of us on the quarterdeck could not see anything. "Three masts", the lookout yelled.

Wales yelled back, "frigate?"

"Aye, frigate. Sailing south by southwest." The lookout paused. "It's coming this way."

Roberts grew animated and kept his eyes toward the approaching sails. "Get Cheddar and reef the sail on the gaff rig and get two men up to the spar. Tell the gunners to man their positions. Black crew up, everyone else below, be quick, no doubt they've got their glass on us."

Cheddar reported to the quarterdeck wearing a huge black hat. Another black seaman called Neptune took the helm. With the large sail behind the mainmast down, our speed slackened and the men in the rigging at the spar began making a pretense of trying to make repairs. As Roberts had ordered, we flew no colors. These stratagems would combine to guarantee a visit from the patrolling *Onslow*. As I made my way through the hatch, five black pirates went to the deck and gathered along the starboard rail, none of these men were bearing arms, and our gun ports remained closed. Cheddar paced the deck frantically, yelling and pointing upward, urging the men in the rigging to get the ship back under full sail. He ordered Neptune to steer a course as if to flee from the *Onslow*, which was narrowing the gap separating us and at its current pace in these winds it would soon catch us.

After an hour of tension, the 'missing' sail and the spar were 'repaired' but the *Onslow* was only several hundred yards away and gaining.

Momentarily, Neptune came down to report, "two hundred yards."

Captain Roberts turned smartly to me and pulled his jewel-hilted dagger from its scabbard. "Here Glasby, just in case." I saw no reason to carry a weapon but stuck it off to my side, securely situated in my belt. I had no desire to get into an argument with Captain Roberts, especially now. The anticipation among the crew was becoming contagious and I was not immune from such feelings.

"Gunners ready?" Wales asked, and a chorus of voices manning the starboard guns chimed in unison, "gunners ready." Minus the starboard gunners and the black men above, I was looking over an expanse of 140 eager faces, some tattooed, some faces blackened with gunpowder or charcoal, all wild-eyed and all carrying gleaming cutlasses and primed pistols. Even if the men were filthy, they seemed to be in compliance with Article Five, given the immaculate condition of their arsenal. There had been no consumption of alcohol since the order the day before. A man sneezed freely and two more promptly coughed. "Shut the fuck up," someone warned, his threatening tone ominous and effective.

Captain Roberts crouched on the first step of the ladder leading up to the deck so he could see his army. He had donned his long crimson coat, a silk scarf wrapped around his head, and his trousers were neatly tucked into his black leather boots.

He spoke conversationally, with an air of supreme confidence. "My brothers." He shifted his gaze from port to starboard and back again. "The instant our guns fire, swarm the decks. Speed is essential. Stay alert and don't push and shove going up the ladders. It will be chaos until we gain the upper hand, which we will. Be mindful not to shoot Cheddar and Neptune. The rest of the deck crew will be scampering up the rigging to get out of harm's way. I almost pity those poor bastards."

Instead of raising his voice, as one might expect, he lowered it, speaking conspiratorially, which drew his rapt audience forward like wheat in a steady breeze. There was a childlike enthusiasm radiating from the warlord and we knew he had no pity for the men we were about to slaughter. "No man born of woman can fight like a pirate. Make these sorry shits feel your wrath, show them your power. Today, my demons, my devils, my furies, my friends, my partners in blood, today we beard the lion."

The two ships were drawing near. I could feel it.

There would be no 'vaporing', no oboes, drums or blasting trumpets. The musicians, or most of them, were armed for battle.

A few men grunted acknowledgment, a few cocked their pistols, a handful whispered to themselves or to each other. Some of them were destined to die today and I caught myself studying them as if by looking hard at their faces I could derive some morbid clue as to who would live and who would not.

The silence was broken by a voice from above, someone not familiar to us, hailing us from the frigate, someone commanding, "heave to, prepare to be boarded." The *Good Fortune* shuddered as our hulls met and the sides of the vessels scraped one another, oak rumbling against oak. There were gentle swells on the sea and our vessel swayed to and fro but we were used to this and paid it no heed. I heard more strangers shouting and talking from above and the footfalls of men coming over the sides.

A boarding party of indeterminate size was moving about leisurely, directly above our heads, blissfully unaware of 140 pairs of eyes looking up at the dark underside of the deck which would soon flow with rivers of blood, eyes following black shadows and rays of light, leaking through the cracks in the planking. Death would claim these interlopers when our hold exploded, sending forth torrents of hard men accustomed to such things, men not afraid to risk their own death to butcher their foes. There was one rule and one rule only, kill as many of them as fast as you can before they kill you.

Roberts took a deep breath and I held mine. My heart was thumping in my chest.

At last he yelled, "fire!"

The wooden doors over our gun ports squeaked and squealed open, all thirteen of them. I swear it took forever. Our gunners took aim, more from habit than necessity, touched the linstock to the touch holes and the heavy guns dutifully responded, roaring thick smoke and blasting solid shot into the gun deck of the *Onslow*. The first volley, at point blank range, damaged or disabled half a dozen guns and decapitated one of their gunners. Stunned sailors lost a limb, some lost two, having had the misfortune of standing or kneeling in the path of flying iron balls the size of a child's head or massive oak splinters and sometimes, shards of bone from another human being, made into missiles by the simple application of the law of cause and effect.

Muffled moans and pitiful pleas were drowned out by the battle cry of Roberts who led his howling pirates to the slaughter, swarming up the ladders and flying from the hatches like immense hornets.

One heavy gun on the *Onslow* managed to return fire but there was no volley. The solitary shot went whizzing through our hull and splashed harmlessly in the sea fifty yards off our bow. I know this because I saw a thin black blur as it flew past. The dazed men from the *Onslow* were ill-prepared for the raging mob emerging from the hold of our ship. A warrior needs time to get his mind ready for battle and our adversaries had to forego that luxury. Our gunners were dutifully and methodically reloading and I could hear their excited voices as the jubilant master gunner barked commands and assigned targets.

I timidly followed the last of the men into the open air and what I saw on our deck nearly made me retch.

At most, twenty men had boarded us, a few carrying muskets, some with fixed bayonets, but even that seemed more due to chance than preparation. Their captain, identifiable by his uniform, had a severe head wound and was lying prostrate in a pool of blood, having been wounded or killed.

Pistol shots cracked randomly, some of our men carried as many as six into a fight, there being no time to reload. Cutlasses battered muskets and the clang of metal hitting metal merged with the sound of men grunting or slashing or being slashed. Everyone was moving, but slowly, as if underwater. I had never witnessed men fighting for their lives in such numbers and in such close quarters. A severed hand slid across the deck, palm up, and when it hit the woodwork around one of the open hatches, it came to rest. I caught myself waiting to see if the hand would close. A distraught man, mumbling to himself, was frantically trying to load his musket. His ramrod shook violently and he was seated with his back to the foremast. One of the negro pirates, holding a boarding axe in both hands raised it high in the air and hacked deep into the man's shoulder, exposing a lung and sending droplets of blood high into the air like agitated champagne rocketing upward when the cork is popped.

Two pirates were stabbing a man in the stomach with long daggers. The dying man grimaced and struggled in vain to gather greasy strands of uncooperative gray and blue innards, mewing in agony and resignation.

A pirate with the cognomen Teredo, who had joined the crew a few weeks ago and claimed to be from somewhere near the Isthmus of Panama, picked up a discarded musket and rammed its long bayonet through the chest of a man, skewering him to our mainmast. Teredo, who looked to be part Moskito Indian, was also the name of the warm water worm that gnawed away at the hulls of seagoing sailing vessels across the Caribbean. Maybe the dark-skinned pirate was like this worm, or persistent, or hard to get rid of, or all of the above. I did not know him well enough to know how he came by his name. He was neither tall nor powerful but he was twisting and tugging and struggling to free the bayonet with all his might. He stopped his efforts abruptly and tumbled forward into the lap of his wounded adversary, apparently the result of being shot in the back of the head. I say this because there was a portion of the back of Teredo's skull missing when he collapsed, a hole large enough to hold an orange.

Lead balls buzzed through the air and rattled in the rigging, hitting spars, gunwales and, from time to time, finding a man with an audible and sickening thump.

Lines were snapping, men were hollering and screaming, white acrid clouds of powder smoke were making it impossible to tell friend from foe, and bits of I know not what struck me in the face. The air was filled with powder smoke that reeked of rotting eggs. I straggled up to the quarterdeck and realized unwounded men from the *Onslow* were retreating pell-mell to get off our ship and back to their own. Some of the sailors and soldiers who had not boarded the *Good Fortune* were attempting to fire from the relative safety of the *Onslow*. Here and there a pirate fell dead or wounded but the surprise and fury of our assault had made the death toll decidedly one-sided. I had an iron grip on the wooden railing to hold myself steady until the railing was shattered by a musket ball an inch from my hand. The shock and jolt knocked me backwards, stinging the nerves in my hand and wrist. It was only later when I realized I had almost been hit.

It would have been difficult to walk across our deck without stepping on a dead or wounded man or slipping in thick pools of blood, shimmering and glistening bright red in the sunshine.

Another powerful broadside erupted from below, causing more death and destruction. I knew our gunners had switched to using canister and grapeshot, their intent to kill or injure men, not to disable or damage the frigate.

I pulled myself up with my good hand. Captain Roberts was the first man in our boarding party to reach the higher deck of the larger *Onslow*. To my left, a short, balding soldier tumbled backwards over the port side of our vessel and dropped into the water, sending sheets of water flying. He had a hatchet buried high in his chest, beneath his chin, and he clutched at it as he fell.

I heard gibberish coming from Wales, who was positioned immediately below me, then he said, quite distinctly, "it's a race." For the life of me, I thought he had lost his reason and I could not ascertain who he was addressing or what he meant.

A shirtless and shoeless pirate casually walked across the deck, delicately stepping over bodies and debris, carrying a severed head by a set of braided pony tails. He brought his trophy backwards then launched it in a smooth arc into the air and toward the water. The pirate laughed when he saw the splash and turned about, heading toward the deck of the *Onslow* where he could presumably find someone else to dismember. This would not be the last time I saw such a grisly scene.

The men who had initially boarded our ship were dead or dying. Less than five had gotten back to the *Onslow*. Counting the standard crew of a frigate this large, reinforced by the soldiers they were carrying, this meant there were still as many as 220 men to confront. Whoever gained ascendency on the decks would triumph. Basic mathematics explained what Wales meant about it being a 'race'.

Some of our gunners emerged and joined the fray while others remained in position by their heavy guns and fired muskets into the gun ports of the *Onslow*. Roberts and his raiders were massacring any man brave or foolish enough to venture out from the hatches of *HMS Onslow*, the bulk of the crew trapped below decks. Two black pirates in our rigging swung downward on lines from the topmast, gracefully landing in the midst of the melee. They easily found weapons but there was no person to stab or cut or torment.

On our empty deck, the captain of the *Onslow* was still not moving and he was surrounded by his dead comrades and a smaller number of dead pirates. I saw faces of men I knew.

Captain Roberts was bent over at the waist, yelling furiously down the forward hatch, "strike your colors or we will blow your ship to matchsticks. Your captain is in our hands. I am Captain Bartholomew Roberts and I assure you safe conduct. Strike your colors."

Pirates were pacing the deck of the *Onslow*, wary, alert, their breathing labored. All were in a killing frenzy, including some with deep cuts and other serious wounds.

Roberts rose and turned to the *Good Fortune*, cupped his hands, and yelled "hoist the black flag."

Pirates on the *Onslow* gravitated toward Captain Roberts as we awaited word from the trapped survivors of the largely undamaged frigate. From where I stood it was clear that the men inside the *Onslow* had one option. I was admiring the taffrail of the *Onslow* when its aft hatch opened an inch, then another. The terrified survivors were helpless and they knew it. If these men ventured out, one or two at a time, they would be shot or hacked to bits. If they did not surrender, their ship would be lit on fire and they would drown or burn.

A shaking hand rose up waving a white handkerchief and I yelled, "captain, behind you," pointing at the fluttering handkerchief visible from the hatch. As the crumpled cloth rose higher, Captain Roberts, surrounded by his men, lowered his cutlass and raised his dark eyes to the black flag floating against the azure sky.

The disembodied voice of a stranger spoke conversationally, in contrast to the massacre just ended, "sir, the ship is yours. We strike our colors. We only ask for our lives and to care for our wounded."

Captain Roberts conferred with the unidentified man. Wales took charge of the pirate crew and assigned men to guard prisoners and others to initiate the process of securing their hard won prize.

In short order, eighteen soldiers joined our ranks, helping to replace eleven pirates killed or mortally wounded. In addition to Teredo, and the negro Ajax, we lost Pineapple, who was one of the cooks, and we lost the burly man with the big feet who had wrenched me from my hiding place on the *Samuel*. The Frenchman Jacques, another who had helped in my capture, was shot once in the thigh and stabbed in the stomach. It took two agonizing and interminable days for the stab wounds that perforated his stomach and his intestines to bring on his death.

Our adversaries had forty men killed outright. By some miracle, their captain regained consciousness. He remained under guard on the *Good Fortune*, where he would be joined by the remnants of his command. They would be permitted to limp back to the relative sanctuary of the coast.

At two hours past midnight we had settled into our new forty-gun frigate.

The captain of the *Onslow* had been led to believe he was in pursuit of easy pickings, a brigantine with a handful of negroes as its crew, men who by all appearances and preconceptions were scared witless, unarmed and incapable of flight. No doubt he and his officers were calculating their tidy profits on the nearby slave markets as they approached. The closer they got, the more they believed they had found a bit of plunder to fill their purses. Intent upon taking the *Good Fortune* as a prize, they had not contemplated firing at her with their array of heavy guns. The commander of the *Onslow* believed black men were superstitious and ignorant savages and this 'knowledge' made him incapable of entertaining the idea that he was not about to encounter a flock of lost sheep, but a pride of African lions. Had the captain not been blinded by this fallacy, Roberts could have forfeited the lives of himself and his crew. The English captain rightly believed his ship was superior, and it was, but his defeat was assured by his mistaken belief that he and his all white crew had been ordained by God and nature to possess unquestioned superiority over those born with black skin.

The captain's hubris cost him his ship, a third of his crew killed or turned pirate, and it nearly cost him his life.

Captain Roberts gambled that this would be so and he won, his brilliant *ruse de guerre* was astoundingly successful. The crew was in awe of him. At every turn in the frantic, bloody, violent episode, Captain Roberts had been at the forefront, exposing himself to danger, leading from the front and lending more credence to the crew's belief that he was, indeed, pistol proof.

As soon as our gear was stowed the drinking and music commenced. The revelry would last until dawn. During the early part of the night, some of the negroes found three or four drums. The rattling of the rigging in the majestic ship could be heard as the drummers began a slow tattoo on the drumheads. After a moment, one of Cheddar's friends started a sorrowful chant. He sang a phrase and ten or twelve men would repeat it, their voices growing exceptionally strong and powerful as they sang. A circular space cleared around the mainmast and the Africans claimed it for themselves, their songs and the drums echoing into the night. One man hefted a half pike and pantomimed seeking game, putting his hand to his forehead as if shielding his eyes from a bright sun. He was followed by men chanting and dancing behind him when he suddenly raised the pike and stabbed at his invisible prey.

Highlett joined me and as the dance seemed to end, he nudged me and said in a reverent voice, "you know, some of these fellows were warriors, sons of chieftains, all of 'em had to be hunters. They are unafraid and I thank the gods they are on our side. They do not do this often and they take this more seriously than most of our shipmates realize."

I'd sensed the gravity of what we'd witnessed and it moved something deep inside me, a shared loneliness for these men who had been taken from their loved ones, their homes, fields, and the savannahs they would never see again, at least not in this life.

"So Mr. Highlett, they dance to remember?" I ventured.

"Yes sir, I suppose. These men are not far from their homes and their dead ancestors. One of them told me not long ago, 'when a man dies, as long as he is remembered, he still lives.' Think there's any truth to that Mr. Glasby?" He turned and looked at me in the flickering shadows.

"I guess, in a way, that man has a point." I was thinking of how hard it must be for these men to resist the urge to take over the ship and sail back to Africa. That was a sentiment after my own heart. It was far more important to me than being remembered after I died.

Before he retired to his new cabin to let the crew enjoy their hard won victory, Captain Roberts asked the men if any objected to christening our new frigate the *Royal Fortune*. He was answered by cheers of acclamation. He bowed in gratitude and bid everyone a good night, but not before calling for three huzzahs for Cheddar and 'his crew'. Cheddar had become the man of the hour. If Roberts retired early to allow Cheddar to reap the praise of the men, as I strongly suspected, it underscored his unselfish willingness to let someone else share the glory. Harkening back to the trial of gunner Thomas Jones, I was reminded that Cheddar had performed valuable services for his captain once before. Roberts, no doubt, remembered that debt.

I stood on the expansive deck and looked at the night sky glistening with thousands of distant stars. Every few minutes, a glowing burst of orange or blue or yellow would race across the sky, fragments burning quickly and brightly. For those black men who had drummed and sang and the men who danced, I suspect these brilliant meteors were omens of a sort.

With the heavy guns brought over from our former vessel, the *Royal Fortune's* armaments consisted of mounted guns made up of 4 twelve-pounders; 18 eight-pounders; 6 six-pounders and 8 four-pounders. There were seven guns situated in the main and foremast, all two and three pounders, with a pair of swivel guns mounted on the mizzen.

We were sailing west, back to the Caribbean, white spume flying, comfortably and confidently in sole and unfettered possession of one of the most powerful warships in the world.

That was an omen even a boy from Boston could understand.

Chapter 7

The Vicar

WITH THE POSSIBLE EXCEPTION OF some of the new negro pirates, I suppose everyone else was looking forward to a return to the West Indies. If I was ever to escape, it would have to be in a place where I had a fighting chance of eluding Roberts and company but no matter what, I still had to make it back to Boston. As a result, it never occurred to me to make an escape bid in far off Africa, a place notorious for savagery and deadly diseases. This fanciful dream, for it was not yet a plan, assumed that Constance was still alive and unmarried. If not, which I dreaded, I still wanted to reclaim my freedom before I succumbed to some unnamed illness or found myself at the end of a noose. As musket balls whizzed by me during the fight to take the *Onslow*, it did not occur to me that a stray ball nearly ended all my earthly woes. It was after the fighting that this sobering realization took root.

It took time to grow accustomed to the palatial size of the new ship, particularly the sumptuousness of the captain's cabin. The ornate interior and size of the great cabin was tangible proof that sea captains truly were the equivalent of seafaring royalty.

Learning the nuances of the big ship; how it handled, drifted and performed in varying wind, currents and seas would take longer. The sailing characteristics and eccentricities of the *Royal Fortune* were of the utmost importance to the man responsible for getting the ship from place to place. Seahorse, thankfully, had an affinity for assessing a vessel and I found his insights beneficial as they pertained to my duties. He was an excellent sailor.

During a routine early morning meeting with Captain Roberts, Wales and the enigmatic Hunter Sharp, Wales asked me an odd question, or should I say he asked me a question oddly. "Glasby, have you noticed that we have men on board who enjoy the," he fumbled his words, embarrassed, "how shall I put this?"

"Do you mean men who like the intimate company of other men? Is that what you want to 'put'?" I had grown accustomed to dealing with Wales and knew how far I could go when it came to sarcasm. "Sodomites," I added gratuitously. It was a hanging offense in the British Navy.

For who knew what reasons, this subject seemed to make Wales uncomfortable so he was relieved by my straightforward remarks. "Yes Glasby, we're free men you know, to each his own and all that." He rolled his eyes.

Enjoying his discomfort, I ventured, "why Wales, I never would have guessed. Is this little confession about you? Or perhaps the strangely quiet and stranger man, our friend Mr. Sharp?" I looked at Hunter who looked back at me as if we had never met. I held his gaze and slowly shook my head.

Wales replied defensively, "me? Not me Glasby, never had the urge. But I would not like to say 'never', suppose it depends on the bloke." The captain was trying to drink his tea without spitting it out on the enormous mahogany table around which we sat.

Wales forced himself to sound unconcerned. "You know the Vicar, delightful chap. Always willing to lend a hand." Wales turned to his captain for support.

"Always helpful," Roberts confirmed.

"Aye captain, always willing to be helpful." Wales repeated. "He's a cheery lad, drinks, but not to excess. You know the Vicar's always spoutin' off about the Good Book, likes to quote the Bible he does. Even heard him utter a prayer over a dead member of the brethren when we took the *Onslow*, which we all admire..."

I interrupted, "Wales, everyone knows about the Vicar and the Albino. What does this have to do with me? Do you want me to teach the Vicar how to navigate? If yes, by all means, so you can drop me off and let me go back to Boston." I could scarcely believe I said the last line. There were no secrets on a pirate ship, they must know. Besides, no one said anything about navigation or teaching for that matter. My remark, thankfully, fell on deaf ears and of course everyone knew how desperately I wanted to get home. Picking up the main thread I said, "or perhaps you want the Vicar to teach me about the Bible? I assure you there is nothing he can teach me that I do not know."

"Sodomy is an acquired taste", observed Mr. Sharp, out of nowhere. He shrugged at our collective silence and asked for rum. Captain Roberts poured from a sparking crystal decanter nestling on a bright silver tray, another of our recently plundered trophies of war. Mr. Sharp raised his glass and gave a toast "to sodomy" and promptly drained it in one large and audible gulp.

Wales blinked slowly and deliberately, twice. "Rum for breakfast. Alright, back to you and the Vicar, Mr. Glasby. This is not about navigation or the Bible. The Vicar has very sincerely asked that someone help him to read. Given the nature of the task and the nature of the Vicar, we, that is, the captain and me, thought it best to ask you first, just to avoid any misunderstanding. You know, to avoid any awkwardness."

"Just so he can read the Bible?" I wondered, wrinkling my forehead.

Captain Roberts spoke up, "not so he can read the Bible, no Harry. If a man can read he can read anything. We've found medical books on board and the Vicar says he would like to study them and put some of his skills to use helping the less fortunate, especially the sick and injured. You may have noticed his penchant for helping afflicted and wounded men, a trait we have admired since he joined the crew, which if memory serves was after we took the *Pink Rose*. We have no surgeon but we have the kindly Vicar, we have discovered books on medicine— and we have you," Roberts said. Roberts was definitely not the only crewmember who lamented the lack of a surgeon. The absence of medical care had been especially acute in the immediate aftermath of the battle with the *Onslow*. Even if the severely wounded were beyond help, comforting them as they lay dying mattered.

"Can I refuse?" I asked half-heartedly. The Vicar was friendly enough but not too friendly and the Albino was, like Mr. Sharp, quiet as can be. I knew the Albino was English and naturally he grew up being ridiculed and a favorite of gawkers. For being born as white as a sheet and for being a sexual outcast, he found peace and solace among pirates, the irony of which did not elude me. Naturally, the crew chided him about his ghostly appearance, as they chided each other, but not maliciously. His unnatural relationship with the Vicar hurt no one and if it offended anyone, they kept it to themselves.

The Vicar and the Albino were not the only men who behaved in such a way.

Most pirate articles strictly excluded women and boys, meaning young boys. That left a number of hearty men who sought relief or companionship, or whatever they needed, with other men. I knew of these men and these relationships and rarely gave the subject much thought. I was not especially eager to learn more but teaching the Vicar to read would give me something constructive to do and with any luck, I might get him to a point where he could actually learn something about medicine. Any medical care was better than none.

"I will agree to do this on one condition, I shall be paid fifty pounds," I offered sheepishly and without conviction. Fifty pounds was an enormous sum.

"Deal," a beaming Wales said, slamming his open hand on the table, quick as that. I realized I had underbid but a deal is a deal. I needed money if I was to escape and since I adamantly refused to become a pirate, I was not able to claim any share of the vast sums we had stolen since my capture. It was proposed I would get half in advance and half when the Vicar could read a full page of the Bible. We finished breakfast and the Vicar met me in the forecastle early that afternoon.

Surprisingly, the thoughtful Vicar could read many short and simple words, which gave us an enormous head start, and to make the endeavor even less onerous, if not downright enjoyable, he turned out to be a splendid pupil. From the outset, he insisted I refer to him by his Christian name, Henry. I agreed on the condition that he refer to me as Harry.

"Henry, you are making remarkable progress. I heartily commend you for working so hard." We had been studying once or twice a day, every day, for three weeks, sometimes for two or three hours. Henry gave himself no respite during his free hours, applying his zeal and energy to the task and inspiring me in the process. "Didn't you tell me you had some schooling in London?" I asked.

"I told you I was in the St. Mary's foundling school but you never asked me if I had any schooling. I did not. The 'school' was more like a prison. Maybe worse." Henry closed the thick medical book he had in front of him, momentarily at a loss for words. "Harry, I believe I can trust you." Before I could confirm the accuracy of his belief, he lowered his voice. "My mother sold me to other men, for money, to buy gin. The Lord took her when I was eight and after her pauper's funeral I lived, if you could call it living, in narrow alleys, mostly by the docks. I had been begging there for months when the Lord intervened. A kind and honest man, with the best of intentions, took me to St. Mary's to keep me from starving. God preserved me and I went to sea on a merchant vessel when I was twelve."

I didn't know what to say. "I'm sorry Henry. I was in London once. I cannot begin to imagine what it would be like for a young orphan. Is the school where you were introduced to religion?" I did not want to dwell on the abominations he suffered as a child and I knew a thing or two about the evils of drink.

Henry avowed that it was and told me that God helps those who help themselves. "My first captain was a brute. I may be the only sailor you'll ever meet who was happy to be taken by a press gang. That's how I was introduced to the Royal Navy. Do you know what it's like to be trapped in a situation with no way out?" He was absent-mindedly stroking Jack's head. Jack was the Vicar's enormous Havana brown cat. The nicked edges of the beast's ears twitched independently of one another while we talked.

"I most certainly do know what it's like to be trapped." Feeling even more uncomfortable, I asked Henry about the gold rings he and the Albino wore.

He held up his hand, wriggling his fingers, showing me his ring. Jack raised his head in silence, protesting the disruption then laid his thick head back down, eyeing me with disgust that disintegrated into disinterest. Cats were valued for killing rats and Jack had earned his keep.

"I found the Albino in Tortuga and I'll never forget that day. His Christian name is Robert and he hails from Wiltshire. Speaking of abuse, you would not believe the horrid way he was treated growing up. Mankind is terribly cruel to those perceived as 'different'. Men learn to behave this way but they can be monstrously cruel, even at a young age. We were both running away."

Boys in Boston taught me about cruelty after my father's murder. Jack resumed dozing and I envied him for his inability to worry about aspects of life that have come and gone.

"We went on the account because for men like us, well, for men like us, it allows us a chance to live without fear, or should I say, less fear. Did you know Sir Francis Drake was a vicar before he became a famous pirate?" Henry fingered a colorful glass trade bead he wore around his neck on a strip of leather, the bead was the size of a grape.

"I thought Drake was a privateer," I said, "but no, I'd never heard of Drake being a man of God."

"Privateer, pirate, what's the real difference in the end? How did all that work for Captain Kidd," observed my student. He had a point. There was still a lively debate about whether or not Kidd had been made a scapegoat for the rich and powerful men who backed his doomed foray as a privateer. "No matter what, we are all men of God."

Henry glanced at Jack, keeping his eyes downcast.

"Harry, thank you for helping me. I've learned a great deal and I owe it all to you." He looked up at me and awaited my response. His compliment and the sincere manner in which he delivered it made me feel slightly embarrassed.

"That makes two of us, Henry. Daresy, I've learned a lot too."

Henry smiled and gently lowered Jack to the deck. "Jack likes you too, Harry."

"You don't say. How do you know?"

"Jack and I have long talks, I just know." Henry was not being flippant about the cat.

We went back to reading. Before we finished, he told me he had another Bible verse for me. "The fear of man bringeth a snare; but whoso putteth his trust in the Lord shall be safe." Henry said the verse was from the Book of Proverbs. I thanked him for all the verses he had shared with me and made him promise to bring me another the next time we met. We had become friends and I was proud of what we had achieved. He was among the most honest and genuine men I have ever known.

"Harry, while you've been helping me I've been trying to teach myself to write. I have far to go but open your hand." I did as he asked and Henry laid a scrap of parchment in my palm. Before I could open it, he admonished me, "my writing is like that of a child but I wanted to give you this as a token of my esteem. Wait til I go before you read it because you will tell me how wonderful it is to encourage me and I will be uncomfortable and you will grow uncomfortable because of my discomfort. I will keep reading and I will practice writing and I will thank God for you and when the day comes that I can write properly we can look back at this piece of paper and laugh about my progress."

"I'm the one who's uncomfortable but I'll wait. I'm curious not because of how you write, as that does take practice, but I'm eager you see what you've selected. You have a knack for things like that, but go now and take that useless cat with you."

It was the last time I saw Henry alive.

The next day, before dawn, I was making my way to the quarterdeck when a breathless Seahorse rushed up to me. "Wales wants you, urgent like, follow me." I did not ask why but we rapidly went into one of the areas where a number of the men slept. I saw Wales and Sharp, each holding a lantern. Mr. Sharp set his lantern down and commenced digging through a sea chest. The Albino was standing near us, half hidden in the shadows, his arms folded tightly. He was watching Mr. Sharp intently and he looked like he had been crying. He was in great distress so I knew something terrible had happened but I had no idea how terrible. Wales nodded a curt greeting and I nodded back.

"Can anyone tell me what's going on?" I said.

Wales, using his thumb and index finger, held up a thin-bladed knife by its wooden handle, a knife with fresh blood on the blade.

"Here 'tis," Sharp said, handing Wales something else, a small item on a string.

Wales asked, "ever seen this before?" I admitted I had, it was the glass trade bead the Vicar wore around his neck.

"It's Henry's, I mean, the Vicar's. Where is he?" My voice sounded hollow and I dreaded the answer.

The Albino put his head in his hands and commenced weeping.

Wales watched the Albino and said to me, with evident emotion, "the Vicar is dead. The Albino killed him."

Chapter 8

The Albino

MR. SHARP TOOK THE ALBINO away, to my momentary relief. All of this was too much to absorb at once. I gingerly stepped around pools of blood on the deck which seemed to extend in every direction. Any number of people had traipsed through the blood, spreading it around, making it difficult to see if the killer left any marks with his shoes or his feet. Wales saw me examining the mess and said, "we already looked. I had the Vicar carried to the forecastle. When you see his body, you will know why there is so much blood, so come then." When Wales referred to Henry as a 'body,' I nearly choked up, struggling with all my might to keep my composure.

On our way forward, I saw seething anger in the faces of half a dozen sleepy-eyed men. The Vicar was uniformly well-liked. My thoughts were churning, why on earth anyone, much less the Albino, would want the Vicar dead. It made no sense, none of this made sense. The Vicar and I had become friends and I was shocked and deeply saddened by his murder. When we arrived in the forecastle and I saw what had been done to this inoffensive soul, I retreated into a dark place. I was furious and perplexed. Someone had removed Henry's clothes, making him appear even more vulnerable as he lay in repose on the bare wood.

The killer had hacked Henry's face, made deep cuts on his neck and there were too many stab wounds in his chest and abdomen to count, at least twenty that I could see. His eyes were glassy and half open. Wales confirmed that the knife found in the Albino's possessions had a blade which matched the width of the stab wounds.

"Wales, this was the work of some madman in a sort of frenzy."

"Agreed", Wales said, "look at his hands."

I bent over slightly and took the Vicar's right hand. His skin was already cool to the touch and I detected the onset of stiffness. There were wounds between his blood stained fingers, one was two inches deep, the others were fairly superficial. He had been wounded when he tried to fight off his attacker and he had no such wounds on his left hand. But I noticed something else and I drew Wales' attention to it.

Wales looked up from the mutilated corpse and said, "if the Albino killed his mate, why would he put the knife and the Vicar's necklace in his own sea chest? Some in this crew are idiots but a sane man would toss the knife over the side, necklace too."

Understandably the killer wanted to shift blame to the Albino but putting the knife and the necklace in the Albino's sea chest convinced me that we could start this process by putting the Albino on the list of those we believed to be innocent. Wales and I saw eye to eye on that score. But the Albino would have useful information and we needed a place to talk. "Can we question the Albino in the captain's cabin?"

Wales shook his head, "the captain is still sick. I had Mr. Sharp take the Albino to the quarterdeck. I don't want the men getting to him. You can talk to him up there."

Sharp, appearing sober, alert even, was standing protective watch over the Albino who was sitting down, his back against the gunwale, his frail childlike hands in irons. We had the space to ourselves. Wales ordered the shackles removed and Sharp complied, dropping them with their characteristic clanging. I waited for Wales to question the distraught man but instead, Wales whispered something to Sharp. I am not sure why I had taken this task upon myself but I had a burning desire to get to the truth. The sea was rolling gently and bluish gray pre-dawn light cast everything in a monotone.

Wales gave me plenty of latitude, sensing the intensity of my desire to find out why this had happened. I knelt down and looked at the dazed Albino. He seemed oblivious to my nearness. "Robert, I am very sorry for your loss. Henry cared deeply for you."

"I didn't kill him Mr. Glasby. Henry and I loved each other." The Albino appeared ghostly in the dim light, almost transparent.

"He loved you too. If you didn't kill him, help us. Who did? Why would anyone do this?" My voice cracked, somewhere on this ship a murderer was praying for invisibility and sanctuary.

"I wish I knew Harry. As far as I know, he had no enemies. You see someone wants you to think I did it, you see that?" Robert was pleading, his pale pink eyes, darkened by crying, made it hard for me to concentrate.

It occurred to me that maybe the killer's real target was Robert—the Albino. Someone killed the Vicar to pin the crime on the Albino, believing the Albino who would surely be executed for the deed.

"Is there anyone who would want you dead? Fights, debts, arguments, what?" I put my hand on his arm, "anyone?"

Robert hung his head. "The night we took the frigate and everyone was celebrating, something happened. It's happened before."

"What? Just tell me."

"I was with Henry." Robert was struggling.

"Yes? Confession is good for the soul". When I said that, he wiped away a tear.

I tried coaxing him, to encourage him to trust me. "Henry is dead, some think you killed him. Tell me what happened."

The Albino looked to see if anyone was within earshot. He spoke timidly and I had to strain to hear him, "a soldier from the *Onslow* saw us. It was dark so he lit a lantern, Henry and I had no clothes on. We were doing something. The man saw us and called us vile names, blew out the lantern and left. I don't know his name or what he looks like. All I saw was his light. He was upset or angry, I know that."

"Would you know his voice?" I asked, encouraged by the details of the incident.

He pondered my question. If he was pretending, he was quite convincing. I had an overwhelming instinct he was trying to be honest with me and with himself. "Maybe," he said. "Maybe I would, the man had an accent I didn't recognize. That's how I knew it was someone new, but I'm not sure."

"Good enough," I said, satisfied he was telling all he could remember. Before I stood up I already knew what I was going to do next. The sun was crowning over the edge of the sea which was good; I needed light. "I need you to take off your clothes."

He rose awkwardly and looked at me with unabashed skepticism. I moved slightly to turn my back to the deck and block the eyes of any man now awake, giving the Albino the illusion of privacy. He pulled off his shirt, then his trousers, silently and without protest. Sharp held his clothes, looking at me like it was my turn to be the crazy one.

The nearly naked man stood and looked at me blankly. He could have posed for an alabaster statue carved by Greek sculptors.

Wales gently told the pirate to get dressed, then had him put back in irons.

"The soldiers," I said to Wales. It was more of a command than a request.

"Yes, the soldiers" He responded eagerly, "where?"

"Up here, I want them up here."

In short order, we had all eighteen soldiers newly recruited from the *Onslow* assembled on the quarterdeck. As word of the killing spread, most of the crew assembled on the main deck, watching intently. One by one I had each soldier remove his clothes. I was very deliberate and when I finished with one, I started with another, watching their eyes for hesitation, trepidation, or any sign that might reveal a guilty state of mind.

I was almost positive I would find nothing of significance on the quarterdeck and my suspicions were correct. When the last soldier dropped his shirt, I went to the rail and loudly told the growing crowd to draw near and listen to what I had to say.

"One of you sorry bastards murdered my friend." I let that sink in, they knew the Vicar was dead, they knew how he died, and now they knew it mattered to me. Most of the crew knew who I was but I kept my head down and no one paid much attention to me, or so it seemed. I took a moment to gather my thoughts. "The Vicar was a good man and the Albino is without blame, on both of these propositions, there can be no dispute. The Albino is innocent and the Vicar's murderer tried to make it look otherwise. For these bloody crimes, the Vicar's killer will pay, on my solemn oath, I promise you he will pay." Men glanced at each other and stared back at me but all were silent. Randomly pointing my finger at one, than another, I yelled, "confess, confess your sin and be forgiven. I'm going to the galley. You know you did it and I know who you are. If you do not confess, you know damn good and well I will find you. You have five minutes, not a second more. Bring me the ring. Confess and you can beg for mercy, but bring—me—the—ring. The rest of you, stay right where you are until Wales comes back." My outrage was not contrived, it was righteous and I wondered if it would work.

I stormed down to the main deck with Wales close on my heels leaving the befuddled soldiers and half the crew to mill about. We headed for the hatch to access the galley and like the Red Sea, men parted to let us pass. One way or the other, I would have the murderer.

We sat, waiting in the gloom, listening to the wooden joints of the ship creak and moan. I watched dust motes drift by like lazy gnats and was annoyed by them. I traced a round water stain left on the wooden table by a mug or a cup and saw dried blood around the base of my fingernail. Wales was watching me and asked sympathetically, "do you think he will come?"

"It doesn't matter Wales, the murderer is on this ship and if he doesn't come, so be it. Either way, I'll have him."

Wales looked up as I was talking. He must have seen someone block the light and cast a shadow as he came down the hatch. I half turned to see who it was and rubbed my bloody finger on my trouser leg.

Someone was coming, but he was hesitant and that was a promising sign. His thin form was silhouetted by the morning light so we could not yet see his face. When he drew closer, he ran his hat round and round, barely holding the brim by the tips of his fingers, fidgeting. He was slightly built, with tousled curly hair and a sparse growth of auburn hair on his chin, barely visible fuzz on his cheeks. I'd noticed him spending time with the musicians although he did not play an instrument, but beyond that, I knew next to nothing about him.

"William Every," Wales said.

The man looked sorrowful, trying vainly to hide behind his twirling hat, then to Wales, "yes sir, they call me 'Fly.'"

"Fly."

I said the name like I'd been chewing a piece of rotting meat. My hands were clenched in fists and the venom coursing in my veins commanded me to make him suffer. "You sorry son of a bitch. I let you come down here so those cut throats up there wouldn't take your balls and make you eat them."

He laid his hat on the wooden table. He was so scared he didn't know what to say and now he had no place to put his empty hands.

"The ring, I want the ring," I demanded, my voice shaking.

He wiped a sweaty palm on his baggy trousers and reached in his front pocket. I kept my eyes fixed on his face. He stared at the table, avoiding my eyes. He laid a plain gold band on the dark wood and using his right index finger, he nudged it toward me. The ring sliding across the wood made a scraping noise.

"I see your hands are clean, 'Fly', now take off your shirt."

"Yes, sir," his voice was barely audible.

"Now," I barked. Fly twitched and flinched when I spoke. He was procrastinating and I knew why.

He wrestled his long-sleeved shirt over his head and began crying. His pale chest and shoulders were crisscrossed with long ribbons of scratches and red gashes.

Wales was menacing and for an instant I thought he intended to strike the man. Through his teeth he hissed, "Mr. Every, why? Why did you do this terrible, terrible thing?"

Fly was trying in vain to moisten his lips. I still believe if I had been in reach of a knife I would have gutted him then and there. Wales let out an exasperated sigh, "pull yourself together you slimy turd, why did you kill the Vicar?" Wales asked with such seething intensity it would have frightened a hangman.

It took the man a few long seconds to get his wits together.

"I was drunk, sir. I used to hear them two at night, breathing hard and moving about. It worked on me it did, I saw the two of them doin' things. I was on the deck drinkin' late and ran out of rum. I remembered seeing the Albino somewhere so I thought the Vicar—I thought the Vicar might be alone. He was, he was asleep." Mr. Every stopped, lost in thought. He must have been reliving what he had done just a few hours ago and I was forced to imagine the horror of it all in my mind's eye.

Every's nose was running and he sniffed, then he raised his hands just above his waist, palms down, performing some odd pantomime. "I guess I put my hands on his legs, he was not wearin' trousers. I saw no harm, I meant him no harm. All sudden like, he started clawin' at me and cryin' out." Mr. Every kept moving his hands up and down while he described what the Vicar did. I was certain he was unaware of what he was doing as he described the murder. "I put my hand over his mouth but he fought, he was hurtin' me. Somehow I got my knife—he kept tryin' to get away. He fought harder and I was afraid someone would hear him cry out, I had to make him be quiet, I just wanted him to be quiet."

I confronted him with the obvious. "You put your hand over his mouth and you cut him, he fought harder so you stabbed him. Then, when he was quiet, pardon me—after you murdered him, you stole his ring and his necklace. You put the bloody knife—your bloody knife—and the necklace—you stuck them in the Albino's sea chest to make it look like he did it. Then you hid in some dark corner. You stupid fucking idiot. So, why keep the goddamn ring?" Mr. Every, I noted, did not deny or refute any of the accusations I had levied against him.

"I don't know, I really don't. I had feelings for him, I guess. I would never hurt him, I told you I was drunk. I'm sorry." He was pleading for sympathy and I had none, his pathetic begging demonstrating to me, at any rate, that Mr. Every was not sorry he had senselessly murdered someone, instead, he was overcome by self-pity. My loathing for the man increased with each breath he stole from the stale air in the galley.

Wales stood resolute, he too was disgusted. "Fly, did you put him in your mouth? You left that out. You wanted to suck him didn't you?"

All Fly could do was nod. He was sobbing too hard to make any more words.

Later that morning, Wales took me to see the captain. The Albino was there with Mr. Sharp and Lord Ringrose.

I asked the captain how he was feeling and he put his hand on his stomach and said he was feeling better. He told me what Wales had conveyed to him about the murder and particularly about our close examination of the Vicar's body. "Wales told me the two of you noticed that the Vicar's gold ring was missing but you noticed something important didn't you?"

"Aye," I said, "I did."

"You wisely made sure the crew saw you examining the soldiers, one by one. What a master stroke Harry. Were you convinced it wasn't one of the soldiers?" Roberts asked.

"It could have been. I just knew, at first, I knew only that we were searching for a white man. If none of the soldiers had any marks, I would have started with the white men in the crew, one by one, until we found the scratches. If the killer was watching us on the quarterdeck, and he had to be, he knew I was coming. He knew why I was coming and he knew once we made him remove his shirt it was all over. I gave the killer the chance to turn himself in. It saved a little time, for him and for us. Whoever he was, he would not want to remove his shirt with the men watching."

I was taken aback at how intriguing this subject was to the captain.

"The Vicar was fond of you," Roberts noted and looked over at the Albino. "Was there a particular reason you looked at his fingernails?"

"When I was teaching him to read, I noticed how strong and clean his hands were. Most of the men have filthy hands. When I saw his ring was missing, that's when I thought to look at his fingernails. They were packed with dried blood and skin, the skin of a white man, but not 'white skin' if that makes sense, without doubt it was not the bleached white skin of an albino. I knew from the skin it was not the Albino and of course, it could not have been any of the negroes. Finding the dagger and the necklace in the Albino's sea chest told me that it was likely anyone but the Albino—I just used common sense." I saw Sharp and Lord Ringrose looking at their dirty hands and fingernails. When they saw me watching, they tried to pretend otherwise and I nearly laughed at them but this was not the time.

Roberts seemed satisfied, "Harry, did anyone ever tell you Jones had a ring?"

"Jones? Thomas Jones?" There could be no other Jones.

"Yes, Thomas Jones. The same Jones who tried to beat me to death while you stood idly by and watched—that Thomas Jones. Thomas and Pedro exchanged gold rings. You seem to notice things like that. You didn't know?" The captain was enjoying himself at my expense.

"No sir, I didn't know. In my defense, I believe I had only been your prisoner for a few days. So, when Jones came at you that night, you knew he and Pedro were....." I was unsure what they were.

"Of course I knew," Roberts grinned. He was feeling better. Ringrose was carefully watching me, his filthy hands clasped behind his back.

"How?" I asked, "how did you know about Jones and Pedro?"

The captain arched an eyebrow, the one with the scar, "I know everything Mr. Glasby, I know everything, because I must, you see. To be a captain under the black flag, the more you know, the longer you live. I must say, you have been a great help to us and today, today you have not only been of enormous help, but you probably saved the Albino's life. I daresay the crew will love you, as they should. Tomorrow, Wales will deal with young Mr. Every. Until then, I am going to rest. I find the quiet to be restorative."

"There is something you should know, all of you." I turned from the captain to address the Albino who had listened to all this attentively. I had been at this long enough to know, to some degree, how these men thought. "The Vicar fought his attacker, he fought like a pirate."

That such a kindly soul had gone down fighting would resonate with the crew, men who esteemed bravery in a fight the way they esteemed unwavering loyalty to a shipmate. It might also erase any stigma that might linger due to the Vicar's particular brand of loyalty to his mate.

The Albino's eyes were rimmed with tears but he offered me a weak smile of gratitude, which I returned. "Thank you Harry, that means a great deal to me. As the captain said, I owe you my life. If you gentlemen will please excuse me, I too find quiet to be restorative and I prefer to mourn in peace."

Chapter 9

Marooned

THE *ONSLOW* HAD BEEN CONSTRUCTED with a dozen small cabins, six on the starboard side, six on the port side. When we took the ship and made her the *Royal Fortune,* the other interior bulkheads were removed to provide ease of movement while under way and during a fight. Normally, I was informed, these modifications to our internal configuration would have included eliminating the tiny private cabins since pirates take the issue of equality seriously. On a frigate, these cabins are reserved for officers or important passengers. Our crew, on their own initiative, said they wanted to reward the Lords for their dedicated service so after taking the *Onslow,* the cabins were kept intact and one had been left vacant.

During the afternoon, after I had exposed Mr. Every, Wales pulled me aside and gave me the remaining cabin. He said the men were grateful and impressed by how I handled the Vicar's murder. After expressing my reservations about the propriety of this development, I set aside my unease, thanked Wales and went to gather my belongings.

I moved what little I owned into the cabin and immediately realized the solitude was helping me focus on Mr. Every's upcoming murder trial. Indeed, it was due to my sudden elevation to cabin dweller that certain aspects of the trial had their hazy beginnings.

The small enclosure, which resembled a water closet, was barely long enough for an average size man to sleep comfortably and if I stood with my back to my bunk, I could extend my arms and press the narrow door with my flattened palms. My cabin was on the port side, toward the bow, and the adjoining cabin, aft, was occupied by Lord Lutwidge. In other words, he was my next door neighbor.

As I was getting situated, Lutwidge cornered me in the passageway as I was coming out. His praise for my role in the resolution of the murder was effusive and his professed joy at having me in the cabin next to his did, I must admit, lessen my self-consciousness about being given special treatment.

"By the gods Glasby, we'll make a pirate of ye yet. If it was up to your fine friend Skeffington Lutwidge, one has to wonder why you could not find yourself sitting on the privy council."

I told him I was fine being the first mate. My refusal to sign the Articles and become a pirate was known by all and thus, it did not behoove me to mention it unnecessarily.

Lutwidge was in one of his moods and he ignored my reticence, "a man needs ambition. Who but Captain Roberts could take a fancy to a fine warship like this and go the next step and make it his own? Our perplexing world has clever captains, brave captains and it has cruel captains but a man cannot be a captain without ambition. Bartholomew and I share a belief in the merits of discipline and good order. Smart, cunning, brave, audacious, decisive, all this and more, eh?" Lutwidge said.

"No one doubts the abilities of Captain Roberts," said I, not meaning to sound impatient.

Lord Lutwidge was fastidious about his distinguished appearance which was enhanced by his towering height. If you put a powdered wig on him he could have passed for a peer. He had that regal air about him and he used it to good effect. He laid a friendly hand on my shoulder which was his way of saying he was about to impart what he called his 'wisdom pearl'.

"Aye, able he is—but there is a great deal more to the man. There is a natural sense of justice about him which most ambitious men lack. Curious that. He can drub, cut or shoot a man during a fight and no one can deny him that power. Oh, he can be replaced by an unhappy crew but how likely is that? Really. He is ambitious but the men are convinced he covets their well-being as much as his own. That's why he will let the trial of Mr. Every run its course tomorrow. It's on the crew, not the captain."

Lutwidge had a way with words but now he had mentioned something of pressing interest, tomorrow's trial.

The trial of Thomas Jones for seeking to avenge the shooting of Pedro was the first of many such proceedings I had witnessed, and Roberts demonstrated his respect for the process by deferring to the judgment of the men, a practice Lutwidge was lauding. Most trials were for minor offenses like fighting or gaming. Occasionally, the crew staged a mock trial for their amusement or as a safe way to air a grievance. Pirates, like all sailors, dearly loved to complain. Above all, they loved to gossip.

"Lord Lutwidge, how will the crew exact their revenge on Every, for surely he must die." The image of Every hanging from a yardarm had not been far from my thoughts since he confessed in the galley, or, to be more accurate, since he removed his shirt at my insistence, thereby confirming his guilt.

"Thanks to the ingenuity and guile of Harry Glasby, the Fly will die." Lutwidge was almost giddy about the prospect. "Every will receive a death sentence, of this you may be certain."

"Will he hang?" Any man but a pirate would have recoiled at the enthusiasm in my voice.

A thoughtful frown appeared on my new neighbor's face. "According to cherished pirate custom, a condemned man retains some measure of freedom even to the last. Mr. Every will choose how he wants to begin his voyage to Davy Jones' locker," Lutwidge said.

Given the heinous nature of the murder, the ham-fisted effort to frame the Albino, the affection the crew felt for the Vicar and the tendency of pirates to embrace the suffering of another for their amusement, this struck me as a punishment that failed to fit the offense. "So they will not boil him, flay him or burn him first?" I protested with unconcealed frustration.

A bemused Lord Lutwidge, his smile back in place, replied, "ah, you have the heart of a pirate but you still lack his soul. I call this progress. Alas my young angel of vengeance, Every will not be boiled and you must realize the dangers involved in burning a man at sea. Now, if we were ashore, burning him might be feasible and, in this case, appropriate. The only other option is marooning. But as you know best, we are in the middle of the Atlantic, so that is unlikely."

Marooning. Lutwidge retold the story of Captain Edward England who had been marooned by his own crew last year on Mauritius, far away in the Indian ocean. England's shortcoming was being too kind and polite to his victims. England was stranded with three loyal crew members and little in the way of provisions. After four months, they constructed a small boat using driftwood and logs and sailed a hundred leagues to Madagascar. This cautionary tale was oft told but the primary reason I was not listening attentively was because I was thinking about something else

Captain Roberts helped me find the charts I was looking for and because he declined to ask me why I wanted them, I figured he knew what I was contemplating as his agile mind worked that way.

The court was to convene the following morning after sufficient time had passed for breakfast.

I awoke refreshed but found I did not care to eat so I settled for a steaming mug of coffee to alert my senses. Wales, despite his role in the investigation that led to the Fly's capture, took charge of the trial, behaving with measured neutrality, as the rules required, but there was an added dose of zeal which told me Wales wanted the Fly's head on a platter. The accused sat slumped and staring at the deck as if he was in a stupor. He was newly shaved and donned a cotton shirt, white as the clouds.

The crew was subdued and sullen, there were none of the usual catcalls or wise remarks and if Every had any friends or allies, they were keeping a low profile. Wales said what he had to say and moved along with diligence. When it was Mr. Every's time to speak, he stood as if carrying a burden and clasped his hands low in front of his body, in the attitude of a young priest about to console his flock. The spectators listened with polite attention and Every wisely omitted any reference to the grisly details of his sordid crime.

I encountered hundreds of pirates in my time. Pirates, as a rule, do not trust anyone who does not consume alcohol. This is a not so subtle way of saying that nearly all pirates drink and they expect everyone else to drink too. As expected, Every was going to claim that the 'rum did it'. It was the same worn out excuse used by scores of pirates in the real world when the authorities asked them to explain their wicked ways.

Mr. Every appeared smallish, helpless, pitiful even, but he did speak clearly, so we could hear him easily enough. One striking feature was his arms, they were hardly bigger above the elbow than they were at the wrist, the arms of a girl.

"I swear on my worthless soul I drank so much rum I was insensible. Like you, I counted the Vicar among my friends. Sober, I would never harm a friend." As if on cue, a tear started running down his smooth cheek. "I've never harmed any of the brethren. I was in the forefront of the fight to take this very frigate. I've barely lived eighteen years. I beg forgiveness from the Albino—and from each of you. If you find it in your hearts to allow me to live, I will never ever drink again, never, ever. And to repay you for your forgiveness, I will stand with you through thick and thin. So help me God." He seemed disoriented, as if he was trying to decide whether to say something else and after a pause, he feebly turned and sat. Maybe it was my anger but I thought his performance was ridiculous.

There could be scant doubt he had touched some on the jury as well as a few in the crew, most likely the ones who were rapists or got violent when they drank. Some crewmen harbored a deep resentment of men like the Vicar and the Albino, so one less shipmate who liked the company of other men was fine by them.

Fly was wise to be brief for the more he said, the more one realized how superficial his plea. Better yet, his glaring omissions said much about the murder and the murderer.

It was incomprehensible that there could be any outcome but death. But an easy death was not the only outcome, nor was a quick death the one I sought for the murderer of my friend.

For the second time in as many days, I was about to address the men. I had asked Wales to allow me the final word. Several spoke briefly about Every's work ethic, which was average at best, and one man vouched for the fact that Every had consumed a large quantity of rum the night of the murder. When questioned by one of the jurors, the witness conceded that between him and the accused, it was the witness who was the most intoxicated. The small concession sparked a few chuckles amongst the men.

When I rose, the sporadic light-hearted laughter, suggesting an air of frivolity, served to make me even madder. The Vicar's blood was still on my clothes.

I began in a conversational but slightly mocking tone, keeping my rage in manacles until it was time to let it loose when I reached the end of my summation.

"Insensible? Mr. Every swears he was insensible, and that is the exact word he used. After you watched me make the soldiers strip, Mr. Every knew he was caught. He crept down to the galley and told me and Wales he had been listening to the Vicar and the Albino at night *for some time*. What he heard inflamed his lust. This urge of his was not something that occurred to him out of thin air the night of the murder. It was something he had wanted and wanted and wanted. We know what happens to the flame of lust when you pour rum on it. But insensible? He readily admitted he knew the Albino was not in the berthing area and he was able to sneak about in the dark without waking anyone. Insensible? He told me and Wales the Vicar was not wearing trousers and when he tried to put the Vicar's cock in his mouth the Vicar stirred." I let that foul image sink in, no one was going to snicker now.

I started again, louder and with more emphasis, as rage began to strain against the shackles.

"When the Vicar discovered Every pawing at him, Every could have run. But rather than flee, Mr. Every here," I shot my finger sideways at Every but refused to look at his face, "put his hand over the Vicar's mouth. Insensible? All he had to do was run." I said the last line in a staccato, hitting each word as if it was a stepping stone across a brook.

I repeated it, again drawing out the words, "all he had to do was run." I'd started to shout but drew back.

"Instead, he drew his blade and slashed the Vicar's face, slashed his throat and all the while the Vicar struggled. The Vicar struggled for his life and he fought his attacker. The Vicar was a pirate. He knew how to fight and as I told the Albino and the captain, the Vicar fought, he fought like a pirate. Even with deep cuts on his face, his neck and his hands, he fought. The wounds on the Vicar's hands said so, as did the bloody wounds the Vicar put on his killer. With his bare hands no less. If Mr. Every was 'insensible', how was he able to creep about in the dark without crashing into something, then to cut, slash and stab the Vicar twenty-five times? If Mr. Every was insensible, how, pray tell, would he have been able to wrench the Vicar's gold ring off his finger? Then, to top it off, the killer had the foresight and sensibility to hide the Vicar's necklace and the bloody murder weapon in the Albino's sea chest. Had it not been for the wounds left by the Vicar, you might be condemning an innocent man to die." My voice had risen to a crescendo and I let loose, shouting with abandon.

A voice called out, "'twas you who saved the Albino, Mr. Glasby."

Ignoring the anonymous praise, the timing of which could not have been better, I forcefully resumed. "Ah, yes, the Albino. Mr. Every would have happily let the Albino die to cover up his own guilt." I pointed my shaking finger at the Albino, who never failed to stand out in a crowd, especially since I had asked Cheddar and Neptune to surround the Albino with the blackest faces they could find. He looked like a snowball in a wagon load of coal.

When I spoke, spittle flew from my mouth, my rage was in full and unfettered flight.

"Mr. Every swears to God but that's the same God invoked when he signed the Articles. He butchered the Vicar, a man who dearly loved God. He sought to blame his evil deed on the one man the Vicar loved above all others. It's an affront to your sensibility gentlemen. Let us be sensible, the ultimate crime warrants the ultimate punishment."

I took a deep breath so I could conclude as reverently as possible. Looking out at the mesmerized crew, I sensed something I had never sensed before—it arose from their faces as they reacted to my words, it was a connection with an intensity unlike any other. We were sharing a sort of rapture, and because of my words and my intensity, they were going to do what I asked. The realization enabled me to finish with a flourish. My conclusion was not borne of any conscious affectation but rather it arose as an affirmation that we, all of us on this ship, were of a like mind about how this unpleasantness must end.

"The Vicar was learning to read so he could better help you and me when we were injured or fell ill. He nursed many of you when you were sick and wounded. His life has been stolen by this pathetic excuse for a man."

I gave the signal to Seahorse who handed me some rolled up charts, the ones I had borrowed from the captain's cabin.

"It's not whether Mr. Every must die. No gentlemen, that is not the question. The question is how. Musket, noose?" I shook my head back and forth slowly and deliberately, "no, not the musket, nor the noose. Mr. Every murdered one pirate and due to his cowardice and, one must presume, his shame—he nearly had another pirate killed. Fuck the noose and fuck Mr. Every. I say we maroon the bastard. For Albino the pirate and for Vicar the pirate we give Mr. Every a pirate's fate. And I've found just the place." I raised the chart high over my head and waved it like a cutlass. "I've found a chain of islets and atolls, some no more than rocks. The largest is Tristan da Cunha and we are on a course that will take us there. I know this, I know because I set us on such a course this morning."

I saw some of the men grin at my presumptuousness in charting this new course.

"On these barren rocks, there is no bird, no beast, no herb, no water, and no trees and we will reach this place in two days. I say we row Mr. Every ashore and maroon him. I say it is fitting, in this case, that we leave him a flask filled with rum. I say it is fitting we take away his shirt to expose the bloody marks that insured his capture—and if the jury think it fitting, we leave him a loaded pistol. He can drink himself into insensibility and he can roast under the judgment of God's bright sun or he can blow his brains out. If he wants to be insensible when he pulls the trigger, he can drink his fuckin' rum."

I stepped down in disgust but I was also experiencing a form of elation.

I cannot adequately explain it but the force of my presence continued to resonate long after I grew silent. My rage looked back at me where it blazed in the eyes of men who had no scruples about letting rage have its way. In different circumstances, the faces I saw would have struck sufficient terror in me to stop the beating of my heart, which was pounding, not in fear, but with unbridled joy.

Our longboat took Mr. Every ashore when we reached the tiny island. They left him a quart of rum, a pistol, some powder in a flask and a ball. Wales told me giving a loaded pistol to a murderer about to be marooned was not prudent. A week later, long after I watched Mr. Every's shape diminish into nothingness as we sailed west, Wales said they gave Mr. Every a musket ball. The ball was too large to fit in the barrel of the pistol. The idea about the musket ball was attributed to the Albino. Wales bemoaned the fact that he could not claim credit for this final insult, saying it was nearly as brilliant as my performance at the trial.

As for me, the day after Mr. Every was marooned, I scrutinized the chart and saw a tiny anonymous speck, the dot where we left Mr. Every, a dot a league from a moderately bigger rock. Some explorer or mapmaker had dubbed the moderately bigger rock *El Chivo*. Adjacent to the nearly invisible and unnamed dot where Mr. Every was left to die, in neat and compact script, I wrote *Vicar's Island.*

Chapter 10
New Barcelona

AFTER THE CREW VOTED TO leave the Guinea Coast and return to the West Indies, we received reliable and unpleasant news from some passing fishermen that the English were stepping up efforts to combat marauding pirates in the Caribbean. The offer of a pardon and the growing naval presence were not proving sufficient by themselves, so it became imperative to limit pirate access to friendly ports, accommodating harbors, and above all, to eliminate what were once deemed to be 'safe havens'.

According to the captain of the fishing boat, the new governor in Nassau, Captain Woodes Rogers, who was having personal struggles of his own, had managed to tighten England's tenuous grip on Nassau and New Providence. This was no mean feat, considering the daunting task of hunting hundreds of pirates who could be hiding anywhere in the 700 islands that make up the Bahamas alone. Many people often fail to realize the extent of the Caribbean Sea, an area that is truly vast.

When I say much of the news of late was gloomy, I am referring to the perception of Captain Roberts and his men, as some of the most daring and successful captains had been hanged.

Take Captain Charles Vane, an evil man known personally by several on our ship. Vane was nearly killed by a hurricane and washed ashore with a handful of pirates on some unnamed island. He had the misfortune of being discovered by a merchant captain who knew his face. Vane was taken back to Jamaica in chains, where he was tried and where he met the noose. Not long after, Calico Jack Rackham was hanged in Jamaica, at Port Royal, his carcass gibbeted on the small islet at the entrance to the harbor. To this day they call the islet Rackham's Cay.

The hanging of Vane and Rackham came as good news to someone in my predicament, but I had learned long ago to keep my own counsel and I kept my views to myself.

Port Royal, Jamaica no longer provided safe refuge. Even with a powerful frigate, we dare not venture near Nassau in the Bahama islands. Despite news that their fellow rogues had been executed, the men were uniformly homesick for the West Indies. The men longed to go ashore.

One of the rewards of piracy was to debauch in a friendly town or settlement and sit at the right hand of Bacchus. Loot burned like hot coals in the pockets of the men, but they realized finding a suitable port, one filled with taverns and brothels, was no longer a simple matter.

The imposing stone fortifications in Vera Cruz, Portobello and Cartagena bristled with heavy guns, insulating them from attack. Spain's coastal patrols around Darien were on the rise. I've already mentioned the situation in the Bahamas and Jamaica. Ports and harbors friendly to pirates, so plentiful in years past were now foreclosed to us, so choices were few.

On the eve of the tragic murder of the Vicar, Roberts talked with his privy councilors and one of the Lords suggested a visit to the port city of New Barcelona, more formally known as Nueva Barcelona del Cerro Santo. When this suggestion was put to the crew, it met with overwhelming enthusiasm. The sizeable city is on the northern coast of the South American mainland in a wide area loosely controlled by Spain, but far enough from the coastal patrols further west and north to be relatively safe. More importantly, it was far from the English strongholds and thus, the Royal Navy. Having sailed with pirates for over fifteen months, I knew full well that a few gold coins would find their way to the right people and remove any threat to our brief but lucrative presence. This tribute would pale in comparison to the amounts thirsty and lust-filled men would squander on themselves when they stepped ashore.

November 1, 1721 was a Saturday.

During breakfast, Captain Roberts, joined by Lords Lutwidge and Ringrose, were discussing members of the crew who posed a particular risk when ashore. Drunkards like Robert Devins, a decrepit man none present could remember seeing completely sober. Robert Johnson was another.

Wales was busy and he came in and out, efficient as always but more animated than usual, there being an unmistakable air of excitement which had been building since we put Mr. Every ashore to rot.

As an obvious flight risk, I dare not entertain the thought that I might be permitted ashore so when the subject of me being allowed to leave the ship came up, no one was more taken aback than I.

"Glasby, when is the last time you were in port?" Lutwidge asked, gnawing the edge of a hard biscuit.

"Not sure my Lord, seems like years," I said.

Lord Ringrose rubbed his protruding belly and announced, "anyone who solves a murder deserves some sort of reward."

Roberts leaned back and eyed me, "you missed your calling as King's counsel. Splendid effort, the Vicar would have been moved, as I was, as we all were. Give us your word you won't make a dash for the mountains or flee into the jungle and you can go. Wales will be happy to appoint two men to help you resist temptation. Even for a navigator, it's a long way to Boston." He and the Lords were in a generous mood.

"You have my word," I lied, knowing all the while that the aforementioned mountains and jungle would make escape nearly impossible and with two men guarding me I would be compelled to behave as if I were their pet.

"Your word is good enough for me," Roberts said, rubbing his hands together. "When Wales comes back, I'll make sure he finds someone suitable to keep you company."

Thanking the captain and the Lords, I gave assurances I needed no escort but neither did I object to having someone keep me company.

Hours later, a voice from the top mast cried out 'land'.

During those hours, I was ensconced in my humble cabin, where Jack had taken up residence. He had gravitated toward me a day or two after his master vanished, although I realized that the inclination of a cat to demonstrate affection is limited by the laws of nature and a cat's inherent selfishness. Sympathetic to his sudden status as an orphan, I may have encouraged him by giving him bits of cooked meat and other morsels, worrying if I fed him too much he might go easy on the rats. Using a wooden wedge, I jammed the door shut so no one could burst in on me, something which happened regularly.

Later that balmy afternoon, I joined scores of impatient pirates on the rails as we glided past the shoals and reefs toward the harbor entrance. Men on the bow were ready to take soundings so we could anchor as close to shore as possible. With Jack watching over me, I had hurriedly scribbled a letter in my cabin. The neatly folded paper, which I had purloined from among our charts, rested comfortably in the cinched waist of my canvas trousers, covered by my long shirt.

The letter read;

Constance, my love. Yes, it is Harry. It is in haste I write these words. I have so many questions I know not where to start. If Providence and good Fortune will it, this letter will reach you and you will know I live. You were told in July of last year that pirates who raided the Samuel took me and other men. I have since learned if I had been married, they would not have taken me (one never knows) fate is fickle. If you bore our child, it is only right and proper it should bear the name Glasby. I will marry you yet—if you will have me. Despite the long months at sea, my love for your remains as constant as the tides. The pirates I am forced to serve are a tough lot but they have not mistreated me. I am kept under a close watch and if I were to seek to escape and be captured, this would change. When wronged, these men can be as cruel to each other as to their sworn enemies. Yet I pray that the day will come when I am the master of my fate and your devoted husband and, if I daresay, a father. I learned earlier today I will be permitted ashore. We disembark shortly. It matters not where we are and I fear this letter may be found so know only that I am far from Boston. I am safe and I am sound- at least in body. My mind? My suffering is nothing when compared to yours. I have money (little) and will use it to pay someone to convey this letter. Perhaps I should just put this letter in a bottle and drop it over the side. My agony lies in not knowing if the letter makes it and the certainty that if it does, you have no way to send a reply. Hold this letter as I do yours (I know it by heart). Hold it until I return. Hold fast, hold tight. Love forever and beyond, your H.

The bow and stern anchors were dropped, the longboats made ready. People in the town watched our arrival skeptically, some gathered on the jetties, wondering who and what we were. I admired a tall church tower and men capering on horses. Roberts' beloved musicians were on the deck performing and many of the men joined in on a song about the ghost who guarded Captain Kidd's buried treasure. Legend has it that Kidd captured a girl named Hannah who stumbled upon the pirates as they were hiding their ill-gotten plunder. Pirate lore says a ghost is the best way to safeguard buried loot. In need of a ghost, and ridding himself of a hostile witness, the dastardly Kidd opted to have poor Hannah killed rather than sacrifice one of his men.

Ever since, so they say, Hannah's ghost screeches and wails at dusk. Her shrill cries can be discerned from Hannah Screecher's Island, all the way across the water to the mainland, where the story thrives.

> And if a lover would win her hand,
> No lips e'er kissed a hand so white,
> And if a lover would hear her cry,
> She sings most every night.

The Albino grabbed my left arm and a pirate named Rodrigo Javier Delgado de la Fontaine grabbed my right. He answered to Papi Chulo, Papi to his many friends. I had known Papi for many months and found him to be quite sociable. Most of his time was spent carousing with the musicians, not surprisingly then, Papi was among those merrily joining in. As they sang, more joined in and the sound of pirates harmonizing and serenading themselves grew stronger and more hearty. Toward the end, I found myself humming along and tapping my foot to the tune.

Wales, the country, not the quartermaster, was famous for its tenors and we had our share.

> But if a lover would win her gold,
> And his hands be strong to raise the lid,
> 'Tis here, tis there, tis everywhere,
> 'In the chest,' says Captain Kidd.

> They lifted long, they lifted well,
> Ingots of gold and silver bars,
> And jewels and plunder from wild sea wars,
> But where they laid them, no man can tell.
> Known only to a thousand stars.

The ballad ended with a hearty cheer for the musicians, especially one incredible fiddler by the name of Nicholas Brattler, who happily waved his violin in the air and took his bows.

"Harry, Wales said you are to guard us while we're ashore. Is this so?" The Albino asked.

"I think you have that backwards *mi amigo*. What about you Papi, how did you get stuck with me? And why did you shave your head?" I counted a dozen red scratches left by his razor. I was pleased to have these men as my guardians and come to think of it, going ashore would be a welcome respite.

Papi playfully pulled on his trimmed beard. "Señor Glasby, the last time I was ashore I had the head lice for weeks."

"Even lice love the Papi," I said, "yet you keep your hairy beard, you're loco, as we all know." The first batch of men were congregating by the gunwale. They were elbowing each other as the first longboat was lowered to the water. None bore firearms, but all had knives and daggers, some had a blade on each side of their belt and another hidden in each boot. No doubt Spades was somewhere trying to arrange wagers on how many of our men would be injured in the brawls ahead.

"Did Wales select you to be our interpreter Papi? Unless 'Señor Roberto' speaks Spanish," I said, referring to the Albino with my thumb.

"Señor Glasby, mere interpreter? You of all people know better. Wales appointed me as the most esteemed and regal ambassador of the *Royal Fortune* and you are to be my deputy ambassadors, my able assistants." Papi's dark eyes sparkled.

"Ambassadors," the Albino sniffed, "let's see what the fine people of New Barcelona think of that, you knob rubbing ruffian."

There were four tall ships anchored in the bay, but none as large as the *Royal Fortune*. I saw Dutch colors on a brig and a dreary slaver flying a Portuguese ensign. There were two caravels and a small number of dilapidated fishing boats. We had an hour of daylight left. There was a jetty to the east and an uneven row of splintered piers which provided a perch for lazy pelicans to observe our arrival.

Pirate James Starling manned an oar in the launch. He had served with a number of captains and answered to the name Diamond. A few months ago he was amongst a crew captained by John Taylor. Taylor had seized the Portuguese East Indiaman *Nossa Senhora Do*

Cabo ferrying a hoard of diamonds somewhere in the Indian Ocean. The fabulously rich prize also carried priceless silks, muslins, opium and twenty pounds of gold.

The share of every member of the crew included forty-two diamonds *for each man*, except for Starling. They drew lots and the befuddled Starling was presented one enormous diamond, a rare and priceless gem worth thousands of pounds. Convinced he had been cheated, he angrily smashed the stone with a hammer and shortly thereafter, he left the ship in consternation.

We were deposited at the end of a pier. I had not spent any meaningful time in a port for over a year and I thanked Diamond as he prepared to return to the *Royal Fortune*. This pattern would be repeated throughout the evening as men were ferried back and forth.

Diamond threw me a stiff salute and yelled, "hope you find a nice wagtail Mr. Glasby." His mind and mine were not working in the same direction but I accepted his admonition and wished him the same.

One of the men jauntily walking with us put his hand on his heart and proclaimed, "I could forebear no longer nor could I await the tide, but sailed happily into the mouth of the strait."

I quietly asked the Albino, "what's that all about?"

"He's going to fuck a ladybird tonight. There will be many ladybirds getting boarded before the dawn. The ladybirds will become rich and the pirates will return to sea with empty pockets. You keep an eye on ol' Papi, he will charm the birds from the trees," the Albino said. I had not seen the Albino this happy since the unfortunate demise of the Vicar.

As I took in the configuration of the waterfront I was reminded of the harbor in Boston.

"Albino, pardon me for asking but are you, you know, are you interested in women? I thought you preferred the company of men?"

Asking such an intimate question with relative ease demonstrated how far I had travelled since departing the *Samuel*.

"Only when at sea Harry. If I was the captain, I would let women sail with us. Perhaps one day."

At least my question had not caused offense.

"So you dream of being a captain?"

"No Harry, being captain is too much responsibility for a humble man like me. But who does not dream of having women at sea?"

Saturday was market day in New Barcelona. The abundant array of fresh fruit and exotic vegetables was astounding. Pineapples, nuts, lemons, oranges, beans, melons, grapes, limes, tamarinds, cocoa-nuts, pomegranates, and delicious looking wonders made of cornmeal and flour. The air was filled with the savory aroma of meats, poultry, fish and soups. Flowers too scented the air and the bold and brilliant colors were most pleasing to the eye.

The Albino stopped and grasped my hand, turning it palm up.

"Yes?" I said, not resisting him, "are you about to tell my fortune?"

The Albino piled Dutch Lion Daalders, doubloons and Portuguese moidores into my hand and tried to close my fist. I fumbled ever so slightly when two or three of the gold coins fell to the paving stones. I was in no need of funds as I carried silver reales Wales paid me when I agreed to provide reading lessons to the Vicar. They were in my leather purse and I would use them to buy food and with any luck, to pay to get my letter on its way to Boston.

"What's this? This is an enormous sum Robert, please, I can't take these." I motioned to give the coins back but he put his hands behind his back, pleased with himself and smiling broadly.

"To me, and perhaps only to me, my life is priceless Mr. Glasby. Sadly, when the Vicar was killed I inherited all his property. I have more than enough to satisfy my humble needs. Please don't offend me by refusing." He was on the verge of getting emotional.

Papi spoke, "Señor Glasby, the crew will see to it that your money is not good tonight. What you did to uncover the crime of the dastardly Fly is talked about more than you realize. A man's reputation among other men, be it good or be it bad, is earned. Your riches include having many loyal friends, but it is also good to have gold, *sí?*"

I cautiously opened my hand and peered at the beautiful heavy coins. "*Sí*," I said.

The town was not at all what I had envisioned in my mind's eye. The brick, timber and stone buildings were solid and well proportioned, most in a respectable state of repair. There were workshops and storehouses and taverns and a long chandlery where sails were made and mended. Thick candles and lanterns gave off a warm yellow light which cascaded from the open doors and windows, projecting a genuine sense of warmth and hospitality. I told my friends I could not recall the last time I was able to walk forty feet without having to turn or stop. As we meandered, my ear caught the sounds of diverse languages, some I recognized and many, I did not.

'Ambassador' Papi was indispensable, not merely due to his Spanish, but for his gentle manner and effortless charm. The plump women who served us food adored him and, by fiat, any surplus adoration fell to me and the docile Albino. One of life's great pleasures is the simple act of eating delicious food with family or friends. Experiencing these delights, I realized just how much I had missed them since my abduction. We ate like kings and I eventually gave up trying to pay for my food.

I have always felt that walking with nowhere to go has a special quality, especially in a place I have never been before.

After darkness descended, the main streets were filled with people, men, women, young and old, but nary a passerby could avoid staring at the Albino. He seemed content to ignore their unrestrained curiosity, their gestures and their barely whispered exclamations. It was comforting to see white-haired old men and wrinkled women with bent backs. Scampering children, on the other hand, made my heart ache, some of whom curiously crept up to the Albino to get a closer look at his ivory skin. They were desirous of touching him and from time to time, he would invite the little ones to do just that. These bold and innocent adventurers with their brown skin and black hair giggled with delight. I envied them for seeing the world as a place filled with amusing and entertaining wonders.

I felt for the letter under my shirt and despaired at the impossibility of finding a means of getting it from the southern edge of the Caribbean all the way to Boston. I might as well be sending it to the moon.

I was making myself miserable thinking of Constance.

"*Aqui,* gentlemen, if you please." Papi guided me by the elbow and we crossed up and over a well-worn stone step and entered a dimly lit tavern. The walls were adorned with bits and pieces of wrecked and weathered ships, sails, rigging, and hardware of dull brass. While somewhat ramshackle at first glance, the overall effect was indicative of someone who loved the sea and most of the tables were already occupied. I recognized faces from amongst our crew, yet not nearly as many as I would have guessed. The remainder were strangers. Papi told us there were many such places in the town but this one had been recommended to him by one of the women who had served us food.

Papi proudly said we were patrons of *La Taberna Marinero Solitario,* owned and operated by the widow of a long lost and likely long forgotten Spanish sea captain, a man who sailed into a hurricane and never returned. If the story was not entirely true, it was common enough.

A statuesque black woman greeted us as we situated ourselves at a round table. Her ebony skin was so smooth, it seemed to reflect light. The beaming Papi pointed at me and the Albino, said a few words in Spanish, and laid a gold coin and some reales on the scarred wood. She returned with a thick glass bottle and three pewter tankards, sliding each to us in turn, then filling them gracefully. Papi and she privately exchanged a few words and she laughed, leaning over to kiss the Albino on the crown of his head. "Beautiful man," she said. When she held his white head between her black hands the effect of the image was other worldly.

We had been served a fine Madeira wine yet I had never drank anything stronger than ale. Drink stole one's sensibilities and undoubtedly the effect it had on my mother was among the many reasons I did not indulge.

I knew the women moving about, stroking sailors, whispering in their ears, telling them lies, would, for various amounts of coin, do all the things sailors desire. I heard ribald tales, growing up in Boston, of the sinful happenings on Negro Hill. I saw men stagger in and out of taverns and brothels in Boston when the wharves were my home. Many is the time I watched drunken men beat each other bloody with fists and feet and sometimes clubs, the worst, however, were the flickering knives. Many were maimed and some were even killed in these senseless drunken duels.

Sailors spent hours regaling each other with embellished tales of having a bounce with a beautiful bangtail on the Ratcliffe Highway north of Wapping. I held nothing against these poor women, the men who lay with them or the bawdy tales the men would tell in the weeks and months ahead. All I wanted to do was find someone to take my letter.

When it came to these women, there was more than coin at stake in these nocturnal adventures. Many a customer was destined to endure the agony of the 'blue boar' and the myriad diseases that lived and thrived in these bawdy houses. I did not want to become a 'straddler', a man forced to walk with his legs bowed like a keg because of the burning in his groin. Women known to harbor these illnesses were called 'fire ships'.

While I was daydreaming, Papi nudged me. Before I could ask why, he raised his drink and said, "*mi amigos*, to the Vicar."

If Papi had said anything else, I am convinced to this day I would have made my excuses and declined.

As the Albino solemnly raised his tankard, I joined them without thinking and we said in unison, 'the Vicar'. "May God watch and protect his soul," Papi added, as he quickly made the sign of the cross on his chest. His gesture was not inappropriate. I drank some of the wine, asked what it was and expressed my compliments and my thanks. This should have been the end of my drinking but the next toast was to my health and again, without really thinking, I drank. Acknowledging the kindness of my friends and sharing in a moment of camaraderie was a pleasure without risk, or so I thought. As I look back on that night, my feet were on the slope, it was steep, and I was beginning to slide. It was to be a long descent before I hit bottom.

We drank to Wales, Captain Roberts, to famous pirates, infamous women, our homes, our friends, and several of the saints. Papi seemed to know them all—the saints that is. Papi's English deteriorated but the tall ebony woman let him wrap his arm around her thin waist. She had a sinuous, languid way of moving that I found intriguing. She did not seem to merely walk, she drifted from place to place, like a dark and heavy fog. Papi beckoned her to lean forward and when she did, he stroked her satin smooth cheek and muttered to her, making her laugh. I asked him what he said but he refused to tell, scolding me for asking and saying loudly, "Harry, my friend from Boston, there are some things a man keeps for himself."

So we drank to secrets.

After the second bottle arrived, Papi passionately kissed the tall woman, or she passionately kissed him, either way, it was a long and passionate kiss and it made me think of Constance. I had not forgotten about the letter but the warm atmosphere and the comfort of being with friends, combined with the wine, gave me an excuse to tell myself I could search for a courier tomorrow. I was further down the slope than I realized.

As we finished the second bottle, the tavern was filled with rowdy men. It grew harder to decipher and identify the languages from one table to another. In the back of the room a small crowd of men were enjoying an raucous dice game. The disgruntled moans and celebratory cheers of the gamblers indicated who was winning and who was not. I thought for a moment I heard the high-pitched voice of Spades chanting the number four.

I went outside to relieve myself and on my return belatedly realized I could have taken my sizeable hoard of gold and kept on walking. The Albino and Papi were busy talking about the things that sailors talk about in harbor taverns. Patrons, men and women, were smoking long clay pipes; pungent tobacco smoke hung in long lazy wisps rising up to the dark wooden rafters. I was not drunk but I would be soon and I didn't much care.

The Albino was the first to climb the narrow wooden stairs. A short muscular woman took him by the hand and led him away. Her oval face, lustrous black hair and bronze complexion marked her as a remnant of some unnamed tribe who had struggled to survive the European invasion. Papi paid no mind to the exotic girl or the Albino's sudden departure.

"You like the wine, no? Let us enjoy a rattle skull. I think you will like this too. Do you wish to gamble Harry?" Papi seemed to feel like his job was to entertain me, not to serve as my warder.

He explained that a rattle skull was a concoction made with dark porter, rum, lime juice and nutmeg. I told Papi a rattle skull was someone who talked too much and made no sense. We debated which came first, the drink or the result. He claimed Lintorn Highlett was a rattle skull, with or without drink, and we laughed about that because it was true. I told Papi Highlett was one of the first of many pirates I had come to know but that I was not destined to be a pirate, I wanted to get home.

"Some day, some day Harry, it will be your fortune to return home. This I know." He spoke to a passing woman in Spanish and the woman returned with more drink. We used our rattle skull to make a toast to Papi's assurance, which I knew was just his effort to brighten my outlook. "*Gracias* Papi, and you, what fate awaits you?"

He looked at me with deep resignation.

"Papi? Papi will never see his home. That is why Papi lives each day like it is his last. My days are few, this I also know." He raised his glass and the sparkle returned to his eyes. "It is one of the hazards of going on the account. If you are not destined to be a pirate, that bodes well for you Harry. But enough about the future, let us find the Albino. I think he is on Gropecunt Lane, what do you think? Shall we?" Papi's chair scraped backward on the stone floor and I dutifully followed him to the stairs. As we climbed, the noises in the tavern faded.

We emerged on a landing lit by a tarnished silver chandelier, shimmering with small glass mirrors and pendants of crystal, some of which were broken or missing. A slight sea breeze propelled the suspended pieces into one another and they tinkled in response. I heard a young woman's muffled laughter, the sound much like the crystal pendants delicately colliding, these feminine sounds were pleasing, comforting.

I had a tight grip on my tankard but found myself unsteady after the short ascent.

"Wait here," Papi whispered loudly. He turned a corner in the warren of narrow halls lined with a series of closed doors. I was scared when he disappeared, of what precisely, I am not sure. I was too scared to walk into the city and flee, I was too scared to go back to our table and sit alone, I was scared of what might happen if I remained and above all, I was scared of myself.

Papi magically reappeared, his white teeth gleaming, and he grabbed me by the wrist.

"Come, come, I found our friend."

We took one turn, then another and the high-pitched laughter grew more distinct. Papi pushed on a thick wooden door with black iron hinges and we entered a high-ceilinged room, dimly lit by a smattering of candles and five or six dirty oil lamps. The room was spacious and had four narrow windows that overlooked the street, toward the port, one of which was partially open. The familiar and distinctive smells of the harbor filled my nostrils. There were other smells too, scented flowers, smoke from lamps and the heavy perfume favored by whores behind the closed doors lining the hallways.

A metal bath filled with hot water dominated the room and held the Albino and a woman, knees up, facing the white pirate. His head was laid back, his pink eyes shut, his white silver hair plastered to his head. He raised a glass in silent greeting.

There were two other women in the room, nude except for their stockings and a few items of gaudy jewelry. The pair were embracing on a plush tattered settee, their pale legs entwined. They looked us over first, then they kissed, their agile tongues twisting, mouths open. The one nearest me cupped her companion's ample breast and pinched her nipple, provoking a long sigh. The women on the divan were white, the woman with the Albino was a beautiful mulatta.

Transfixed and without embarrassment, I watched the two women kissing, embracing and fondling each other and felt myself become uncomfortably erect.

One of the women on the settee stood, she was by far the younger of the two and possessed a profile like those found on cameos. Her fine brown hair was tied in intricate braids and the braids were tied with white satin ribbons, delicate ringlets hung on either side of her face. She was slender with wide hips and small high breasts, accentuated by perfectly round pink nipples. She was missing a tooth and had tiny scars on her cheeks from the pox. She guided me, gently, to sit by her friend, introducing herself as Gertie, her thick Dutch accent added to her allure.

The plump-breasted woman languishing on the couch was a decade older than Gertie. Her peasant's face was dominated by a dark beauty mark on her right cheek, the mark more of a distraction than an enhancement. She took my hand in hers, laid it on her breast, urging me to feel.

Papi had departed and the Albino was resting but I was too enamored to give my friends much consideration.

Gertie asked me my name and I told her. "Mr. Harry", she said softly, "this beautiful lady is Charlotte. Do you love her amazing tits? Señor Papi says you are a good man and a good friend and a good sailor. It must be hard being so long at sea." As Gertie talked, Charlotte wrapped her fingers around my manhood, kneading it and easing me into the corner of the divan, my back against an ornately embroidered and fringed pillow. Gertie reached around me and playfully grabbed the pillow, situating it on the floor and pushing me back with her hand on my chest. The women expertly untied and unbuttoned my trousers, pulling them to my ankles, exposing me. Gertie slid off the edge of the couch and kneeled at my feet, putting a hand on each of my knees and nudging them apart. Charlotte put her hand on my face and leaned forward to kiss me on the mouth. I let her probe with her tongue and I responded in kind. She told me to enjoy, telling me I was very handsome for a sailor.

Charlotte knelt next to Gertie, leaned forward, and took me between her breasts, moving up and down while she watched my face, gauging my reaction. I laid my head back and closed my eyes, silently willing her and Gertie to continue.

I heard water swish in the tub and Gertie cleaned my face with a warm wet cloth, this simple act of kindness was extraordinarily pleasurable. She positioned herself on the cushion and maneuvered Charlotte aside, washing my upper legs and massaging my private parts with the warm cloth, this too giving rise to pleasures I had nearly forgotten. Gertie probed the moist tip of me with her pointed tongue. She said something to Charlotte in Dutch and I was worried something may have gone awry because she sounded stern.

"Please ladies, don't stop," I pleaded. Gertie giggled, tossed the cloth aside and took my length deep into her mouth. I entwined my fingers in her braids, her mouth tightening as she slowly moved her head up and down. When she paused to push a strand of her hair from her cheek, my shaft glistened from her saliva.

"Not to worry, Harry", the Albino said, "they know their business.

"Papi sends his regards", Charlotte said.

Gertie took me deeper, her nose touched the patch of hair below my waist. Charlotte manipulated and teased my balls and tugged them as I felt my imminent release build. I let out a sustained moan and felt light-headed, pulsating again and again, spewing my seed first into Gertie's mouth and then across her face at a jagged angle.

In that delirious instant I knew, with clarity, why men would pay so much to enjoy these forbidden pleasures.

The women kissed again, making certain I was watching. Charlotte licked Gertie's cheek and ran her tongue up to the corner of her eye. Then, inching close to my face, Charlotte playfully ran her tongue around her lips. I had the odd temptation to rub the offending beauty mark off her face.

Gertie retrieved the damp cloth to finish wiping her face, then used it to clean me.

Charlotte cupped her hands under her heavy breasts and raised them, "Papi warned us you might resist, but I told Papi you could not resist these; Papi did not argue." She pinched her brownish nipples and pulled them outward until I thought she might hurt herself, abruptly she leaned forward and kissed me fully on the mouth. "Gertie and I very much wish to see you again Harry. And this," she gave me another tug, "with this you can give a woman much pleasure".

Gertie said Papi would meet me downstairs but there was no need to hurry. I did not know if I was supposed to thank the women and told myself it would not be polite if I left and said nothing. When I clumsily pulled up my trousers I saw my folded letter on the floor, practically under the settee. I nearly gasped. I had forgotten about it and my neglect and the reason for my neglect made me feel terribly guilty.

The curvaceous mulatta gracefully emerged from the tub, thin sheets of soapy water cascaded down her chocolate skin. Gertie peeled off her stockings and slipped into the tub. The Albino chided me, his voice distant and detached, "Harry, please don't desert tonight, Captain Roberts would hang me."

"I'll wait for Papi", I assured him. "Ladies, please be as kind to my pale friend as you have been to me. I offer you both my sincere thanks for a memorable experience. I can see myself out." Gertie delicately waved her fingers at me from the tub, Charlotte blew me a kiss and made a lewd remark about my cock. The Albino chuckled but he looked like he was on the verge of sleep. As if reading my thoughts, he said "Harry, if you don't see me again tonight, watch yourself."

"Don't worry, I'll be fine," I said, "you know, if they filled that tub with milk, you'd be invisible."

Somehow I found the landing, then I found myself at the table where our night had started. There was no sign of Papi but without me asking, the tall black woman set a decanter of rum in front of me. Papi or the Albino would find me and get me back to the ship but while I waited, I drank the rum. To pass the time, I relived my experiences with Charlotte and Gertie until the images began to blur, only to be replaced by hazy images of Constance. I drunkenly wondered if she would be angry with me for what I had done with the two women. The more I drank, the harder it was to make sense of it all, but my apathy was comforting and I was steadily growing numb.

My next memory was trying to force my sticky eyes open as I lay flat on my back in the dark confines of a narrow alley. My shirt was ripped, flecked with blood, my sore buttocks rested in a shallow puddle of muddy water. One of my shoes was gone and I reeked of urine and realized I was lying in pool of filth. It was just before sunrise and hungry sea birds were making a racket. My head throbbed. I saw vomit on my pants and assumed it was mine. My hand traced a lump on my forehead near the hairline which was tender to the touch and the size of a quail's egg. I ran my dry tongue around the inside of my mouth to make sure I still had all my teeth.

It took a supreme effort to stand up.

Once I did, despite my dizziness, my hands rushed to my shirt and my belt. I turned around several times forcing my eyes to focus and nearly fell down in the process. I was still under the effects of the alcohol. Someone had waited until I was too drunk to defend myself or I had passed out, either way, I had been given a battering and left lying in filth behind the tavern.

As feared, I lost more than my dignity; my purse was gone but worse than that, my precious letter had been stolen.

"Bloody hell, " I muttered, "bloody hell."

Chapter 11

The Sun-Dried Governor

WRENCHING OFF MY REMAINING SHOE, I hobbled down the gently sloping alley, doing my best to avoid the waste thrown from night jars out of second story windows. When I reached the edge of the harbor, I sat on a wooden crate with my throbbing head between my soiled hands, wondering who robbed me and how my two guardians had failed so miserably. In the distance, a pair of dogs barked at each other or perhaps they alerted because some miserable soul had wandered, unwelcome, into their territory. It was likely these same early morning routines were being honored in Boston.

I had been clubbed, or pummeled, or kicked in the lower ribs on my right side and considered the unpleasant consequences of having a broken bone or two. It hurt to breathe through my nose and when I tried to clear it, I stared forlornly at a bloody wad in the remnants of my ragged shirttail.

To my surprise and relief, a longboat was headed toward me. As it drew closer, I stood up to make my presence known, my balance having improved somewhat. I had a terrible thirst and something noxious bubbled in my intestines, the ensuing gas pain was enough to double me over in agony. This would be a long day.

Seahorse crouched in the bow and the launch was carrying far more men than I would have deemed prudent. I girded myself for the insults I had earned and tried to help pull the boat up as men tending the oars raised them in unison. Seahorse disembarked, gruffly directing men hither and yon. The longboat should not have been ferrying this many men this early, especially on a Sunday. In fact, the longboat should not have been on the water ferrying anyone, something was amiss.

"I suppose you are taking these men to church," I said.

"I thought you knew, "Seahorse said, looking me up and down and making a face at the stench arising from my person. "We received word about an hour ago that a French pirate hunter is in Cumana."

"Cumana? Cumana is only forty miles from here, more or less," I told him. We had sailed past Cumana the day before.

Seahorse was paying little attention to me. He was distracted by his duties, "yes, yes. We're rounding up the men. The captain is talking to the Lords and we're getting underway. If we have to sail without anyone of consequence, like you, we might try to come back; otherwise, *adios*." Seahorse looked at the lump on my forehead and seemed on the verge of asking me more but kept such thoughts to himself. "Harry, stay with the boat. When it's full, send it on and it will come back, we have to get moving. Do you know where Papi and the Albino might be?" Everyone was in a hurry to flee, that much was clear.

I told Seahorse I last saw them at *La Taberna Marinero Solitario*. He was not familiar with it and asked me if I would go back and search for them. I pointed in the direction of the tavern, describing the facade and convinced him it was not far, moreover, I was in no condition to move quickly, pointing at my bare feet. My excuses frustrated him, of that I am certain, but not wanting to argue, he took off at a trot.

Despite my decrepit condition, knowing of the ship's imminent and hasty departure, I began calculating the odds of making good my escape. The *Royal Fortune* was about to sail under duress, undoubtedly some in the crew would be left behind. If the information Seahorse gave me was true, and had I known it sooner, I would never have shown my face on the waterfront. Instead, I would be hiding somewhere, waiting for the ship to weigh anchor and sail without me.

This unnamed French warship might be equally aware of our presence and already headed this way. Roberts would be lucky to escape the mouth of the harbor. If the French got to us first, the *Royal Fortune* would be trapped and unable to maneuver. We had not been in port long enough to take on food, wood and water; all that could wait. I cursed whoever had stolen my money. Despite my bad luck and my poverty, all I needed to do was hide for a day or two and take my chances. I could not let concerns for the Albino and Papi dictate my decision, but I knew Roberts and Wales would blame them if I was not on board when the ship departed. The image of my friends being flogged gave me pause, Papi could probably take it but the Albino would not survive such an ordeal.

These competing considerations were interrupted by the shattering boom of cannon fire.

A small puff of white smoke was lifted by the morning breeze and carried away from an open gun port on the ship. I turned to the town and saw pirates in ones, twos and threes hurrying to the launch. Others from our crew were getting into small canoes and row boats, shouting and gesturing, presumably to find oars so they could get moving. Scattered townspeople appeared but none interfered, realizing it was not safe and that with any luck, they could retrieve their stolen canoes later. Men were active in our rigging, unfurling sails and one man high in the main top was peering east with a spyglass, the early morning light reflecting brightly off the lens. Unquestionably, the lookout was peering in the direction of Cumana.

The rising sun would make it difficult to see me if I ran east, particularly if I went back into town and used the warren of twisting lanes and hidden alleyways to head for the jungle. Roberts would sail west or north to avoid battle with a French warship, his direction of flight would depend on the winds and the current.

Appreciating the risks, I decided to make a run for it, excitement helped clear my head and momentarily enabled me to forget my aches and pains. Nagging worries about my friends and my lack of funds notwithstanding, a golden chance like this might never come again.

"Harry," it was the Albino calling out to me; louder the second time, "my dear Harry." He was waving at me with a grinning Papi by his side. The noise of the cannon or the search parties had somehow roused them, each man carried two large bottles, one in each hand, Papi held his up triumphantly for my approval. My so-called guardians looked refreshed and rested which made me angry, not merely due to my disheveled condition, but due to the fact that their emergence thwarted my impulsive decision to run. I stood stiffly and glared at them, wondering how much bad luck one man can have.

Within thirty minutes, the bow of the *Royal Fortune* was pointed north, the longboat was being stowed and the few men not otherwise occupied were asking anyone who would listen what was happening, where we were going, and whether Captain Roberts had a plan.

My services would be needed soon but no one had sought me out, nor did anyone even seem to notice me; this was not usual procedure. As we inched out of the harbor, I started to feel that familiar nervous chill. Then it dawned on me, the audacious Roberts was going to sail east, toward Cumana.

The wind was light and we had to wear at first so initial progress was slow.

Joining some of the crew on our busy deck, I too was eager to learn why we were sailing toward danger when common sense said we should be heading the opposite direction. This French vessel had to be among the growing number of warships looking to kill and capture pirates. I saw Highlett gawking at my bare feet, tattered shirt and stained trousers. I was tempted to tell him I had not shit myself despite the noxious odor that said otherwise.

"Mornin' Mr. Glasby, heard you had a fine time last night."

"Morning to you Mr. Highlett, you likely know more about my fine night than I do. Never mind all that, you can fill me in on what I did some other time. Why are we steering an easterly course? I was told a French pirate hunter may be near Cumana."

Highlett patiently informed me that Cumana was the oldest Spanish settlement on the entire continent. He reminded me of the enmity the French had for Captain Roberts, given his past successes in seizing and burning their vessels. None of this explained our course and when he finally took a breath, I said as much and he had to confess that Captain Roberts had yet to take him into his confidence. An English ensign was raised on the main topmast head and I pointed it out to Highlett. He excused himself as if suddenly remembering he had other duties, which was quite likely, but it was plain we were both in the dark about why Roberts was headed toward Cumana. The wind freshened as we exited the harbor entrance and the bow began to rise up and down gracefully.

Wales tersely summoned me to join him on the quarterdeck, a reminder that, like it or not, I had duties too. When I reached him, he grimaced and turned away at the stench, "Jesus Glasby, it looks like someone had their way with you last night. I knew there were risks in letting you ashore." I wanted to tell Wales he had no idea of the risks involved in letting me ashore but I was more interested in why we were sailing east. When I pressed him, he brushed me off and told me to get cleaned up before I made someone retch.

Standing my ground, I asked again and Wales deigned to confirm the accuracy of our present course, saying only that I would be needed on the quarterdeck as we neared Cumana harbor. He refused to tell me exactly *why* we were headed east or what we might achieve by going into a harbor where a French pirate hunter was lying in wait for us. Frustrated, sore, tired and short on patience, I excused myself and said I needed to find some shoes. I went below, gulped some cold water and went forward to relieve my grumbling bowels. That done, I went to my cabin and found Jack resting comfortably but eyeing me warily. I tossed my ruined shirt toward him and found a replacement. He moved his head slightly to avoid my shirt but otherwise he ignored me, as always. "Stay here Jack and do forgive me if the noise you are about to hear makes it hard to sleep, it's none of my doing, as you know." I scrambled back up and rejoined Wales and Captain Roberts, who was busily giving very specific orders to the helmsman.

In contrast to Wales, Roberts was delighted to see me and said so, "pity about the shoes, whores you know." He spoke with the giddy air of someone going to a summer garden party. His comment about shoes and whores made no sense but I was not inclined to explain my many shortcomings or to inquire as to how he continually seemed to know my every deed and thought. His cheery mood was itself a bad sign.

"Yes captain, as Wales told me a few minutes ago, it would appear we are on a course for Cumana." I waited on him to speak. He raised his brass telescope and after scanning about, he lowered it and said, "yes."

I wondered if he might be mocking me. "Why for God's sake?" I blurted. "I was told we left New Barcelona in the utmost haste because a well-armed French pirate hunter is nearby. If so, are we not sailing in the wrong direction?" I stared in disbelief at the captain as he blithely continued searching the horizon.

"Harry, this wind is favoring us more than I dared hope, you can see the ensign. We believe the French ship is the *Trident*. If this belief is correct she carries fifty guns, maybe more— and she has a full complement of gunners to go with it. By the way, we are all humbly grateful you were able to make it back aboard. The ancient harbor in Cumana is known to some of our older hands and we can approach in such a way that may give us an advantage. I had a talk with the Lords this morning and we'll know very soon. The likelihood of blood on the decks is high. As your captain, I beg you to let me deal with matters of grand strategy while you find some shoes."

I looked at Wales, wondering if he too had lost his mind. Wales looked at my dirty feet and said, "see if you can find Mr. Sharp, he'll take care of you." If we were going to be blown to splinters by the *Trident* it was of little import that I be killed with or without footwear.

Sharp was below fiddling with a pistol. I told him what I needed, adding as an afterthought, "Wales sent me." Sharp apologized for the lack of shoes and to make up for it, he offered me a cutlass and a firearm which I politely declined. Ominously, Mr. Sharp said there might be shoes available soon enough, depending on how we fared against the French. He tried once more to supply me with a weapon and I told him weapons would be better employed by men who knew how to use them. He looked at me, thought for a moment and said "you make a good point."

Men who knew how to use weapons were carrying long pikes, swords, axes, and brass embossed pistols, the latter tied by the handle with silk sashes and slung over their shoulders. They were congregating below decks near the hatches. Gunners were positioned by their assigned cannons and talking excitedly amongst themselves, making preparations as men do before battle to occupy their minds and their hands. Roberts was seizing the initiative and it seemed likely we were going to attack a French warship. Everyone but me seemed to think this was some sort of gay frolic.

With my own well-being foremost in my mind, I made my way back up to select a safe vantage point. I looked at my feet and considered jumping overboard and trying to swim to freedom, watching the outline of the dark green coast through the haze. I had been a strong swimmer in my youth but it was too far. Maybe I had lost my mind and everyone else was sane.

While going up to the quarterdeck, I was stunned to see the outline of a huge French vessel at anchor less than a league distant, its stern facing us, docile and vulnerable, its bow pointed toward the waterfront. The voyage from New Barcelona should have taken longer in my humble opinion, but we must have caught a swift current that shortened the time. Captain Roberts stood close to the helmsman, his eyes darting left and right. Wales gestured for me to accompany him so I went down to the main deck and saw a longboat being readied.

Wales told me to join him in the longboat, explaining, "we're going to pay a visit to that beautiful French lady." Incredulous, I asked what in God's name we were doing, and he told me to be calm, all would be revealed. The *Royal Fortune* was headed directly into the harbor but when I did a count, I could see twelve men on our decks and three or so in our rigging, none were armed.

We were getting closer. My mind was still not working to full capacity and while I should have been terrified, I was not, probably due to my inability to pin down precisely what we were doing. As far as I could tell, we were engaged in some daring intelligence gathering mission since attacking this French behemoth was out of the question.

The surface in the harbor was calm and the sparkling blue water exceptionally clear, sunlight playfully reflecting off the small undulations created by the light breeze. All was quiet except for a gull or few flying overhead. Wales beckoned me, again, to follow him and I stood fast awaiting some further signal as to our intentions but receiving no reply, I climbed over the rail and clumsily got into the launch, stifling several moans in the process. One of the men seated nearby said something in perfect French, causing the other occupants to join in some light-hearted laughter. The only word I understood was *merde*.

We rowed directly into the thin shadow of the looming French warship. I could see the thick anchor cable holding the French ship in place. "*Trident*," Wales said below his breath, reading the name of the ship as we passed its stern and came up to her port side.

Looking back at the *Royal Fortune,* I studied her to see if she looked like an English merchant ship. I saw nothing to the contrary but I could not shake the notion that we were on a fool's errand. Had we not been so dangerously close to the French ship, I would have asked the confident pirates in the longboat what we were doing.

Wales waved up to the deck of the French warship and a well-groomed man, presumably an officer, leaned over and shouted "*bonjour*, a good Sunday morning to you." All I could see were long double rows of gun ports lining the *Trident's* gracefully curving hull.

Crouched in the stern of the launch, Wales stepped over a large coil of heavy rope which I had not noticed, almost as if he were intending to shield the rope from view.

"Top of the morning to you, *monsieur*. We are searching for pirate Captain Bartholomew Roberts and our sources tell us he may be near. A fishing boat passed us this morning and told us Roberts may be hiding in New Barcelona."

My jaw wanted to drop but by sheer force of will I kept my mouth clamped shut. A distinguished looking man joined the young officer, the two standing shoulder to shoulder. The older fellow was sipping a hot drink from a delicate porcelain cup, presumably tea or coffee. We were near enough I could discern the blue pattern on the white of the china. The two Frenchmen exchanged words between themselves and I presumed the younger man was translating. The young man smiled and turned back to face us.

"*Oui*, pardon, yes, we are sailing to New Barcelona. The Captain Roberts is there. Will you care to assist us, there is a very big reward."

Wales answered, "as I said, our captain is searching for Roberts. It is you who would be assisting us, *oui?*" This bizarre banter suggested we were going to have a competition to see which captain could be the most arrogant. My palms started to sweat but Wales had not yet reached the summit of his morning bravado.

The young French officer found our hubris amusing. He smiled condescendingly and asked Wales, "good sir, who is your captain?"

Without a moment's hesitation, Wales shouted, "Glasby, Henry Glasby. Captain Glasby is not well but I shall speak with him and return with his instructions." Wales and I were fortunate I was unarmed. He glanced at me out of the corner of his eye and one of the men elbowed me in the side. Naturally, his elbow struck me precisely where I might have a broken or cracked rib. I groaned and bent forward involuntarily causing Wales' eyebrows to arch skyward.

He probably thought I was going to vomit and if I had, it would not have been due to the fact that I was still hung-over.

The unsuspecting men above us missed my genuflections. The Frenchman yelled to Wales, "*tres bien*, please give our humble compliments to your *Monsieur* Glasby, perhaps we might lend our surgeon." The young man could not have been more congenial.

"You are advised to keep your surgeon sir." Wales was enjoying himself a bit too much and the French officers looked at one another quizzically. The younger one shrugged his shoulders, no doubt chalking up the slight misunderstanding to the complicated mysteries of the English language.

"I will send back word from Captain Glasby," Wales promised. The Frenchmen waved and resumed their private conversation.

Scarcely a hundred yards now separated the two warships. Wales had the launch begin the return trip, then, as we neared the anchor cable of the *Trident*, he quietly said "feather oars". One of the men in the launch surreptitiously reached over the side of our boat and tightly affixed one end of the coiled rope we carried to the *Trident's* anchor cable. He tied the knot with two or three rapid motions just below the waterline. Oblivious, the older French gentleman raised his delicate cup toward us in a friendly salute. As far as they knew, we were a large English merchant ship, possibly interested in pursuing Bartholomew Roberts and our Captain Henry Glasby was not feeling well. At least that last part of the outrageous lie had validity.

Someone on the *Royal Fortune* gave the order "heave to." When we were back on the deck, I kept thinking the watch on the *Trident* is certain to spot our line now securely affixed to their anchor cable. Even if they did, I wondered if they would be able to ascertain its purpose in time to matter.

Finally, I figured out what Roberts was planning and the hairs on my arms stood up.

The captain welcomed Wales back on board like they had not seen each other in ten long years.

By some pre-arranged code, Seahorse barked "aye captain" and the English ensign began to plummet downward. Armed men roared up from our open hatches to the accompaniment of the ship's musicians.

Roberts had donned his red damask coat and he wore tight fitting black trousers with shining Spanish silver buttons running up the side of each leg. He waved his hat over his head, a giant feathery plume gracefully swaying in the air. Four pistols, bound around the grips in silk strips, hung behind his neck and over his shoulders.

He shouted, "raise the black."

War had been declared and the *Trident* was about to learn that the pirate they were hunting had saved them a good deal of searching.

Our end of the stout line connecting us to the *Trident's* anchor cable was hurriedly run through pulleys and eight or nine men strained to draw the two ships closer. When the line snapped taut, droplets of seawater were hurled upward and more cascaded along its length into the harbor. Six more pirates joined the effort and with each rhythmic heave, the gap between the ships grew ever smaller. Roberts had also correctly calculated that he would have the flood tide working in his favor.

I removed myself to a position near the bow of our ship where I could be out of harm's way.

A solitary man on the stern of the French ship raised a spyglass. He did not need the glass to see the enormous black flag, with the dancing white skeleton, rising to the top mast. The man with the glass suddenly burst into a frenzy, pointing and gesturing toward the anchor cable. A burly French seaman started hacking their thick anchor cable with a small hand axe, but it was too late, it was far too late.

I grimly watched the gun ports of the *Trident* and awaited the devastating crash of her guns, certain her volleys would be followed by swarming masses of armed Frenchmen intent on repelling our boarding party.

The tranquility of the moment suggested I was to wait for the French assault in vain. Moreover, Roberts had no intention of firing a warning shot or issuing a preliminary demand to surrender.

Most merchant ships have a crew of twenty or less, sometimes as few as eight or ten. The *Trident* had fifty guns and, on any given day, a crew that might exceed three hundred. We were outgunned and outmanned but our broadside of over twenty heavy guns and all our swivel guns on the starboard side were arrayed against the undefended stern of the *Trident*. When armed ships, side by side, exchange a series of broadsides, anything can happen, especially if a mast is hit or a large sail shredded or disabled.

Solid shot, in any event, normally goes flying in one side of the hull and out the other, crushing, damaging, maiming, or killing anyone in its path.

A ship is several times longer than it is wide, so round shot sent through the bow or the stern travels through the *entire length* of the ship, a phenomenon called 'raking'. The effect of a single broadside can be devastating, depending on how close the ships are when battle commences. I could have thrown a grenado onto the deck of the *Trident* at this point, but our men were heaving on the line and even when the distraught sailor finally severed the anchor cable, our momentum and the incoming tide would carry us directly into our quarry in a matter of seconds.

Using my fingers, I quickly calculated the number of twelve and eight pounders we had on our starboard side. Among the array of misfortunes about to befall the *Trident* was the fact that Roberts had no desire to make the warship his prize. Therefore, he had no incentive to avoid damaging the structure of the ship or its hull, in fact, quite the contrary. Our gunners had the luxury of aiming for the head and the heart, the goal being destruction of their target.

Worse for the *Trident*, she could not get underway to maneuver or escape. This was the fate I had feared for the *Royal Fortune* when we were anchored in the harbor in New Barcelona.

The command "fire" reached my ears from our open gun ports and I stiffened. We had reeled ourselves so close to the French ship I could hear men about to be slaughtered yelling for their lives, one man screaming, "*mon Dieu, mon Dieu.*"

Our first volley was *double* round shot. The shock and recoil of our heavy guns firing in unison was extraordinary. The concussion made something in my ears implode and uniform patterns of delicate ripples fanned out on the surface of the calm blue water. Our versatile swivel guns, packed with canister and grapeshot, began firing at the decks to keep the French from firing at us with muskets.

The decks of the *Trident* were nearly devoid of human life, which meant the bulk of their crew must be below, where they would be ripped to meaty shreds by our heavy guns. Why were they not massing on their decks?

Our gun crews hastily reloaded and sharpshooters in our rigging fired muskets at any Frenchman unlucky enough to venture into the open, although they had yet to send anyone into their rigging. Any stern chasers the French might have used against us had been rendered useless, along with their gunners, by the storm of shot unleashed by the sudden wrath of the *Royal Fortune*, tearing out the *Trident's* guts.

How many volleys would it take to turn the inside of the *Trident* to an abattoir?

Seahorse raised a speaking tube and yelled, "strike your colors." His demand had clearly been conveyed by the lolling black pirate flag, scores of armed men poised to leap aboard the *Trident,* and the certainty that the fusillades ripping their ship's vitals were not about to abate of their own volition. The master pirate gunner, a lanky but intensely serious man called Powder, kept shouting, "fire at will." His gunners happily obeyed, trying to outdo one another in speed and efficiency.

Wales was to lead our boarding party and still the decks of the *Trident* remained devoid of defensive preparations or discernable activity.

If, by chance, a French sailor on the *Trident* was of the view that he and his shipmates were going to be slaughtered by our heavy guns, he was in for a rude awakening. The real slaughter, the personal kind, was about to commence. Seahorse kept yelling at them to strike their colors and surrender.

Why were these obstinate Frenchmen ignoring the inevitable; was their captain mad, insensible, already dead?

Through clouds of thick gray smoke, I finally spotted a small cluster of French sailors bracing for the pirates who, with grappling hooks, had pulled the ships together. Due to the curvature of our hull and the configuration of the *Trident's* stern, it was no simple matter to board her. Nevertheless, there was six or seven pirates for every French sailor bold enough to offer battle. One way or the other, those brave French sailors had to know they were going to die. These lonely men destined to be massacred must have been crouched against their gunwales or, perhaps, a hardy few had emerged from their hatches, dodging grapeshot pouring from the swivel guns and well-aimed fire from pirates overhead.

With bile rising in my mouth, I watched these poor men die and I pitied every one of them. I pity them still.

There have been times in my life when I've regretted my decision to watch men murder each other; such vivid memories weigh heavy on a man's thoughts long after the events giving rise to them have ended. The starboard side of the *Royal Fortune* abutted the stern of the *Trident* at an odd angle, giving our men a narrow avenue to depart our ship, clamor up and over the taffrail of the *Trident* and descend on the men who would perish in a vain effort to defend themselves and their ship.

Wales went first, as if besieging a fortress, propelled upward by strength and agility, surprising in a man of his thickness. He was followed by Neptune, the latter armed with a cutlass three feet long. Neptune overpowered a man valiantly trying to force them back, gaining a crucial foothold for the horde of eager pirates to follow. What began as a trickle turned into an inverted avalanche. As pirates reached the quarterdeck of the *Trident*, a group of our men still worked with grappling hooks to bring the two ships side by side, to better align them. This configuration would allow pirates to assault over the rail and crush any who remained alive.

These bewildered Frenchmen were not anticipating a sortie from above or they would have posted more men at the top of their stern. A uniformed man did dare to lean over as Wales and Neptune were in the midst of scaling the scrolling woodwork on the *Trident*, only to be hit in the face by a musket ball. The man was knocked backwards, leaving a cloud of pink mist where his head had been. Many of our marksmen honed their shooting skills on a regular basis and were armed with only the finest muskets, muskets handcrafted in France.

Papi led three men up and over the stern. Almost instantly, the body of a French sailor went cartwheeling over the side. Within seconds, another French sailor was heaved into the sea, splashing into expanding ripples left by his predecessor. Our cannons were still delivering fire into the stern and increasingly, into the port side of the French vessel. Massed men on our deck were impatient to eliminate the gap that separated them from bedlam and glory, and that gap would vanish in less than a minute.

I watched in mute wonder as Wales parried the swift thrusts of a graceful and slender Frenchman armed with an elegant sword, the rapier equipped with an enormous and elaborate cross-guard at the hilt. Wales quickly shifted his weight and sidestepped the attacks of his adversary, a well-trained swordsman. I swear he wore a smile under his thin moustache until the moment he slipped and fell in a puddle of blood, losing his balance and his confident smile. Wales raised his heavier blade and sliced the man from shoulder to waist in one massive stroke. As the mortally wounded man faltered, Wales brought his blade up in a long backstroke that nearly severed the man's head, blood spurting in arcing jets from his neck.

Pirates began to hunt in packs, one led by Seaman Starling. He and two other pirates had a man pinned against a gunwale and the man threw down his pistol. Reaching to his side, the Frenchman withdrew a long knife and dropped it to the deck, raising his hands to surrender. I saw an extremely agitated Starling yelling but I could not hear his words. The man at Starling's side, an extremely ignorant pirate I believe they called Cromwell, grabbed the unarmed man, twisting his arms behind his back. Starling rushed forward and slashed the pinioned man's throat from jowl to jowl. Blood gushed from the man's wound as he toppled forward. Cromwell hastily picked up the man's discarded pistol by the barrel, Starling grasping the butt. They began a violent argument over who was to keep the trophy, pulling back and forth on the prize like two disgruntled children. I looked away in disgust.

Our musicians had ceased vaporing but they were still playing, their selection of somber tunes lending an eerie aspect to random acts of murder and mutilation being perpetrated for no real purpose. I doubt there had been more than a dozen Frenchmen on the deck at any given time. There were so many pirates that most of them had nothing better to do than strip the bodies of the newly dead and throw their naked bodies into the harbor, the color of which had gone from turquoise to a shade of pink, at least in the water at the base of the two ships.

A black pirate was kicking a wounded Frenchman who was curled up in a ball, desperately trying to protect his midsection. The pirate suddenly stopped and dropped to his knees, pounding the man's head with the thick metal handle of a short cutlass. He pummeled for all he was worth until the man's head was the consistency of a bloody sponge. The pirate stood up, drew one of his pistols and carefully placed it an inch from the man's forehead. He fired. I was certain the man had been killed twice over but then, for good measure, the pirate kicked the man's corpse as hard as he could four more times. The pirate, covered in blood from his elbows to his ankles, walked over to a hatch and sat down where he methodically began reloading his pistol.

People were moving on the deck but all were pirates. Their killing frenzy unleashed, they hammered and smashed the hatches in the hope of finding more victims. At long last, I recognized the voice of the handsome French officer who had conversed with Wales just a few minutes ago. Wales was facing the officer, aiming a pistol at the Frenchman's heart, the officer moved slowly and cautiously, his hands held shoulder high, palms out.

He nodded at Wales, then, in French, he gave the order to 'strike the colors'. Who was left alive to hear the order I do not know but two Frenchmen rose up and grabbed the line to lower their ensign. The officer, who was unmarked and seemingly unwounded, gracefully bent to one knee and slowly extended his arms, cradling his delicately curved saber. The cannon fire and musketry ceased.

I edged closer to the *Trident* and heard the kneeling man say, in a firm voice, "sir, we are at your mercy, please stop the killing." Wales said "*merci*," shouted appropriate orders and grasped the sword.

To my horror, the bloodletting was not over, in fact, it was about to get worse.

Captain Roberts materialized on the deck of the *Royal Fortune*. He was incensed to the point of being incapable of speech and as soon as I recognized the body, I knew the reason why.

Seahorse had been carried back to the *Royal Fortune* where his shipmates laid him gently on his back. He had a small bullet hole above his left eye. There was no exit wound and surprisingly little blood on his face. Some Frenchman had shot him with a pistol. We had one fatality in the massacre, but it was a man who had faithfully served the captain with the utmost loyalty. Some lives mattered, most did not, but as ever, some pirates mattered more than others.

While Roberts seethed, someone brought him news that two women, a white woman and her black slave, had been found hiding in an empty water cask in the hold of the French ship.

Five French sailors, two of whom were copiously bleeding from gashes and sword thrusts, were dragged before Roberts and laid at his feet, the scene reminiscent of a human sacrifice. Dozens of pirates were tearing the *Trident* to pieces, looking for valuables, clothing, weapons, drink, foodstuffs and provisions.

The French officer who had surrendered the ship along with his ornate sword, was holding and comforting his ailing captain. The old man had suffered a serious wound to his thigh. Wales brought them on board the *Royal Fortune*.

Captain Roberts launched into a screaming tirade, deriding the captain, over and over again, for not striking his colors immediately and thereby wasting the lives of his crew. The deranged Roberts probably did not care about the lives of his foes, but he was unhinged by the loss of one of his most reliable lieutenants. The young officer could not keep up and interpret the diatribe for his distraught captain, but it was evident that everyone understood what was being said.

Raging like a tempest, Roberts taunted the French captain about his apparent inability to hear. "We have a way of helping with that," Roberts shouted. Roberts motioned to Neptune who drew a short knife from the top of his boot. Two men pinioned the sagging French captain against the mainmast. Roberts said "do it" and Neptune cleanly sliced off the old captain's ears, one after the other. Following a few pitiful obscenities in French, the disfigured man fainted, rivers of blood flowing down his neck and onto his shoulder boards.

Fear and anger warped the face of the grim young French officer. He was no coward, anyone could see that, but he had no means of defending his captain and his outrage and shame must have been unbearable.

Roberts demanded to know why there were so few men on the *Trident,* were they suffering some epidemic? Deadly illnesses among those new to the West Indies was common enough and so grave were concerns about the ravages of these plagues among seafaring men that ships known to be infected were rarely attacked. If the French crew was infected with some sort of virulent fever, it might be conveyed to our men with disastrous consequences.

"No illness, it is Sunday, we let the crew attend mass, they are in God's loving care," the young man wearily explained, employing the flat tone of the defeated. When word of this catastrophe eventually reached any French crewmen safely ashore, their prayers of thanksgiving and salvation would, in future, be undeniably heartfelt. No doubt their priests would try to convince them it was a miracle. By choosing to attend mass, they had avoided being shot or hacked to pieces. I had noticed there were no launches or longboats which might have been used to flee with the women, whoever they were. Their longboats must have been used to ferry most of the Roman Catholic crew to shore.

This business about holy mass also explained why the *Trident* had not gotten underway to sail the short distance to New Barcelona in their search for Bartholomew Roberts, the man responsible for their ongoing agonies. Had our attack been on any of the other six days of the week, the battle may well have ended the same but the journey would have been longer and more difficult—for us and for them.

We were still perplexed as to why the French had waited so long to surrender, especially since they had insufficient men and thus lacked any chance of success.

"Who are these women?" Roberts yelled. He took the flat of his cutlass and struck the young officer so hard the poor man tumbled sideways to the deck. Before he could recover, Roberts hit the man again, this time on the other side of his face. Roberts ordered that the battered man have his hands tied, "damn you *monsieur*, is it the woman?" Roberts wanted to know the identity of the woman as he strongly suspected that the presence of the lady, whoever she was, might shed light on the failure of the French to surrender in a more timely fashion.

The young French officer, his left eye the color of an eggplant and swelling shut, his hands bound behind his back, rose to his feet, unsteady yet defiant. His attitude suggested he had no intention of telling Roberts about this 'woman' or anything else. In these circumstances, being stubborn would come with a very steep price.

Roberts resented the defiance in the battered Frenchman and took three big steps. He straddled the bleeding French captain and aimed his pistol at the back of the unconscious man's earless head. "Who is the Goddamned woman?" Roberts yelled, "I will kill every one of you bastards if that is your wish."

Balefully, the French officer looked to his captain and back toward Roberts. The pistol was cocked and all I could hear were the cries of the circling gulls. Balling my fists in anticipation, I counted one, two and then boom, Roberts fired before I could get to three. Roberts jammed the smoking pistol in his coat pocket, paced about and pulled another pistol, aiming it skyward and raging about the 'woman'.

Roberts was fortunate that looks could not kill. The dark brooding eyes of the young French officer conveyed anger, but I could sense that there was something more.

The officer spoke, "the helpless old man you mutilated, this gentle and kind man you senselessly murdered, he was my captain. And he was my father. Fuck you Roberts, fuck all of you." He tried to spit at Captain Roberts but his mouth was too dry. Roberts, unfazed by this revelation, reared back, raised his arm and struck the man on top of the head with the butt of his heavy pistol, a blow severe enough to crack the man's skull.

The officer collapsed in a crumpled heap.

Roberts murmured at his uncooperative and unhearing adversary then shouted for all to hear, "fuck you, you French piece of shit. Someone please tell me, who is the woman or I will have this man," pointing at Neptune, "cut out the eyes of that man," pointing his pistol at one of the other prisoners. None could doubt his threat.

It would have made sense to bring these women on board and question them directly. Roberts had his own way of doing things and that was his problem. Certainly the slave woman would have told us the truth without recourse to such extreme methods.

Most of our boarding party and all our gunners, in other words, all but a few of our men, crowded the main deck to watch the battle of wills between the young officer and Captain Roberts. Roberts, it seemed, felt obliged to demonstrate his mettle to his men so as to justify and solidify his position as their uncrowned king. Somewhere it must be written that to lead very bad men you eventually become a very bad man yourself.

"Take one," Roberts ordered. Neptune grabbed the head of the unfortunate and terrified sailor from behind. He held him tightly and with his free hand, raised a curved blade from his boot, heading directly for the man's eyes. As soon as the prisoner was touched, he shrieked and squirmed, twisting his head back and forth, eyes shut, as if he had been set on fire. "*Non, non, non,*" he cried. He pleaded with his young officer, sobbing and begging, calling him Louis. Louis had heroically made it to his knees, thin rivulets of blood trickling down the side of his head, some of the blood getting into his eyes and making him blink the one eye that was still functioning.

Despite his utter helplessness, Louis remained silent. I knew in that moment that Louis knew he was about to die.

"Maybe she is your mother?" Roberts said with sarcasm. Neptune relaxed his grip on his hostage. For the first time, I detected a glint of fear in Louis' countenance, "would she like to join your father?" Roberts prodded.

Louis looked at Neptune and back at Captain Roberts as if he was contemplating a plan. More likely, Louis realized there was no plan to be had, his senses beaten into nothingness. He did not know what to do—except to bring an end to his suffering and humiliation by provoking his own death. Whatever the reason, his stubborn silence was deafening.

From the deck of the *Trident,* Hunter Sharp yelled, "sir, captain, sir, wait, we're coming aboard." Sharp had bright beads of clotted blood in his unkempt beard and in his hair, but he himself looked unharmed, other than being winded and out of breath. He came to the gunwale, ignoring the dead and wounded scattered on the decks of both vessels, politely adding, "please." Drawing in several deep breaths to regain his composure, he looked at the mass of intrigued faces and addressed his captain.

"Beggin' your pardon captain, I heard you askin' after a woman. The Lords are watching over two. They are fine, for now. I suppose you heard about Seahorse?"

"Yes, Mr. Sharp, there he lies. About these women, who the hell are they? Can anyone tell me that?" Sharp was nodding in anticipation of the question and one could see he was in possession of the information.

Struggling to breathe normally, Sharp said, "the black one is called Sarah and she is a slave. The lady, she keeps faintin', her name is Elizabeth. She is mistress to the owner of some plantation," he paused for effect, "on Martinique. Lord Lutwidge told me to tell you they found someone far more interesting," Sharp said. Having just solved the needlessly prolonged mystery about the 'woman', Sharp had unexpectedly upped the ante by offering up another.

Louis hung his head and closed his good eye, whatever we were about to hear, Louis knew.

"Martinique you say?" said the captain, clearly intrigued.

I looked up at the black flag and saw 'ABH' and 'AMH' emblazoned over the white skulls, a Martiniquan head.

"Aye captain, Martinique. Seems to be the reason the *Trident* did not surrender from the start. Lord Lutwidge instructed me to ask what you would do if we found a man who put a bounty on your head. He wants to know what you would do with Governor de Montigny." Mr. Sharp awaited the response.

Captain Roberts was incredulous. We all were. The captain jubilantly slapped the side of his leg and burst out laughing, most of the crew joined in, except Sharp, who stood still as a statue. This had evolved into a Sunday overflowing with surprises.

Roberts looked around at the men making sure all eyes were on him. "Lord Lutwidge well knows the answer to that Mr. Sharp." Even the more obtuse members of the crew had to have been infused with a sense of high drama at what was certain to unfold.

"His Lordship told me you would say that," Sharp said, finally allowing himself a crooked grin. The crew took delight in Lutwidge's wit, some laughing, others making rude noises and crude suggestions. The mob was warming to its task and Roberts would be the willing instrument of their wrath.

"God help him," Wales said, as he saw who was coming.

Everyone, including our prisoners, stared transfixed at the knot of men coming on board. Seaman Starling, the murderer called Diamond, and Papi of all people, were escorting a finely dressed man who stumbled awkwardly between them, blindfolded, his elegant hands tied in front by a piece of torn red silk. Their blindfolded captive had hair reaching his shoulders, the black strands flecked with gray, and a pointed well-trimmed beard and thin moustache to match. He was understandably disheveled, his elegant yellow waistcoat was hanging open and in other circumstances, some might wonder if he was drunk.

He was the Honorable Florimond Hurault de Montigny, the Governor of Martinique.

The trio paused once they had hoisted the Governor onto our deck. Papi moved his hand up to his own face and raised his eyebrows to silently ask Captain Roberts if the blindfold should be removed. The beaming pirate captain smiled at Papi and shook his head.

"Not yet Papi," Roberts said, his voice equal parts glee and menace.

At the sound of Roberts' voice, the Governor moved his head back and forth, disoriented and terrified.

We waited.

"*Oui*?", the Governor said, his voice shaking.

"So sorry *Monsieur* Governor," Roberts said. He silently gave Papi the go ahead and Papi jerked the blindfold off, the Governor eyeing his captors and squinting uncomfortably in the glare of the sun.

Roberts took off his dark gray tricorn hat, equipped with a huge white feather, and waved it in front of his knees, the same thing he had done when we first met. "Governor, or may I call you Florimond? Permit me to welcome you aboard the *Royal Fortune*. It is a delight to have you as our guest, allow me to present my crew." He waved his hat in a broad arc encompassing the bloody sooty and grinning faces of a hundred and fifty pirates. A man might prefer facing a village of starving cannibals. Two or three pirates raised their hands and incongruously waved at the Governor.

"And as you must know, by now, sir...verily, I am the one they call Roberts. Bartholomew Roberts. I am pirate Captain Bartholomew Roberts." Roberts was in rare form, performing for the crew, gloating at his good fortune.

Eight hours ago I awoke in a puddle of shit and now I was being forced to witness the abuse of innocent men and possibly women. I cringed at the memory of gory tales I had heard about pirates burning, beating and cutting prisoners for hours on end.

All I heard in that tense moment was the sharp snap of a canvas sail in the breeze, high up in the rigging. Even the gulls knew it was a time for quiet.

Roberts, for whatever reason, looked over at me, his unexpected scrutiny making me most uncomfortable. He ordered Sharp to take off the Governor's tall leather boots. When Sharp complied, Roberts said graciously, "please give them to Mr. Glasby, some whore took his shoes." The crew found this quip and the gesture most amusing. Mr. Sharp tossed me one boot, then another, each of which I caught awkwardly against my chest, straining to hide my embarrassment and regain my balance.

Louis made a teetering effort to rise to his feet.

Roberts took a boarding axe from one of the men and kicked Louis in the stomach. The Frenchman keeled forward, falling once again to his knees, his bloodied head bent forward. Roberts raised the axe in both hands and brought it down on the crown of Louis' head, cleaving it in half. The bones of his skull and the gray mass of what, moments ago, had been his brains, were visible for all to see.

Roberts tossed the boarding axe aside and it cluttered across the deck.

The shocked Governor, his mouth agape, intoned officiously, "you will hang Roberts, you will see the Devil soon."

Roberts replied, "today, Governor? Why today even the Devil fears me. I will never hang but I am more than ready to meet the Devil, more importantly, are you?" Roberts was relishing this Greek tragedy, intoxicated by the power he had over these men and a captive who in normal circumstances would have been the one holding the scepter of power.

The Governor bowed his head and humbly asked for a priest. He was told we had a Vicar once but the Vicar was dead. He was admonished that he should not have missed mass today. "Say your prayers Governor, I'm sending you to your God." Roberts had someone toss the end of a long length of hemp rope over the yardarm on the mainsail and Roberts himself tied a noose large enough to fit over a man's head. Without any fanfare, Roberts put the crude noose over the Governor's head and pulled it snug around his neck.

Would the blood ever stop pouring from the gaping hole in the remains of Louis' head? A pool as large as his body had gathered where he lay.

Roberts began to prance, gesturing and pointing with his hands, "I'm Bartholomew Roberts, proud Welshman, gentleman rover, and you *were* the Governor of Martinique. You made a very big mistake and that mistake has nothing to do with going to mass. You made me your enemy. So Governor de Montigny, will you confess your many sins and beg our forgiveness?" Roberts was mimicking and mocking the rituals and methods used during the hanging of pirates.

The Governor managed to thrust out his chest, "I made you my enemy? You jest but you jest poorly. You've made yourself an enemy of mankind. As for me, I do not fear death, I am promised life everlasting by my Lord and Savior who forgives all. Jesus, the Christ, in his mercy and goodness, he offers even someone like you his love, although you, a vile murderer, are most unworthy. That is the miracle of his gift— is it not? Will you confess your sins and beg forgiveness, all of you?" The Governor had reclaimed some of his bearing and his voice rang steady. He was being brave, not haughty, "I even forgive you as my sins are forgiven, washed away by the blood of the lamb and forgotten. God's mercy is without end but I sense that you are without mercy, *oui?*"

"Men like you see men like us as scum," Roberts said, clearly riled by the Governor's profound ability to speak the truth, an ability that arose either because of his dire predicament or even more impressively perhaps, in spite of it. "You use God and your priests and your power and your money to enslave us and make us serve you, all the while you preach it's 'God's will' It's not us who should be asking for forgiveness, it's you sir. You and your popes and your kings and your princes who could give two shits for any of these men. These are free men. Until we die, and we all shall die, we will live free and we will happily kill anyone who would take that freedom from us. You sir, you are a fucking thief. We may all die tomorrow but men will know we lived as we wanted, not as we were ordered to live by pompous shits like you. If there is a hell, I will see you there, but not today, not on this day. Today you will do the Marshall's Dance." Most of our men cheered, some whistled, but not all.

Not me.

The Governor was rudely hoisted up in fits and jerks. When his cream colored silk stockings left the deck the small feet they covered kicked in violent spasms until he was left suspended about fifteen feet above our heads. The soles of his feet were black from the grime and blood on our deck. His legs twitched for a full minute and he wet himself, choking and gagging, his eyes bulging grotesquely. I had seen this before and was vividly reminded of what I saw as a boy in Boston, yet those dark times seemed as if they were two lifetimes ago. I had often worried and wondered if I would ever have to see such a horrible, repugnant sight again. And in my heart of hearts, I wondered if this would be me one day, was this to be my fate?

Roberts dared not talk of freedom to men like me. I was not free, but I would be. I had to escape these vile men. As the life ebbed out of the devout Governor, I made a promise to myself that I would be a free man or a dead man but I would never become a murderer.

The terrified French sailors were freed and when they realized they would live, they wept. They would spread the story of today's spectacle and embellish it, as all men do. Not that the story needed embellishing. The *Trident* was stripped bare of anything of value from sewing needles to barrels of powder. The shattered remains of the vessel were set on fire late that night, serving as a funeral pyre for the mangled bodies of the dead and murdered men on board.

After consulting with the crew, it was decided, unanimously, to return to New Barcelona. Five men had not made it back to the ship and they would be retrieved. We had unfinished business to attend to, which no doubt included a few more days of riotous drinking, carousing and of course, whoring. Roberts had to arrange for the ransom of the fainting Lady Elizabeth. From what I could gather, a local merchant secretly paid Roberts for the distraught woman. Whatever he paid, it is likely the sum paid by her lover for her safe return was far greater. The maidservant Sarah was granted her freedom and with Papi's help, Sarah found herself living and working at *La Taberna Marinero Solitario*. As it is with men, one woman's nightmare is sometimes another's salvation.

During the four days we remained in New Barcelona, I never left the *Royal Fortune* or, to be more precise, I was not allowed to leave. Nor did the Governor. He hung above the deck, visible from shore, drying in the sun. I saw him that desolate Sunday and for many more days thereafter, until he was nothing but bones and tattered strips of cloth. I kept his supple leather boots and wondered if this would bring me more misfortune. Only time would tell.

Meanwhile, I thought of the horrors I had witnessed and one other thing, I thought of escape.

Chapter 12

Escape

DURING OUR RETURN TO NEW Barcelona, I was keenly interested in the fate of the men who remained behind, it was assumed they'd been dead drunk or sleeping so soundly they failed to hear the searchers and the early morning cannon blast. Nothing was said to suggest any of the five were suspected of desertion. Not only were the five easily found, by all outward appearances, they were genuinely relieved to be back among their shipmates. To a man, they lamented missing the attack on the *Trident* and the gory scenes that unfolded on our deck. I did my best to avoid having to hear the constant retelling of the barbarities I'd witnessed.

Our water, wood supply and foodstuffs were replenished to overflowing. Merchants and vendors invariably sought to collect inflated prices from pirates on the theory that pirates had fabulous sums of money and were, to one degree or another, at their mercy. As was known by everyone, there were fewer and fewer ports where an active pirate ship could acquire much needed victuals, drink and supplies.

Despite the impediments created by outside forces, the ferocious reputation of our captain and his crew continued to sow fear among any potential adversary. The gently swaying and decomposing remains of the Governor removed any doubt as to the risks inherent in making an enemy of the ruthless Bartholomew Roberts.

We paid market prices.

As ever, after a few days and riotous nights, the townspeople were genuinely happy to see us go and it was rumored the taverns were on the verge of running out of ale and rum.

Before we weighed anchor, three new men signed the Articles and joined the crew.

There being no foreseeable end to this never-ending madness, I firmly resolved to escape, whatever the cost. Missing two golden opportunities in New Barcelona helped give me impetus, but it was primarily the sight of an old man having his ears cut off and other helpless men shot, bludgeoned and hanged. My decision made, it came at a cost. As I pondered my nascent plan, I convinced myself that the captain and Wales were growing suspicious. Their uncanny ability to gather information often bordered on sorcery.

The flood of worry kept me awake at night and made it difficult to concentrate.

As sailing master, I was among the first to know we were destined for Hispaniola. We needed to careen the hull and this unpopular bit of drudgery was long overdue. It had been decided the ship would depart the Caribbean once the hull was scoured and repaired and we would return to safer hunting grounds off the Guinea Coast. As news of the atrocities in Cumana spread, details of our whereabouts would circulate among ambitious men who wanted the glory of bringing Roberts to justice, whether motivated by duty or the reward, the outcome would be the same. Consequently, another cross-ocean voyage beckoned.

A clean hull maximized speed, an essential element in our success as well as our survival. The Crown's anti-piracy program was gaining ground and it seemed that Royal Navy ships were roaming these seas in growing numbers. When a pirate crew was captured and the captain and some or all of his men carted off to the gallows, the news found us, along with tales of how they were overtaken, sometimes how they were betrayed and ultimately, how well they died. Our crew drank toasts to fallen brothers, sang songs in their honor but never seemed to believe it could happen to them. I suppose it is thus with all bad men. It was not discussed openly but even a fool would have to realize that as one crew after another was defeated, the odds against those who remained grew worse.

It was with pride and trepidation that Bartholomew Roberts was uniformly acknowledged to be atop of the list of wanted pirates. Hanging the Governor of Martinique would have accomplished this even if Roberts was not also seizing dozens of merchantmen annually.

As for me, once across the Atlantic, it would be well-nigh impossible to flee, so I had to get away before the ship sailed east.

Careening the hull was a labor intensive process that would take two weeks or more, given the size of the *Royal Fortune*. Hispaniola is large and mountainous and if I could get a sufficient head start, and if I was lucky, I might be able to avoid capture.

We sailed northwest unmolested and I did my best to avoid Roberts. He had to know I condemned the abuse of the Frenchmen and the murder of the Governor and by his forbearance, he acquiesced in my decision to retreat within myself. Thankful for the distance, I spent my free time ensconced in my cabin, talking to Jack and reading *The Life and Strange Surprising Adventures of Robinson Crusoe of York, Mariner*, one of three books that had defied the odds, survived my involuntary servitude and provided me with companionship. I sought to draw inspiration from the hardy Crusoe, with his cleverness and ingenuity. Alas, what confidence I could muster was fragile at best. Trying to be brutally honest with myself, I would not allow any assessment of my prospects to be unduly influenced by the resourcefulness of a man who lived only in the imagination of Daniel Defoe. Oddly enough, Crusoe spent twenty-eight years on his island, only to be rescued in the end by mutineers looking for a place to maroon their deposed captain. Reading about Crusoe's adventures did allow me to think about something other than my escape and the risks it entailed. At least in that regard, the book provided an escape of sorts.

Three days before we dropped anchor, my fears had so magnified themselves that I thought the entire crew was aware of my intentions. I attributed their conspiratorial silence to a vile practical joke, one being played at my expense. Insomnia put me on the verge of delirium. I could barely eat but I knew I would need strength, so I ate what I could and stashed the remnants in a small canvas bag. Every few hours, I would chance upon two or more men talking. If they stopped and looked at me, my racing heart seemed to say, 'Harry, they're on to you, best give it up.'

Owing to my misfortunes in New Barcelona, money became a thorny issue. This concern was self-inflicted and to some degree, a product of my stubborn nature. Having steadfastly refused to accept the spoils of piracy, should I take money and if so, where would I get it? If and when I happened upon any natives, money might be used to bribe them into hiding me or staying silent if confronted by the search party who would come hunting. If I eluded capture, funds would be needed to reach Boston. Roberts would not abide his sailing master walking off into the hills, never to be seen again. My skills made me valuable— maybe indispensable. Remember the six mile wide island I found? Few afloat could perform such a feat and the upcoming Atlantic voyage was not without risks, even under favorable sailing conditions.

These considerations led me to pray that if I was unsuccessful, the captain might spare my life, even though recent events had dampened that marginal hope. Roberts seemed to grow more reckless and violent with each passing week. My gambit could cost me my ears or my life.

If I stole money and failed to get away, I would face the serious charge of theft. Many find it hard to believe that stealing on a pirate ship is prohibited and while it is, how is such a rule enforced? I saw men every day with maimed and disfigured noses, many more with the unique scars left by a brutal flogging, all for stealing a trifle from the property of a fellow pirate. The rule against thieving was rigidly enforced which may have explained why it was so rare.

Based on a fair estimate of what someone might demand in the way of a bribe to risk hiding me from angry pirates, I could only acquire such a sum if I resorted to theft. Asking for money from someone like the Albino was an option, but he had already generously given me a fist full of gold and he was sure to ask me why. What could I tell him that would eliminate suspicion? He would not believe I had taken up dice or cards. Worrying further that the captain and crew would accuse the generous Albino of aiding in my escape, I discarded the idea. If I was caught, even if the crew did not execute me, the thought of being flogged or having my nose sliced made me sick to my stomach.

Escaping without money seemed a more prudent course and it would behoove me to avoid contact with strangers during the venture whether I had money or not. Once free on the big island, I would work out some means of finding a vessel to carry me north to Boston. Good sailors were always in demand.

I descended back to earth on hearing the lookout; from one hundred feet in the air he could spot a sail twenty miles distant.

We were nearing shore. Our journey had taken a week owing to the weather, the amount of cargo we carried and the poor condition of the hull. My hands began to sweat and my mouth was as dry as old gunpowder. I could not banish nagging doubts about my vow of poverty. I knew where some of the men hid their coins and gems and it was no secret where Wales kept the ship's bounty, not that getting it would be easy. Assuredly, the penalty for stealing from the ship's treasure would be monstrous if I were apprehended. The vivid vision of my feet dangling off the deck was horrific.

Captain Roberts silently approached me from behind, "excellent work Glasby."

"Thank you sir." I stood stock still with my hands clasped behind my back so Roberts would not see them tremble. Had I given myself away by the tone of my voice? Was he aware of my intentions? I pretended to look across the empty sea although none on the deck could yet see land. Roberts began conversing with someone else but I was so startled by his presence I could barely hear as my blood thundered in my ears. It was then I told myself that if I wanted to stay alive I had to breathe good air into my lungs and let the bad air out. My nerves were frayed like rotting anchor cables being picked apart for oakum. When you are under intense stress, telling yourself to act naturally rarely works, but I did my best.

At least the weather was fit. During late autumn, the heat, humidity and insects on some of these islands could be formidable. I would fare better than Mr. Every, although settlements in the southern part of the island are few and far between. I discounted the risk of being done in by the elements and all things considered, a late season storm would put the ship at risk but it might also hamper the ability of searchers to find me. I could last a few days without food and I had some inclination of what sort of sustenance might be provided by nature in the guise of fruits, berries, and roots. Water would be readily available and the canopy of trees would provide shade and make it harder to see me from afar.

Captain Roberts, on a prior visit to Hispaniola, had marooned a small and tight-knit group of French pirates who declined to do their part whenever we encountered French vessels. At first they were just a nuisance but then other pirates, who are very superstitious, petitioned the captain to get rid of them, insisting that the Frenchmen were harbingers of bad luck. If you are perceived to be the source of bad luck on a sailing vessel, particularly one manned by pirates, your days are numbered. In the aftermath of the burning of the *Trident*, I overheard men discussing the profound wisdom of marooning these men. They reasoned that by ridding the crew of the accursed French pirates, we had enjoyed good fortune during the devastating attack in Cumana, proving that superstition can exert enormous influence over the mind of a simple seaman.

Success in Cumana stemmed in large part from the happenstance of it being on a Sunday morning, with most of the Catholic crew at mass. We were lucky in that respect, of this there can be no doubt. So who knows, maybe the crew was right.

Luckily for the French pirates, marooning was a convenient way to be rid of them, as there was no intention of bringing about their death. Had it been the latter, a remote and deserted island would have been chosen.

At last we drew close enough to the beach to make out the mist-shrouded mountains and the lush greenery of the coast, the crew prepared to go ashore.

I am proud of my abilities at sea of which you have heard much about, but when it comes to escape, I am not so capable. The desire to put life as a reluctant pirate behind me grew to such an absurd impossibility, it nearly caused me to lose my ability to properly and effectively reason.

On the first day, I was permitted ashore for a few hours but dutifully returned just before nightfall. Intuition told me this was not the time or the place. Our scouts found a sheltered cove farther west to careen the ship. We had to sail three leagues to reach this location and I resolved to wait until the ship was careened and about to sail before I departed. That would ostensibly give Roberts less time to search for me. Miraculously, my doubts began to dissipate which came as an enormous relief and I finally managed to get some much needed sleep.

As I ponder my reasoning now, hindsight suggests I should have made my escape bid the first day we were ashore, before the ship moved west. There were two reasons why this would have increased my chances.

One, as mentioned, the ship landed and took on water, then departed abruptly to careen the hull in a more protected harbor nine miles away. In this scenario, I would not be leaving the ship as much as it would be leaving me. The crew would be busy and I could have put considerable distance between me and the ship by running for all I was worth. Even if my absence was noticed before the ship set sail, something I had to assume, I would already be miles from shore.

The second reason pertains to something that was wholly beyond my control as well as beyond the capacity of my overactive imagination.

Fate can be harsh no matter the choices one makes.

There were a multitude of things I considered in forming my plan, too many to count, but a man cannot know what he does not know.

Two other crewmen, disgruntled men who had had their fill of cross-ocean trips, men convinced they would die in Africa, had conspired to desert. Being thieves, their goal was to take as much money and as many gems as they could carry. Even though they had their own booty, they stole from some of their shipmates, thinking that the ship would sail on and let them go. After all, in their twisted minds, Thomas Jones and his friends were not pursued.

These two pirates were wholly unaware that one of the most able sailing masters afloat was about to make a run for it *in the same spot and at the same time.*

When, at last, the hull had been scraped and all was in good order, I slipped ashore with a working party minutes before sunset. The scariest moment is always just before you start. Despite my hand wringing or maybe because of it, there was little left to think about so I scuttled off, my back to the sea and my head and eyes aimed at the jungle. The captain intended to sail early the next morning to intercept some merchant ships bound for Cuba. When it became apparent I'd absconded, the crew would demand that the ship pursue the merchant ships. Any pirate alive would choose a rich prize over a missing navigator; just kidnap another.

Many of my woes arose from Roberts' incredibly reliable intelligence apparatus and that is why I had such intense worries that he knew I was plotting an escape. After all, he knew of approaching merchant ships which were days away. But he knew more than that, much more, and it pertained to something right under our noses.

Heading inland with my bag of scraps and my fingers crossed, each step I took was a tiny victory. I'm surprised I didn't bump into my fellow travelers as they too elected an inland route, wholly unbeknownst to me but not unbeknownst to our ever omnipotent captain. I made the summit of a ridge rather quickly and this minor accomplishment lent itself to the irrational notion that I was free. The moon had not risen so it would soon be pitch dark, a fact that made movement difficult but not impossible. Moving stealthily and optimistically onward, I descended the ridge to a dry creek bed. Exhilarated by my progress, I lay quietly for half an hour before going up the next hill, one higher and steeper than I had appreciated. Tugging on saplings and roots, I labored long and hard and emerged on a worn dirt path at the summit of the second mountain ridge. At this point, I firmly believed I had eluded the pirates and the sweet ambrosia of freedom beckoned.

In reality, the opposite was true.

Silently disgorged from a black wall of impenetrable brush, two young islanders materialized a few paces away. One carried an ancient Spanish lance and a dim lantern, the other a bow and handful of crude arrows. Using broken but passable English, one loudly ordered me to "stop you, right there." For a split second I considered running into the jungle but I did not know if these boys were alone, where I was going or how far they might track me. These uncertainties were too much to bear and I meekly raised my hands in surrender.

My stern captors, their youthfulness notwithstanding, jostled me a hundred yards down the path, poking me in the backside with the point of the lance. To my befuddled amazement, there stood two haggard looking men from our ship. My initial impression led me to conclude they were members of the search party sent to find me. Their heavy ankle chains, which we had taken from slavers, and the fact that they were unarmed, supported an alternate theory. In short order I was chained to my fellow miscreants and we sorry three marched unceremoniously down a steep winding path to an insignificant fishing village. No one said a word, what was there to say?

When I say fishing village, I mean four rickety wattle and daub huts and two crude outrigger canoes with nets drooped over some mangrove branches. Had I the means, I would have cut my throat to avoid returning to the dismal life I had so earnestly sought to abandon. Never have I felt so low. The only time I ever felt this foolish was when I woke up in the alley in New Barcelona.

Our longboat rocked sideways in the gentle surf, surrounded by several agitated and angry men busily swatting clouds of feasting mosquitoes. They had no choice but to wait and they were eager to set sail and let the mosquitoes feed elsewhere.

Someone said with genuine wonder, "well I'll be damned, there's Mr. Glasby."

My dispirited fellow captives helped row us back to the *Royal Fortune.*

Wales greeted me.

As he escorted me below decks, he confided that one of the escapees had tried to recruit a third man for their scheme. This had taken place a month ago, before we visited New Barcelona. The third recruit opted to remain with the ship but he had demanded two pounds to keep his mouth shut. The escapees either forgot about his demand or decided not to pay him but at any rate, the odd man out revealed the plot to Wales after we burned the *Trident.* When we landed in Hispaniola to careen the ship, Wales paid local islanders to watch and wait for the pair as they made good on their escape attempt.

Amazingly, and contrary to my endless worrying, no one had the slightest suspicion about me. I was a bonus. The confused watchers, who were told to be on the lookout for two men, observed me from a distance the moment I snuck off the beach. They must have followed me by smell or by sound as they could not have seen me in the approaching darkness. On the other hand, they had to believe I was heading inland and would eventually reach the pathway on the ridge, which was where I was captured.

The bronze colored boys who caught us on the trail were brothers. They were given rewards of two pieces of eight for each of the crewmen and four pieces of eight for me. When I asked Wales why the payment for me was four and not two he gave me a hard knock in the forehead with the knuckle of his forefinger. "Glasby, cause of what you carry in your coconut, because you know your way around the seven seas. Without that, you are absolutely and totally worthless. You know Harry, if it wasn't for those two thieving lunatics, you would have made it." His commentary about my fellow escapees only added to my sense of impending doom. My career as a pirate would soon be starting its third year, that is, if I was lucky enough to avoid being shot or hanged. If my life was to be spared, what else might they do to teach me a lesson?

I touched my ears, wondering how I would look without them.

But first, the three of us would stand trial.

As ever, the fate of Harry Glasby was in the hands of pirates.

Chapter 13

Valentine

ONCE WE LEFT HISPANIOLA THERE was no longer any justification to keep us manacled. The trial was to take place an hour after sundown the next day. Given the phase of the moon and consequent darkness, Wales claimed it would be hard to hear and see on the deck, so he moved the proceedings to the galley.

The idea of writing another letter to Constance swirled in my head but I thought it would be a waste of time. We were at sea, heading across the Atlantic, and I was facing a trial which could end with my execution. She had likely given me up for dead long ago, a supposition that did nothing to improve my gloomy outlook.

When Jones was flogged for trying to avenge Pedro and Mr. Every was marooned for the murder of the Vicar, I had to concede that justice was done. I'd sat in on pirate trials involving rather petty offenses and the process was surprisingly fair and more importantly, fair-minded.

During one particularly long period at sea, some of the men had been drinking and started a mock trial for their amusement, something they did from time to time. Lintorn Highlett donned a dirty white wig and presented himself to his raucous audience as Sir Lintorn of Highlett, Lord Chancellor of the High Seas Court. God only knows where they stole the wig.

The defendant, a foul-mouthed and grumpy sort called Chamberpot, was notorious for cursing God and Christ so the men charged him with blasphemy. Someone purporting to be Lucifer testified for the defense, giving a litany of fanciful reasons why Chamberpot should be not be condemned. Chamberpot was defiant to the end and regaled everyone with a long, colorful and imaginative string of insults and vile curses. The jury was enjoying themselves and heaped effusive praise on Lucifer for his 'candid' testimony. Based on the evidence, they said they had no choice but to sentence the heathen to death, saying such a sentence was necessary to teach the rest of the crew a lesson and to save them from the fiery furnaces of Hell. As the verdict was being announced by the inebriated Lord Chancellor Highlett, in flowery legal lingo with great gusto, five men entered the proceedings. Two of the five happened to be from Beaufort in the Carolina Colony, Chamberpot's home, and one of the others was a very close friend. Before anyone could explain, Chamberpot's friend became enraged that Chamberpot was about to be executed, hurling curses and making threats about the absurdity of it all. His outburst and the predictable response from some of the drunken crew caused a near riot that included several fist fights. A juryman was stabbed before order was finally restored, his wound, mercifully, was not fatal.

Wales, upon hearing of the fracas, issued an edict banning mock trials for six months. Several weeks passed and Wales gradually softened, lifting the moratorium on conditions that a few basic safeguards be implemented to eliminate the risk of any future misunderstandings.

Long afterwards, many who were present that night continued to refer to Highlett as Lord Chancellor.

The outcome of a pirate trial was rarely a surprise but this could also be said of trials in the so-called civilized world. Procedures were in place, I surmised, to give the men the sense that their law was superior to the brutal discipline meted out by Royal Navy officers, especially captains, and to assuage the curious and erroneous perception that Admiralty Courts hanged accused pirates on mere cobwebs of proof or on incompetent and perjured evidence.

Growing up in Boston, I knew as well as they did that many alleged pirates were acquitted. Others, especially young men, were justly condemned but often as not, pardoned or reprieved. Reality did not jibe with the self-serving pirate belief that due to gross injustice and endemic inequity in the world at large, they were allowed to turn their backs on society and murder, rape and steal. One doubts that pirates spent much time pondering their blatant hypocrisy or the hypocrisy of men living in the cities and villages they left behind. Men everywhere are keen to judge others harshly while overlooking their own sins and shortcomings. I recall the Vicar saying something about that concept more than once.

My fellow escapees and I had no illusions about the seriousness of the accusations against us, we were apprehended literally going over the hill. At least one of my decisions was paying unforeseen dividends, the decision to resist the urge to steal as a means of funding my flight. The same could not be said of my fellow defendants, Thomas Burgess and Henry Jennings.

I was vaguely familiar with the men whose botched escape resulted in my apprehension but I'd never had a meaningful conversation with Burgess or Jennings. Neither was liked and since this gave them something in common, they stuck together. Even for pirates, who live on the fringes, these two were on the outer edge. Burgess had a habit of finding ways to avoid work. When on watch he pretended not to understand simple directions and feigned ignorance about basic knots or how to handle our complement of sails. These were basic skills novice sailors quickly mastered. The work never ends on a sailing vessel and it can be physically demanding to say the least. In wet cold weather, it could amount to a form of torture and a malingerer like Burgess was a bosun's nightmare. Few would argue the proposition that many seafarers became pirates primarily because they are lazy and Burgess certainly supported such a contention.

As far as reputations went, things were worse for Seaman Jennings. He was not as lazy as Burgess but he had been accused of thieving from members of the crew in the past. He was devious and cunning even for a pirate and the accusations had never been substantial enough to warrant an actual trial. In other words, he was fairly good at it.

Jennings was the apparent master-mind of the escape which is stretching that phrase to the breaking point. He and Burgess had endeavored to recruit Francois LeSage to join the party believing he knew the terrain and it was known that many on the island spoke French, so having LeSage would have been smart.

No one in the crew was speaking to LeSage.

On the one hand, he declined to join the plot but on the other, he agreed to keep it secret for a bribe of two pounds. When the bumbling and deceitful Jennings neglected to pay the bribe, LeSage told Lord Copplestone of the plot. In the grand scheme of things, LeSage as informer proved he was someone who could not be trusted. His demotion to the bottom of the pecking order was justified and had he been tossed over the side in the dark of night, none would have mourned him.Many whispered that any man who could be bribed for a mere two pounds was also too stupid to be a pirate, a self-righteous claim if ever there was one.

Adding to the animosity of the crew, the few pieces of eight found in Jennings' purse were far less than the sums reported missing. The victim might be lying about how much was stolen but more likely, Jennings had used the money he and Burgess had stolen to bribe others, perhaps other pirates or people on the island.

Sharp privately brought up something even more serious shortly after I was brought back on board. He seemed to suggest Jennings and Burgess may have broken into the ship's locker and hidden far more loot somewhere on the island. When I told him I had no knowledge of such a thing, he changed the subject and never mentioned it again. If true, this was something beyond petty thieving and it would implicate Wales for gross dereliction. It was the duty of the quartermaster to keep the ship's locker secure and account for the division of valuables and plunder from time to time. This strict accounting is why pirates were said to be *on the account*, indeed, I had seen the ledger books Wales used to make distributions among the men. No one would believe Wales had been in league with Jennings or Burgess and Wales served as quartermaster precisely because he was trusted by everyone. Beyond that, he had unlimited access to the ship's treasure, he was too smart to trust a pair of incompetents, and finally it was Wales who personally set the trap that snared the fleeing thieves.

Since Sharp had never before confided in me, at least to such a degree, I concluded he was fishing for information. He wanted to know whether Burgess or Jennings had done or said anything that might shine some light on what they had stolen and, equally if not more pressing, where it might be hidden.

As for the captain during these tremors, there were few times since my initial capture when the crew held Roberts in higher esteem. While memories are short and pirates, on the whole, are fickle, the coup against the French in Cumana had been truly masterful. My repugnance at the savage treatment of the prisoners notwithstanding, I had served Roberts as well as I could and knew he cared not one whit about my opinion of his conduct.

Captain Roberts did not say a word to me about my failed escape attempt or the pending trial, which struck me as ungrateful in the extreme. Speaking plainly, I was deeply resentful and truly terrified by his silence.

Having been kidnapped and made a virtual slave by a gang of murderers and thieves, I felt more than justified in believing there was something fundamentally unjust about my treatment.I confess that my tendency toward pessimism spiked when I was discovered, serving only to confirm the nagging and persistent belief that my attempt to get away would fail. Luckily, the only unbroken mirror on the ship was in the captain's cabin or I would have stood in front of it repeating to myself, "I told you so." Roberts had a rare gift for seeing the bigger picture and any effort by him to intervene on my behalf, when two other men were on trial, would be perceived as favoritism and usurping the authority of the crew. It was their ship, not his. He served at their pleasure, they knew it and so did he. And so did I.

The day of the trial was eventful but not in a way that might presage any hope for some sort of last minute reprieve.

We happened to pass another pirate vessel only to learn that the merchantmen we hoped to seize en route to Cuba had already been stripped clean.To make matters worse, because things can always be worse, their cargoes were rich in silver ingots.So much so that the pirate sloop we met was riding noticeably low in the water.Few things make a pirate more irate than learning he just missed a rich prize. We sailed on but the atmosphere was tinged with disappointment and anger. Some in the crew started to complain that they'd missed easy pickings because of the three deserters.

I decided it was best to eat in my cabin, avoiding Roberts, Wales and the belligerent crew who would soon be called upon to sit in judgment.

When the men situated themselves that night, Wales sought to start fresh so as not to let the bad news about the silver and consequent ill will dictate the course or outcome of the proceedings. Plugs of fresh tobacco were distributed and new clay pipes. These comforts may sound mundane but smoking below decks was strictly forbidden due to the risk of fire. A large bowl of rum punch was produced and through these humane gestures, I could sense that the mood was beginning to lighten. Wales entered from the rear of the assembly and threaded his way to the front, pausing along the way to exchange pleasantries and pass on a word or two of good cheer. Roberts elected not to attend, another unmistakable sign to the crew that this was their domain, not his. As a sign to me, it did not bode well. Who better to sing my praises then the beloved Captain Roberts?

Wales' opening gambit was to profess relief that he had not spent all day carrying heavy silver bars which would have aggravated an old back injury. When the ballyhoo subsided, he resumed, "sail under the black flag with me boys and I promise you that for every lost treasure there are two more. You don't stop casting your nets when they come in empty—do you? Do you? No, no sir. You cast your nets again and again until you bring home your catch. Is there any end to fish in the sea? Could you call yourself a fisherman if you burned your nets? Would you call yourself a man if you stopped looking for rich treasure?" As he asked each question in turn, he paused and waited for the crew to respond with a resounding "no", a few punching at the hazy air with their fists.

He traded his empty mug for another, overflowing with punch.

"Now lads, to the matter at hand, I must ask you this. Who calls himself a pirate that quits and deserts his mates and steals the treasure they fought for—money they earned by risking life and limb, facing grapeshot and lead and the high gallows with the short halter?" A cascade of boos and catcalls echoed throughout the galley.

"Harry Glasby, Thomas Burgess and Henry Jennings have burned their nets," contended Wales. He went on to remind the crew that Burgess and Jennings were also charged with thievery. More boos, whistling, hisses and shouts.

At the mention of my name, someone sitting behind me leaned forward and roughly slapped me on the side of my head. I did not turn to challenge my assailant. As the galley quieted a thin voice in the back yelled "more punch" which made everyone stomp their feet in unison and chant "more punch, more punch."

Wales raised his hand. He adopted a tone of seriousness and I sensed he had a purpose beyond entertaining a crew who, moments ago, were wrestling with angry and resentful thoughts. "We have a form of justice the world must surely envy. Without formal commissions we admit to having no wigged and robed counsel, with their feeing, with their haughty airs. They look down their long noses at us but we hold our noses at them because these fucking barristers spew nothing but shit." The crew cheered but Wales' somber deportment was unchanged, "we will not admit the bribing of witnesses- we will not see to the packing of juries- we will have no torturing of the accused or his witnesses, which does nothing but wrest the sense of law and purpose away. And we admit to no God awful punishing, puzzling, perplexing terms made unintelligible and twisted into uselessness. We will not see words cut and sliced and murdered by the razor sharp tongues of those who despise the truth unless it suits their own ends."

The crew cheered, louder and more boisterous.

Most of these men knew people, including members of the crew, who had been tortured and brutally punished by sheriffs and magistrates and jailers using processes created and devoted to the privileged few to retain that privilege. The law did not apply to powerful well-connected aristocrats, theirs was an apparatus primarily designed and used to control the masses by the mighty.

Wales had found his rhythm, "our tribunal sessions are not burdened by numberless officers, wrinkled ministers of rapine and extortion with ill-boding aspects that would scare the shit out of our beloved Astrea, the goddess of justice." The men chanted the name of Astrea.

The crew had forgotten about missed treasure and apparently, even the wretched misery that was part and parcel of their everyday existence. They were thoroughly enjoying the buoyant revelry, the pipes, the punch, and that hard to define euphoric feeling that even though they were pirates living far beyond what rich men called 'the law', they, in truth, had far more justice in them then the aristocrats who lorded it over them in England, France, Spain and dozens of nations who claimed to be God-fearing and civilized.

They were permitting themselves, despite the brutal life they had chosen, to feel a sliver of pride. It was no wonder they loved Wales as they did.

The trial commenced and it gave those with grudges against Burgess and Jennings a chance to have their say. Guilt was not at issue, it was the punishment that had to be determined.

After hearing from a small number of witnesses, amidst the smoke and clamor, the jury huddled together to agree on their verdict. It took mere minutes and I sat, stoically, as I watched them talking and nodding to each other.

Wales struck me as being more mindful than ever when he cleared his throat and sang out, "my brothers, my brothers—these sorry men before you were arraigned upon a statute of their own making and the letter of our law being strong against them and the fact of their guilt plainly proven, it is my solemn duty to announce that this jury is now ready to pass sentence."

I viewed the proceedings as I might watch a school of sharks feeding, as if by some weird transmutation I was a helpless fish and thus, already dead. It had never occurred to me to speak in my own defense. Perhaps someone, someone other than me, should have pointed out that I had never signed the damned Articles and remind them of how I saved the Albino and found the Vicar's real killer. Someone might remind the jury that I had forsworn any loot since the day I was made their prisoner. I refused to beg for my life because I had no expectation that my life could be saved, nor did I believe there was anything I could say that would sway the jury.

I assure you it was not pride or vanity. I made the choice to accept my fate believing fate had embezzled my right to make choices. The pessimism which convinced me I could never escape infected me now more than ever, whatever tiny threads of hope I possessed had been dropped on that narrow path on the dark ridge in Hispaniola.

Burgess and Jennings, guilty of stealing and desertion, made feeble pleas for their lives. Jennings tried tears but pirates are rather immune to the tricks people begging for their lives employ. If anything, Jennings aroused the ire of the crew by acting so pitifully. They would have respected him more if he had exhibited some courage or even bravado. The notoriously lazy Burgess started to say a few words but he was hard to understand. It was not nervousness, the man was just inarticulate. As far as I could tell, he was trying to blame Jennings for the whole mess, but the shouting and boos got so loud he shrugged his shoulders and sat down, too lazy to even plead for mercy.

The crew wanted and expected us to be condemned to death. In their twisted universe, there was no other outcome or punishment that made sense. Jennings and Burgess were thieves and deserters, as for me, I had the ill fortune to get caught up in their wake.

Through the haze and the tumult, I noticed juror Valentine Ashplant stand up and whisper something important to Wales. It had to be important because Wales listened intently and then began nodding. Ashplant had been one of the original Lords although he no longer sat on the privy council. He seemed to avoid the captain and the other Lords, the root cause of their presumed falling out having been long forgotten or perhaps simply buried. It was common knowledge among all but the newest recruits that Valentine Ashplant was not a man to be trifled with, nor was he quick to anger. He was a man of mature bearing and quiet dignity. If the resolute Mr. Ashplant put his mind to a task, he finished it with determination and deadly earnestness. Ashplant, with his long arms and wide back, was among the very best at furling heavy wet canvas sails during a storm.

Nothing fazed him.

Ashplant slowly wrapped his fingers around the bowl of the long clay pipe dangling from his mouth, "I have something to say." He looked in the eyes of the men to make sure they were paying attention. They were.

"By God," he drew from his pipe and opened his mouth a crack in one corner, letting loose a thin white jet of smoke, "I say here and now, Mr. Glasby shall not die. Damn me if he shall."

Inexplicably and without fanfare or bluster, he sat down, staring straight at me.

A bewildered member of the jury mumbled that the Articles demanded death for deserters. The crew seemed more interested in what was happening with the jury than with me. Wales stepped forward, casting a sideways glance at Mr. Ashplant and interjected. This had to fall into the realm of better late than never. "Men,

Valentine makes a valid point, Mr. Glasby never signed the Articles. You were there, or you most assuredly know how Glasby became sailing master of this ship." Whether it dawned on any of the men, it certainly dawned on me, if I was gone, who would be the first mate, who would steer their damned ship?

Two or three of the unsteady jurors had consumed more than their share of the rum punch,hard men who easily lost their temper. They were angry at Ashplant, me, even Wales, the kind of angry a man gets over some paltry thing that leads to fights and stabbings, irrational explosive anger that allows a pirate to beat a helpless man bloody or to wait his turn to rape a sobbing girl then strangle her and throw her in the sea. Going on the account provides an angry man who causes pain, suffering and death for his own merriment an excuse to indulge in behavior that civilized men rightly abhor. Living in the midst of such men is not living, it is akin to seeing some part of yourself dying a slow death.

When horror becomes commonplace, a man must be careful or he can lose his soul.

Ashplant rose again as if burdened by the antics of too many rowdy schoolboys locked in a windowless room. There was something majestic about this enigmatic fellow who, for whatever reason, had anointed himself my champion. His wide-set eyes burned with some inner resolve that radiated like beams from a ship's lantern on a foggy night. Ashplant pushed back his thick bushy hair and puffed again on his pipe, no one was going to hurry him. The smoke enveloped his head and his protruding ears and made the light behind him dim dramatically.

Everyone was silent. He looked rough men and dangerous men dead in the eye and made sure they understood he was immovable.

"God damn ye gentlemen, I am as good a man as the best of you. Damn my soul if I ever turned my back on any man in my life, or ever will, by God. Mr. Glasby is an honest fellow, notwithstanding his misfortune, I love him. May Old Roger damn me if I do not. I hope he will repent of what he has done, but damn me, if he must die, I will die along with him." The crew was absorbed and transfixed by his commanding voice, not to mention his unshakeable resolve.

The silence was so profound it was almost tangible. A man behind me hacked and coughed, made worse by his vain attempt to stifle himself.

No one moved, no one dissented. My savior, Valentine Ashplant, dared anyone to challenge him. With his smoldering pipe hanging from the corner of his mouth he squinted his hooded eyes to avoid the smoke. Gently crossing his arms across his chest, he slowly and deliberately used his right hand to draw a pistol from his left side and vice versa, moving gracefully, the polished ebony handles of his matched weapons reflected the light. He held them like long black feathers and pointed them at his fellow jurors, each man leaned a bit left or right as if to avoid his aim. Everyone knew those elegant pistols were primed and loaded.

Ashplant laid his flintlocks on the table and the jury foreman, the relief evident in his voice, cheerfully asked of no one in particular, "now, that argument is most persuasive, eh lads?" Heads started to bob with one eye on the foreman and one eye on Ashplant. The foreman got a quick round of acquiescence from the jurors, including the angry holdouts. That done, the jury foreman faced the astounded crew, crying out with evident relief, "being as it is well supported, this jury with due reconsideration, finds that Mr. Glasby shall be and is hereby acquitted."

Ashplant pulled out his pipe, looked at me and winked.

The Albino was beaming and he threw me a small salute.

As if to relieve the tension, a great and sustained cheer erupted. The angry men and the rest of the crew would have the death of

Burgess and Jennings but thanks to Valentine Ashplant, I was spared.

By the Articles and by custom, a condemned man generally had the right to select his manner of death. By their election, Burgess and Jennings were tied to the mizzenmast at sunrise the next morning and simultaneously shot, even in death they remained together. Along with a somber and mostly sober crew, I watched while their bodies were untied and dropped over the side. I do not recall anyone uttering a word, nor did I see Mr. Ashplant on the deck to witness the executions. Later that day, I saw him leaving the captain's cabin, which was a bit odd in and of itself. I extended my hand to him, "allow me to thank you Mr. Ashplant."

He shook my hand warmly, using both of his, "Mr. Glasby, you are most welcome. Sometimes, a man just wants to do something good, your time will come." I watched him duck his head and go back to his business and I tried to decipher exactly what he meant.

Wales tried to assure me that neither he nor Captain Roberts had a hand in this odd turn of events but Wales hinted, broadly, that the captain would not have stood by if I had been sentenced to die. I pressed Wales about Ashplant emerging from the great cabin and Wales said it had nothing to do with me or the trial. There was something else troubling Wales but I could not put my finger on it, whatever it was had nothing to do with me.

The circumstances of my capture and unexpected commutation of my sentence made it painfully obvious that if I attempted to flee again and was caught, there was little chance of avoiding execution.

We sailed east, to Africa, and I navigated as before, each new day melting into the next.

Chapter 14
Cape Lopez

ONE HUNDRED AND EIGHTY PIRATES and one kidnapped navigator called the *Royal Fortune* home. The men careened the hull with uncharacteristic zeal, realizing that this monotonous task helped reduce the time we would spend traversing the Atlantic. Once at sea, a vessel the size of the *Royal Fortune* could be sailed by a crew of two or three dozen, depending on their experience and the sailing conditions. The routine resumed. Pirates not standing watch or working, as always, amused themselves with drink. The ban on mock trials had been lifted and to their credit, the ship's energetic musicians seemed to perform without respite. Despite the prohibition on gambling nary a day passed when I was not invited to play cards or toss dice.

Jack's quiet presence gave me comfort and I like to believe he derived the same from me.

On account of my routine duties I saw much of Wales but less of the captain, yet they gave me a wide berth, as did the crew. The high repute afforded me after the Vicar's murder had diminished considerably, reaching its nadir during my trial, notwithstanding Valentine Ashplant's miraculous intervention. The harsh reality that some of the men had advocated my death fueled my animosity and fed my self-pity.

We were about a week from the Guinea Coast and I was in the great cabin making some routine calculations. During the day, it was not rare for me to have the large space to myself, but I avoided going there at night.

I heard someone enter and sit at the large table. It was Roberts, casually sipping a cup of tea.

"Good morning captain", I said, "I'll be done here in a few minutes."

"Take your time Mr. Glasby. When you finish, join me please. I want you to know I would have given you a reprieve had it been needed."

Laying my divider on the charts, I turned to look at him. He was facing the stern windows overlooking a vast expanse of blue. His superficial nonchalance angered me.

"You, or Wales, one of you-you fixed it with Ashplant," I countered.

He motioned me to sit. I ignored his invitation. The wounds inside me that were healing had been reopened.

"I'd wager a hefty sum you know Mr. Ashplant and I are not close. We have no quarrel, Mr. Ashplant and I. No, the good Samaritan acted wholly on his own accord, as he is wont to do. I'm grateful to him, as you must be, for saving me the trouble. Trials are the business of Wales and the men, you know that Harry. Your alleged offense was most understandable. Had it not been for Burgess and Jennings you would have eluded us no matter how many men we sent looking. Much like your friend Mr. Ashplant, I would not let the crew deprive me of my navigator any more than I would offer them my right hand. I would very much like to know why Ashplant intervened. It's a great mystery. Will you not sit?"

I sat across from him, feeling somewhat conciliatory given his remarks. Why it had taken weeks for him to tell me these things was another mystery.

"Captain, you and your crew have amassed a fortune. Here we are, back in Africa with the heat, insects, deadly illnesses and abject misery that shrouds everything. Everyone knows piracy in the West Indies eventually ends in death. If being on the account is a life sentence, and a short one at that, maybe coming back here is sensible. When will you, Wales, all of you—when will you have enough? When will you stop? Ever?"

"Ah, so you can go back to Boston?" He avoided my question.

"You will never give this up will you? Enough—there is no such thing as enough for men like you. Your obsession will cost you your life and the lives of some of these men. Possibly all of them. You dare speak of Boston. What do you presume gives you that right? You say you would have saved me from execution. A man like you, especially a man like you—knows why I tried to get away. Tell me, captain, how much is enough?" He could be under no misapprehension about my indignation.

"What awaits you in Boston? Or London or Port Royal? Justice, family, servitude? Peace? Let me tell you about the king's justice Harry. Long ago I sailed with a man. While in London he was accused of petty theft. He was a stubborn man, like many, but he was afflicted. He heard voices, so he said. He refused to plead to his offense. They threatened him and still he refused, he claimed the voices commanded it. The executioner bound his thumbs with whipcord and pulled so tight the cord snapped. The man's resolve only increased, still he refused. They used the cords again, without success. They took him to the press yard. You know the press yard?

They tie a man flat and put more and more weight on his chest until he enters a plea—or dies. This can last for *days*. The prisoner is kept alive on coarse bread and water. Before this poor man could be tortured anew, his voices wisely told him to plead not guilty." Roberts drained the last of his tea. "He was tried before a jury and acquitted. He was not a thief. At least, let us say, he was not the thief in that particular case. Did we bind your thumbs and threaten you with being pressed before your trial?"

"When will you have enough captain?" I insisted. I was willing to acknowledge that his condemnation of English justice was impossible to refute but I wanted to know about Roberts. "Must I bind your thumbs or press you to get an answer?"

Captain Roberts smiled and faced out to sea.

"There are many forms of injustice Harry. This ship is my home. These men; Wales, the Lords, men like Sharp, even Cheddar and Seahorse, they are my family. Where could we go, any of us? Would our money get us into society? Some men buy respectability and the amount needed is proportional to the sins they commit to obtain that money. As you well know, we have taken hundreds of prizes. Toward that end, people have died. Regrettably. I would need a vast fortune, perhaps such a fortune does not exist. Men like me do not row ashore, get a wife and run a sugar plantation. I'm not Henry Avery. I've heard of men, like the famed Captain Avery, who took their fortune, their shares, and made a life, but such men are few. We hunt, yet is it not we who are the hunted? They have the money, ships, the men. We have freedom, freedom that most can only dream of, but we can only run, fight and hide so many times. What matters is how we live until our day comes. With any luck Harry, you will return to Boston. I hope so. You don't want this life and I don't want the life you seek. I made my choice and I will live with it until fate says otherwise." He looked into the bottom of his empty cup.

"I have no freedom, what choices are left to me?" I thought of Constance and wanted to demand why he believed he could steal my liberty just so he could range the oceans and live a life that suited him.

"Wherever fortune takes you Harry, freedom and power oppose one another. Neither is absolute. There is no infinite freedom and there's no absolute power. Today, the power we have over you denies you the freedom you cherish. Power gives a man freedom and it is power that takes your liberty. You think I'm your jailer and yes, I suppose you're right, I'll give you that. Captains come and captains go. When I'm gone, there will be another captain and then another. There's always someone who has more power. That's life. To be free, whatever that might mean, you must have power. For men like me to claim our freedom, we assert our power over those less powerful. You say that's wrong, you say I'm a thief, and I say it's wrong to torture a man or to press him with stones in the name of justice. Do not be misled by what arrogant men call virtue. Virtue without power will only be mocked. If all men are evil, and all are, then we should embrace the power we have taken for ourselves lest we become slaves to a master claiming, falsely, that he is just. As for me, I shall not be mocked." Roberts stood and walked to the stern windows, propping his foot on the sash. He looked at me thoughtfully. "Harry, a man is a grasshopper or an ant. Fate, fortune, providence, whatever you name it, choices are few. You are young. All I can say is, when you can, choose wisely."

Pontificating in general was easy but he was uncomfortable talking about me. His countenance said he realized his treatment of me was improper. "I chose to make you my sailing master and I chose wisely. That has been your fate. So far. Be thankful you were not born a black heathen in this Godforsaken land, lying naked, chained, full of despair, in the foul smelling bowels of a slaver waiting to be delivered to a short, brutal life of whippings and toil. That should tell you much about power and freedom. Sometimes it's just fate, or chance, or luck."

The captain seemed to have finished so I excused myself to go up to the deck to make sure the helmsman had us on the correct course. Much of what Roberts said made sense and if a man looked at the world expecting it to be fair, such a man was likely to suffer more, not less. I was not certain how the future would unfold but I took the captain's remarks about choices seriously.

The weather was glorious and we sailed on, making excellent progress.

Three days from the coast sails were spotted off the bow. Shortly, it was identified as a three-masted snow flying French colors, under full sail, heading west. If it was a merchantman, it would have changed course to outrun us. With less than a league separating us, the French ensign was lowered and a large black flag raised in its place. Roberts was pacing the deck with his spy glass, passing the time with Lord Lutwidge and Lord Copplestone.

"Raise the black", Roberts shouted, "we have visitors."

A cheerful Lutwidge elaborated, "she's the *Bachelor's Adventure.* Those are the colors of Captain Ling, presuming, as we must, that the crew has not jettisoned him for a proper captain."

The snow trimmed her sails and we did the same. A longboat was lowered from the snow, carrying nine men, four manning the oars, including two of the biggest men I had ever seen, negroes, shaved heads, menace in their every movement. Once on deck, introductions were made.

Captain William Ling stood five feet and maybe two inches tall, with slits for eyes, like a sleepy sow, short thick fingers like sausages, great gold rings in his fleshy ears, the gold glinting in the sun. His effusive praise for the 'great' and 'feared' Bartholomew Roberts went to the very precipice of sincerity and Roberts returned his compliments on behalf of himself and our crew, sincere enough, if not somewhat muted in comparison.

Ling's quartermaster presented himself as George Rounsivel, another man deeply honored to make the acquaintance of the great Roberts. Lutwidge embraced a man called Palgrave Williams and told us he and Williams had sailed together under Captain Davis. Reunions at sea among pirates was fairly commonplace. And when circumstances permitted, often joyous. During the introductions, Ling presented Wales with two canvas bags filled with pleasantly scented soap, sparking a round of predictable comments.

The two giants were addressed as John and Cudjo. The latter had dozens of tiny marks and random scars from his midsection to his forehead. These were not tribal marks. Captain Ling said Cudjo led a slave uprising on a ship which had been about a week from Guinea, bound for Jamaica. It emerged that the revolt had been some time ago, Ling telling us Cudjo had been his right arm for many a year. A crewman on the slaver shot Cudjo with 'dust shot', fine particles designed to painfully stop a slave but not designed to damage him to such a degree he would decrease in value on the auction block. I was likely not the only one wondering how much a specimen like Cudjo might bring at a slave auction. Ling boasted that Cudjo, "wrestled the empty gun from the crewman and pounded the weapon, and the man, to bloody bits and pieces." Thanks in part to Cudjo and others, slaves took control of the ship but none of them knew how to sail, much less navigate. They drifted helplessly for over a month when a French privateer found them, taking both the vessel and its cargo back to Africa to be sold once more. Cudjo and John were the only two allowed to join the crew of the privateer. Months passed and they managed to escape when the privateer docked in New Providence, in the Bahama islands.

When Ling advised that the captain of the privateer was dead, Cudjo raised his enormous hands and pantomimed strangling someone.

Quartermaster Rounsivel lamented the changes brought about in New Providence by Captain Governor Woodes Rogers, telling us that recruiting fine men such as these had become damn near impossible. Predictably, Rounsivel commended John and Cudjo for being like devils in a fight, a gratuitous observation which generated polite nods from our contingent.

Roberts suggested we adjourn to his cabin for 'refreshments', the mention of which made Ling's eyes open a sliver and his thick pink tongue lolled fore and aft over his lips.

While everyone was being made comfortable, Bolivar, one of our black pirates, offered to bring us a bowl of punch. Ling averred that punch would be grand, he then launched into lavish praise not just of the captain's cabin, but the entire ship. According to his expert assessment, the *Royal Fortune* afforded Roberts the means to defeat any but the largest of the Royal Navy's warships in a one on one contest.

Bolivar returned with Mr. Sharp and a huge silver bowl filled with dark liquid. They placed the bowl in the center of the table and it took both men to carry it.

Ling asked Bolivar without looking at him, "what have we here?" Ling's eyes were on the punch.

"Captain Ling, we have the best wine, rum, port, porter and brandy in my very secret punch recipe and when you finish, we have more. It's the eggs and sugar that make it special. Please enjoy." Bolivar bowed slightly and vanished. Mr. Sharp quietly took a chair along the bulkhead so he could absorb the valuable bits of intelligence that would flow back and forth amidst jokes, toasts and a myriad of shared grievances.

Ling lamented the lack of adequate drink in these parts. It was evident he could barely wait to sample Bolivar's punch.

As the guest of honor, Captain Ling was provided a silver cup which he filled with punch and drank to the health of the man to his right. He then refilled the cup, passed it on, and the process was repeated until the bowl was almost empty. Tobacco and a trencher filled with pipes were laid on the table so any present could help himself.

Ling was encyclopedic in his knowledge of currents, tides, coves, reefs and shoals in the waters around Cape Lopez and beyond. I found myself enjoying the conversation. Before the first of many punch bowls had been refilled, I invited Ling to review the charts I had, scanty as they were, to identify and record as much of this invaluable information as his patience and time permitted. He answered my questions with genuine enthusiasm and gentlemanly grace but still seemed able to keep his punch glass filled.

The gathering extended into the night.

Lutwidge affably tried to befuddle Captain Ling with a litany of Latin words and phrases. Ling, a man with a seemingly endless capacity for intoxicating liquor, had an equally endless capacity for Latin words and phrases. Moving to Greek, Lutwidge finally had to confess defeat. One of our party had Cheddar summoned and we listened patiently to see if he, Cudjo and John could communicate. They did not make it far, the languages they used were as different as French from Arabic. The only words they had in common were words for ship and pirate, words which had been imported to Africa as more and more ships, and more pirates, arrived to take slaves to the New World. Ling insisted Cheddar remain and we relived the details of how we had taken the *Onslow* and made it our own. Ling's men listened politely but I'm sure they had heard most of the story before.

Ling wanted to know how a bright young man like me had fallen in with such miscreants. There was an awkward silence before Captain Roberts said, quite matter of factly, "I seized Mr. Glasby like I would seize a brace of Spanish pistols. He's the finest navigator I've ever known. In fact, we were talking not long ago about how I hoped he would return to his home in Boston one day. Until that day, Mr. Glasby must steer our ship." Ling laughed and offered to trade two carpenters for me. Roberts told Ling, "if you throw in a sober surgeon, I'll consider it."

This comment prompted the discussion to drift into the realm of how impossible it was to find good surgeons. It was agreed that the only way to get them was to seize them, as no sane surgeon would ever volunteer to serve on a pirate ship.

Roberts was relieved to learn there were other pirate crews up and down the coast, particularly in the Cape Lopez area. He had been expressing his desire to hunt in concert with other ships for the added power and safety it entailed. The need to adapt by adding a consort was, according to the remarkable Captain Ling, a veritable necessity if one were to avoid a fatal rendezvous with Royal Navy Captain Ogle, the commander of *HMS Swallow.* According to Ling, this Captain Ogle had been sailing these waters for many months, pursuing pirates who fled the deteriorating situation in the Americas and deemed the Guinea Coast a safer alternative. Ling hinted broadly that Ogle's tenacity would soon render Africa an equally dangerous place and advised that his crew insisted on leaving before it was too late.

Uncharacteristically, the outgoing Captain Ling, when asked again and again, resolutely declined to share his intentions and destination with any of us, frankly explaining that if Ogle got his hands on the *Royal Fortune*, the whereabouts of the *Bachelor's Adventure* might be compromised with fatal consequences. We only knew that Ling was sailing west.

A pirate captain might keep his plans to himself for many reasons, not the least of which was to avoid competition. But the reticence of Captain Ling and his men to divulge their plans was something new, something different and altogether foreboding. Ling's fears were ominous because this was the first time a fellow pirate had deemed it necessary to keep quiet about the future as a means of avoiding the expanding reach of the Royal Navy. Maybe there was something about this English Captain Ogle that made it so.

Retiring to my cabin as Ling and his men noisily departed, it struck me that I was the only man on board who viewed this news with cautious optimism. Having never heard of the man before and with no idea of his physical appearance, the powerful premonition that I was to destined to meet Captain Ogle took root. When I nudged Jack aside so I could recline, I whispered, "pleased to meet you captain, I am Harry Glasby of Boston." When a man is a prisoner, a wisp of hope is better than none.

As always, Jack ignored me.

Chapter 15
The Choices of Others

SUBSEQUENT EVENTS WERE TO RESULT in the dramatic augmentation of our forces, although why Captain Ling was not invited to combine with us was never made clear. Pirate captains are even more fickle than the crews they lead, trust being in short supply. One might correctly draw the same conclusion about all sea captains, each goes about his business as he deems fit, the counsel of others is typically unwanted and unheeded.

The massive African continent, in the north and west, resembles the ear of the great elephants who give their tusks to the ivory trade and call the vast land mass home.

Leaving Ling and his men to their own devices, we sailed between the Island of Princes to the north and St. Thomas island to the south on January 4, 1722. It was at the former, the Island of Princes, what many call Principe, that Captain Howell Davis was lured ashore and killed. The death of Captain Davis catapulted Bartholomew Roberts into the small cadre of men who are called both pirate and captain. Roberts, showing flashes of the bravado that would make him famous, harnessed the angst of his new crew and led them in a bold attack on Principe to avenge the death of his predecessor.

Luckily for the current inhabitants of the Island of Princes, Captain Roberts was not of a mind to duplicate that memorable feat.

Our lookout spotted St. Thomas at ten o'clock on a crisp morning, the wind fresh but the weather thick. Principe and St. Thomas are northwest of Cape Lopez about two hundred miles from the mainland and separated from each other by one hundred miles of open sea, not far removed from the Equator. The peninsula of Cape Lopez protrudes from the mainland where the lower portion of the ear attaches to the elephant's head. From there, far to the north of Cape Lopez, the coast turns westerly, where the great Niger river flows in rivulets and channels and empties itself into the sea at the Bight of Benin.

If a man were able to walk along this inhospitable coast from the Niger river, continuing west, he would pass fortresses and ports built to facilitate the burgeoning slave trade. Places like the Slave Coast and the harbor at Whydah. Moving on, our imaginary explorer would walk to the Gold Coast where he would find the imposing Cape Coast Castle looming high over the sea. By the time he reached Cape Palmas to gracefully curve in a northwesterly direction, our footsore adventurer would have travelled a thousand miles. It is still another five hundred miles to Freetown in French Guinea and even further to the Gambia River and Cape Verde in Portuguese Guinea. If our man was still alive, a most unlikely prospect, and if he went as far as Cape Verde, at long last he would have reached the far western edge of the elephant's ear.

By virtue of my duties, these exotic places and their relationship to one another were etched in my mind.

Gliding past St. Thomas, we were spotted by two French vessels, one of ten guns and one of sixteen. They would have been better served to make a hasty escape, as both vessels were very fast, but choices were made and the curious French captains did not flee, believing us to be a large but harmless merchant ship. Roberts did nothing to dispel their enormous error until the black flag was hoisted, our deck cleared for action and the guns run out. Confronted by pirates, the men on the French ships barely had time to curse one other, assign blame and say their prayers.

By four o'clock both ships had been commandeered without any resistance.

Fate had gratified Roberts' desire to take on a consort by a factor of two.

The *Comte de Toulouse* with her sixteen guns was renamed *Ranger,* the smaller craft was dubbed *Little Ranger.* A carpenter was compelled to join us, a sound decision as work had to be done to convert the vessels. Several French seamen volunteered to remain with us. The dispirited captains and their remaining men jammed into two longboats and sailed away toward St. Thomas. As far as I could tell, the joy of suddenly and easily obtaining not one but two new vessels overcame any lingering reluctance on the part of our crew to risk a run of bad luck by taking on a small cadre of French pirates. Practically speaking, with three ships to sail, the need for experienced sailors was evident.

During the exchange, we learned that *HMS Swallow* was at Cape Verde, two thousand miles distant. According to the Frenchmen, Captain Ogle's ship was a powerful two-decker of fifty-two guns, christened in 1720. Ogle also had a consort, the *HMS Weymouth.* The *Weymouth* was docked at Cape Verde to nurse her crew, half of whom had been stricken by disease and deadly fevers. Such fevers were omnipresent along the coast and made Africa a dangerous place for Europeans, so much so that one seaman in three perished within four months of arriving. As to the ravaging effect of these illnesses on the men of the *Weymouth,* I was destined to learn more. For the present, the French sailors said Captain Ogle had spent some time at the Island of Princes, the island north of St. Thomas, as recently as the autumn of last year. The island had a good harbor and a small fort two hundred miles from the fevers of the coast. Ogle, who sounded like a very capable captain, spent weeks in the area, sailing to St. Thomas and patrolling the coast in search of pirates, pirates like Captain Ling.

With the crew of the *Weymouth* battling disease and the *Swallow* lying idle at far away Cape Verde, the reduction in pirate activity in these waters created opportunities an energetic man like Bartholomew Roberts was unlikely to forego.

Our flotilla reached Cape Lopez the next day where we encountered pirate Captain James Skyrm commanding a brig he called *Fancy's Revenge.* He came aboard with his lieutenants and explained their intention to careen and repair the hull. His vessel was leaking so badly there was legitimate doubt as to whether they could make it to the coast. Skyrm's worry was evident on his lined face and in his sunken, hollow eyes, the whites of which were a pale shade of yellow. Adding to his woes, their pumps were in dire need of repair and they lacked the necessary replacement parts or expertise. Skyrm was blunt, two hundred men were on the verge of mutiny and they were desperate for our assistance.

Fate and fortune were surely at work here but to what end?

Roberts had just seized two swift sailing vessels which were as fit as if they had just been put to sea. Skyrm commanded an experienced but disgruntled crew who faced the disagreeable prospect of long days of toil on a desolate shore, notorious for its tropical diseases and clouds of insects. Even if everything went perfectly, all they could do was render a worn out vessel marginally seaworthy.

None doubted how this was going to end. After the appropriate toasts, offers of sweetmeats and roast fowl, a handshake deal was struck. Roberts would take advantage of the Royal Navy's absence and sail north to Whydah where unguarded merchant ships sat in the harbor taking on slaves. During our foray, the delighted crew of the soon to be abandoned *Fancy's Revenge* would move themselves, their possessions, and most of their guns to the sleek French ladies they could proudly call their own. When the *Ranger* and *Little Ranger* were ready, everyone would rendez-vous at the Bight of Benin, located north of our present position and midway between Whydah and Cape Lopez.

The *Royal Fortune* set sail the next morning, our crew anticipating the presence of easy prey with unabashed relish. By the jovial tunes coming from the musicians, they too had succumbed to the nervous excitement.

As to Whydah, it would be a matter of how many vessels were in the harbor and how much they carried in the way of valuables. Low risk and high reward, the dream of pirates since the advent of the sailing ship.

With his recent successes and the imminent prospect of seizing new plunder, Roberts held counsel with Wales and the privy council in the hope of finding the cause of the crew's increasingly sullen behavior. "Wales, are the men losing their minds? Must we endure their incessant drunkenness, gambling, provoking behavior and haughty attitude. It's as if each perceives himself a captain, a prince or a king. They have become, to be fair, a company of ungovernable brutes." Since leaving Hispaniola and the execution of the two deserters, the crew had become more belligerent. No one disputed this but neither could anyone pin down the cause. Our voyage

across the Atlantic had been long but uneventful. I thought again
of the toll boredom takes on sailors. Was being idle enough to erode
the bond between men who heretofore would follow Roberts to the
gates of Hell?

If anything, his assessment of their attitude was too charitable.

Much as fire is an ever present danger on sailing ships, so too
are cabals and outright mutinies. During these hurried conferences
with the Lords, the word 'mutiny' was so incendiary it could not be
mentioned, but it had evidently become a pre-occupation for our
captain and those most loyal to him. They sometimes met thrice
daily.

Wales cornered me, more than once, to solicit my views. I gave
them willingly, but explained to our quartermaster that I knew as
little as he did. I promised him if anything changed, I would bring it
to his attention. Meanwhile, was it any wonder, I surmised, that men
who are naturally violent and spend their days in a drunken stupor
think they are capable of great deeds? I told Wales and the captain
that the ease with which the two French vessels were seized seemed
to feed the men's inflated opinion of themselves. I went on to assure
them that, as far as I could ascertain, the crew's fundamental respect
for Captain Roberts had not been seriously undermined and there
were no active plots to have him replaced, at least not by force.

Roberts and Wales were only slightly relieved by my assessments
but what real value was my opinion? On the one hand, as sailing
master, I was at the captain's elbow, on the other, I was not really
'one of them'. They conceded, with the hesitant acknowledgement
of the Lords, that the crew, motivated by reasons good or bad, could
demand a vote to replace their captain. This might require a cabal
but not a mutiny. The fact that these discussions were so prevalent
was indicative of the crack in Roberts' armor and the effect of that
crack on the thoughts of the small number of men who ran the ship.

One could liken it to a surgeon who has a chronically sick patient but cannot figure out the nature of the malady, much less determine a course of treatment or a cure.

When Roberts talked to me of freedom, power and choices, he had mentioned the tendency of captains to come and go. We knew of a ship that had three captains in a week and other crews that replaced their captain, found the new man wanting, and promptly restored the prior captain to his position. Since I had departed the *Samuel*, the idea of this crew electing another captain had rarely crossed my mind and then only as a remote possibility.

Wales, and maybe the beloved Valentine Ashplant, were the only pirates I knew who might look favorably on my release. Even so, Wales' loyalty to Roberts was unquestioned. Wales would never be the captain of the *Royal Fortune* as long as Roberts lived, regardless of what the crew said. Wales would do almost anything to support the authority of his captain. Even if the men rose up and demanded a new leader, if Roberts and Wales were excluded, there was no one who had the stature and skills to take the helm.

Skyrm's men were removing the forecastle on the deck of the *Ranger* to allow for the placement of more heavy guns. Had Roberts been more patient and less distracted by domestic concerns, the flotilla could have sailed to Whydah in force, a move that would nullify resistance and give us more firepower in the event we had been wrongly advised as to the whereabouts of Ogle's warships. It would also mean any loot had to be divided with Skyrm and his crew, a most unsavory prospect. Pirates are not creatures who like to share. Inevitably, pirate logic foresaw more prizes in the weeks ahead and if anyone but me thought otherwise, they kept it to themselves.

"You seem lost in thought Glasby, please trim the sails so we might get underway." Captain Roberts was jaunty to a degree suggesting he was anything but. It was not like him to put on airs. We sailed north by northwest. Rancor among the men seemed to have dampened, for the present, by the certainty that we were not seeking a random victim somewhere at sea, but multiple prizes trapped in a harbor unaware that pirates would descend like ravenous wolves in three days.

The harbor at Whydah is surrounded by a coral reef and within this reef are bays and inlets that are capable of sheltering dozens of ships. These are natural characteristics of the entire coast and many of the creeks have sufficient depth to provide protection for marauding vessels such as ours. Few European navigators are willing to explore these waters as the depths vary from many fathoms to three feet, sandbars and shoals posing a threat to even the most cautious captain. The natural harbor at Whydah is an exception and the southwest approach afforded us a ready means of entering without risk, which is not to say we dispensed with using precautionary throw leads.

If it was my task to get us safely into the harbor, it was left to Roberts and the men to convey their intentions.

We sailed into Whydah like a roiling black cloud bank, one that promises imminent catastrophe with blinding bolts of lightning and unstoppable winds, the malevolence one finds in the killer hurricanes prevalent in the West Indies. There are disasters wrought by nature and there are disasters wrought by man. Roberts had the cannons run out on both sides, although none were manned. He amassed the crew on our starboard side, drums pounding, trumpets blaring, with long red and black pennants streaming from our masts in the stiff breeze. The cacophonous vaporing of the musicians and the pounding of the drums was enough to make any man's heart beat faster. Whether one's heart beat faster due to excitement or fear depended on where one stood.

We spilled the wind from our sails by bracing the yards, positioning twenty or more men on the yardarms of the mainsail and topsail, with a handful on the bowsprit, each man in the rigging armed with a long musket.

Lest anyone be in doubt as to nature of this unwelcome onslaught, as if such doubts were possible, our black flag lazily floated from the topmast. White against black, the tall figure of a pirate on the left was joined by a skeleton holding a pike on the right, their arms raised triumphantly in the center, hoisting an hour glass aloft. Not everyone who saw the black flag lived to tell about it but none who saw it had any uncertainty as to its message. Surrender or die.

As we made our brisk entry, we saw eleven tall ships in the roadstead.

All eleven surrendered. Meek souls do not captain slavers but even a brave man knows when he has been deprived of his power. The captains were summoned to the *Royal Fortune* and by turn, each was rowed to our hull and duly welcomed with dignity and respect. There were ships flying English, French and Portuguese colors. Roberts was adorned in his finest, omitting the silk sash that held his pistols. His gleaming cutlass rested on top of a solid wood table he had ordered for the meeting. Some of our men relaxed and smoked their pipes, others meandered about, but all gave the dispirited captains sufficient space to gather without making any overt gestures or needless threats.

Once the principals had assembled, Roberts dictated his terms. How much would each captain be forced to pay to avoid seeing his ship burned to the waterline? This was an arena in which Captain Roberts excelled, using his guile, charm, audacity and courage to cajole, bluff and threaten, as needed, when needed. Bartholomew Roberts had a rare and uncanny breed of intelligence that enabled him to push men to their absolute limit. If one of the captains was lying, Roberts knew. If one of the captains seemed willing to make greater concessions, Roberts knew. Throughout the process, he used his knowledge and his intuition to push the men harder. The captains too were knowledgeable men and they knew their adversary was not someone to be trifled with.

As the entreaties wore on, Roberts gained enough information and insight to identify the rivalries and jealousies that existed among the eleven captains. When the time was right, he would exploit these differences in order to obtain as much ransom as he possibly could. He would not leave any gold in the harbor.

Just after three o'clock, each captain had ransomed his ship by promising to pay eight pounds of gold dust, or about five hundred pounds sterling per vessel. Delivery would be expected within two hours.

It was agreed, for lack of a better word, that we would also take the finest of the French ships in the bay, a vessel that had operated out of St. Malo in France. This craft had been outfitted as a privateer. The privateer bore a reputation as a particularly fast vessel which made it an attractive addition to our fleet. As ever, this made the need for more crewmen acute. The last part of the bargain addressed this need. We were to take on forty slaves and turn them into sailors, presumably they would one day become pirates. As always, any white seaman who volunteered to join us was most welcome.

In the end, we took thirty-five negroes, their physical condition being suspect given the length of time many had been held in the cramped lower decks of the slave ships. Some of these poor creatures had been held as long as ten or eleven months and a handful of these unfortunates could barely walk without assistance. A slightly larger number of white sailors opted to become pirates, a number I attributed to Roberts' reputation and the desire of many a man to flee duty on a slaver and get away from the risk of death by disease. I did hear Roberts telling someone to make sure none of the new men were Irish.

If anyone worried that the influx of new men might exacerbate the delicate situation between Roberts and his crew, those concerns went unmentioned. At a minimum, Captain Roberts, even with his reputation, would have to earn the loyalty of the new men, no matter what. By taking the gold, the French ship and a few dozen slaves, he was off to an impressive start.

When the unhappy slaver captains disassembled to withdraw, a grizzled and weather beaten man calling himself Captain Henry Kane growled about something to one of his fellow captains about Boston.

From time to time, when a group is talking among themselves, your ears hear the sounds but there is no understanding unless or until your name is spoken. When this odd trick of the mind happens, your name somehow reaches out to you among the babble. Had Captain Kane said Harry Glasby, I would have been only slightly less astounded. A shudder went through me; Boston, all that I lived for was in that long ago, far away, yet not forgotten place.

Eagerly approaching this wizened fellow, I clasped his forearm to arrest his departure, "sir, did you just say Boston?" His look was venomous. He stared hard at my hand with his bloodshot eyes and I let go of his arm.

"Who the bloody fuck are you?" he said, turning to spit a brown wad of tobacco on the gunwale, the gob slowly rolling down the wood. Loathing a man instantly is not one of my habits, yet the image of Neptune cutting off the ears of this irksome creature made me grin, my expression causing Captain Kane to wonder out loud if I was suffering a mental lapse. Kane kept leaning away from me in his zeal to get off the *Royal Fortune* as fast as his bowed legs would carry him.

I was able to convince Captain Kane I was sane, more or less. I apologized insincerely, restated my inquiry, and added by way of explanation, "I am Harry Glasby of Boston. I was kidnapped by these pirates while en route to Scarlett's Wharf in July, 1720."

If he believed me, Captain Kane's apathy was unnerving. This man had ice water in his veins and he confirmed it by his retort. "Do I look like I give a shit about Harry, what was it?....Glasby? We all have our fucking problems—sir."

"I am not a pirate, I was forced. I have urgent business in Boston. Please sir, I beg of you, do you know Boston or anyone who might?" The pleading in my voice made me ashamed at my vulnerability. His eyes softened ever so slightly yet I hesitated to say more. He did not deny saying Boston so I must have heard him correctly.

He began with a small concession even though it was phrased as a rebuke. "What I said to Captain Shoemake about Boston is of none of your concern. Nor is my business any business of your Captain Roberts, a man whose name is well known to all. His remaining days are few." Captain Kane was sure Captain Roberts was well out of earshot. Yet I could see Kane feared goading the famous pirate. This small revelation emboldened me, inasmuch as the remark about Roberts' days being few could be Captain Kane's undoing.

I had to employ a slight bluff of my own to widen the opening in this hard man's shell. "We know of Captain Ogle and I would be happy to tell Captain Roberts you are of the opinion that Ogle is the better man. Or you can tell me of Boston. Sir." Before the words left my mouth, it was apparent Captain Kane saw the flaw in his admonition and the potential for harm that a word to Roberts might procure.

For once I realized stories of explosive pirate tempers, torture and brutality would work in my favor. Roberts had cut off many an ear.

Prideful to a fault, Captain Kane bypassed any preliminaries, apologies or explanations, telling me his bosun was from Boston, a young man called Campbell. He begrudgingly said he would have Campbell return with their ransom payment and ask for me. I repeated my name and assured Captain Kane that Roberts had no interest in my inquiries, all he wanted was payment. The sight of Captain Kane's back as he departed the *Royal Fortune* was most welcome. Unrelated to me or Captain Kane, the dreadful cost of offending pirates would be made manifest in a few hours. Meanwhile, my anxieties did not give rise to any doubt about Kane's promise to send Campbell back with the ransom.

Lord Lutwidge slid up to my side so we could watch the defeated captains rowed back to their ships. "This day's fine addition to our rapidly growing fleet already has a new name, did you hear?" I told Lord Lutwidge I was blissfully unaware. He chuckled and said, "she is now the *Caerphilly Castle*. I would have chosen something different."

Lutwidge swore me to a vow of silence. He was most eager to boast that he had been offered the captaincy of the new vessel but, being magnanimous in all things great and small, he politely suggested another more capable man who everyone agreed had the makings of a strong leader, the importance of which could not be overemphasized in the midst of recent tensions. I asked Lutwidge if the new name of the French vessel was in some manner an homage to Captain Roberts; most everyone knew Caerphilly was the largest of all the great Welsh castles, a symbol of stolid strength and perseverance.

"Ah ha, well done sir. You are correct about the castle. It is Welsh but the intention is not to honor the bold Bartholomew Roberts, no my dear friend. The newest ship in our armada is to have our newest captain. My heart already aches for the pain his absence will inflict, as it will, no doubt, make a mourner of you too."

Reflecting on the day's cascade of surprises, I was not paying much attention to Lord Lutwidge or I likely would have been spared the need to ask, "who?"

Lutwidge draped his long arm over my shoulders and spoke into my ear, "Wales. And he is taking our former Lord and your savior Valentine Ashplant to be his quartermaster."

I was speechless.

Regaining my senses, I implored him, "what? Wales is to captain the new vessel? We cannot afford to lose Wales." I was stunned and distraught. Despite everything, Wales had never treated me with anything but respect and his unerring sense of fairness had earned him mine in return and, I daresay, my honest affection.

Compounding my visceral unease was the simultaneous loss of Mr. Ashplant. As I expressed my regrets, or tried to, Lutwidge interrupted me to announce that he, Lord Lutwidge, would serve temporarily as quartermaster on the *Royal Fortune* pending a formal election, where, he suggested, it was certain the position would be his for the duration.

Lutwidge was not fond of long hours and hard work, and while he could talk a man half to death, he lacked one of the most important traits of a leader; the ability to listen. His estimate of his value to the smooth operation of the ship was far higher than the value assessed by this fractious crew. Lutwidge was fond of me, I will give him that, and having him as our temporary quartermaster caused no immediate concern. Much depended on the merits of any other candidate but these developments could wait, I desperately needed to find Wales before he left.

One of the men told me Wales was in the captain's cabin then another said look in the galley. I was not in a mood to see Roberts so I first went to my cabin to retrieve an item of importance and bumped into the beaming Wales as he hurried out of the galley, his arms filled with wrapped packages, wooden boxes and a canvas bag hanging over his shoulder.

"Wales, for God's sake, I will not congratulate you. You cannot leave me. Lutwidge is not able to bind this crew as you have done. You must not go, your timing could not be worse." The words poured out of me. He laid his burdens on a table and pulled me aside. He apologized profusely and expressed his agreement that I was right about the crew but only a strong hand could govern the men on the new ship, many of whom were ignorant slaves whose only exposure to sailing was having been chained for months in the hold of a slaver. Lying in a coffin would have taught them as much about sailing. He even conceded my point about Lutwidge.

As we talked, Ashplant, Copplestone and some of our more experienced pirates were making selections on the slavers. The negroes needed clothes before they could be put to work. *HMS Swallow* was rumored to be at sea and haste was essential.

I begged Wales to take me as his first mate, believing he might have the heart to release me some day.

He patiently explained, "Harry, I expected such a request. I am not naive. I know why you want to serve under my command, so does Roberts. I asked to take you. Roberts said he was willing to give me most anything I needed but giving you up was, and I quote 'not fucking likely.'"

Fate was watching me, as ever, like a hawk watches a distant mouse from a tall oak tree. When the hawk finally gets bored, it will swoop down unseen and use its talons to rip the mouse, or in these more immediate matters, the powerless Harry Glasby, to tiny pieces. Where were these 'choices' Roberts loved to discuss?

I resumed begging, tugging on the sleeve of his shirt in panic and desperation. When it dawned on me these entreaties were useless, I sarcastically referred to Roberts as "Captain Not Fucking Likely". Wales laughed and wrapped his hand around the back of my neck, assuring me we were still going to be sailing together. In his view, even if Roberts were to permit me to transfer to the *Caerphilly Castle* it would not necessarily improve my lot.

Hanging my head, I nodded. He was right.

"Take this, please," I said. I had been holding one of my books behind my back with the intention of making it a gift to Wales in recognition of all he had done for me. Predictably, he insisted he could not take it and professed to have insufficient time to read books. We danced this dance until he relented. He thanked me, stepped forward, and took me in a powerful embrace.

He let go of me and looked about to see if anyone was near. He told me he had much work to do but he whispered to me that there was one last thing he wanted me to know. He told me it was important. Pulling me behind an oak column, we were hidden in shadow. I stood there while he told me a most incredible and unbelievable tale. As he talked, my eyes grew wide in baffled astonishment. When he finished, all I could do was stare. I was struck dumb by these revelations and by his decision to share the information with me, of all people. Before I could respond or ask questions, he joyfully embraced me one more time and promised he would treasure the book as a remembrance of the adventures we had shared.

As he walked away, reminding me not to forget what he said, I recovered some of my wits and yelled, "don't burn your nets Wales, never burn you nets." He said nothing more, ascended the ladder and waved the book in the air.

The book he used to wave goodbye was authored by Captain Woodes Rogers and published in 1712, *A Cruising Voyage Round the World*. Boldly written in the front piece; "*To my beloved friend and new first mate, a navigator without equal, a man destined to be the master of his fate, a man who the world will one day know with respect if not awe, future Captain Harry Glasby, I humbly give this book as a small token of my esteem and gratitude, s/ Captain Samuel Cary, the 11th day of November, in the year of our Lord, 1718."* If nothing else, Wales would know how much he meant to me when he read Captain Cary's kind words, words that now seemed to have been penned eons ago and words that were haunting in the extreme.

My emotions had me locked in a tight grip but I remembered I needed to get back to the deck to await the arrival of Campbell, wondering how much shock a man could absorb in one day.

I tell you now, a man's abilities in this arena exceed his puny estimation of its upper limits.

Today was a day for revelations, they hit me one after another. Fate was in rare form. The next tremor was being ferried in a battered longboat carrying a young man from Boston, a man who grew up on Marlbrough Street. Situated on this same street was a tidy brick townhouse owned by the parents of one Miss Constance Sacker.

One by one the gold arrived in thick canvas and sturdy leather bags. None of the captains were willing to humble themselves by bringing payment in person.

Boston bred Alistair Campbell inspected the *Royal Fortune* through the pale blue eyes of a curious lad who grew up on pirate legends and adventurous sea stories. Our frigate with all its guns was, I must admit, most imposing.

Mr. Campbell firmly shook my hand, asking about my health and pledging to tell me whatever he could about Boston, his beaming countenance soaking in the sight of brutally rough men working to make ready for another sea voyage. Campbell was adorned with a shock of dark reddish hair and light red circles on his cheeks, superimposed on skin the color of fresh cream and as smooth as the finest silk. His prominent nose and high cheekbones were decorated with rows of freckles. He looked like he had been sent to our ship on a brisk December morning to pick up freshly baked bread or a basket of apples.

We were about the same age but his wonderment at the workings of the flagship of Bartholomew Roberts and his fresh-faced boyishness made him look much younger. Were it not for his height, he could pass for fourteen.

He began by warning me, "Captain Kane said to deliver the gold first then to answer your 'fucking' questions." Campbell's accent was making me homesick already and his disarming ability to be direct yet accommodating made him the antithesis of his master.

"First time on a pirate ship?" My question was framed more as an observation.

An immediate and cheerful "yes sir." He answered as if I was blessed with the gift of reading minds.

If he wanted to believe I could read minds and tell the future, that might give me a leg up. "So, I can tell you are from Boston. Do you remember the last wharf you visited?" I needed him to pass a quick test. He kept staring beyond me at the men, looking at them like they were polar bears dyed purple with wide green stripes. His feeble effort to maintain eye contact was almost endearing.

"Yes, Oliver's Wharf. Captain Kane gets slaves, sails to Jamaica, then up to Boston and back to Whydah. This is his fifth such voyage, my first. Captain Kane is very frugal as you know, and he is going to be upset for many weeks about all this. Your captain took some of our cargo so we will be longer in loading, then we sail." He was, of course, referring to the pitiful human beings on his ship as cargo. I suppose thinking of them that way was so very mundane to Mr. Campbell and his shipmates, men who casually wielded the power of life or death over warriors, shamans, mothers and scores of terrified children. Time did not permit me to ask why he had signed on a slave ship.

"What street do you call home? When you are not at sea," I asked, hoping against hope my face would not reveal my trepidation.

229

"Now or then?" He wrinkled his brow.

"I'm not following you Mr. Campbell." He was confusing me, mainly because I was exerting most of my thoughts to shielding the real purpose of my interrogation. Being guarded about my intentions had become ingrained in me since my capture.

"My home is on King Street. Before I signed on with Captain Kane, we lived on Marlbrough Street." He looked at me now, to see if I was listening, tilting his head sideways a bit.

Constance and her family lived on Marlbrough. The blood pounded in my ears.

"Ah yes, Marlbrough Street, very close to Oliver's Wharf," I offered.

Campbell tilted his head the other way, "no offense but Oliver's Wharf is not what most would deem 'close' to Marlbrough. Are you well sir?"

"Yes, fine. It's just been a taxing day. I'm sorry, I misspoke. Was the home of your youth near Winter Street by any chance, I have friends there." I quickly amended my statement from 'have' to 'had'.

"Why how can you know these things? Our home was very near Winter Street. Are you wanting to know of your friends?"

"Did you know the Sackers?" I asked.

"I did," nodding his head, then amending his reply. "I do."

Feeling faint, I blinked hard a few times and struggled to keep my composure. No wonder Mr. Campbell had asked me if I was well. He was young but he was not blind.

"Mr. Campbell, I am curious to know if you ever knew a lady named Constance Sacker." I realized by our exchange he lacked guile and I could have put this simple inquiry to him when he first shook my hand.

"Why yes. My sister Sarah was her constant friend, pardon the expression. Constance was a bright and spirited girl, as is Sarah.

Did you know Constance has a child herself? Sarah told me, said she had a husband, lost at sea I believe he was. Very sad. The Sackers left Marlbrough Street and I know not where they went. Seems they left in a hurry. We ourselves moved to King Street but let our house to a pleasant family. You know Boston is growing, hard to keep up with all the changes. Can I ask you something?" He chattered like a red-headed woodpecker but he was most amiable. I was desperate to know more about Constance and the news he had provided had restored me to my senses. She was alive, widowed and a mother.

I might as well be on some distant orb as on the deck of this pirate ship floating off the coast of Africa.

Boston, Constance, my child, all were so far beyond reach but knowing Constance lived rejuvenated me like a cask of fresh water delivered to a man becalmed in a canoe on the equator. I knew if Mr. Campbell started asking me questions about life as a pirate our conversation could last for hours.

"Yes, of course you may ask me whatever pleases you, but do you by chance know anything more about Constance? Did she marry again, is she in good health, does she have a boy or a girl?" I forfeited my reticence and thought Mr. Campbell must decipher the personal nature of my interest at this juncture but we had no time to waste and I yearned for more.

He looked up in thought. He put his hand to his chin, "hmm, not sure. Far as I know she is fine but I do not want to mislead you. I know nothing about her child. Sarah is still in Boston, did you know her?" Campbell delicately changed the subject to signal he had divulged all he knew.

"I do not believe I know your sister Sarah. I thank you so very much, I do. Pray ask your question and I will do all I can to give you an honest reply."

His eyes lit up, "were you present when Captain Roberts hanged the Governor of Martinique?" Campbell eagerly looked up to the very yardarm where the Governor perished.

I traced the path of his eyes then looked down at the Governor's shining black boots.

I lied to him and the untruth came rather easily, "alas, I regret to say I was not." His sagging expression revealed his disappointment.

Looking up, I remembered watching Roberts murder the Governor. I felt a twinge of guilt and opted to give Campbell something for his troubles. I pointed up, "but that yardarm, they tell me. That is where the Governor hanged—for many weeks. His body disintegrated, it fell to tatters." I let that image sink in and young Mr. Campbell made a perfect circle with his mouth, staring upwards into the rigging. He had his pirate story and could leave with some satisfaction.

Extending my hand to get him to depart, he took it and held it, saying "oh yes, Captain Kane wanted me to tell you one more thing. He said to tell you that if your story is true and you were forced, he wishes you Godspeed and good luck. Captain Kane is a hard man but he is sincere, he means well."

"Please tell Captain Kane to accept my gratitude for his help and as for you Mr. Campbell, I have no doubt that one day you will captain a ship of your own, with great efficiency and alacrity." He beamed at the compliment, which was sincerely given, let go of my hand, climbed easily over the gunwale and threw me a salute and a wide smile. He was rowed back to his slaver in the darkness.

Men milling about on our deck were grumbling but in a way that piqued my concern. According to their complaints, Captain Roberts had been too lenient with the slaver captains. Sentiments such as these were easy to generate and if this idea simmered long enough, it would be impossible to extinguish. Wales had, time and again, used his masterful skills to defuse problems like these before they erupted. Then, to top it off, the mood dangerously intensified when word spread that one of the captains refused to deliver payment.

A spark had fallen into the powder.

During negotiations, Captain Fletcher of the *Porcupine* was among the most sullen of the extorted captains. His absence might be due to some innocent misadventure or, if Fletcher was a raving lunatic, his blatant and prideful defiance could perhaps be intentional. My intuition was telling me this was Fletcher's way of telling us to go fuck ourselves. I was not the only man on the *Royal Fortune* with intuition.

Unwilling to give the taciturn Fletcher the benefit of the doubt, a group of men led by pirate Starling, the one called Diamond, began to demand that the *Porcupine* be set afire.

Captain Roberts, upon hearing of the growing discord, walked purposely toward the would be arsonists and berated them like errant children. He was furious with Diamond who was plainly drunk. Boldly reminding them they were free to elect a new captain any time they wanted, he said Fletcher may have been delayed but no matter what, there were still slaves on the *Porcupine.* Given time, Fletcher might yet pay the ransom. We were not set to depart until dawn and, he reminded them, we have eighty pounds of gold, much needed new men and a new vessel.

Diamond brazenly asked how a new vessel or more men would increase the crew's shares when the gold was divided. The faces of the men behind Diamond were lit by the flickering light of lanterns hanging in our rigging. It was eerie and the mood tense. Where was Wales when we needed him?

Despite having turned into a turd we would all be better off without, Diamond had a point. Once the gold was parceled out among the crew, it would not amount to more than the average seaman spent during a few raucous nights ashore. While I had my doubts about Diamond's ability to make those precise mathematical calculations, I waited to see if Captain Roberts was going to give him the same medicine he had given Pedro.

Roberts, his face in partial shadow, glared. "The *Porcupine* is not to be molested." He paused a few seconds then roughly elbowed his way through the group, bodily shoving Diamond back a full step in the process. When Captain Roberts was out of sight, the rabble moved aft and I could hear their excited voices, one or two laughed, and there were bursts of curses about Fletcher this and Fletcher that. Their petulant reaction was to be expected but something told me the men were not just venting, they were plotting. It was inconceivable that Diamond and his erstwhile brigands would defy the explicit orders of Captain Bartholomew Roberts. We were in transition and had yet to find a new bosun to replace the fallen Seahorse. This was not the time to see if the elegant and erudite Lord Lutwidge had the wherewithal to take immediate and forceful action.

Four or five rowdies began lowering buckets into the empty longboat as it was clumsily lowered into the water. Diamond urged them on. My eyes searched for the silhouette of the *Porcupine,* its dim stern light the only sign of life. We were anchored a little more than one hundred yards away. The dread rising in me made it hard to breathe.

Diamond and the longboat filled with his drunk cohorts made a beeline to the moored ship. While the men rowed their voices carried over the water long after they passed the halfway mark. Due to darkness, I could not see the men climbing up her side. Seeing them was immaterial because I knew full well their plan. The buckets they loaded and carried with them were filled with tar and pitch. Soon enough, I was able to make out their bobbing heads and shoulders contrasted against the night sky. Had I known there were eighty slaves chained in pairs below decks, I may have sounded an alarm but under no circumstances was I going to inform Captain Roberts. The insubordinate men who were preparing to burn the *Porcupine* were murderers and they had friends who were murderers. I further rationalized my cowardly decision with my belief that it was too late to stop the fire.

As if on cue, thin twisting yellow and orange tongues of flame began to appear. Roberts would know it was Diamond and his friends and he would deal with them according to his ways.

Accelerated by the tar and pitch, the *Porcupine* began to blaze. By the light of the fire, the longboat returned, carrying eight boisterous self-satisfied pirates. The doomed ship's sails were reefed and they burned like torches soaked in oil. Most of the deck was engulfed with roaring flames by the time our longboat was raised.

The spectacle drew a crowd. Diamond and his myrmidons passed bottles back and forth, hooting and slapping each other on the back. One pointed out a pair of chained slaves who had miraculously made it to the stern and after a moment's hesitation, both tumbled into the harbor. This was greeted with cheering and cackling. The harbor was home to enormous sharks who fed on bodies thrown into the sea; the daily roll of the dead provided the sharks a steady source of food.

Anyone left on the *Porcupine* had the choice of being drowned, devoured by sharks or roasted alive. As slaves plunged over the side, two by two, we could hear their pitiful screams amidst the roaring inferno. The heat became so intense it warmed our faces. The sky around the flaming vessel lit up like an image from Hades.

Curious men lined the rails of the other slave ships. They watched the conflagration in silence. Unlike the defiant Diamond, who raised his bottle of Kill Devil and yelled "fuck Fletcher" to another chorus of cheers from his inebriated gang.

A tottering pirate next to Diamond pointed toward the bow of the *Porcupine* yelling "look, look, look at that damned bastard."

In the rigging of the foremast, two men were struggling upward. One seemed immobile and the other man was stepping on the ratlines, pulling and dragging the man tethered to him by an invisible chain. How any man could still be alive in the searing heat was beyond comprehension. As they rose higher, the flames followed. One of the pair screamed, it was impossible to know which. It was evident that the man doing the pulling would soon lose his grip or his will or surely he would be overcome by the smoke and the heat. Below him, the limp form dangled, tethered to his ankle. Still the other climbed, heaving to bring the second man along, one or two feet at a time. It was mesmerizing to watch the slow ascent and impossible to turn away.

Diamond led his supporters in a chant that started slowly and grew faster and louder— "up, up, up." Still the struggling man went higher. By some otherworldly effort, he very nearly made it to the top of the foremast.

As I knew, as that desperate man knew, he had no place to go.

Gunpowder in the *Porcupine* began to explode with muffled energy, more men jumped off the sides, yet the man in the mast and his insensible companion defied the laws of nature.

The sight is among a collection that have long since poisoned my dreams. The negro in the foremast did not lose his grip or tumble. He made a choice. He wrapped his arms around his inert burden and dove. It was oddly graceful. They fell in a slight arc and when the pair landed, enormous clouds of red and orange sparks shot up from the deck, burning themselves out and drifting quietly downward.

The men with Diamond cheered the shower of sparks and drank and relished in the slaughter they had wrought. The inferno of death entertained and amused them. These were pirates who inflicted pain and suffering because it gave them enjoyment. I had an overwhelming urge to kill them, especially Diamond.

The brilliant light of the flames shown across the harbor and reflected off the smooth black water. Out of the corner of my eye, I saw the yellow light flickering in the passive faces of many of our negro crewmen. Cheddar was watching. There was an anger and a sadness in his eyes. I wanted to speak to him but for the life of me I didn't know what to say.

We sailed at dawn and left the *Porcupine,* now a sooty, hissing, smoking hulk. We never learned the reason behind Fletcher's refusal to pay.

We did learn that *HMS Swallow* sailed into Whydah harbor on January 15, 1722, three days after our visit. Roberts' luck held but for how long?

In Whydah harbor, I learned that often times the choices affecting us the most are not ours. Far too often, men are at the mercy of choices made by others.

Chapter 16

A New Captain

CHALONER OGLE, DESCENDED FROM AN ancient and respectable family, had spent a lifetime at sea. Of his remarkable capabilities as an officer in his Majesty's Navy, there were few equals. Many was the time I pondered the myriad possibilities had anyone but Ogle been the master of *HMS Swallow*.

As you will see, his fate and mine were deeply intertwined.

From official dispatches and reports, I would later read that Ogle had determined, after his arrival in Whydah, that Roberts would need to refit the French vessel we had seized, the vessel now sailing under the steady hand of Wales. Ogle claimed the foresight to pinpoint the Bight of Benin as our likely destination. As he would later say, "I judged they must go some place in the Bight to clean and fit the French ship before they would think of cruising again, which occasioned me to steer away into the Bight and look into those places which I knew had sufficient depth of water."

With due respect to Captain Ogle, this report was written after the fact. It was far more probable that someone in Whydah gave intelligence to Captain Ogle about our destination. When one considers how badly the slaver captains wanted to see Bartholomew Roberts hang, it is a near certainty. Roberts humiliated them and sailed away with eighty pounds of gold dust, but it is the humiliation that men remember the longest. One can barely imagine the lust for revenge churning in Captain Fletcher.

Subsequently, when we learned eighty slaves perished on the *Porcupine*, the poignant irony of 'one pound of gold per life lost' sobered those of us who still clung to their frayed conscience.

The memory of those two wretches climbing the foremast and their horrid demise still haunts me.

Whydah had been behind us a scant three days when Ogle arrived in dogged pursuit.

On the second day of our eastward journey to the Bight, the *Caerphilly Castle* drew near and sailed in the attitude and with the delight of a porpoise. These graceful mammals were well known for their antics, diving in and out of the waves as they playfully shadowed swift sailing ships. Not all my memories of life off the coast of Africa are filled with horror. Wales drew close, pulled ahead and fell back, getting the feel of his new vessel and putting his crew through their paces. There was an unmistakable sense of confident joy in his display of seamanship. Aided by a spyglass, we took turns watching a buoyant Wales as he stood confidently by his helmsman. Without question, the skilled builders of the French ship had one thing in mind, to give her the gift of speed.

I missed him.

Unaware that the *Swallow* was so near, Roberts retreated to his cabin and made it known he did not want to be bothered.

Diamond made a pretense of pretending all was well. All was not well. There had been fissures in the crew before Whydah, before the grumbling about the amount of ransom paid and before the blatant disobedience that led to the horror of the *Porcupine*. The defiance of the villains who burned the slave ship would have been unthinkable in months passed. Some wondered aloud if Roberts had lost his grip.

Simmering calamities we had unsuccessfully tried to ignore were bubbling back to the surface. The black pirates refused to have anything to do with Diamond and his fellow conspirators. Roberts lacked a strong right hand to govern his divided crew and being ensconced in his cabin did nothing to help. The absence of Wales loomed ever larger, then the unthinkable happened.

The fissures grew; wider, longer and deeper but not in a manner any of us could have predicted.

Wales vanished.

Three days out of Whydah we awoke to the stark realization that sometime between nightfall and a blood orange dawn the *Caerphilly Castle* had disappeared. Even the unflappable Lord Lutwidge was dumbstruck. We refused to believe Wales would desert us, but what of his crew? Had he had been imprisoned or killed? Dare we hope he had he been deposed by a disgruntled faction who pressed for an immediate election and, for reasons we could not know, voted for another. Whether or not Wales still lived, his crew selected a course which paid no heed to Bartholomew Roberts. That much was indisputable. Unlike a horseman who rides away, there is no trail to follow when one vanishes at sea. Aside from countless questions about what the hell had happened, the ramifications of this betrayal were daunting.

The endless sea, our constant companion, seemed to mock the *Royal Fortune* and those of us living within its wooden skin. Circumstances can change in an instant. Two days ago, Bartholomew Roberts was in command of five hundred pirates in four fearsome sailing vessels. Lookouts in our masts hoisted long brass telescopes to see if they could work a miracle and find the missing ship. They peered at their shipmates moving about like entranced sleepwalkers and were themselves too mortified to shout the news that there was no news.

The power of our small fleet, working in unison, would have dramatically reduced the threat posed by the *Swallow*. Even without Wales, the armament on the three remaining ships and the vessels' ability to maneuver during a fight would put the *Swallow* on the defensive. If the fire power of Ogle and Roberts in a sea battle were equal, Roberts had no one but himself to answer to and he could fight or flee. Ogle's choices were influenced by the fact that he had to answer to the Admiralty and ultimately to his king. Navy captains who flee from battle have been prosecuted and executed for cowardice.

Battles can be won by outnumbered and outmatched men if they are properly led and a wise sage will tell you it matters not how many guns you possess but how you use them. In the swirling mist of these newest uncertainties, I was not alone in wondering if our crew would take the next step and elect a man to replace Roberts. We had to be near the precipice. Roberts was wondering too.

Conversely, and despite small disadvantages, Ogle did not have to worry about being unseated by his subordinates. The very idea was laughable. All the headstrong and gallant Ogle needed to do was find us and blow us to bits or better yet, wrap us in chains and haul us in.

Lutwidge, Lord Rose, the anemic Copplestone, and dozens more had been instrumental in helping make Roberts the most successful pirate captain ever to sail the Atlantic. Could this group of veterans protect the captain from defeat from within? How many of that loyal group were still present? Considering the men who had been pirates when I was taken the headcount was surprisingly easy. Less than half remained; too many had died or departed. Without Wales, the Lords had become a rustic collection of jovial relics, no longer a ruthless force to be reckoned with.

Despite the adversity and risks, Roberts' ledger, literally, as it was written scrupulously in a logbook, recorded more than four hundred and fifty prizes, a tally made more impressive by the short time it took, a mere three years. Considering all the things that could go awry in each of these encounters, he accomplished this feat with relatively little loss of life and in general, he made the welfare of his men a priority despite his sweeping powers, his temper and their periodic tantrums.

Mourning the inexplicable loss of the *Caerphilly Castle*, I sought refuge in the galley, soundly cursing Wales because he had not been more insistent that I go with him. I soundly cursed Roberts for insisting I remain, his "not fucking likely" echoing in my thoughts.

The imperturbable Jack sat quietly in my lap, the last inch of his tail flickering aimlessly from time to time. I envied his inability to worry.

Someone rudely put a hand on my shoulder, startling me, then sat across from me with a mug of tea. Jack's eyes opened and his back stiffened. He let out a long low growl.

"What's wrong with that fuckin' cat?" Diamond asked, his mean eyes in narrow slits, his grimy face covered with uneven stubble. There was a fresh cut across the bridge of his nose and yellow bruising under one eye suggesting a recent altercation.

I waited a few heartbeats to answer. "His name is Jack and he doesn't like you," I said, scratching Jack's ears. That usually calmed him.

Diamond gave Jack a surly look and in a tone to match asked, "how do you know that Glasby?"

Diamond's uninvited presence was annoying. I had no idea what he wanted and given my sour frame of mind, I didn't care. I waited again before speaking just to make Diamond squirm. "Jack and I have long talks, I just know." Diamond was uninterested in my welfare and had he the chance, he would have gutted Jack just to spite me. Jack knew it too. He squirmed free and walked away, his tail raised in the air, drifting lazily from side to side. In many ways, Jack had more brains than the poor excuse for a man seated across from me.

Ignoring the jibe, Diamond pushed his tea to one side and leaned forward. He reeked of stale alcohol and I drew back to avoid his stink which extended well beyond his gravedigger's breath. Men like Diamond had been making my life a living hell and he could not have chosen a worse time to intrude on my solitude. He was on edge about something and that made me happy. He licked his lips, first on one side, then the other before telling me, "those fuckin' niggers are after me."

I expected him to say more because everyone knew this and no one but Diamond cared.

Exasperated by my nonchalance, he rolled his eyes and broke the silence, "I know you don't give two shits Glasby. You and Roberts are cozy. Wales is smart, he's gone. Roberts no longer has this ship." He pushed his greasy hair away from his face. His hands were filthy.

"So?" I said, apathetically acquiescing in his litany. He was right, I didn't give two shits about him.

Diamond launched a tiny bubble of spit that landed on my hand when he talked. Everything about the man was repulsive. In his effort to intimidate me, he stammered in a mocking tone, "so, so, so. You're not as smart as they say. Roberts is done. We need a captain who can lead. And one who can deal with those jabberin' apes."

Jack sat calmly at the end of the galley, watching us, his long tail curled around his front feet. "Diamond, you may not be as stupid as they say. You may be right about our negro shipmates." I wanted to goad him and scare him at the same time, "but Captain Roberts has most of the crew and that's all that matters, none of this concerns me."

He visibly struggled, which pleased me to no end. I am not sure why he wanted to talk to me or even what he thought I could do for him—or against him. He was impulsive and lacked the wherewithal to tackle complex problems. His demeanor indicated he was giving up on me and I was grateful. He jabbed his index finger in my direction, "just stay out of it Glasby. When we get a new captain, we'll still need you to steer. Got it?"

Laying his palms flat on the table, he pushed himself up, keeping his eyes on me.

"You mean 'if' we get a new captain. Meanwhile, you would be well advised to watch your back." I tipped my empty blackjack in a mock toast.

He looked around the galley and told me to go fuck myself.

As he turned to stomp away, I said in a firm voice, "you forgot your tea." I wanted him to know he could not bully me. He turned his head and opened his mouth to speak but something in his dim mind told him to let it go and he left me alone. As Diamond left the galley, Jack's head slowly turned as he watched the annoying man climb up the hatch. One of his ears twitched and the moment Diamond was out of sight, Jack came back and nestled quietly, resting against my ankle.

Roberts emerged later that morning and when we met up with Captain Skyrm, there were some transfers to round out the crews. Two or three of Diamond's friends went to the *Ranger*. The tension was easing, helped by the mutual respect Skyrm and Roberts exhibited toward each other. The former lacked experience but he was confident and eager to learn. The captains kept their men busy making modifications and repairs but not so busy that they could not commiserate and enjoy themselves. All things in balance.

Without much ado, and without any apparent dissent, the *Royal Fortune,* the *Ranger* and the *Little Ranger* sailed south back toward Cape Lopez.

The crew of the *Swallow* had been kept lively too and they were getting closer.

Twisted slivers of indigo and flaming pink lit up the morning sky on February 5, 1722. After a three week chase, Captain Ogle found us anchored in the lee of the Cape. He had been patrolling for months. His glee must have been beyond measure.

With a strong wind out of the southeast, Ogle had to go northwest and away from us to avoid the hazards of a sandbank described on my charts as Frenchman's Bank. When the pirates saw the unidentified ship veer off, they concluded it had spotted our masts and turned away in fear. Ogle's maneuver was due to conditions, not superior tactics. But sometimes it is better to be lucky than smart.

Roberts had abiding faith in Captain Skyrm who was eager to prove himself.

On receipt of a signal from Captain Roberts, the *Ranger* with her thirty-guns got underway to pursue the mystery ship. Maybe Roberts thought that since we'd done tolerably well in Whydah, it was the *Ranger's* turn to have a prize. Given the known presence of the Royal Navy in the vicinity, it seemed imprudent for one of our ships to go off alone, prowling after an unidentified ship. Pirates can be cocky too. No matter how one viewed the decision, clearly made in haste, Roberts was the duly elected captain and I was just his disgruntled navigator.

Ogle raised his telescope and watched the approaching *Ranger* in stunned disbelief. She was coming to him and she was coming alone.

Maintaining his course, Captain Ogle had his crew deliberately slow the *Swallow* to allow the *Ranger* to catch up. It was a brilliant stroke. The details may be found in the captain's log, "we spilled the wind from our sails by bracing the yard, leading the mainsheets aft and bringing the tacks of the mainsail and foresail on board."

Any chance that the men of the *Royal Fortune* might sense the threat and join the fray had evaporated like spit on a hot cast iron frying pan. The hunter had lured its unsuspecting prey toward the horizon and both ships were moving farther away from us, to the north and west. Fate allowed the antagonists to sail beyond our sight and our hearing which assured that we would be unaware of the pending clash of arms.

Royal Navy lookouts reported that the pursuing pirates had rigged the spritsail yard under the bowsprit to prepare for boarding. One might be willing to forgive the laissez-faire attitude of the pirate captains, considering the fact that even yet, the *Ranger* was still clueless about the true identity of the *Swallow*.

Skyrm, curiously, flew an English ensign, a Dutch pennant and the black. By 10:45 a.m. the pirates were within range of the *Swallow's* chase guns, mounted in her stern; by 11:30 a.m. the *Ranger* was within musket range. No shots had been fired.

A robust sixteen-year-old named Robert Williams was at the helm of the *Swallow*. He had departed Watford in Hertfordshire, England, three years before and he struggled to keep his eyes on his business and stop looking over his shoulder to see if the oncoming pirates had realized their colossal error.

"Make ready, Mr. Williams," Ogle said.

"Aye, captain," Williams chirped, biting his lower lip to curb his excitement. He knew his ship, his captain and he did not need to be told what he was about to do. Williams had not been pressed into service, he'd eagerly enlisted in the Royal Navy. This clever and earnest boy had dreamed of these glorious scenarios, in one guise or another, for most of his short life.

Seaman Williams and his captain shared the knowledge that their port side gun crews were coiled like springs, poised, primed and eager to pummel the *Ranger*.

"Starboard the helm please," Ogle ordered.

The coiled spring that was Mr. Williams started turning the ship's wheel the instant his captain made a sound. The boy let loose of his lower lip and a broad smile extended across his face. The distinctive screeching and thumping of the gun ports being winched open innervated the entire crew. Heavy cannons on the port side rumbled as they rolled out. The *Swallow* gracefully and steadily obeyed the man-boy at the helm, cutting to the left and across the bow of the *Ranger*.

A small group of men on the deck of the *Ranger* wondered why the other ship had briskly cut in front of them. Before anyone could do or say much, someone in the rigging starting screaming unintelligibly. The words 'bloody' and 'bastard' were prominent in the outburst. An astute pirate sprinted to lower the jolly roger, at long last recognizing that this was judgment day come calling. There was little else the stunned pirates could do. The ineffectual gesture of lowering the pirate's telltale ensign was noted in the *Swallow's* log. Defiant to the end, once battle was joined, the black flag was raised again.

Round shot, some balls weighing as much as twelve pounds, tore into the *Ranger*, chain shot ripped through the rigging, spars, masts and sails. Royal Navy gunners were effective and professional. Their lives depended on it.

Due to the wind and the course of each ship it took some time before young Williams could bring the *Swallow* back into position to fire a second volley. The Royal Navy warship with its heavy cannons and well-trained gunners bombarded the *Ranger* without mercy or respite with a jubilant boy at the helm. Williams was standing on air yet he performed his duties in such a workmanlike manner that an old salt would have said "well and truly done lad." Williams' greatest wish was that his mother could see him in his moment of glory. She hated the Navy.

It was recorded that the *Ranger* surrendered at 1:30 p.m.. Its main topmast had been splintered and twenty-six men killed or badly injured. Captain Skyrm's left leg was shredded off at the knee by a six pound ball fired during the first broadside. Despite his grievous wound and the consequent pain, blood and resulting shock, Skyrm steadfastly remained in command and positioned on the quarterdeck until the bitter end.

His men tossed the black flag in the sea, not as a gesture of defeat but to destroy evidence of their piracy and to deny Captain Ogle a trophy.

That night, in the middle of a thunderstorm and a heavy downpour, Ogle's victorious crew secured their prisoners, tended to the wounded, made some hurried repairs to the damaged *Ranger* and made ready to sail their newest prize to the fort at the Island of Princes.

Having overwhelmed the *Ranger,* Captain Ogle and the *Swallow* set a course for Cape Lopez to attend to unfinished business.

As the sky turned murky and gray, we sat on the *Royal Fortune* anxiously and impatiently awaiting the *Ranger's* return. To make things worse, we endured slanting sheets of pelting rain and gusting winds brought about by the tropical storm, anointing it as the most likely explanation for the *Ranger's* troubling absence.

The weather was unrelenting. With or without inclement sailing conditions, we were bound to wait for Skyrm's return.

We waited four dark, wet, dreary days. Our crew stayed occupied by discussing the theory that the storm claimed the *Ranger* along with a dozen other explanations. I do not recollect anyone floating the possibility that the Royal Navy had a hand in this conundrum. Perhaps the storm was worse further north and west. These debates and boring anecdotes of odd weather were discussed for hours. The men had nothing else to do really, except drink.

To my astonishment, on the third day, Roberts asked me and Lord Lutwidge if we had any information that might indicate Skyrm had intentions of linking up with the *Caerphilly Castle*. Still reeling by the loss of Wales, it was hard to dismiss the thought in the absence of contrary intelligence.

On February 9, 1722 Ogle again arrived off Cape Lopez. He spotted the *Royal Fortune* and the *Little Ranger* while we sat unawares. None of us could have known we were vainly awaiting the return of a captured ship.

Due to the late hour, there was insufficient time for the *Swallow* to mount an attack. The storm decided to worsen, making poor visibility worse. Captain Ogle beat to windward, a demonstration of his capacity for patience as opposed to any want of courage. His Majesty's ship had the greater firepower but as to the audacity of the captains, neither had an edge, but fate and the elements were working in concert with Captain Ogle.

February 10 arrived with a thick haze that obscured the horizon. Despite heavy mist, the *Swallow* sighted us anew.

Ogle's luck held.

Roberts was enjoying a lively breakfast of salmagundi in his cabin with what remained of the Lords. Copplestone was absent and purportedly recuperating from another strain of malign distemper. The rain continued to fall but the wind was not as severe and I remained below, talking with the Albino. As had been true for several days, most of the bored crew had been drinking far into the early morning hours. Those not still drunk or unconscious were severely hung-over. This had become routine and Captain Roberts refrained from putting a stop to the behavior for fear of driving a bigger wedge between himself and the men.

I saw someone headed to the great cabin and overheard another pirate saying a ship was approaching.

The Albino and I looked at each other and hurried up to the quarterdeck. Most were certain it was the *Ranger,* as men so often believe what they want to be true. Others were equally certain it was a French slaver or perhaps a Portuguese ship. Ogle was flying a French ensign to confuse us and his ploy was working.

Suddenly a new member of our crew, who was standing near us and staring out to sea, began exclaiming with all his energy that the approaching ship was none other than *HMS Swallow.* I wrinkled my forehead at the Albino, wondering if the screaming man had lost his mind or was just another excitable drunkard. The Albino looked at the yelling pirate and shrugged his shoulders.

The man, in a state of high excitement, frantically rushed past us and stood at the top of the ladder which went down to the main deck. I thought he bore a resemblance to one of the men who joined us in Whydah. He waved his arms and screamed, on the verge of tears. We had a terrible time understanding him.

"I'm Robert Armstrong, I deserted from that fuckin' ship, that's not the *Ranger,* it's the goddamned *Swallow.*"

I looked upon dazed and upturned faces and there stood Captain Roberts. At least he was alert and sober.

Roberts bounded up to the quarterdeck to calm Armstrong and to inquire about the sailing capacity of his former ship. Armstrong was about to collapse.

"Sir, she is best upon the wind," Armstrong sputtered. The last thing a deserter from the Royal Navy wants to see is his former ship. Such would be true even if Armstrong had not compounded his desertion by turning pirate. Armstrong was telling us that the *Swallow* was at her best when the wind struck her abeam.

"Full sails," yelled Roberts.

I wish I could tell you the men dutifully sprang to action and gallantly scampered up the rigging. Despite the urgency, hardly anyone moved.

Oblivious to his unresponsive crew, Roberts went below while a few dazed men struggled to get us underway, drunk, hung-over and wet. Our captain re-emerged in his finest. At 10:30 a.m. we weighed anchor and a steady wind filled our sails.

Having long served with Bartholomew Roberts, we could communicate by some unnatural method that required no words or signals, just thoughts and glances. We had done this countless times.

Thanks to Armstrong's warning, there was every reason to believe we could outrun the *Swallow* even though the direction of the wind was marginally in her favor.

Instead of making a course for the open sea, where we could put some distance between us and the *Swallow*, Captain Roberts, true to form, ordered us about. Roberts always played as if he had the best hand, even when he did not. He put us on a course heading straight for the warship. An audacious maneuver of this nature was far from surprising considering the man who held our fate in his hands. Many later claimed Roberts said he wanted to test the firepower of the warship. I heard him say nothing of the sort and the firepower of a man o' war was hardly a mystery.

My own theory about Roberts' motives was based on recent events coupled with our long history together. I knew this complicated man as well as any living being.

Depending on our speed and the skill of the Royal Navy gunners, we might survive one broadside and make it to the open sea. It was an enormous gamble. I believed then that Roberts was tired of running and tired of worrying about the moods of the men. He wanted to teach these grumblers a lesson. It was his way of disciplining those who had turned on him, the drunks, the gamblers, the shirkers and the plotters. I don't think Captain Roberts ever really entertained the idea that he could be beaten. Had he the crew he had two years ago, his confidence might have been justified.

Pirates are prone to incessant griping and they tend to sulk when not active. Idle hands and all that. But during a fight, a pirate captain has the power of life and death. The breadth of his authority over the men who serve him is virtually unlimited. Sea fights are chaotic and confusing. There is little time for reflection, debate or a hurried conference to weigh options. Instant obedience to orders is the rule and there are no exceptions. Roberts could, if needed, kill any man who faltered or hesitated and his unquestionable willingness to do so made him a force to be reckoned even when the odds were not in his favor.

With his bravery and the aplomb and poise he exhibited, especially during times of danger, Roberts may have carried a slight edge into the duel with Captain Ogle.

The encounter, no matter how it ended, would be dubbed for posterity The Battle of Cape Lopez.

Beside the inevitable and imminent contest between Ogle and Roberts, there was another fight brewing and this fight would govern the outcome either because of or in spite of inspired leadership. This fight would be a struggle between a weakened pirate crew who had turned drinking into an avocation against well-trained and well-disciplined British seaman. The latter were courageous, hardened and ably led. They were also fresh from a decisive and resounding victory. More to the point, there were more of them and they had more guns.

And they were sober.

Roberts knew all this. Despite making errors from time to time, he was still at his most brilliant when things were at their worst. He was able to stare death in the face. Roberts would use this battle as a means to chastise his crew and make them fight for their very survival. If they survived, he would, once again, be their undisputed lord and master.

'If' may be the most significant word in the English language. If the men did as he demanded, I had ample reason to fear he might succeed in pulling off another miracle. My mind traveled back to the day we took the *Onslow* and our bold foray from New Barcelona when we crushed the unsuspecting *Trident*. Woe be to any man who dared to make it his mission to bring down this supremely elusive pirate, the seemingly unbeatable Bartholomew Roberts.

Despite his luck and his skill, Captain Ogle may have finally met his match. We would know soon enough.

Our canvas was soaked and heavy and the wind thick yet the same conditions affected the *Swallow,* whose size and displacement brought her sailing speed into question. The variable in this equation was Roberts. If we could escape, it would count as a victory. For pirates, victory may be measured in a multitude of ways but each variant must include living one more day. I kept hearing that phrase in my head, over and over and over.

With the events and revelations from our foray in Whydah impressed upon my mind, I had resolved not to live one more day *as a pirate*. I had had enough.

If the *Royal Fortune* withstood a fusillade from the *Swallow* and broke away to parts unknown, the nightmare of my existence would continue. For me to escape, the Royal Navy had to seize our ship. If, by sundown, I still drew breath, there was a chance I might reclaim my liberty. Like I said, 'if' is a mighty word.

The Royal Navy was not my foe.

My enemy was cloaked in a velveteen crimson frock, a red feather waving from his tricorn hat. Suspended around his neck, on a heavy gold chain, hung a large diamond encrusted cross.

His Majesty's Royal Navy and Captain Chaloner Ogle would bring me death or they would bring me salvation.

After thirty minutes, at 11:00 a.m., the ships were within pistol range of one another and I could easily discern Captain Ogle calmly observing us from his quarterdeck. The black pennant waved from our topmast. A Royal Navy seaman lowered the French ensign and hoisted the King's Colors. Before their war banner reached the top of the mast, the roar of the Swallow's heavy guns broke the silence. As a young boy, I was wading in the cool shade of a long wooden bridge outside Boston when a heavy freight wagon passed over. The rumbling was the same. The guns of the *Royal Fortune* answered with a volley that shook the oak planks under my feet.

Chain shot ripped away bits of our rigging, our mizzen topmast was hit and a long section of it began to fall aft. The aim of the gunners on the smoke-filled gun decks of the *Swallow* was superb and they were reloading with practiced efficiency. I know this because I could see some in their number moving about and their reputation said so. None of the damage was disabling and we sailed on, exchanging sporadic cannon fire and vying to avoid putting ourselves in a position where we would have to absorb the full fury of their broadside. Our gunners fired and reloaded and bore up as men do when they have no other choice.

By 1:30 p.m. the rain had lessened and the *Swallow* was poised to maximize its advantage in firepower. A well-aimed shot carried away our mainmast.

Roberts cursed the Royal Navy while I watched our upper mainmast hanging in the twisted shrouds, tangled in the lines and held up by badly frayed rigging. Yielding was a concept foreign to Bartholomew Roberts; it was something other men did. He stood impassively while the black gun ports of the mighty *Swallow* belched fire, smoke, and deadly missiles. My nerves, like our mainmast, were about to shatter and splinter. I shivered and shook in my anger and impotence, standing an arm's length from the man who defied his King. Roberts, the man who would not be mocked. He was preparing himself for the frenzied fight that would ensue when boarders roared like a tidal wave onto our decks. Knowing the fighting prowess of a pirate with his back to the wall, the prospect that we might emerge victorious, while unlikely, was still a very real, and for me, a dreaded possibility. I readied myself for the pointless carnage that would drench the oak planks of our deck in blood.

I was terrified. Roberts, damn him, would never surrender. He feared the noose but he did not fear death. He epitomized that rare breed of fighting man who relishes the battering he will mete out to his foes even as he, himself, is slaughtered, his blood mixed with the blood of his enemies. If there is a line between glory and insanity it is a fine line indeed.

Ogle and his adoring subordinates later reported that The Battle of Cape Lopez was fought in driving rain, complete with sheets of lightning and crashing thunder. To top it off, they claimed we were surrounded by a series of tornadoes. One such dispatch reported to the Admiralty that Bartholomew Roberts was struck by the last full broadside, felled by grapeshot which tore out his throat, propelling him across the tackle of an eight-pounder. Four or five men were present on the quarterdeck when their invincible pirate captain collapsed and it was only natural they were stunned to the point of disbelief.

Bartholomew Roberts writhed on the deck of the *Royal Fortune*, blood poured from a round hole in his neck, as men he had long commanded watched the life flow out of him. I was not stunned or saddened. My reaction was instantaneous, overwhelming and unrestrained relief. The ever-present stone on my chest, like those used in the press yard, had been lifted. Many were the times I had seen the inside of dark, dank and forbidding prison cells. I felt as if I had been left in such a cell and at long last, the black iron door swung open. I thought about power, freedom, choices and fate and a voice inside me proclaimed that while Boston remained a very long way away, I could finally contemplate the first significant step on my journey home. If it took the death of every pirate on the *Royal Fortune* to make that step a reality, so be it. For in this moment, this penultimate moment, I was alive.

Helmsmen Long Bill Stephenson, a reliable and sober man, left his post and grabbed the dying Captain Roberts by his red coat. Roberts lay slumped over the gun carriage, unawares and motionless, while the distraught Stephenson admonished him "to stand up and fight like a man." Stephenson turned the captain sideways. Upon spotting the wound he looked up and murmured in disbelief, "grapeshot, he's been hit in the throat, it's grapeshot." Stephenson's red-rimmed eyes filled with tears.

In my mind's ear, I heard another voice. It was Captain Roberts repeating one of his favorite ditties—"damn to him who ever lived to wear the halter." I had heard this remark on many occasions along with strict orders that if he ever went down in battle to put him and his weapons over the side. If he died a warrior's death and cheated the hangman, he did not want his corpse and his weaponry to be put on display by his enemies. Never did I begrudge him his pride, for all brave men must have it.

Roberts got his wish. He did not live to wear the halter.

Looking down, I discovered Roberts' brace of pistols and his long silk sash in my hands, stained with blood. I went to the side and threw the pistols as far as I could and wiped my palms on the sides of my legs to get the captain's blood off my hands.

Captain Roberts was tied in a canvas shroud with two cannon balls to carry his body to the depths of the sea. When his limp form was tenderly released over the side, the heart of the crew went with him.Roberts' pride was preserved, his second wish fulfilled.

Men gathered on the deck and I watched them in silence. Stephenson was not the only one with tears welling.

It will not surprise you to know my eyes were dry.

With Roberts dead, Wales gone and Lutwidge nowhere to be seen, I suddenly found myself the unwitting and unwilling captain of the *Royal Fortune.*

Chapter 17
Dum Spiro Spero

SOME IN THE CREW, LIKE their captain, preferred a fight to the death, figuring they were destined to die sooner or later. Better to go down fighting. One such diehard, a ruffian named James Phillips, had threatened to blow us all to hell if our vessel was ever seized. Roberts made the same threat when he took the *Samuel*. After all, Captain Roberts may have avoided the halter but the Royal Navy would be pleased to kill more of us today and a large number of those who survived at their leisure. Men like Roberts and Phillips either had a flair for the dramatic or they truly preferred blowing themselves sky high in lieu of donning the hemp necklace. Not everyone wanted to go out that flamboyantly in the event Phillips was serious.

Papi rushed across the deck shouting, "Harry, Harry, what now? Many are wounded, some will die." He had a dirty cloth rag tied around his head covering a bloody wound. He seemed unfazed by his injury but the amount of blood gave me pause.

"Papi, go below immediately. Take someone and get to the powder. You must hurry. If that rum soaked braggart Phillips gets to the powder before you do, we'll all die." Papi and a black pirate called Merlin hurriedly scuttled down the aft hatch. With luck, Phillips would be in his usual state of drunkenness, unaware of our predicament. I trusted Papi and thought Roberts would be gratified to know his threat to blow up the ship still resonated.

The *Swallow* was off to starboard and closing to within sufficient distance to use their grappling hooks and unleash their boarding parties, for they had two. We couldn't out maneuver them because of the damage to our sails. Tailored blue coats, white scarves and gold epaulets identified the officers who would lead the attack when they reached our decks. Theirs would be a triumph talked about across the seven seas for generations. There were about forty sailors in each group, one forward, one aft, armed with cutlasses and half pikes. Given the enormity of their task, they had to be hand-picked and when I raised the glass I saw men not boys, fighters, not terrified merchant seaman.

Overheated cannons in the belly of the *Swallow* fired volleys of iron into the *Royal Fortune,* round shot crashing into the thick oak timbers and star shot tearing more and bigger gaps in the rigging.

We were not accustomed to being on the receiving end of such overwhelming and irresistible force.

I desperately wanted to live.

"Neptune, Deadeye." They turned from the *Swallow* to await my command.

"Strike the colors," I said.

Neptune responded, "aye aye, Mr. Glasby," and the two wriggled into the mass of lines and ropes and began bringing the black flag down for the final time. Their prompt obedience to my order rather surprised me.

I ran to the starboard rail facing the *Swallow*. I cupped my hands to the sides of my mouth and called out with all my might, "we yield. Have mercy. We ask for quarter. The ship is yours." The officers must have understood me because they looked at each other and began conversing among themselves.

I yelled again, as loud as I could, "we yield."

Papi later told me Merlin found the drunk Phillips carrying a lighted match, headed to the magazine, cursing and swearing to take us to the Devil. I did not press Papi for details as to how they prevented Phillips from carrying out his suicidal threat.

Roberts' black flag seemed to hang fast in the twisted debris, a stubborn gesture of futile defiance. With renewed effort the colors and a mass of rope and broken spars disengaged and dropped in a crash against the rail, tumbling ignominiously into the sea. British sailors streamed aboard, disarming the first pirate they encountered. Others went to try and retrieve our colors before they sank. The Navy's zeal to accumulate evidence for the trials we were bound to endure had, unbeknownst to me, sent Lords Lutwidge and Ringrose in a mad scramble to the captain's cabin. It was their aim to destroy the Articles and the accounts so meticulously kept by Wales. A man's signature on the Articles and his name in the ledgers would be most damning.

Firing from the heavy guns had ceased. I heard voices unfamiliar to me, and I heard the voice of defeat. Royal Navy sailors barked at men to drop their weapons or to go here or go there. These men moved swiftly and the process, while not complicated, proceeded in a professional and orderly manner. I waited in vain to hear one of our men telling a sailor to 'go to hell' or hurl some vile insult or lament. Why were the men so subdued? Had Roberts' death turned lions into lambs?

I should have been dancing with joy but I was overcome by a deep sense of melancholy. I felt hollow, like my insides were gone.

The killing was over, for today anyway, but I knew the King's appetite for justice had to be satisfied by an Admiralty court and who knew which of these men would hang.

Cheddar and another black pirate emerged from the forward hatch. I had seen them together before and knew they were friends. Cheddar was wielding a cutlass and when he stood, he held his chin high as if daring anyone to impede him. He walked to the port rail and stood between my line of sight and the second man. I could see that Cheddar's friend had something in his hand. They came to a stop a long pace from the gunwale. Cheddar lowered his chin to his chest and raised his cutlass, his long arm outstretched, pointing the weapon at the horizon. Copious amounts of blood ran in rivulets down the blade onto his hand and wrist.

The second man swung his burden back then propelled it forward, launching it over the side. It was a head. It had been carried by its strands of matted hair, dripping crimson circles the size of doubloons on the deck. Droplets of blood flew through the air as the head tumbled, splashing into the sea. Cheddar uttered a few words I could not hear and casually tossed the bloody cutlass into the water. As if nothing was amiss, the two went back down the hatch.

The head belonged to Starling, the one they called Diamond. Now the head belonged to the deep. What I witnessed gave me a sense of sanguine satisfaction for which I make no apologies.

Most of our crew decided now was a good time to get drunk. Sailors from the Royal Navy were in firm control by virtue of numbers alone. Facing no resistance, our conquerors shed their orderly facade. They began riotously looting. They ripped into the belongings of our men, ransacking below decks and carrying armloads of clothing in scenes eerily like the ones I had seen when the *Samuel* was seized. As was true then, I was powerless to stop the melee, only this time, the thievery of the victors served to blur the invisible line that separated us from them. None of the officers did anything to stop the frenzy and one or two actually joined in.

What I observed rendered the Royal Navy's assertion that pirates were lawless cretins suspect. Discipline can be a moody beast. Hypocrisy was rarely in short supply when it came to men in authority and Captain Roberts would have appreciated the irony.

A Royal Navy captain, in full dress uniform, flanked by two officers and followed by two burly men with flat faces and crooked noses moved solemnly in my direction, climbing up the ladder in single file. The eyed me suspiciously as they advanced, except for the captain, who looked like a man who has just won a huge sum at the gaming tables. Once assembled, they stood smartly on the quarterdeck as the mayhem went on unabated, with three or four scampering sailors doing their best to avoid the notice of the captain and his aides. There were aspects of the deteriorating scene I found somewhat comic. I wondered if the captain could discern the lack of fear in my face, a look he may have mistaken for disrespect or defiance.

The captain stepped forward and in that voice characteristic of educated Englishmen said, "I am Chaloner Ogle, Royal Navy, you have me at a disadvantage."

I cannot explain why, but I threw back my head and laughed, rudely and without embarrassment. The unexpected release certainly suited me better than melancholy.

My behavior was far too flippant and with effort, I quickly regained my bearing.

"My good sir, look about you. It is you who has me at a most unequivocal disadvantage. You are aware that Bartholomew Roberts is not only dead but he has, even in death, escaped your king. His ship—this ship—is yours. I humbly submit to being your prisoner." I raised my hands, palms forward, the universal sign of being unarmed, grinning like the village idiot.

"I lament not having the honor of meeting the great Roberts. He has been a most worthy adversary." I noticed Ogle did not refer to his adversary as 'captain' but whether it was an oversight or a slight, I cared not. "We have come far in our endeavors as you sir, are well aware. Pray, whom do I have the honor of addressing?"

"My name is Harry Glasby, of Boston in the Massachusetts Bay Colony. My apologies for laughing, I meant no disrespect. Meeting you, at last, is not only an honor but a tremendous relief, the enormity of which you could not possibly fathom. As you will see, I was made a prisoner by Bartholomew Roberts on the 13th day of July in 1720 off the coast of North America. I was forced to be his first mate and to that end, with the death of the captain, I was thrust into a position to strike our colors." I extended my hand and looked the captain in the eye. "I have prayed for this day. I wish only to go home. You sir, and your men, have saved me. God Bless King George and His Majesty's Royal Navy."

As soon as I said it, I worried I may have overdone it a bit by bringing up the king.

Captain Ogle shook my hand, a bit warily, his reticence entirely appropriate, then the two officers did the same and politely told me their names. Ogle consulted with one of his aides, holding his hand up to shield his words. He nodded, lowered his hand and said, "Harry Glasby. I believe we gathered intelligence from survivors of a French ship that you were a pirate captain of some standing. The *Trident*, if memory serves." The captain looked at the same officer who nodded in confirmation.

Damn you Wales.

I shook my head in denial and disbelief. The responses that came to my mind sounded absurd or incomplete. "Begging the captain's pardon, what I have told you is absolutely true. Time will reveal that I am innocent." When I thought more about what Ogle said,

JAMES H. DRESCHER

I realized I stood before him acting in every manner as if I *was* the captain of the *Royal Fortune*. Meeting their skeptical gaze, I had a hurried and startling glimpse of my own hanging.

A clever but guilty man might well claim to have been kidnapped and forced into piracy but I detected a glimmer in Ogle's eyes that gave me hope. The glimmer could also have been a reflection of pride in his otherworldly intelligence network. If he knew such trivial details about Cumana there could be very little he did not know. I was right about one thing, during the trials that were to follow, more than half the crew would contend they were forced into piracy against their will.

Despite the unpleasant distractions, I expressed my fervent sentiments that they would tend to our wounded, that we would not be abused and I acknowledged that we would be made their prisoners until such time as all this could be sorted by an Admiralty court.

From the edge of my field of vision, I spotted a fresh faced sailor with a large brown cat tucked under his arm, striding to the starboard rail. To Captain Ogle, I said, "excuse me for a moment sir." Then, to the boy sailor, "hey, you there. With the cat. What do you think you're doing?" I was afraid Jack was about to be pitched over the side.

Captain Ogle cracked a thin smile. The self-conscious sailor ran his hand from Jack's head to his tail, the latter swung lazily. By all indications, Jack, who could read men's minds, sensed he was in no danger.

The sailor was tongue-tied under the gaze of his captain. He was unsure whether he had permission to speak. I was under no such impediment and renewed my inquiry. "What are your intentions?" My demand even struck me as odd. It was just a cat, but it was my cat and I would not willingly allow Jack to be harmed.

Looking at the water, at the cat, at his captain and back to me, the young man shook his head vigorously, "oh sir, 'tis not what you think sir. They told me below this cat hunts rats. They said his name is Jack." His arched eyebrows suggested he was either wanting confirmation of what he had been told, permission to proceed onward or most likely both.

Relieved, I said, "so you are not putting him over the side?"

"Oh, no sir." He shook his head. Jack watched me, drawn by the sound of my voice.

"What a relief. That cat does answer to the name Jack. Well, answer is not the word, he is rather independent. But he's a good hunter. Are you pressing him into the service of His Majesty's Navy?" I was not aiming to be trite.

The sailor, who himself may have been the victim of a press gang, gave Jack another stroke, "yes sir, I believe you can put it that way."

"I beg you to promise he will be well treated. He was once a friend to my friend and I owe him that." They would not know or care if my debt was to my friend or to the cat.

"As long as Jack obeys the captain and serves King and Country you may rest easy as to his future sir." Even if Captain Ogle was enjoying all this, the young sailor wanted to be away.

Wisely believing the fate of a pirate cat was beneath the dignity of the hallowed Captain Ogle, one of the officers interceded, "carry on Ladner. You must have other duties to attend to."

"Aye sir." Ladner and Jack proceeded to Jack's new home.

We were disarmed, searched and left with just enough clothing so none of us could claim that we were taken prisoner naked, not that our well-being was of concern to any but us. Miraculously, I still wore the governor's boots.

One more incident underscores the whimper that heralded the demise of this leaderless gang of drunks. Pirate John Mansfield got roaring drunk that long afternoon. He had deserted from the pirate sloop *Rose* and joined our crew for drink and gold, in that order. He awoke, brain-coshed, from a rum induced coma only to see the *Swallow* floating alongside. He began crying out, "look mates, a prize, a prize."

Mansfield and the rest of us were escorted under the watchful eyes of our captors to the hold of the *Swallow* where we joined the morose and dejected survivors of the *Great Ranger*, many of whom were wounded. The stump of Captain Skyrm's mangled leg was wrapped in blood soaked rags and mercifully, he was unconscious. He lay near the bulkhead on a tattered wool blanket. His men had positioned him so others would not kick him or step on his wound. They greeted us in sullen silence, having already been confined in the hold for five days.

Excluding Diamond, our engagement with the *Swallow* claimed the lives of one captain and two pirates, a fellow called Ugly George and an immensely powerful African known as Fornido.

The Royal Navy collected 152 new prisoners and of this number 52 were negroes. By my calculations, Papi and nine more were wounded seriously enough to need immediate medical attention. Ajax had absorbed shards of oak from a broadside while working on a gun crew. Other gunners commended his courage in remaining active despite his injuries, a testament to his tenacity if not his sobriety. The multitude and severity of his wounds proved to be fatal.

Pirate John Kelligrew hailed from Cornwall in England and claimed to be a 'son of a gun'. His mother had married a British seaman and she gave birth to baby John on the gun deck of a warship while situated between two eight-pounders. She was visiting James Kelligrew, her husband. The story was accepted as true by the pirates on our ship because there were other such births known in Royal Navy lore. Seamen were denied leave to reduce desertion, but whores and wives were permitted not only to visit warships when in port, but to stay on board for extended periods of time.

Kelligrew had been struck by solid shot. Those nearby surmised the velocity of the ball had been slowed by going through our hull and striking part of a heavy beam. It bounded off something solid but it was still moving fast enough to crush Kelligrew's ribs. The massive bruising was deep purple, the color of port wine, and it started at his naval and ended at his armpits. Kelligrew's breathing was labored at best and he took his last late that night.

Born between the guns, killed by one.

Captain Skyrm and his dispirited crew consisted of 102 men. With the one-legged Skyrm bravely refusing to yield and fighting for survival, ten men in his crew were killed during the battle.

All told, Ogle had 254 prisoners, 70 of this number were black.

Captain Ogle suffered no fatalities in either engagement.

Confirming that the *Little Ranger* presumably remained at Cape Lopez, Captain Ogle sailed south to ensnare another prize. When we arrived, Ogle's men found the smaller vessel deserted and discovered that the valuable contents of the pirates' shattered sea chests had been ransacked. What had been a floating storeroom was now a ghost ship. All our men were affected by this wholesale theft and they were furious. I told Captain Ogle a pink known as the *Neptune* had paid us a visit the night of February 9th and her captain, a man calling himself Hill, had breakfasted with Captain Roberts on the fateful morning of the 10th. We knew little or nothing about Hill. Ogle said the *Neptune* either belonged to or sailed on behalf of the Royal Africa Company.

Hill and his men absconded with considerable amounts of gold and other valuables and I passed the details to Ogle. I was left to wonder why the owners of the chests were so troubled by the larceny. Offended might be a better word. They were going to a place where none of that mattered and quite obviously, the loot had been obtained by theft in the first place. I suppose they would argue that they worked for the plunder and assumed certain risks to take it, supposing further that the men who walked off with it took no risks and just carried it from one ship to another. No matter one's view of the perfidy, it would have been a tidy sum.

We never found out what happened to the devious Captain Hill, the *Neptune,* or the small group of men who had been minding the *Little Ranger.* More likely than not, those men, fifteen or twenty in number, fled with Hill. It is conceivable that Hill had them murdered, netting more money for Hill and his crew. If our former shipmates were alive, their decision to scurry was a wise one if viewed dispassionately, something the prisoners found hard to do in the stench of the cramped hold of the *Swallow.*

The ransacking of the *Little Ranger* did something else. It obscured the severity of the theft perpetrated by Burgess and Jennings. Hill and his accomplices may have obscured more than that; they may have diverted attention from the fate of the Whydah gold dust.

I wanted to murder Captain Ogle when he stopped at St. Thomas and had his men careen the hull of the *Swallow,* the very same hull that formed the walls of our temporary prison. Listening to the men scrape and clean the hull was akin to torture. Naturally, the laborious procedure took longer due to a resumption of torrential rains and powerful thunderstorms. At least we were not at sea and the weather reflected the dark mood of the pirates. After stocking up on firewood and water, the *Swallow* got underway on February 18 with the *Royal Fortune,* the *Ranger* and the *Little Ranger* making up our fleet. The *Little Ranger* had the dubious distinction of being the only undamaged vessel.

All in all, Captain Ogle must have felt like a triumphant Caesar.

As was done with Ajax and Kelligrew, each time a man perished he was unceremoniously dumped over the side. There would be no blessing of souls, no benediction, not even a few yards of canvas for a shroud. Dead pirates were bothersome refuse and live ones were not faring much better. Fifteen bodies were dumped in this perfunctory manner by the time we sailed into the harbor at the Cape Coast Castle on March 16.

The returning conqueror was greeted with a grand salute of twenty-one guns firing from the massive walls of the stone fortress. Whatever his private thoughts, Captain Ogle *was* likened to a Caesar. All he lacked was a horse drawn chariot and the head of Bartholomew Roberts hanging from his bowsprit.

For many shivering in the hold, it would be the last time they would hear cannon fire and I daresay, they were made despondent by the sound. One man's triumph is another man's defeat.

Two days earlier, I discovered that one of my fellow inmates had carved *dum spiro spero* in the wooden hull using a small blade or possibly an orphan nail. Remembering that Lord Lutwidge had some acquaintance with Latin, I sought him out and asked if he could decipher the words.

"I can," he said, "*dum spiro spero*. It means 'while I breathe, I have hope.' Did you do this Glasby?"

"No, I didn't."

"Any suspects?" Lutwidge asked.

I slowly shook my head. "If not you...", my voice trailed off. Lutwidge stared at the carving then sat back on the deck to await our arrival at the fortress, holding his head in his filthy hands. It was the shortest conversation we ever had.

Chapter 18
The Governor's Boots

WORDS ARE NOT SUFFICIENT TO describe the squalid conditions we endured in the *Swallow's* hold.

We lived alongside swarms of vermin from biting lice to black rats the size of rabbits with the tenacity of pit dogs. It was dark, damp and it reeked of men, rotting wounds and our accumulated waste. Many were the times in the bleak days ahead I was plagued with unsettling visions of what it must be like in a slave ship. One of the negroes contended conditions were more humane on such a ship. Discussion of the fate of the seventy Africans among our number was conducted in snippets and whispers. Pirates descended in any quantity from a black ancestor would be sold into slavery.

How would proud and defiant men like Cheddar and Neptune and their warrior kinsmen ultimately fare? Unless one has been a slave, comprehending the anger, fear and frustration that lies at the heart of such a dismal existence is an impossibility. I had more exposure to this status than most white men, I must confess, having been a prisoner and made to work against my will, but in the end,

I never gave up on the prospect of having my liberty restored. I viewed my misfortunes as temporary and that outlook helped sustain my well of hope, a well which never did go dry, even during interminable hours such as these.

To be born a slave is one thing, to have sipped from the cup of freedom and then forced back into bondage quite another. We sometimes forgot that our black shipmates, almost to a man, were born free, captured and sold into slavery. By adopting a life of piracy, the Africans in the hold had enjoyed freedom of a different sort, with immense power and a sense of worth that comes from being perceived and treated as a near equal. The Royal Navy would take their freedom and their dignity and my pity for these men weighed heavily on my conscience. Born with dark skin, they were destined to be treated more like cattle than human beings with a soul. If it was any consolation, cattle are not hanged for piracy and no matter what these negroes had done as brigands, being sold as a slave was better than being dropped from a scaffold, although even that proposition is subject to legitimate debate.

A few desperate pirates begged to be allowed to help crew the vessels as we sailed to the Cape Coast Castle. The unremitting horror of our circumstances fostered an inability to think rationally. When their requests were summarily denied and they grew more disconsolate, I revealed the circumstances of my father's murder, omitting the detail that his killers were pirates. Any one of us, if allowed to roam about freely could cheat the hangman by leaping into the sea, seriously damage a vessel, or seize a marlinspike and kill a sailor. It only takes two pirates to conspire and three to spark a revolt. Pointing out how much worse our agony would be if we were sailing to London or the West Indies did nothing to allay the malaise. One of the few who did not complain was Captain Skyrm. How he survived with his crudely amputated leg is among the few actual miracles I've personally witnessed.

The *Swallow* anchored on March 16. Our captors kept us on the ship until the next morning. We were never told why but that last night in the hold felt like an eternity. After being ferried to shore in a pair of longboats, we once more set our unsteady feet on solid ground. The sight of the sun, trees, sea birds, and the cloud speckled sky served as a welcome elixir. The sky was so blue it hurt my eyes.

The towering walls and forbidding stone structures of the fortress exuded strength and power, for that is its purpose. Former slaves, some of whom had been in this fort before, did their utmost to warn us about what lay beneath. We derided their tales as far-fetched, deluding ourselves with the belief that nothing could be worse than the hold. A wise man knows it can always be worse.

Imagine you are forced into a wooden crate and the top nailed shut. Your joints and muscles begin to ache and eventually you reach the point where you agree to shoot your own mother to be released; minutes would seem like hours, hours like days. Without explanation, you are suddenly released, your unbearable agony subsides and your sense of well-being is overwhelming. But your celebration is short-lived as your tormentors push you into another crate. A smaller one.

The hold was bad but the dungeon was worse. The Cape Coast Castle existed primarily to warehouse slaves awaiting transport. Carved and blasted from the rock beneath the fortress were chambers lined from floor to ceiling with bricks. We were marched through the 'door of no return', winding down a steep passage. The tunnel had a vaulted brick ceiling just out of a tall man's reach. At the bottom were cells where we would linger until the trial. Lacking windows, a man could wake up believing he had been buried alive.

As for the seventy negro pirates, they were put in another such place or diverted directly to waiting slave ships.

We had been reduced to 180 prisoners.

The barbaric nature of our subterranean existence in these veritable tombs did not cause any of our number to go insane but you will know that my descriptions are true when I tell you that four men died within two weeks.

James Joseph, a young man from Newport in Rhode Island, was not wounded, had no fever, no sickness and there was not a shred of evidence to suggest why he suddenly left us. He was a fiddler and his abundant good nature and sense of humor earned him the name Jollyboy. While those of us who clung to life were becoming inured to degradation and death, the early morning discovery of the dead Jollyboy provoked anger and sadness. Jollyboy, we concluded, gave up hope and willed his death. His well of hope ran dry. The men interpreted his death as an omen, as if an omen could make the present or the near future any worse. Yet we began to wonder, who would be next?

The Albino recited one of the Vicar's favorite verses, from the Book of Psalms, "The Lord is nigh unto them that are of a broken heart; and saveth such as be of a contrite spirit." A somber but disembodied voice intoned, from deep in the foul blackness, "lot of fuckin' good the Lord did Jollyboy."

The anonymous observation was not contested.

The following day, eighteen Frenchmen were removed and they were either released or given over to France on the theory that they, as foreigners, were not subject to the jurisdiction of an English court. Not all the men who spoke French were citizens or subjects of France but no one spoke up to refute this assumption. Vive la France. We were delighted less in their sudden good fortune than the consequence that we had more room in which to lay. Rumors flew that this development signaled an important uptick in activities above. Just as a starving crew talks incessantly about food, we talked of nothing but the trial. How would they try so many? What chance did we have to avoid conviction and death? Many would wear the halter and Spades tried to generate some betting on this topic but found no takers. Those who had been pirates the longest did not engage in these discussions. They knew they were doomed and our conditions were so horrid they just wanted to get on with it.

I was grateful Wales and Ashplant had vanished.

Two days after the Frenchmen were taken, one of the guards summoned me. Naturally, I wanted to know why and naturally he told me to shut my mouth and follow him.

On emerging from the dungeon, my restraints were removed and I was taken to a nearby room and told to wash my filthy hands and face. It was the first time I had washed since our capture. I waited half an hour and a different man in the uniform of a Navy midshipman introduced himself and said he was to escort me to an office on the first level of the fort. As we walked, I saw white and black men working, none paid us any mind. We entered a tidy room with two wooden tables and around each table sat four identical chairs in perfect order. One wall was taken up by a large archway which led into a storeroom of immense proportions. Stealing a look into this chamber, I admired the orderliness of the shelves, stacked with supplies; candles, lanterns, blankets, buckets, cloth, canvas, ropes, shining copper pots and black ironware. These goods were used to purchase slaves. A small fire burned in the fireplace and the aroma of wood smoke was pleasant. Before the midshipman left, he bade me sit and asked if I would "care for a cup of tea".

I replied in the affirmative. He inclined his head in a polite bow, said "very well sir," and departed. A very young and exceptionally tiny black girl brought me tea, sugar, and a delicate silver spoon on a black wooden tray inlaid with bits of carved ivory. She smiled warmly and I smiled back, her round chin level with the top of the table. I must have looked hideous with my matted hair and unkempt beard. It was the best cup of tea I have ever had and I would have gladly given a tidy sum for another.

The polite midshipmen returned, asked if I enjoyed my tea and motioned for me to come along. We stepped outside and crossed the inner courtyard of the fortress, exiting through a narrow doorway adjoining the main gateway. The heavy iron portcullis was closed. The walk was refreshing and the sea air divine. Our brief journey terminated in a beautifully manicured and idyllic garden. Adding to my astonishment, a uniformed Captain Ogle was casually admiring some bright pink blossoms. He looked up as we approached and put his hands behind his back. He was bareheaded and his hair hung neatly down his back, tied by a thin black ribbon. There was a brief exchange of courtesies and the midshipman was dismissed.

Ogle asked whether I had "ever seen such magnificent flowers?"

"Every flower is beautiful in its own right," I said, adding "sir" after an embarrassing lapse. I had every intention of doing my best to please him but I would not reduce myself to groveling.

He nodded curtly, "well said. I do apologize for the conditions of your confinement. Once we landed, responsibility for your well-being was handed to another. Please, walk with me so we might enjoy the sights and senses of this delightful oasis." He held out his hand to direct me to walk at his side. As much as I wanted to know the reason for our conference, I let him proceed according to his desires.

During our conversation, he paused to gaze at flowering blooms and exotic plants or to ask for my thoughts and comments about matters of horticulture and gardening. Of course the purpose of this unusual visit had nothing to do with the incongruity of a colossal English garden in the shadow of a slave fortress.

The mild March weather was pleasing and the sun warmed me, easing much of the aching in my back and legs.

We passed under a trellis blanketed with hundreds of miniature white roses when Captain Ogle commenced a series of questions about the *Caerphilly Castle* and its captain. I answered fully and truthfully, making plain that I knew very little. I believe he already knew the answers and I hoped as much. If so, my veracity would be more easily established.

He then launched into a description of a play he had seen on Drury Lane in London called "The Successful Pirate". The light-hearted farce was penned by someone unknown to me. I admitted I'd never seen a play, which he found amusing, telling me I must see to that one day. He wondered why pirates rarely took their ill-gotten gains and settled down to a life of ease and luxury. I said I'd often wondered that myself. According to him, the play was about English pirate Henry Avery who amassed a large fortune and thereafter lived such a life. I had heard stories about Captain Avery but found it odd that anyone would take the time to write a play about a pirate, much less that someone would pay money to see it.

Now seemed to be an opportune time to test these waters.

"Captain, will I have the chance to see a play one day? By now you know of my plight and no doubt your magistrates inquired into my innocence when talking to the Frenchmen. I never bore arms and never accepted plunder. I did Captain Roberts' bidding to preserve my life so that I might one day regain my liberty. My only bid for freedom nearly cost me my life but they captured me and the merciful intercession of a respected pirate saved me from execution. As I reflect on that dark time, it was a close run thing."

He raised his index finger and touched it to his lips, saying after a moment, "ah yes, I believe that would have been Mr. Ashplant." His eyes gently awaited my reaction to the intimacy of his knowledge.

I was momentarily speechless.

"Why yes, Valentine Ashplant. Sir, how could you know this?"

Ogle smiled and scratched his cheek enigmatically. "You innocently say you never accepted plunder. I believe with certainty you used the word 'never'." He waited and I wondered. I felt as if I was walking down a dark stairway and was uncertain if I would miss the final stair. Among Ogle's seemingly vast array of sources, what if some bastard had told lies about me to further his own ends?

"No, never. They presented me the Articles when I was kidnapped and I refused to sign. A man once gave me some coins in reward for services I performed but that is a very long story. I managed to lose those coins and that too is a long story and not one I am particularly proud to share."

"Mr. Glasby", he said my name sympathetically. "I am not interested in your ill-fated adventures in New Barcelona. But I am compelled to ask if those are not the boots of the murdered governor of Martinique?" His tone indicated he was amused, as opposed to a ploy to ensnare me in a falsehood. It bordered on playfulness and I felt myself redden.

My eyes shot down as if learning for the first time I had been equipped by the creator with a pair of feet. All of us wore whatever we had on when we were made prisoners. My face was now hot and I felt like a child caught in a prank. Captain Ogle waved his hand to signal that he did not care about the boots or the technical inaccuracy of my claim. I resolved to be more careful about using the words 'never' and 'always'. He began praising my navigational skills as if to underscore his disinterest in the history of my boots and to signal that we were moving on with his agenda. He went on for some time about me and grew quite effusive. Was he trying to curry favor with me when he had all the cards? As far as I could surmise, I had nothing to offer him or the authorities.

After a moment of quiet, all was revealed.

"Mr. Glasby, what do you suppose happened to the gold necklace and diamond cross Captain Roberts wore the day of his demise. Such a thing of beauty could be of substantial value. Is that not so?" Ogle spoke to me like a friend but nonetheless, there was a gravity in his voice that was not present when he talked of flowers.

"I've not thought of that until this moment captain. I vividly remember the jeweled necklace. He wore it that afternoon but the men who put Roberts over the side might have information about the fate of the cross. And before you ask, I do not recall who handled his body. I myself threw his pistols into the sea." I felt it important enough to add, "and we were still under bombardment, as you yourself will recall. I had little time for trifles."

"I do recall. And my apologies. I wanted to remember to thank you for striking the colors, which we retrieved and which counsel for the crown will use in presenting its case to the judges we have assembled. Pirates represent lawlessness but we intend to extend to each of you the rights afforded to all. You will be tried fairly and on that you have my word. Captain Herdman of *HMS Weymouth* has been appointed as President of the Court. He will be assisted by the Honorable James Phipps, General of the Coast. A Secretary from the Royal Africa Company, Edward Hyde, and two merchants will sit in judgment. Oh, forgive me, I've overlooked Lieutenants Fanshaw and Barnsley of the Royal Navy. Are any of these names familiar to you?"

I responded that these personages were wholly unknown to me.

Captain Ogle seemed to accept my response. "My role is merely to give evidence. The same as yours. If you speak truthfully I rather believe things will go well for you. I am not without influence." He uttered this last bit with a hint of conspiracy.

"I will do my best. As any innocent man would. I do not believe, sir, that you summoned me here to ask about my boots.

You know the *Little Ranger* was looted and your men, with all due respect, were running amok on the *Royal Fortune* so any valuables we had were confiscated. I will ask about the necklace if that is your wish."

Captain Ogle scratched his cheek again, "what about the gold?"

He was looking at me with the keenest intensity but I no longer felt quite so vulnerable. I had something of value after all.

Before I could reply, he added, "the gold taken during the raid on Whydah."

I was confounded, "are you saying the Whydah gold was not recovered and seized by your crew?"

"Mr. Glasby, the trial starts March 28 and when it ends I must sail to Jamaica. I am prepared to take you there. You may keep the boots if you wish. They do seem to be of the highest quality." His wan smile about the boots gratified me but much more significantly, he blatantly sidestepped my question about the gold dust. I now knew what he wanted.

His interest in my testimony and the gold proved to be precisely what I suspected, nearly word for word, and I told myself to be careful so as not to appear smug.

"In return, I ask very little. If you are asked about the Whydah gold, just tell them, truthfully, that you do not know its fate. If we arrive safely in Jamaica, you will disembark with your freedom. Given what I know about your resourcefulness, you will find your way to Boston. Shall we return to the fortress and drink to our understanding?" He was presuming much.

Rendered speechless once more, Captain Ogle, mistaking the cause of my silence, inquired as to whether his offer caused me offense. I vigorously shook my head.

"No sir, none whatsoever. Your generosity and the prospect of getting back to Boston are truly overwhelming. I do not know where the Whydah gold was taken and will say so as often as necessary. As to your other offer, I respectfully decline as I do not drink."

I had dreamed over and over again of being acquitted by the Admiralty court but getting myself from the Cape Coast Castle to Boston was such a daunting task I had rarely given it much consideration. Applying for a position on a slaver, an idea I abhorred, was heretofore my only means of getting back to the Americas. But to sail with Captain Ogle, as his guest, all the way to Jamaica? It was too good to be true.

Captain Ogle's barely concealed joy at my willingness to give him assurances about my testimony was amply conveyed by his countenance. He gently gripped my arm in warm familiarity, "I am told pirates do not trust a man who does not drink. Is that so?" He was back to using the same light-hearted tone he used when chiding me about the boots.

"Captain, pirates are an interesting species. You must have heard that Bartholomew Roberts did not drink with any regularity, as you seem possessed of all there is to know as if by magic."

Captain Ogle expressed surprise at this bit of news and told me he would be pleased to know more about this interesting 'species' and the departed Captain Roberts during our cruise to Jamaica. He informed me they had made a room for me in the fort and that I would no longer be under guard once the trial ended. Til then I must remain confined so as not to arouse undue suspicion or jealousy. I asked why this offer was extended to me alone as all the men on the *Royal Fortune* would have known, to some degree or another, that we had the Whydah gold on board. He explained that as a consequence of my unique position as acting captain of the ship when it was seized, coupled with my reputation for honesty, circumstances made me the most logical witness to speak about this matter —*if it came up*. When he put it that way, I began to suspect he had had similar conversations with the President of the Court and possibly some of the appointed judges. That might explain why he asked if I knew them.

We walked together and headed in the direction of the fortress. The garden would have made a good sized farm in the Massachusetts Colony. While I was buoyed by these developments, I felt a twinge of guilt about the men suffering in the dungeon to a degree I found discomfiting. I asked Captain Ogle if I could tell my fellow inmates about the trial date and the appointment of the judges. He had no objection and said he assumed I would tell them with or without his blessing. I asked him to indulge me in one more favor. Would he allow me to take some oranges I had seen growing in the garden to the men. He happily assured me that oranges and melons would be delivered within the hour, enough for everyone.

I went back to the men and gave them the news. They were keen to learn about the trial, despite knowing, as they did, that many of them had only a few weeks left to live. After I told them what I knew and answered their questions, I'd completely forgotten I'd asked Captain Ogle to have fresh food sent to the dungeon. My memory was revived by the distinctive sound of the door being unlocked and the footfalls of two dozen slaves descending down the passage.

Responding like happy children at the surprise receipt of buckets of oranges and dozens of melons, the laughter of my fellow prisoners echoed off the stone walls and high ceilings. These walls had probably never heard such sounds. Since the tumultuous events of the tenth day of February I had not allowed myself to see my fellow prisoners as much more than pirates. But these were men I had lived with, befriended, men who did small kindnesses for me and men who told me of their sufferings and abuse. Men who taught me by their experiences that those to whom evil is done often do evil in return.

Not all the men were bad and very few of the men were evil and some of the very worst had not survived. The evil men who remained would hang, or not, and I would not care. But most of the men were just that, men. They had made a mother smile, had suckled and then grown up in a world that oftentimes treated them like they were worthless or deserving of their suffering. They had loved or tried to love and somewhere were people who, at one time or another, loved them in return. When the men laughed, I saw their faces not as men but as the children they once were. It was not just the wholesome sweet fruit, it was the pure and childlike joy of being surprised. It was the joy in their faces that revived the child who hid inside them. Despite Captain Ogle's assurances that I would likely go free and sail with him to Jamaica, I glimpsed faces of gleeful children smeared with the juice of oranges and melons. I withdrew to a far corner, drew up my knees and let my tears roll.

The trial was conducted in the Great Hall of the Castle and began the morning of March 28 as foretold by Captain Ogle. An ailing Captain Skyrm was carried in and propped up in a hard wooden chair. He looked like he had aged ten years. The rest of us stood. We were arraigned and everyone entered a plea of not guilty. The men on trial no longer resembled monsters of mayhem except for Deadeye, who garnered some quizzical looks from officials and a few curious observers.

We were charged with having "…twice wickedly sinking, burning and destroying goods on vessels under the color sometimes of one flag and sometimes another and committing marine depredations and wanton outrages against his Majesty's subjects, engaging in high seas piracy, an offense recognized in all civilized countries."

The second charge was that the men aboard the "...so called pirate ship *Ranger* did behave as traitors, enemies of mankind and vile pirates by their attack on the *HMS Swallow* on or about the 5th day of February instanter." The defendants deemed responsible for these horrid crimes were pale, filthy, disheveled and dejected. Counsel was assigned to advise us but counsel could not address the court or cross-examine witnesses. When men sought to do this themselves it was awkward and it merely allowed the witness to repeat any damning testimony, of which there was an abundance.

Eighty of the accused pirates were from the *Ranger* and the first witnesses were crewmen from the aggrieved *Swallow*. All eighty agreed to having been on board the *Ranger* and all confirmed they had signed the Articles. Many contended they had been forced into piracy and denied having carried arms, fired weapons or otherwise assisted in the offenses alleged other than to avoid punishment or death at the hands of the 'real' pirates. It was not my concern that most of them were lying. The other excuse for their crimes echoed the pleas of Mr. Every when he was tried for murder. Like Mr. Every, the men seized from the *Ranger* tried to assign blame for their misdeeds on drink.

As the mammoth trial unfolded, the judges ruled it would be necessary to hear the evidence as to each man, one by one.

Next, the men of the *Royal Fortune* duly entered their pleas of not guilty and the court patiently listened to the statements of each man.

Rather than wait until the trial ended, as one defendant after another had been heard to testify, his verdict was announced on the spot. Due to the unprecedented numbers, the trial took four weeks.

A score of those convicted were deemed to have been 'bold and brisk' or 'lively and willingly' engaged in robbery, arson and murder. Much was made of how long a man had been a member of either crew. Any man seen carrying cutlasses, pikes, pistols or other weapons and those who had been manning heavy guns or observed while in the actual act of looting were convicted. Captain Skyrm was found guilty and sentenced to death as were his officers and many in his crew. Incredulously, only four from the *Royal Fortune* were found to have engaged in wanton cruelty or outright acts of violence. Many others among our crew, and all the surviving Lords, were found guilty of piracy and condemned to death.

The musicians were acquitted.

As for the Whydah gold, it was never mentioned.

When it was my time to testify, I told the truth and focused on my plight, giving evidence about my dealings with Captain Roberts and Wales. Many witnesses testified on my behalf and there was never anything to suggest the judges had anything but sympathy for me. The worst part was being asking to testify against men who lay next to me in the dungeon. While I spoke the truth, I said as little as I could, vowing not to volunteer information and endeavoring only to answer with precision. If I did not know or could not remember, I said so and waited for my two hour interrogation to end.

To my everlasting gratitude and relief, as I reflect now on the effect of the evidence I gave, it did not, in and of itself, cause anyone's death.

Robert Armstrong, age thirty-four, the sailor who deserted from the *Swallow* and recognized it while on the deck of the *Royal Fortune,* was sentenced to die. He was the only one to hang from the yardarm of the *Swallow,* the traditional method of execution for deserters. Captain Ogle and his officers, during our journey to Jamaica, would later tell me the convoluted story of how Armstrong deserted and found himself a pirate serving with Bartholomew Roberts.

Twenty pirates were permitted to sign a seven year indenture warrant to work in the mines owned by the Royal Africa Company further west on the Gold Coast. Seven years hard labor underground struck me as the equivalent of a long drawn out burial. It's hard for a man of the sea to go from stealing gold to digging it out of a deep hole in the depths of the earth. Being in a mine evoked unpleasant memories of the fortress dungeon and I struggled to avoid the nightmarish thought of spending seven years in such a place.

Seventeen men were to serve sentences at Marshalsea in Southwark, London, a notorious prison reserved for hard cases. Four of the seventeen would perish before they arrived.

Fifty-four men were sentenced to the gallows.

Two of the fifty-four were pardoned for reasons unknown to me. Captain Skyrm was not one of the two.

I was acquitted.

To my great astonishment, seventy-three other men were found not guilty. During my sojourn in the garden with Captain Ogle, he had said "you will be tried fairly" and I recall being so concerned about my own fate I assumed he was directing his comments to me alone. But then I remembered he also said the Admiralty intended to extend to "each of you the rights afforded to all."

Say what you will about British justice during those days but these facts speak for themselves. We were all treated fairly.

The Register of the Court, the surgeon from the *Swallow,* Mr. John Atkins, read the names of the condemned as written on the death warrant. He intoned officiously:

Ye and each of you are adjudged and sentenced to be carried back from thence to the Place of Execution without the Gates of this Castle, and there within the Flood Marks to be hanged by the neck 'till you are Dead, Dead, Dead. Ye shall then be taken

*down and your earthly body hung in chains. And the Lord have
Mercy on your Souls. Dated at Cape Coast Castle this the 2nd
day of April, 1722.*

The warrants were signed by all the judges and this process was
repeated again and again.

There is no easy or convenient method for a hanging of this
magnitude so the men were divided into groups.

The first six were carried to the place of execution on April 3. Six
more were executed on April 9 and they increased it to fourteen on
April 11. Four were hanged April 13, eight were executed three days
later and the last fourteen were lined up on April 20. It was a grisly
business and a business it was.

I'd seen the Marshall's Dance in Boston and I'd watched in
horror as Captain Roberts hanged the Governor of Martinique. I'd
had my fill of death and witnessed enough hangings. I respectfully
declined to attend the executions but the primary reason was that
some of the condemned, like Lord Lutwidge, were men I did not
want to watch die.

The Lords were in the first group of six on April 3.

Lutwidge lodged a spirited complaint that the rules for hanging
were being ignored, saying, "I have seen many a man hanged but
this way of having our hands tied behind us I am a stranger to,
and I never saw it before in my life." Whoever was in charge of
the Cape Coast Castle likely had little experience in such matters.
There was a huddled discussion and the six men were untied, one
by one, and their hands moved to the front. Lutwidge expressed
his sincere gratitude, saying he felt more comfortable. He went on
to wish that he could express atonement for his many sins but alas,
he did not feel any remorse whatsoever. He did not want to have
his last sin recorded as 'lying'. He suggested that any forgiveness he

might be relinquishing should be allotted to his fellow Lords, whose crime riddled careers made him look like an amateur. He closed by hoping to see Captain Roberts, who he missed sorely, and his soon to be dead friends in Hell. He anticipated arriving that afternoon and would do all in his power to make things ready for any new arrivals who might well follow. Lutwidge had obtained bright red ribbons which he tied in his hair and on his person. He explained to the assembly that when he met with Old Roger, meaning Satan, he hoped to make a favorable first impression, admitting that even if he failed, he would get credit for at least making an effort.

Lord Ringrose had dysentery so his hanging did not go well. Many of the men, I was told, 'put on a good show'. Some begged for forgiveness and others tearfully expressed remorse for their wicked ways. Some said nothing. It is impossible to know what goes through a man's mind as he awaits the signal to be dropped from this life into the next. All the men were visited by a part-time reverend. He enjoyed ministering to those who were contrite, kindly comforting them during their last moments by sending up a prayer which, I suspect, the Almighty received with more than a little skepticism. The good reverend could righteously claim to have saved a fair number of dirty souls even though it was far too late to erase the trail of death, destruction, and agony some of these vile men left as their temporal legacy.

From the records we know a third of those executed hailed from the west of England, the rest from Wales, London and the north, with the tragic exception of Papi. None of the men from the American colonies were executed.

To my immense relief, the Albino was found not guilty.

During our night in New Barcelona, Papi predicted I would one day find my way home but he told me he was destined to die for his life of piracy. When asked on the scaffold if he had any last words, the charismatic Papi announced that he would not change a thing, adding, "I am no grandee, just a poor *corsario* and a most excellent thief. But I swear by the Virgin Mary and all the saints, I never killed a defenseless man or hurt a woman. As for my dear and beloved friends who will die with me on this day, I offer you my thanks for your loyalty and your affection. I humbly hope, in some small way, you knew of my love and affection for you. The closest I ever got to heaven was when I was held in the arms of a beautiful woman or shared the music made by my brothers during our short time together. It is you I will miss the most, you were the family I never had. *Adios, vaya con Dios.*" He serenely assured the officers, officials and sailors present he held no grudge and expressed sympathy for those who, no doubt, found their duty repugnant. He claimed he'd made the most of his days in this wicked world and would do his best to make good use of his days in the next. His final flourish was to kick off his shoes, honoring a solemn vow to die with his boots off.

Papi was in the last group of fourteen hanged on April 20. When I was told what he said and how he died, I hung my head and said a prayer for his soul and gave thanks that I did not have to bear witness to his execution. I would not have done well. His prediction as to his own fate came to pass and I naturally wondered if he would prove to be right about mine.

The average age of the few surviving men in the 'House of Lords' was thirty-seven but the average age of all those hanged was twenty-eight.Four were over forty. Had Roberts lived, he would have been in this group, having been born in 1682. The oldest to hang was forty-five. I must assume that honor fell to Lord Copplestone or Lord Lutwidge. Four were under twenty, the youngest eighteen, a man who, amazingly, had been a pirate since he was a lad of thirteen.

I did not know them all as many served under Captain Skyrm.

As for that indomitable fellow, two guards held the mangled captain upright so he could be hanged.

Eighteen of the most notorious pirates were cut down, coated in tar, wrapped in metal bars and hung from gibbets to sound the traditional warning. This seemed like a gross waste of effort since very few people who might be tempted to become pirates venture by the Cape Gold Coast. The ghoulish gesture probably resonated well in the dispatches and letters sent to London and Greenwich and Portsmouth. It's the same thing they did with the body of Captain Kidd in London. As ever, naval tradition often asserts itself in odd ways.

When justice was sated and these tarred blackened corpses put on display, my understanding as to why Bartholomew Roberts ordered us to bury him at sea deepened considerably.

Chapter 19

Revelations

ROBERTS' DEATH WAS A VICTORY for civilization and a watershed moment for its lifeblood—trade and commerce. Roberts jokingly referred to himself as Admiral of the Leeward Islands but he was astute enough to know that eventually, he and his fellow marauders would be defeated or killed.

The depredations of pirates had grievously impacted powerful men with soft hands and large purses, men who ran banking houses, ports, plantations and governments. Soft hands can still make an iron fist. Pirates were harbingers of uncertainty and business cannot thrive during times of uncertainty. With piracy on the wane, the business of making money flourished as never before.

In May, our fleet set sail for Jamaica.

As the dismal coast of Guinea faded off the *Swallow's* stern, I was reminded of my awkward breakfast with Spavens, Hough and Highlett. In the weeks ahead, I would get to know the officers and men serving under my host. Thanks to Captain Ogle, I spent long and pleasant evenings in the captain's cabin and did my utmost to answer endless inquiries about life with notorious pirates.

Among the officers I was privileged to know, I must give thirty-six year old surgeon John Atkins of the *Swallow* my warmest praise. As Register of the Court during our trial, he vividly remembered the unusual details of my situation. When we met again on the deck of the *Swallow*, he took delight in telling me he was present during the Battle of Cape Lopez, an engagement I longed to forget.

Having read Juvenal, Pope, Horace and Milton, he was truly a deep thinker. He published his book about Africa in 1723 and I later learned of another which arrived in 1735, *A Voyage to Guinea, Brasil and the West Indies*. His philosophy about slavery was extraordinarily radical and he relished testing his unique views with anyone brave enough to rise to the challenge. During these lively debates, Atkins maintained that removing negroes from their homes, where they are at ease, to a strange country, people and language, must be highly offensive to the laws of natural justice and humanity.

His Christian charity was an inspiration to many of us but alas, I was in the small minority who agreed with him.

Atkins told me about the deadly diseases that ravaged the crew of *HMS Weymouth*. Arriving from England in April, 1721, the *Weymouth* cruised the African coast with the *Swallow*. They docked at the Island of Principe, the place where Captain Howell Davis encountered his fatal ambush. According to Atkins, the men lived in tents and the heat and their drinking habits triggered the epidemic.

The first fatality was on September 3.

By October, twenty-six names had been recorded in the book of the dead.

When the *Weymouth* sought refuge at the Cape Coast Castle in late October, forty-five men had passed and the death toll continued through February, the month in which we were captured. Well known first mate Alexander Selkirk, who had survived four years alone on an island in the Pacific, succumbed on December 13, 1721.

The *Weymouth* left England with 240 men and lost 280. The imbalance is explained by men pressed into service from merchant vessels, men reassigned from the *Swallow* and slaves purchased by the Royal Navy.

Had Captain Roberts any inkling of how vulnerable his adversaries truly were, it is more than probable he would have found a way to rally his crew and escape.

Only Captain Herdman of the *Weymouth* and a miniscule remnant of his crew still lived. Herdman had served as President of the Admiralty court. One of the midshipman told me his captain was so desperate for replacements he purchased fifty negroes from General Phipps, one of the trial judges and commander of the Cape Coast Castle.

The manpower shortage was still acute and dozens of slaves were amongst Ogle's prize fleet; the *Royal Fortune,* the *Ranger* and the *Little Ranger.* When I saw these vessels under sail, I was overwhelmed by emotion. My melancholy arose from my belief that Cheddar and Neptune, and many more former pirates, were *sailing their former ships.*

These skilled sailors were proud men but they were destined for the cane fields and sugar factories where they would live an average of seven years. Any defiant soul who ran away faced whippings, castration and death. Recalcitrant rebels were slowly burned, often for days on end.

Atkins was the source of another revelation. After a sumptuous June supper, he told me Ogle had purloined the Whydah gold dust. Gathering my wits, I shared the details of our walk through the Cape Coast Castle garden and my embarrassment about the governor's boots. We were destined to remain in the dark as to why Ogle's perfidy was ignored by his benefactors. Surely they knew. Either way, Ogle had proven time and again that he was intelligent and resourceful, some might say brilliant.

He was knighted by King George I, the only officer in the history of the Royal Navy to be afforded such an honor for his stellar service in fighting the scourge of piracy.

Two days before we reached Port Royal, Captain Ogle, without mentioning the Whydah gold, praised me for my discretion and presented me with a substantial sum in gold and silver coins. He made me promise to send him a letter on my arrival in Boston. I thanked him sincerely for all he had done and wished him continued success and good fortune. Years later, in addition to his array of prestigious awards and accolades, Ogle learned of the reward for the capture of pirates. Pirate captains were worth one hundred pounds down to seamen who were valued at twenty.

Ogle was unaware of the reward when he seized the *Ranger* and the *Royal Fortune*.

Having captured and killed hundreds of wanted men in the space of a few days, including one live captain, minus a leg, the reward paid to Ogle and his crew exceeded the value of the Whydah gold by a substantial amount.

Sir Chaloner Ogle retired as a Vice Admiral to enjoy the rewards bestowed by his monarch and his powerful friends in trade and commerce. I imagined him enjoying his retirement in a splendid English garden.

As was true when I was kidnapped by pirates, there were aspects of my life I kept to myself.

We must now lift the curtain on certain heretofore murky events.

During the long night before they were shot, Burgess and Jennings spent hours alone with Wales. Before Wales departed the

Royal Fortune to assume command of the *Caerphilly Castle*, Wales hurriedly pulled me saide and told me about their drunken midnight confessions.

In Whydah, Wales allowed how he knew in minute detail about the loot the two miscreants managed to carry off the ship. The chest containing the crew's accumulated plunder was practically emptied. Wales told Roberts of the calamity, but he dared not tell anyone else. The captain worried the crew might seek vengeance on Wales, who was responsible for keeping the treasure safe. Roberts also feared he might lose his position as captain if the men discovered the truth, so they agreed to keep the news to themselves. Wales resolved to ascertain the location of the stolen wealth but using traditional methods of torture would be messy and alert the crew that something was amiss. Moreover, the crew would not have accepted the accidental death of two men during the night, one maybe, but not two.

A lighter touch was needed.

Nothing had been found on either escapee when they were hauled back aboard the ship so it was assumed Burgess and Jennings used their own money for bribes—even though it was their idiotic failure to pay a two-pound bribe to LeSage that foiled their entire scheme.

So, where was this vast treasure?

Several bottles of fine rum loosened the condemned men's lips.

Wales did not tell his captain everything.

Only Wales and I knew about the location of the haul and I was too smart and too scared to share the secret.

It would be some time before the enormous significance of this betrayal, because it was a betrayal, was fully known to me.

When I asked Wales why he was telling me, he said it was unlikely he would survive long enough to benefit from his secret knowledge. If he were killed, he could not abide the thought of this vast booty being lost for eternity. Wales believed if I survived it was unlikely I would be hanged, as I was wholly innocent. He entrusted me with precise directions to the treasure and asked me to promise to use the loot wisely in the event I should ever lay hands on it.

We shook hands and I presented him Woodes Rogers' book, reeling from his brisk confession and its implications.

Burgess and Jennings told Wales they buried two canvas bags filled with gold, silver and jewels—topazes, Colombian emeralds, pearls and diamonds; hundreds of diamonds.

The deserters were rightfully afraid if they were captured with this immense plunder they would be murdered forthwith. They had the rare foresight to bury the bags before their apprehension.

Burgess and Jennings were being watched by islanders hired by Wales for this purpose. If the islanders who tracked the escapees had suspected that the bags they carried were full of treasure, it is certain that Burgess and Jennings and the loot would have vanished into oblivion. Luckily it was pitch dark that night.

Still I had to wonder. Had the islanders seen or heard digging and gone back later? Even Burgess and Jennings would not have known the answer.

The question remained, was the treasure still there?

Chapter 20

Cristo Blanco

WE GLIDED INTO THE FAMED harbor in Port Royal, Jamaica on August 24, 1722 while I admired the shimmering sapphire haze over the stately Blue Mountains, just off the starboard bow.

I had never been to this former pirate haven, much changed after the earthquake of 1692, which had all but rendered the Port Royal of old a modern day Atlantis.

Mr. Atkins, the surgeon, shared a vivid description of Port Royal, one written over twenty years prior by another visitor who arrived armed with a pen. The author, Ned Ward, published a pamphlet about his impressions when he returned to London in 1697. He called it *"A Trip to the West Indies"*. According to Mr. Ward, Port Royal was "the dunghill of the universe, the refuse of creation, a cesspit, the nursery of heaven's judgments, the receptacle of vagabonds, a sanctuary for bankrupts, the close-stool for the purges of prisons, as hot as hell and as wicked as the Devil." Is it any wonder that pirates had loved Port Royal almost as much as Port Royal had loved its pirates?

But those halcyon days of hedonism waned way due to the power of nature's periodic wrath and the heavy guns of His Majesty's Royal Navy.

As we drew near, the new reality made itself manifest in the guise of two tarred bodies wrapped in chains, hanging on either side of the harbor entrance. Everyone on board knew they were pirates but I did not bother to ask their names. It was too reminiscent of the grisly scenes we left behind at the Cape Coast Castle. Lest anyone doubt the efficacy of the ongoing war, pirates hung like macabre trophies in the harbors of London, Boston, Charles Town, Nassau and St. Kitts, Once again, in my expanded view of the ways of the world, these displays said more about the hypocrisy of nations claiming to be civilized than they did about the bad men coated in tar and pitch.

The first thing I did was to post a short letter to Constance. I paid a pound to send it on a merchant vessel bound for New York by way of Bermuda. If the letter reached New York it would reach Boston in a matter of days. To give you an idea of how dear that tariff was, during those times a servant girl earned five pounds a year. I addressed it to "Constance Sacker—Boston" but I was unsure of her abode, her present name and her feelings. Realizing she may have found another during my sojourn, I offered to waive any claim to her affections although my own feelings for her were undiminished. I told her I was in Jamaica, had some unfinished business to attend to which would delay me, and no matter what had happened during my long enforced absence, I looked forward to seeing her face again. After much trepidation and uncertainty, I signed it 'your happy and humble friend'. Despite everything, I still carried her letter, a tattered paper I had come to view as one of two sacred talismans. The other was something I kept to remind me of the Vicar.

Word quickly spread throughout the port that a strange young man was interested in sailing to Hispaniola. It was said this impatient fellow was willing to pay a substantial sum for passage. I grew increasingly angry at the greedy captains who were more than willing to take me but demanded a king's ransom for the privilege. One of the landsmen I met told me Pensacola in Florida had been ceded to Spain. He said a Spanish vessel loaded with ironwood, rum and sugar was sailing to Havana and on to Pensacola. It was due to depart in two days. Perhaps the captain would divert his ship to accommodate me.

Senor Salvador Alvarez de Gonzalez was listed in the harbor manifest as the Master of the *Santa Rosa*. All I had to do was find him. I began my search in waterfront taverns and eventually found him, with some of his crew, carousing in the Cross of Diamonds. I am not superstitious but I thought this might be a promising sign. Searching for a man in a tavern in Port Royal is no small task. Before the devastating earthquake, there had been a public house for every ten residents. While the numbers had diminished, there were still dozens and for every tavern, or so it seemed, there was a punchy house full of harlots in close proximity. Captain Gonzalez spoke broken English and with my weak Spanish, we reached an acceptable agreement which included me working on board his galleon. Maybe fortune was smiling on me as he had lost three of his men to fever in less than a fortnight.

It is strange that men must die for me to achieve my ends.

We sailed August 26, a scant two days before a powerful hurricane devastated Jamaica and left five feet of water in Port Royal, killing hundreds. In keeping with a long standing pattern, hundreds more would perish in the aftermath from thirst, starvation and disease.

The *Royal Fortune* and the *Ranger,* now prizes, were part of the fleet of merchant ships, slavers and Royal Navy warships who followed *HMS Swallow* across the Atlantic. The *Swallow,* minus its masts, which were cut down as the storm arrived, survived the torrential rains and horrific winds but the former pirate ships were mercilessly driven under the cliffs at Salt Pan Hill. It took the hurricane an hour to reduce both vessels to matchsticks. If God's wrath toward the multitude of sinners in Port Royal was to blame for the storm, it seemed that the sinners always managed to find an edge. The survivors would mourn and rebuild; that too was part of the pattern.

The men on the *Santa Rosa* could not, of course, know the real purpose of my visit to Hispaniola. In short, I needed a ruse. While seeking transport as I wandered Port Royal, I described a man who I claimed had robbed and murdered my brother, then this vile man fled to a fishing village on the island of Hispaniola. I asked people if they knew the village, or the island, and I even asked now and again if they knew of such a man. Taking care not to overdo it, I never came out and said I intended to seek vengeance and kill this man, that was without a doubt. A drunk sailor got caught up in my yarn and offered to go with me on the condition that if we killed the man, I would pay him a bonus of thirty pounds. The intoxicated fellow was kind enough to forego any fee if the murderer could not be found or otherwise escaped my righteous scheme to obtain vengeance.

During my time ashore, I found a carpenter. In the event I found anything of value, I would need a place to hide it. Sean Maloney had lived in Port Royal for thirty years. When it came to wood, he was a master.

Maloney, using a drawing I provided, modified a sea chest to my particular specifications. It was wood with black iron fittings and ornate hinges, as are most standard chests of similar size and function. It was substantial, standing two feet tall and almost three feet wide. It was a little more than a foot deep, forming a rectangle, flat on the top. What made this chest special was the hidden compartment he added at my bidding. Many chests have a false bottom so that would not do. My sea chest had a cleverly constructed panel which slid up and down slots created for this purpose. When the faux panel was in place, it fit securely in the back and left a hollow space a generous inch deep. A second piece of wood was precisely crafted to fit snugly in this gap and it could only be removed using a sturdy blade or chisel. When this strip of wood was forced back in place, the hidden compartment was nearly invisible to anyone unaware of these modifications.

Even empty the chest had heft but I filled the hiding place with sand. The chest itself was packed with cheeses and a change of clothes. When the loaded chest was carried on the *Santa Rosa*, the men carrying it chided me, in broken English, about its weight. With a straight face, I told them I was carrying cannon balls I had collected during my travels. The pair found this intentionally ridiculous explanation so humorous they would see me in passing and hold up round shot once or twice a day, poking each other and laughing at themselves. Forced to join them so as to avoid any hint of suspicion, I pretended to enjoy the joke which, in reality, I found utterly maddening. It is not because I am thin-skinned or lack a sense of humor, rather, I was deathly afraid of drawing undue attention to the unusual weight of the chest.

When Maloney offered to sell me a lock for an additional fee, I told him that locks are easily broken. Locks also signal to the unscrupulous that the owner of the chest has something valuable he seeks to protect. A chest without a lock offers less temptation. Learning about unscrupulous men is inevitable when you go to sea lest you think that pirates are the only thieves on the ocean. I said no thank you to the lock but gave him the additional fee to insure his silence.

During our short trip to Hispaniola, we saw precious little of the deadly weather, departing in the nick of time and thanks to my skills, we had no problem finding the tiny fishing village clinging to the southern coast.

Captain Gonzalez sent me ashore with one man, an experienced seaman from Barbados named Cristobal. Cristobal and I pulled the small longboat out of the surf where it sat listing from side to side in the shingle. He pointed to some trees where he could sit, sheltered from the sun, as the waves gently washed onto the shore. With Cristobal lounging in the shade, I made a show of visiting with some men in the fishing village. I dare not look to see if he saw me but assumed he was curious about my intentions and further assumed he had heard the rumor about my brother's murderer. My instincts told me he was watching closely. The villagers unwittingly played their part, making gestures while I asked about the terrain, the creek and the local fishing conditions. The villagers said the stream I was looking for was known as 'Murder Creek'. I would use this information about the name of the creek to good effect when I returned to the *Santa Rosa*, with or without treasure.

I carried a large bag with several cheeses, some of which I gave to the fishermen. As long as I returned with the same bag, even if it was full, Cristobal would not be driven to ask questions.

Leaving Cristobal, the white sand, scattered driftwood and broken seashells behind, I used the directions and clues Wales provided and began my trek, taking extreme precautions to make sure I was not being followed.

If anyone ever tries to sell you a pirate treasure map, run. Pirates may forget the names of their parents but they can remember where they hide valuables and none but a madman would be foolish enough to make or even possess a genuine map. If treasure maps lead anywhere it's to some fool's untimely and felonious demise. My rational and practical mind tended to believe Burgess and Jennings might be having it on with Wales. After all, they would have sworn they gave the treasure to Moors driving a camel caravan if they believed the information would procure them rum to sooth the pain of their last night amongst the living.

These were the instructions Wales gave me which to this day remain etched in my memory.

From the top of the first ridge overlooking the creek, find the highest point due north on the second ridge. The second ridge is where I was captured so when Wales told me the story, it was easy to picture. Climb to this point and from there, follow the path west until you reach a crude statue of white stone which supposedly resembles Christ Jesus. The statue, which stands about four feet tall, is white, but with all due respect, it bears no likeness to any accepted image of Our Redeemer, an error easily made by unlearned sinners Burgess and Jennings. The forlorn statue more closely resembles a well fed friar and it stands on the south side of the path, surrounded by flat stones. So, even if the statue was gone, the flat stones would provide the necessary reference point. The deserters were not worried about coming back in years but in days. Standing with your back to the statue at night, find the North Star. Having been a navigator, I did not need the help of the North Star to know my compass. For reasons of self-preservation, I did not want to be digging for treasure or carrying it back to the *Santa Rosa* in the dark of night. Just to be safe, I brought a compass. Walk twenty paces to the edge of the woods and look for a solitary flat gray stone, about the size of a man's head, lying just beneath the dirt. I found this stone by kicking the dirt away with my foot. One of the men, Jennings I think, had carved a crude 'V' on the underside of the stone. The two bags were said to have been wrapped in oilcloth and buried about two feet deep.

After finding the gray stone and turning it over, my heart began to race. There was a V scratched on the underside. I was in the right place. Resisting the impulse to start digging, I walked about a hundred yards up and down the path in each direction to verify that I could dig unobserved. You can imagine my thoughts as I walked.

Satisfied that I was being watched only by the stone friar at my back, I used a heavy metal serving spoon to remove the dirt. To my enormous surprise, the earth had been disturbed by another, as the soil beneath the stone was not at all compacted. I could not cease worrying how tragic it would be to have come this far only to find nothing for my troubles.

While I fretted about having arrived too late, the spoon struck something, something substantial enough to bend the handle. I had dug little deeper than a foot. There was something in the hole and it was neither root nor rock. I know this because whatever it was gave when I pushed on it with the spoon.

I got up, took a few deep breaths and looked anxiously up and down the path. It was tranquil and cool droplets of sweat trickled down my throbbing temples. A few buzzing bees and large yellow and blue butterflies were busy visiting the pink and white flowers on the thick bushes along the path. It was near ten o'clock. Getting back down on my knees I dug deeper and pulled up a waterproof bag which I recognized as having come from the *Royal Fortune*. My recognition of the bag came as no surprise but what did shock me to my core was the realization that it was the very bag Wales had been carrying when he said goodbye in the tumult of Whydah, long after Burgess and Jennings had met their end.

My hands shook uncontrollably. I unfolded the bag. Knotted strands of cordage, singed black around the frayed edges, fell to the ground. It was the remnant of a homespun fishing net. The bag also held the book by Woodes Rogers, the edition signed by Captain Carey. I laughed out loud. No wonder the soil was loose. Wales had been here, or at least someone acting as his agent, and that someone put a burnt net in the bag along with the book.

In no uncertain terms, Wales had left me a message. His days as a pirate were over and he was no longer on the account.

It was a message only I would have understood.

According to the story Wales extracted from Burgess and Jennings there were two bags of plunder. Wales must have taken one. He left the other, a heavy bag, and I strained to pull it out of the hole so I could inspect its contents.

What I saw in the bag was beyond imagining and I vividly recall my knees nearly gave way.

"Bless you Wales, God bless you." I muttered this repeatedly to the butterflies and bees in a subdued voice, then I said a silent prayer, threw the bent spoon far into the woods and joyously kicked some dirt back into the hole.

When I returned to the village with the bag of treasure draped over my shoulder, the sun was not yet directly overhead. The friendly villagers gave me some fresh fish which I squeezed to draw out blood so as to rub spots on my clothes and my arms, being careful again to avoid overkill. I tossed the fish into the brush. When I nudged Cristobal with my toe to wake him up, I was gruff and cursed him for falling asleep. He saw the blood and my demeanor and offered his apologies.

He was afraid of me and as a result, the bag went unnoticed.

Cristobal tried to induce me to speak but I was sullen and silent. He spoke to himself in Spanish and hurriedly pushed the boat into the water, without my help or even an offer on my behalf. I caught him nervously looking at the fresh blood then looking at me to see if I had noticed. Once I climbed in, he began to row. I waited until we were fifty yards from shore. My back was to Cristobal as I was seated in the stern, my eyes glued to the beach. Pulling a dagger from my boot, I dangled it over the side then loosened my grip and let it go into the water, pretending that I did not want Cristobal to see what I was doing. He rowed with admirable vigor but in respectful silence and when we got back aboard the *Santa Rosa,* Captain Gonzalez greeted me and asked me if all had gone well. I fixed him with an impassive gaze and answered with an enigmatic "it is finished". Having never seen a play, I thought my acting had been sufficient for my limited purposes.

My insides were bubbling. I was burning with impatience to get the heavy bag below where I could make a quick inventory of what I carried and secure it in the secret compartment of the sea chest. The captain ordered his bosun to get us under sail and I told the captain I had to piss but would meet him on the quarterdeck.

Carefully climbing down the ladder, I first made sure no one was present in the area where I slept. All was quiet. With my back to the bulkhead, I lifted open the top of my sea chest having situated myself behind a row of curtains the crewmen used to achieve a modicum of privacy.

Listening intently, I waited a few tense seconds before I felt safe enough to pull out the horizontal piece of wood covering the hidden compartment.

The thin strip of wood popped out and I tipped the chest to empty the sand from the hollow cavity, replacing the sand with gold, silver and handfuls of precious gems. It took less than a minute but that minute seemed to last a very long time. Using some of the sand to fill the gaps, so nothing would rattle when the chest was moved about or unloaded, I securely replaced the long wooden plug. I scooped up the bulk of the loose sand in my cupped hands, carried it to the head and dropped it into the sea from which it came.

A fly on the wall, and there were many, would have watched in wonder as a man grinning from ear to ear dropped sand through a hole where men relieved themselves and thought that man a raving lunatic.

With effort, I stifled my smile and worked to dismiss troubling doubts about the wisdom of my decision to dispense with a heavy lock. There were so many gold and silver coins they could not fit in the secret compartment. I wrapped the loose coins in my spare clothes. If a thief stole the coins, the remainder of the immense treasure I had in my possession would, with luck, remain undiscovered.

Later that afternoon I presented Cristobal with the last of my cheeses as a sort of peace offering. He thanked me profusely and I held my finger to my lips to insure his silence. He nodded his understanding and eagerly said "*si, si.*" I was confident he'd told his version of our unusual visit to the beach to anyone who would listen. When I went back on deck and stood at the rail, I stared at the island as we sailed, fighting with all my might to look morose and preoccupied.

While you may rest assured I was preoccupied, I was anything but morose.

Since July, 1720, many were the dreary days and never-ending nights during which I cursed Fate without mercy or reservation. On this magical day and henceforth, had it been within my power, I would have made humble and contrite offerings to appease Fate with the hope that in the future, my previous ingratitude would not rekindle her ire. As I had learned on many unforgettable occasions, Fate can instantly change a man's life or end it without warning or reason.

On this glorious day, thanks to Wales, Providence and a good bit of preparation, I was suddenly wealthy beyond my wildest imaginings.

The foaming sea, the azure sky, the white towering clouds, even the dark mass of green trees on the shrinking coast seemed brighter in color and vibrancy than ever before. I knew the world around me had not changed, just the way I was seeing it.

After a short and uneventful stop in Havana we sailed on for Pensacola, landing in north Florida on September 10, 1722.

During the voyage, now that I was rich, I said many a silent thanks to King George, Captain Ogle and even Governor Woodes Rogers for reducing the threat of piracy in the waters between Hispaniola and our destination. By virtue of the plethora of hanged and tarred corpses standing guard at the entrance to the world's major harbors, the risk of losing my sea chest to pirates was considerably less than it would have been when I was captured two long years ago.

Pensacola was still oppressively hot during the day and hungry mosquitoes moved in clouds and swarms. In my ebullient mood, these unpleasant conditions were mere trifles. There were times I felt like I was walking on air.

As I scoured the seafront in search of passage to Boston, I found myself engaged in conversation with a nondescript man of indeterminate age and pedigree who claimed to have served on the disease stricken *HMS Weymouth* during the time Captain Ogle was searching for Captain Roberts up and down the coast in Guinea. The man said his name was Joe Smythe and he had been invalided out of the Royal Navy after numerous bouts with dropsy and fever. His watery eyes and wax like skin served to corroborate his claims of ill health.

I'd spent countless hours with Captain Ogle and his men, so it was not long before I starting spotting holes in Smythe's ramblings. For one, he had never heard of a surgeon by the name of Atkins. He also had trouble remembering the name of the island of Principe and tried to tell me it was located near the Bight of Benin. Maybe his mind was permanently addled by disease, a common enough trait among those severely inflicted. Smythe did possess a healthy capacity for drink and he was enjoying one ale after another at my expense. One thing was clear, the man knew things about Roberts, the *Royal Fortune* and particularly Captain Ogle that were not common knowledge.

As we passed the time, Smythe heaped praise on me for my hospitality and generosity and said he was devoted to helping me get to Boston. The man was growing tiresome and as night fell, I realized my time had been wasted. A feeling that the man was a deserter had been gnawing at me. It occurred to me that he had not sailed back to Port Royal when I did which left open the basic question. If he was not on the *Swallow* and its small flotilla, how did he get all the way from Africa to Florida?

Smythe sensed my growing unease even though he was drunk. He unexpectedly clasped my hand in both of his and said "why kind sir, I don't believe I've ever had the pleasure of knowing one so kind. You're a true prince. What may I call you?"

His method of taking my hand in this remotely feminine way sufficed to make the hair on the back of my neck stand up and what's more, the look in his eyes communicated something beyond the superficial fellowship of sailing men enjoying a few pints. Smythe's voice was suffused with mock sincerity, of that I had no doubt. I even had the fleeting thought that he had intentions of trying to rob me, which I confess does sound far-fetched. Perhaps these dark and dismal thoughts were triggered by the private knowledge that I had become one of the wealthiest men in the colonies, a status known only to me but one I had yet to embrace. These unsettling worries got the better of me and before I could recover my wits I said, "my name is Harry Glasby."

I realized my slip immediately.

Smythe gently let go of my hand and gawked at me with a mixture of confusion and surprise. The ale made it difficult for him to focus and to make full use of his memory. He pointed his finger at me, shakily, saying my name again to try to cut through the fog. His gnarly finger suddenly shot up in triumph. Something connected. "Hmmm, Glasby. Say now, weren't you captain of that big pirate ship, eh? I knew that name was familiar." He was not shouting but he had raised his voice to celebrate his achievement. Luckily, it was not crowded and no one was paying us any attention.

I spent the next few minutes trying to convince him he had misunderstood me. He knew the name, that much was certain, but not my face. When he repeated my name back to me, I went blank and could not create a similar sounding or remotely credible substitute. Smythe did not push the matter but my conundrum was worsened by my perception that he did not believe my denials. Buying him one more ale and some rum for insurance, I told him I had to answer nature's call. I got up, settled the bill and hurried out the back. The night air was thick but it was cooler and I briskly walked along a bricked lane toward the harbor. There were few clouds and the three-quarter moon had risen, painting a long shimmering golden lane on the gently rippling water.

Once I was certain Smythe had not tried to follow me, I was able to relax and enjoy the serenity which served to calm my frayed nerves.

Sitting on a stone wall, still warm from the day time sun, I looked at the tall masts and rigging silhouetted against the moonlit sky. The air was not as still by the shore. I watched twirling and circling moths, maneuvering in the light breeze as they endeavored to hurl themselves into the light of the stern lanterns.

My future would depend on Constance but any uncertainties about her were slightly offset by the value of the treasure hidden in my chest. It had to be immense and such a sum would make our lives much easier, to be sure. Even a drunken pirate languishing in a brothel would find it hard to spend so much money. It would take sustained effort and two or three lifetimes to squander such a sum. If nothing else, pirates can teach a man how not to behave by the poor example they set.

Smythe had unknowingly done me a service. My face was known to some, my name was known to many. How often had terrified men seen me at sea or even in some random seaport, surrounded by pirates? Such men would often sail in and out of Boston. Men like the fresh faced Alistair Campbell, the taciturn Captain Kane, and all those other men who had seen my face in Whydah, not to mention men like Atkins, Ogle and dozens of men and officers on board the *Swallow*. Who knew in what year or under what circumstances our paths might cross and it would only take one such encounter to unmask me.

To this day, I do not know what became of my shipmates who had been forced to leave the *Samuel* and serve on the consort vessel that long ago day in July. There was my friend Captain Cary, the lucky Irishman Rafferty Moran, and many more. A great many men knew the name 'Glasby' and who among them would not know I had sailed with pirates? It mattered not what they believed about me or even whether they wished to bring me to account for myself during those years at sea.

Had the Admiralty trial been in Boston instead of the Cape Coast Castle, the situation might have been different. But what of the money? How can that poor orphan Harry Glasby, the one we all gave up for dead, how can he claim he was forced into piracy when he keeps spending money? If just one inquisitive eyebrow went up, my world could implode. There were an infinite number of distressing scenarios in which the stolen fortune could be taken from me. For the sake of Constance, I was not willing to take that risk.

I had come too far and risked too much.

Admiring the back of a freshly painted fishing vessel, I saw the stern bore the name *Prescott's Fancy*.

I had a sea chest full of stolen plunder.

My parents were gone, I had no family and with my riches, I could live nearly anywhere I wanted and I could live in style and still sleep at night. Stealing a new name would be easy and would solve many potential problems.

From that moment on I would be known to one and all as Harry Prescott.

Chapter 21
Sophia

GETTING ACCUSTOMED TO MY NEW name took longer than expected. It's uncomfortable, like being forced to wear a larger man's clothes and his equally ill-fitting shoes. A man would say 'Mr. Prescott' and I would look about, waiting for someone to speak up, only to realize it was me they were addressing. This was particularly embarrassing when the name was repeated. On one such occasion, I tried to convince a gentleman I'd served as a gunner and suffered damage to my hearing.

Having learned in Port Royal to be more circumspect about my true desires, I found a merchant ship in need of men and signed on as a seaman. The ship was to sail for Charles Towne as it was then known. Once there, I was confident I could find passage to Boston.

The master of the ship that carried me and my treasure out of Pensacola was Captain Samuel Endicott. Endicott had a foreboding air about him with bushy yellowing eyebrows and stringy hair, greasy at the roots, like tallow. There were deep crow's feet pointing to his gray eyes, a permanent record of his habit of squinting at everyone.

His upper lip protruded like the beak of a turtle and I do not believe I ever heard him laugh. He hailed from Salem and his vessel was the *Palladium*, which proved to be a fast sailer, much to my delight. Insofar as character is concerned, Endicott was a good man, a sound captain and he seemed to think sufficiently well of me. As evidence of this, he tried diligently to retain my services as a crewmember.

After unloading his cargo of molasses, brandy and cloth, he planned to sail to England with rice, indigo and a quantity of deer skins. He never made it. Months later I learned that Endicott and the *Palladium* were lost in a storm near the island of Bermuda, en route to Liverpool.

During my short time with Endicott, I led everyone to believe I had business in the Carolina Colony and intended to return to Pensacola.

One more voyage and I would be home.

Visions of my anticipated reunion with Constance played themselves out in my mind. There was nothing I could do about this and not all were uplifting. Most consisted of fanciful vignettes of her running down a dirt path, lined with blooming flowers of every hue. Gasping, she threw herself into my arms, covering my cheeks with tearful kisses and filling my ears with a torrent of endearments. Less persistent were tableaus of her walking arm in arm along the waterfront with an impossibly handsome sea captain.

Charleston was a growing seaport. A forest of tall masts in the harbor rose up and down with the tides. The wide avenues were bustling with lively vendors, beautiful carriages and fashionably attired women. Stately mansions and manicured gardens were cloisters for plantation owners fleeing heat, humidity and mosquitoes. Gigantic oaks festooned with Spanish moss shaded the wide thoroughfares like tunnels, the walkways lined with wrought iron gates and tall brick walls, many with intricately carved cornices and capstones. The inhabitants put a premium on style and beauty. Boston, in contrast, was home to sterner stock who put a higher value on practicality and function, men and women who by temperament found ostentation a close cousin to outright sinfulness. In the event Constance was attached to an impossibly handsome sea captain, Boston had no strong hold on me and the risk of being recognized could not be eliminated by the expedient of taking a new name.

Charleston, I discovered, had much to offer beyond anonymity. If I was destined to live my life without Constance, it would be in the Carolina Colony.

Ships regularly sailed from Charleston to Boston and I chose the sloop *Isabella* because it was fast and she was to sail for Boston in three days.

During my short stay, I made my first substantial investment. Locating a trustworthy agent to take some of the gems in my possession and sell them at a fair price was not as difficult as I'd imagined. His name was Rutledge Iain Lee and he had the discretion not to ask too many questions. Behind his pleasant and boyish visage was the shrewd mind of a businessman. He was a bright and ambitious man who took the long view, a perspective that may have been influenced by the seven young children who called Mr. Lee father. Mr. Lee conducted business out of a well-appointed but tastefully decorated set of rooms on King Street. Our agreement paid him a commission of fifteen percent.

When I boarded the *Isabella* as gentleman Henry Prescott, I owned a substantial two story warehouse on Bay Street. The property happened to be just north of Broad Street and the provost exchange where scores of pirates had been imprisoned before they were tried and hanged.

It was to be the first of many such investments and as the Carolina Colony prospered, so did I. When my agent died prematurely, much to my dismay, his eldest son, Rutledge Iain Lee, II, took over my interests. Our partnership has been and remains mutually beneficial.

Early October, 1722, found me standing on Long Wharf in Boston.

The wharf was aptly named and it had been enlarged during my absence. It started at the foot of State Street and extended a half mile into the harbor. The sight of so many familiar scenes warmed my aching heart, the sounds, the smells, it was pleasantly overwhelming. My first order of business was to find a secure place to store my belongings. The storehouse I selected was one familiar to me and I took the chance that no one there would recognize my face. The building was unchanged but thankfully the proprietor and I were strangers. I came dangerously close to signing the log and storage agreement as Harry Glasby.

From there, I found a public house and sat outside in the cool air drinking coffee.

Ships of every description moved about in the harbor and all manner of men and horses were busy with trolleys and block and tackle, loading and unloading cargo. I had sat like this for hours on end as a youth. What would these workmen and seafarers think if they knew the man sipping his coffee had sailed with blood-thirsty pirates from the islands and ports of the Caribbean to the wilds of Africa and the brooding Cape Coast Castle?

Walking the cobbled streets, nostalgia and yearning overcame me and I began to catch glimpses of Constance passing in a carriage or commiserating with a group of young ladies as they emerged from a shop. I saw her from a distance as she turned a corner with a bouquet of late blooming flowers on her arm. Procrastinating, I walked by my boyhood home, the jail and the house on Marlbrough where the Sackers had lived. Seeing these places generated little in the way of sadness or regret as I was not the same man who had been

315

in those places years ago. It was like I had lived two lives, one before I was kidnapped and the one after. My resolve gradually increased as my shadow lengthened. I made my way to King Street and a kind old man pointed out the tidy town home which held the family of sailor Alistair Campbell, the talkative man serving under the velvet fist of Captain Kane.

For a long moment, I stood at the main entrance. I swallowed my reticence, reached up, rang the bell and looked both ways. No one was paying me the slightest notice.

A servant girl who I guessed was near fourteen appeared in the open door and asked how she could help me. I stammered that I was Henry Prescott, just returned from the port of Whydah in Africa. Calming myself, I told her I was fulfilling a promise to bring greetings from Alistair Campbell. My unease made me speak too rapidly. Her eyes lit up at the mention of Alistair and she interrupted me and asked if he was well. I assured her that he was very well indeed, overflowing with youthful vigor and blessed with uncommonly good health. I was escorted into a tastefully furnished front room and invited to sit. The happy girl left and I remained standing, looking at pictures and mementos on the mantelpiece.

Excited voices preceded two women into the room, the older of the pair introduced herself as Mrs. Mary Campbell. She politely and formally presented me to her daughter, Miss Sarah Campbell. My anxiety was such that I nearly presented myself as Harry Glasby and the near miss made me even more anxious. Lady Sarah was Alistair's sister, and according to him, she was a close childhood friend of Constance. Sarah graciously touched my arm and guided me to a chair.

From the outset, it was 'tell us this Mr. Prescott' and 'tell us that Mr. Prescott'. They were naturally full of questions about Alistair, Captain Kane, the flora and fauna of Africa and a catalogue of other topics. My disembodied voice provided accurate but necessarily incomplete answers, omitting some of the most interesting details as pertained to the imaginative abuse of slaves, pirate atrocities and the nocturnal entertainment of burning men alive. Somewhere in the midst of this enjoyable interrogation, they insisted I remain for dinner. It would have been impolite to refuse and I still lacked an acceptable strategy for making inquiries about Constance.

Moreover, I was hungry. I willingly obliged. They were thrilled.

We carried on our conversation until it was time to begin our meal. In my guise as their guest of honor, Mrs. Campbell invited me to send up a prayer. I offered praise and thanksgiving and requested the standard blessings to the best of my ability. Concentrating to provide my hosts a suitable prayer, my awkwardness was lessened by a surprise visit from the Vicar's amused ghost, his visage unmarked by the horrible wounds that caused his premature death. In the years to follow, I grew to accept his benevolent appearances whenever I had the privilege of praying out loud.

Our discourse was otherwise rather pleasant but since all my experiences of late involved scores of lost, imprisoned, and hanged pirates, some falsehoods and embellishments escaped from my lips despite the distaste it caused. Just as I was adjusting to my new name, I was learning to temper the truth and adjust it to suit my needs and safeguard my past.

The energetic girl who had greeted me at the door kept us supplied with food and drink. I saw her eavesdropping from the adjacent room, the tedious habit of all servant girls. There must have been a cook somewhere but I never had the privilege of laying eyes on her. The food and the company were excellent and the experience reminded me of what it was like to be back in a world I'd all but forgotten during my captivity.

Eventually, it was my turn to ask questions.

"Miss Sarah, Alistair asked if I might seek out a friend or former friend you might know. She was someone of interest to a member of his crew. As to the latter gentleman, I have no name." I was treading lightly.

She wanted to be helpful, "who is the lady?"

My tongue stuck to the roof of my mouth. I wanted to make a fist and pound the table and yell "Constance Sacker damn it". Instead, I dabbed the corner of my mouth with a napkin and said as nonchalantly as I could, "I believe her name is Constance." The words came out well enough but my heel was bouncing under the table like the wings of a hummingbird.

Sarah leaned forward, "you must mean the widow, Constance Glasby." My eyes would not focus and my breath was labored. From that moment, Sarah's words were like waves crashing over the bow, scud blowing into my face and eyes. I sat, staring at her like I had been hit by a hammer. She appeared not to notice my turmoil and launched into a recitation of all she knew about Miss Constance Glasby.

"Constance now lives on Princes Street, with her mother and her baby. Mr. Sacker, a sea captain, went to sea early last winter and has yet to return. He and his entire crew have been given up as lost. We were so very saddened by the latest tragedy—a persistent and unhappy theme for the Sackers." I made a clicking sound with my tongue to express sympathy and gravely shook my head. Sarah smiled, "Constance, dear soul, married a sailor named Glasby." I raised my eyebrows and stifled a grin.

Sarah looked at me and said, "Harry, that was his name—what a coincidence that, I am sure his name was Harry." She was amused that I shared my first name with the unfortunate Mr. Glasby, but as she became more serious in tone and deportment she seemed to derive some sense of self-importance in providing me with the information I had solicited.

Fortified by momentum, I asked Sarah if she knew what had befallen the unfortunate sailor Glasby.

"Poor Mr. Glasby was murdered by pirates on a return voyage from London. It was very horrible, since he was killed before he could see his child. The murdered man would have been about your age. Did you know him?" I shook my head. "Are you sure you cannot remember the name of the sailor who was interested in Constance? Such a pity. Constance was heartbroken. The last time I saw Constance was at the fish market.She looked well. Her child came along too."

Sarah and Mrs. Campbell started bickering in a futile effort to agree on how long ago Constance had been sighted, was it two weeks or was it three? Their uncertainty and their minor disagreement was good-natured. They were enjoying my company and the conversation.

Having learned where Constance lived and the important revelation about her name, I dare not push for more. As to whether we had a boy or girl, this was most immaterial to me. Was I being too cautious about my inquiries? I decided I had navigated the conversation satisfactorily but what if Constance really believed I had been murdered by pirates?

The Campbell ladies expressed their joy at making my acquaintance and would I please return soon and tell them more about my travels? I was noncommittal without being ungrateful. Satisfied they had not the slightest idea who I really was, the evening had been a colossal success. Telling them I could not remember a more delicious meal and had rarely been in such delightful company, I bowed at the waist, thanked them profusely, and moved toward the foyer.

The servant girl materialized to escort me out.

I waited but she did not open the door. She looked to make sure the Campbell women were not within earshot. She was expectant,

319

as if wanting to ask me a question so I made it easy on her. "Is there something you would like to know that your mistresses forgot to ask?" I was consumed by my own thoughts and uninterested in hers.

"The fish market is on Friday," she said, awaiting my reaction. She smiled slyly, "and I saw your foot goin' up and down."

Damn that child, she had insight far beyond her years. "Day after tomorrow," I said. She knew. She unraveled the mystery, perceived the truth and laid me bare.

"Good luck Harry," the girl whispered. She was a mischievous imp. No servant girl in the colony would have referred to me as anything but 'Mr. Prescott' or 'sir'. I was taller than she by a head and now it was my turn to look behind her to make sure we were not being observed, breathing through clenched teeth. She knew I dare not chastise her for her bold lack of decorum or embarrass myself by trying to force the cat back into the bag.

I pulled a silver shilling from my pocket and dropped it in her palm, which she brazenly kept open, shifting her weight back and forth to tell me to hurry. I fumbled for another and dropped it, making a clinking sound in her hand. She would go far in life. She would have made a good pirate. Telling her I had no more coins, she thanked me, winked and wished me good luck. As I left she stood in the threshold and told me to "come by" any time. She waved and rather than appear churlish, I waved in return and heard her laugh.

I walked hurriedly by the darkened house where Constance slept, passing by three times. Constance Glasby no less.

Days and nights in the hold of the *Swallow* and the bowels of the Cape Coast dungeon had passed slowly but nothing could compare with the interminable Thursday leading up to my visit to the Friday fish market.

I was lodging in a room let to me by a sailor's widow. The frail woman kept asking me if I wanted a girl to keep me company. It was how she put food on her table. To bring an end to her entreaties, I told her I was betrothed and she sullenly let the matter drop.

Friday morning broke with a milky haze blanketing the harbor. The fog would fade as sunlight filled the city and warmed the ramshackle stalls in the fish market. I had been up and about a full hour before sunrise. I selected a vantage point to watch the townspeople come in and out of the rows of wooden and canvas shanties, bustling with busy men and women displaying a startling array of cod, bass, oysters, eels, clams and other delicacies. There is a steady hum and pulse to a fish market I still find fascinating.

My plan was to wait until noon. If Constance did not appear or if I was unable to see her in the crowd, I would 'beard the lion' and march to her doorstep. Perched on a small barrel with hot tea and a biscuit, I tore off bits of the edges and fed them to the grateful pigeons, finding I had no appetite. None of the clever phrases I rehearsed suited me, and besides, they all sounded contrived, which they were. Lacking an appropriate way to introduce myself, and being so uncertain about her affections, the temptation to get up and walk away grew stronger. I told myself I was no coward but my fears seemed to mount the longer I thought about all the things that could go awry.

Brushing crumbs off my new black waistcoat, it occurred to me that no one at the Campbell house said Constance visited the fish market with any regularity. My limbs ached from sitting and as the market grew more crowded, it became more difficult to observe the hundreds of people passing through. Stretching my back, I walked toward the opposite end of the market near a row of clam and oyster vendors. After a few strides, I stopped abruptly. An old man walking behind me stepped on my heels, grumbling and pointing at me with the end of his wooden cane.

I saw a young woman.

She had her back to me and carried a flat-bottomed wicker basket over her left arm. It was empty. She wore a light blue dress with full white sleeves, the hem of the garment reached the ground. Her face was framed by a white bonnet in which she had tucked her hair, thin strands peeking out from the side and the rear, the fine auburn tips randomly laying on her white collar.

This was not among the countless visions I had had about our reunion. Breathing rapidly, I longed to see her face.

She turned her head to point at something and I saw her profile.

I remembered Constance as a thin but healthy girl and the person I watched, transfixed, was a woman, her hips were wider and she had filled out in a most pleasing way. She was speaking to a rotund middle-aged red-faced woman standing behind rows of gleaming cod. I was too far away to hear them but they seemed to be having a conversation as neither of them was paying any mind to the fish.

Commanding my feet to carry me forward, I approached from an angle and when I was about fifteen steps away, the woman glanced toward me out of the corner of her eye but turned back to the talkative fishmonger.

I took a few more steps and she snapped her head again and stared at me in shock and wonder. My fears vanished, maybe because she was alone but maybe because my heart was so full of joy, there was room for nothing else.

My entire face broke out in a smile, I nodded at her and began to raise my hands.

She dropped her basket and grabbed the folds of her long dress and rushed to me, wrapping her arms around me and drawing me close, my chin resting on the top of her bonnet. I embraced her and she began to sob, her face buried in my chest. I put my hand on the back of her head. Retreating a step, she took my hands in hers and looked into my eyes.

She wiped away her tears with her right hand then grasped my hand again, squeezing my fingers.

Through her tears and her disarming embarrassment, she confessed, "I'm afraid to let you go." She reddened as she looked at me and bounced a little on the balls of her feet.

I pulled her to me, "one day I'll tell you all the clever things I'd planned to say." There were times when I was at sea I could not remember her face but she was more beautiful than I had dared imagine. Her dark green eyes sparkled, her mouth a bit wide, her lips full. She had a tiny dimple in the center of her chin and a delicate neck that had not changed since I had last kissed it.

"Harry, I missed you more than words can say. Do you know I am called Constance Glasby?" She was curious about my response to this announcement as she could not know what I knew and what I did not.

Where to begin?

"Yes, I did know that but only learned of it two days ago. Did you get my letter?" I asked so I would know how much to tell her of my travels since Jamaica.

"I did," she said, "it came as such a surprise."

"So you know I was in Jamaica. I'll tell you about the business I had when I left the island." I paused because she was clearly perplexed. "What's wrong?"

"Dearest, your letter said nothing of Jamaica. You wrote of many things but you seemed afraid to tell me where you were." Her reply was confusing and I told her so, asking when she received the letter.

"Harry, my dear Harry. Your blessed letter arrived the week after Christmas."

Christmas was ten months ago. Something was amiss.

"Constance, the letter was sent in August."

I noticed the fishmonger watching us and nodded to her as if to say everything was well. She nodded back and smiled, revealing three or four lonely teeth.

Constance released my hand and picked up her basket. When she straightened she said, "do you mean August of last year or this summer? Your letter was the first good news I'd had after those evil men took you. I could not bear to think about the tribulations you must have endured but your letter gave me such hope."

I struggled to explain, clumsily wrestling with this unexpected riddle. "I meant August of this year. It's impossible. The letter you describe—it was lost. I did not send it. I sent you a letter *this* August, from Port Royal in Jamaica." As the mention of Port Royal I remembered the news about the hurricane that struck the island two days after I left. The letter from Port Royal must have been destroyed.

She shook her head, still smiling. "Harry, I have one letter only. You will see it. If you sent another it has not found me. With you, my dearest, I am convinced that nothing is impossible. Do you know you have a child? We—have a child."

The cloud about the lost and found letter from New Barcelona drifted away.

"Yes, I do and as you must know, that is among the many reasons I never gave up. I learned about our child in a long ago and remote place but as of yet, no one has said—is it a boy or a girl?"

Constance beamed. She found my admission delightful because it was she who had the pleasure of giving me the news. She rocked up on the balls of her feet again. "Harry Glasby, we call her Sophie. Your daughter is Miss Sophia Glasby. She is as beautiful a little girl as God ever made."

Tears flooded my eyes. "Sophia," I said to myself. I was finding it harder to talk, impossible really. My child would no longer be anonymous to me and no longer would Sophie have to live without her father. I leaned close to her ear. "Constance, I'm not Harry Glasby, I'm Harry Prescott. I will explain. I must say, I have so very much to tell you."

"Well, whoever you are, would you like to meet your daughter?" She gently took my hand and we started to walk.

My throat began to close and my eyes were overflowing, tears were cascading down my cheeks. All I could say was "yes", and that in a hoarse whisper.

Chapter 22
The Prince of Wales

I WAS PRIVILEGED TO MEET two more women at Princes Street that unforgettable day, one was known to me before I'd sailed for London.

The second lady, the little one who bore my name, was a joyous wonder. I fell in love with her instantly. Sophie had her mother's languid eyes and pleasant disposition. The scowling Mrs. Sacker, on the other hand, was aloof and guarded in the extreme. Her initial reaction to my return was understandable but I could see she was grateful I'd survived and come home to Boston. Implicit in this cobweb of cautious optimism was her assumption that I would accept my long term responsibilities to care for Constance and Sophie. I thought my physical presence demonstrated everything about my intentions, but it would take time to win her over. Mrs. Sacker slowly came to tolerate me, a process that was hampered by her skepticism about the story behind my new surname. I told her several of my former captors blamed me for the death of their compatriots in Africa and swore to get their revenge.

The family had endured many hardships while I was away and I had yet to tell anyone I had returned with a fortune. In light of my humble origins, it was only natural that Mrs. Sacker was skeptical about my ability to provide for a family, regardless of my noble intentions.

In addition to the loss of Captain Sacker, I was deeply saddened to learn that Eliza, Constance's sister, had taken ill and died in May. How Constance and her mother persevered in the light of these tragedies gave me a much deeper appreciation of the reservoir of strength they shared.

Until Constance and I could marry, Mrs. Sacker, of course, forbade us from sleeping in the same house, much less the same room. She made it equally plain she disapproved of us being alone together even during daylight hours. Behind her back, I referred to Mrs. Sacker as 'the Puritan' but my intentions were not spiteful or malicious. To avoid undue difficulties and misunderstandings, I slept at the lodging house but spent my days with Constance and Sophie. As my love for my own daughter blossomed, I came to understand more fully the power of Mrs. Sacker's ferocious urge to protect Constance, her only surviving child.

Constance and I were married on Wednesday of the following week. My new mother-in-law, Sophie, and my soon to be former landlady stood in polite attendance. Sophie was bored and the two adults were uneasy attending a wedding where the bride and groom brought their offspring. The landlady seemed surprised to realize my claim of being betrothed was true after all. The brief and unostentatious ceremony took place on October 14, 1722.

During those crisp autumn days, I shared many of my adventures and experiences with Mrs. Sacker and Constance. Privately, I told Constance much more. Admittedly, some of the things I'd done were not seemly, nor was there a pressing reason to reveal the particulars of every barbaric scene I'd witnessed. Any omissions to protect myself or avoid embarrassment were few in number, as I deemed it important to be forthright with Constance who had waited so patiently and faithfully for my return. From time to time she chided me for inconsistencies or gaps in my recitation of events but she did so in a warm and understanding manner. Her deference served only to make me love her more. Lest you wonder, I did tell her about my night of debauchery in New Barcelona and left out nothing. She confessed to enjoying the tale and made saucy jests about my embarrassment and the folly of my drunkenness.

We endeavored in vain to decipher the perplexing conundrum of the lost letter. How did that missive survive, much less get to her? When my curiosity was particularly irresistible, I held the paper up to the sunlight to search for blood, dirt, markings or any other sign that we may have overlooked. On every occasion when I subjected it to close scrutiny, I had to put it away in frustration. The letter reminded me of Mr. Spavens, the pirate without a tongue, the letter was unable or unwilling to speak.

Before the marriage, in the joyous hours we spent talking and walking in Boston, I told Constance everything I knew about Burgess, Jennings, Wales and the treasure. She was fearful harm might come to me from the law or from some of my terrifying former colleagues. More than seventy accused pirates were acquitted during the Cape Coast Castle trial and many knew I hailed from Boston. None would have a reason to suspect me of being privy to the great secret about the missing plunder. It was not impossible that Burgess and Jennings had talked to someone else the night before their execution but in all likelihood, they had not. It was also remotely possible Wales had shared information with another before or after he left me in the harbor at Whydah. This too I found hard to believe.

To counter these fleeting fears, I forced myself to ponder only probabilities, not possibilities.

Having a trusted confidant was a luxury I had not had while living with pirates. All the dark and worrisome possibilities gave rise to some heartfelt discussions and being able to talk with Constance was better than any tonic. She had a maturity beyond her years and I valued her opinions on things great and small. With her capable counsel and innate sagacity, most of my fears were banished but to assuage our guilt, for we knew what we were doing was wrong, we considered ridding ourselves of the wealth by giving it to the poor. Even this would generate risk. Among other things, I would lose my anonymity if I gave away such an enormous treasure and news of such extravagant generosity would have traveled throughout the colonies and beyond, possibly to Captain Ogle and the Admiralty in London. Despite my acquittal in Africa, had the Crown made it their mission, I could still be hanged if the truth about me and the plunder were to surface. Keeping the stolen money was easier, safer and, admittedly, selfish.

When I grew weary of talking about pirates my new wife would stroke my forehead and tell me about Sophie as a baby and how she and Mrs. Sacker created a tale to lend legitimacy to what would otherwise have been a scandal. Not everyone believed Constance was married, nor was it uniformly believed I had been lost at sea, but for the most part, people kept their skepticism to themselves and made allowances.

In the world of seafaring men from Boston and beyond, the story of how I was taken by pirates was well known and the news of my seizure had been printed in the *Boston News Letter*. After a year, few would have cared if I still lived and far fewer would have known the truth. Even doubters would have concluded I had perished or perhaps found piracy to my liking.

These reminiscences pained me because of the sorrow I felt for not being present to marry Constance in the first instance. Constance began calling herself Glasby a few days after she was informed about the events of July, 1720, preparing herself for a future that probably would include accepting my death. When asked, she claimed we were quietly married on the eve of my departure for London. She had few options and the lie tasted more bitter with each retelling. She did it for her unborn child and for her parents, who overcame their anger at her sin and did all within their power to lend credence to the charade. The Sackers were proud people but when it came to the whispers of their self-righteous neighbors and the spite of those who live to gossip, Constance's parents gave her the support she needed and the forgiveness that heals all. Sister Eliza had been enormously unselfish and her sudden death caused immense and unbearable pain.

Mrs. Sacker loved Sophia with all her heart. While this did not make up for the loss of Eliza, the love of a child works in ways we are not fully capable of understanding.

I told Constance about the agonizing and uncertain time we were manacled in the *Swallow* and the Latin phrase gouged in the hull. The hopeful sentiment behind that desperate carving applied to her as much as it did to any of us. *Dum spiro spero*—while I breathe I have hope. With or without the miraculous letter that had brightened her Christmas the year before, the letter that proved I still lived, she swore she had never given up hope that I would return.

Naturally, the letter made it easier to keep hope alive and she conceded that some days had been more trying than others.

Constance would not entertain moving to Charleston as long as Mrs. Sacker lived, but she acknowledged the risks of staying in Boston, particularly since we intended to keep the money. The port of Marblehead, a day's journey from Boston, offered us the things we needed. It would become our new home and give us a clean slate on which to build our future.

Mrs. Sacker's reluctant blessing for the Prescott family migration cost me fifty pounds a year and it was money well spent. Our decision, ironically, gave more credence to my story about vengeful pirates. Thanks to the stipend, she could live comfortably on Princes Street and visit us three or four times a year and Constance could take Sophie to Boston whenever she wished.

I purchased another large storehouse in Charleston on the recommendation of my agent, Mr. Lee, and acquired half an interest in such a venture in New York City, Mr. Lee taking the other half. The income from the warehouses alone was far more than we required to meet our modest needs.

We purchased and improved an ordinary and victualling house on Gingerbread Hill in Marblehead. You would call it a public house and inn. As the village grew and the port became busier, we worked hard and the Lord blessed us with two more children, James and Margaret. Gingerbread Hill became known for revelry, gambling and all the other vices that go wherever sailors congregate.

We were blessed and we prospered beyond our wildest imaginings.

We named our popular public house The Prince of Wales. The worst part of being in a busy port and thus being subjected to a steady stream of rowdy sailors was not being able to tell them about my years as a pirate. Inevitably, I patiently listened to legends about the famed and feared Black Bart and his notorious and diabolical crew. If only they knew.

To my knowledge, Captain Roberts had never been known as Black Bart during his lifetime, it just indicates how stories like his are embellished as they pass from one man to the next. Some said the name did not arise from his deeds but from his dark complexion and his hair, an explanation that had far more credence but less flamboyance.

As the years steadily passed, I too began to think of the legendary pirate as Black Bart. I often wondered how surprised and astonished he would be to find his former first mate with a loving wife and three children, tending to the stolen wealth amassed from the hundreds of prizes he took. It was not the life Black Bart would have chosen but I could not have been more satisfied with my good fortune and the love of my family and kindness of our neighbors.

Of course I had to wonder at it all. Alone among the crew, I had refused to sign the Articles and partake of their ill-gotten spoils. Yet by a series of odd events, their booty ended up in the hands of Harry Glasby, a young mariner from Boston who desperately wanted to get home. Some questions have no answers but Fate still seemed to take pleasure in looking in on me now and again.

One sparkling November afternoon I was idling in the pub and an old white-haired gentleman came in and started giving me the look. This was twenty years ago so it would have been late 1758. Marblehead was much bigger and we were so overcome with work I had started to ask Constance her thoughts about selling the inn and moving back to Boston or possibly New York. She loved our life, accurately stated that Marblehead had been good to us and with more finality than she intended, told me that this was the only home our children had ever known. She did not want to start over in a large city and giving it some thought, I had to agree, not out of deference but because she was right. Our roots had grown deeper than either of us realized and Constance had been wanting to build a new home. Another consideration was the realization that grandchildren were on the near horizon. That endeavor, the new home, not the grandchildren, consumed our energies for the following year and the result was well worth the effort and the substantial expense. We had countless moments of shared humor making up stories about the 'widow's walk' that sat atop our uppermost floor.

These decisions signaled our intentions to remain in Marblehead until we died.

I recognized the distinguished visitor instantly but the shock at seeing him after all those years paralyzed me from top to bottom. Overcoming my disbelief, I joyfully sat at his table, saying not a word. The old man did not merely look at me, rather, he looked into me. It was all I could do not to shout his name in boyish wonder.

I asked if he would care for a pipe. His eyes sparkled, he nodded and said he would not mind a pipe so I got up and fetched one, came back, and watched him smoke for a long minute. Despite the wear on his rough hands and scarred fingers, he handled the lit match like a seamstress wields her needle. When his pipe was lit, he waved the match to extinguish the tiny flame and with a flourish, tossed the smoking splinter over his shoulder where it landed on the stone floor, never taking his eyes off mine. He wore an impish grin and as he smiled, his eyes formed curved quarter moons in his wrinkled skin, deeply scored and weathered by long years at sea.

At last I gave in to his desire to have me strike the first strike, "Valentine, how is that tobacco?"

He took another puff or two and pronounced it "damned fine" tobacco. Lord Valentine Ashplant was smoking in my pub.

Mr. Ashplant left Africa with Wales on the *Caerphilly Castle*, defied the odds and still lived. Here he was in the flesh, paying me a friendly visit. Then the blood curdling thought hit me that he had scoured me out to challenge me in some form or fashion about the treasure. As if sensing my poorly disguised unease he blew a thin jet of smoke at the ceiling before providing me with relief. "If you found some plunder, none could be happier for you than I. Rest easy, I come as your friend." He calmly tapped the bowl of his pipe in his calloused palm and scattered the tiny black ashes on the floor. "Yes sir, damned fine tobacco."

He filled the bowl anew and lit it. He leaned in close to my face, even though the place was near empty. "So, ye call yourself Prescott. Jack Spratt and all that but you will always be Mr. Glasby to me." After he hoarsely chided me, he leaned back, arms folded across his chest, beaming with pleasure. He had the pipe wedged in his back teeth protruding from the corner of his mouth, just like he held it that long lifetime ago when I stood trial for escape and nearly got myself shot.

"Harry Prescott," I reiterated with unintended skepticism, as if I too found my new name to be a bit presumptuous. Mr. Ashplant laughed at that and I laughed too. He repeated it with an air of mock formality, drawing out the last name. We laughed again. During the many hours we were to share, we talked about death and we talked about the Devil. We confessed to having occasional and vivid thoughts that maybe we could go to Hades one day and visit old friends. I accused him of cheating death and the Devil and he said he could accuse me of the same. People wandered in and people left but none took much notice of two old salts in the far corner of the dark pub. The only regret I have is that Constance was visiting her ailing mother in Boston.

Valentine said Wales would approve of the name of the pub. I pointed up and said Wales would more than likely tell me I had done a piss poor job of keeping the pub sign properly painted. When I laid my hand on Valentine's arm to thank him for saving my life he told me there was no need for that but he did want me to know why he had come and how he had found me.

For a man of few words, he had come far in more ways than one.

"Harry, you have long wondered why I interceded for you that day. When Wales left the *Royal Fortune* and I went too, we had grave concerns about the men we left under Captain Roberts. No sooner had we started to work the crew of the newly christened *Caerphilly Castle* when a group of men following a rabble rousing shit confronted Wales about some petty matter. They were challenging their new captain, you see. I pulled the ringleader aside, one called LaPlaga, which I was told meant the plague. I told this LaPlaga if he did it again, he would be a dead man. Before you can say clear the decks the crew called a meeting, voted in a new captain and determined to flee the looming wrath of the Royal Navy and to desert dear ol' Captain Roberts. We sailed west. Along the way, we endured a storm that had our bowsprit aiming at the heavens then plunging as if to spear a whale in the depths of the sea. Two men fell from the rigging and died on the deck. Emerging from the storm, we nearly died of thirst and starvation. The stormy seas damaged our water casks and most of them were half-filled with seawater. I've yet to find a man who can steer a ship like Harry Glasby." He said talking about that perilous voyage always made him thirsty and if I didn't mind, could I bring him another ale.

"We had no way to warn Roberts. Had our flotilla stuck together, I am here to tell you, Roberts in the *Royal Fortune*, Skyrm in the *Ranger* and Wales in the fastest vessel that ever sailed under a black flag, the *Caerphilly Castle*—we might have been able to take on the *Swallow* and the *Weymouth* both—but for sure, we could have outgunned Captain Ogle and the *Swallow*. For sure." He sipped from his mug and studied its contents, "damned fine ale. Where was I?"

"You were exaggerating about the prowess of three pirate ships in a sea battle with one of the finest captains ever to sail a man o' war." I chided him, but not too much.

"Aye, the great Ogle," Ashplant said with mock majesty, rolling his eyes. "You know damned well how long Ogle had to pound the *Ranger* then pound the *Royal Fortune* but fighting all three pirate ships at once? In such a fight, you would not want to wager on the *Swallow* my happy friend. Wales and I, of course, we vowed to abandon the *Caerphilly Castle* as soon as we found ourselves in port, a vow dependent on us not getting our throats cut first. While underway, Wales and I took turns sleeping to guard against assassins and had the vessel not been such a brisk one, we would have died of thirst and starvation along with the rest of the worthless crew. When we straggled ashore, I ate a hearty meal then made good on my vow to kill that mutineer LaPlaga, sticking a note on his chest that read 'I have more knives and plenty of paper' in case his mates got up the gall to come after us. But remind me to tell you about the treasure, lest I forget. I'm an old pirate, a thing as rare as a two-headed calf."

He looked off at something in the distance. He was enjoying a memory.

"Harry, you always worked hard and minded your own affairs but when ye helped find the Vicar's killer and saved the Albino, that put you near the top. That Fly was a shit wasn't he? Did Wales ever tell you they gave Fly a musket ball for his pistol when he was marooned?" I nodded to indicate I had been made aware. He raised his ale in tribute to the trick, not to the murderer.

"So you enjoyed the whores in New Barcelona and got yourself pissed. You do recall that much, right?" His sudden change in course threw me off balance.

"Valentine, please do keep your voice down. Yes, I remember. That was not me at my best." I could see Gertie and Charlotte like it was yesterday but asked Valentine how my bungled revelry had any bearing on Wales and the treasure.

He raised his palm to silence me, then pointed to his empty mug, his white eyebrows moving like excited caterpillars. I refilled it and promised I would listen.

"Thank you Harry. You remember when we left New Barcelona to hunt down the French ship, the *Trident* if I am not mistaken, and we bagged that unlucky governor only to return to New Barcelona. I went out one balmy night with the Lords and we were in some dingy tavern deciding which whore was the ugliest. It was a close call that. All in good fun. Some English speaking man, not a pirate, but he looked like a man of the sea, approached our table and asked us if we knew anyone named Harry. Not knowing who or what he was, we advised that it was of no concern to him if we did and to shove off. He persisted and produced a letter. It was recognized as yours and one of the Lords, Lutwidge I suspect, read the letter aloud. The stranger said he found it and thought it might be of importance. Realizing his service to you in bringing us the letter, we thanked him, gave him some pieces of eight for his persistence and he touched his forelock and left, never to be seen again. Nice man by the way. I'm sure the stranger did not give us the letter for a reward but how is one to know?"

At last, the mystery of the letter. Oh how I wished Constance had not gone to Boston. The hour was late, the pub was empty and all was quiet.

"You are wondering where he found your letter. He didn't say, we didn't ask. He may have found it in the street, in the gutter, or rolled up tightly and shoved up your ass. But it said Constance Sacker, Boston. It said she might be having your child. This touched us Harry. We are hard men but we are not unfeeling. We drank to babies, Constance, Boston, and to the Vicar and the Albino. We drank to the damnation of King George and we drank to the finest navigator since William Dampier. That would be you of course. You remember how that all goes. As we were making these glorious and endless toasts, Wales suggested we make contributions to send your letter on to Boston. I said if one goes in we all go in and all for the first mate, our beloved Harry Glasby. You can imagine how we were, after all that drink.

The merry five of us each put down a gold doubloon. That letter was sent my good man and given the sizeable sum we put toward that end, I must ask, did the letter reach your Constance?" He rhythmically thumped the table with his knuckles to emphasize the last few words. He stared at me and waited. Mr. Ashplant had been wondering about the fate of my letter for over thirty-five years, a wonder we had shared.

I guffawed, tossed back my head and clapped my hands making a sharp retort. "It surely did Valentine, it most surely did. How utterly amazed I am. We have been wanting to know how that letter got to Constance since 1722. You might have come by sooner." He slapped my knee and let out a long whistle through a gap in his tobacco-stained front teeth. He was quite tickled. Then a slight shadow fell over his face and I knew he was probably thinking about Wales and the men who tossed their doubloons on the table to pay the freight on that indestructible piece of paper.

I told him, "my belated thanks to you and all the Lords for the thoughtful generosity." The shadow lifted and he said "to old mates" and smiled thinly to let me know everything was fine.

"I would've come sooner but I've been busy. That letter is how I was able to find you, Mr. Harry Prescott. I landed in Boston yesterday, asking for Constance Sacker or anyone named Glasby. Happy you did not move to Philadelphia or Canada or St. Kitts. Marblehead might be a nice place to visit but I digress. Your Miss Constance was not so hard to find and I came on up from Boston. When some nice local woman told me I would find Constance and 'her Harry' at The Prince of Wales, I knew I was on the right path. When the same woman told me Constance married Harry Prescott, now I did have a painful twinge of concern you might have vanished or died. How was I to know, maybe Constance was in the habit of falling in love with men named Harry? You see, women do tend to love a man named Valentine, so I've seen how that works. We're going to need more ale." He slid his mug toward me. He was enjoying himself.

His mug refilled, I slid it back to him, "we have plenty of ale but don't drink too much more before you tell me why you saved me." I was anxious to know and leaned forward with my forearms on the table, my fingers locked in front of me.

Sipping the froth off his ale, he looked at me over the lip of his mug. He had that mischievous look in his eye. He sat it down, licked his lips and cocked his head a little to starboard. "Wales said you always suspected him or Roberts put me up to it. That's not how it was. Roberts and I respected each other but I did not weep when I learned of his demise. It's simple. You were and are a good man. We were not. You had a woman who loved you and a baby who, God willing, would survive to need you. It was not right that we made you our prisoner, that was evil right there sir. I would have killed the first man who raised a hand to you that day or any other. When I laid my pistols down to bring the point home, the men knew Valentine Ashplant was not someone to trifle with, pardon the boast. I don't think I did it for you or your baby or Constance. I did it for me. I did it so I could say I was not all bad. You see?"

His words moved me for I knew them to be true and heartfelt. As always, whenever he said a thing his words were cloaked in veracity and backed by resolve as hard as black mahogany. It was that way at my trial and remained so as he spoke to me at the pub. Had he told me he was riding back to Boston on a unicorn I would have offered him a bucket of oats, believing him wholly incapable of telling a lie.

"Look about you Valentine. I would not be here were it not for you. All men are bad and good in some combination. None who says he is all one or the other is being honest. Some men claim to be all good. Men who make such a claim are among the very worst. They lie to themselves and they lie to us. Even the worst among us has some remnant of good. Well, except men like the headless Diamond, and maybe that Plague fellow, but you see my proposition. You did a good thing my friend. And it warms my heart to say so." We sat in relaxed silence for a minute or two.

I excused myself and brought over more tobacco and lit a pipe and drank some cider. Valentine asked me to explain what I meant when I mentioned the headless Diamond and I told him the story of how Diamond led the rabble who burned the *Porcupine.* Mr. Ashplant had left the *Royal Fortune* and was unaware of the details of that debacle. After I told Mr. Ashplant about Cheddar tossing Starling's head into the sea, he raised his glass and said heartily, "to Cheddar." After we put down our tankards, Valentine added thoughtfully, "Diamond was a right dirty shit but see Harry, he proves the truth of your observation. Thanks to him, we have a good story to tell." I told him I was in agreement and excused myself to answer nature's call and brought back more tapered candles.

"Oh, the treasure," he blurted it like he'd touched his finger to a burning linstock. It was a good thing we were alone.

"Wales and I left the *Caerphilly Castle* behind the moment our feet hit the fine white sand in Nassau. We helped ourselves to all the loot we could grab to give that worthless crew a reason to remember us. It was not much but we had it and they did not, damn them all to the fires below. Of all the murderous bastards you knew, Wales and me took the King's pardon so we could go about our plan without waking up at night with dreams of the halter. You'd be amazed at the number of former friends you had in Nassau. Quietly, mind you, Wales and I found a small vessel to take us straightaway to Hispaniola. He took me ashore at that little tiny fishing village. We found the hole made by the dearly departed Jennings and Burgess. Wales had told me all about them, and he told me about you. He told me that unless by some unforeseen once in a lifetime chance the treasure had been taken by strangers, that hole held wealth beyond imagining. I used to tell him he had a low opinion of my imagination. We were strong men back then. He carried two bags and I carried two more. They were heavy. Those bags were damned heavy. We left you mere crumbs Glasby. And for some insane reason, a book." He took a long drink and watched me.

He watched me for good reason. My jaw hung agape at what he had told me about the treasure.

"You said you left mere crumbs?"

"I'm *not* saying we were unable to carry all the loot in that hole. I'm saying that what you found was just a small portion of the entire treasure. It was our gift to you. Wales and I went to Barbados and got women, loads of 'em. We made enough cream and coffee colored children to man a sloop—maybe two. We got bored with all that whorin' and we bought a sugar plantation. We made sugar and rum. Sounds heavenly don't it? I can still smell the hot juice of the sugar cane when we boiled it, had the smell of freshly minted money. Without much warning or lament, Wales died, as must we all. He died happy. Very happy. Very rich. I promised Wales if he died first, I'd find ye and make sure you were doing well. Had your dear and constant friend Valentine died first, it would be Wales sitting here telling you how happy and rich I was on my deathbed. I believe I've got a few years left. But you see, Wales left you that last bag for the same reason I saved your life. All of us need a little redemption now and again. So, here's to Wales. He had more good in him than he knew. But none of us were as good as you Glasby." Valentine winked. The Navy deserter, righteous murderer, retired pirate and prosperous plantation owner came all this way to find me and to deliver this incredible story and having done so, unbridled happiness radiated from his face.

My eyes welled up at the memories and the kind heart of these old rogues who had been called heartless by many and for ample reasons. The miracle of the lost letter, my trial, the treasure, it was all connected.

The mood had grown somber and there were many things I wanted to ask and many more I wanted to share.

"Valentine, can you tell me what it was that drove a wedge between you and Captain Roberts?" He stared into his mug and I worried I may have overstepped.

"Harry, how strange you should use the word wedge. No man alive knows why I became a pirate. The only other man who knew just died. I was born under another name and under that name I faithfully served in the Royal Navy until the war with France and Spain came to an end. In 1715, I still served and had taken a young and beautiful wife of reputable but humble origins. She was the world to me. Our bosun made lewd remarks about her but he was senior to me and I held my tongue. He was crude, corrupt, cruel and cowardly. To obtain authority over others, he also had to be conniving. Late one night, she left me on the ship and the bosun followed her. He raped her. To avoid the halter, he strangled her. There were no witnesses but everyone knew it was him. After that night, the bastard went out of his way to avoid me and never said another word about her. He knew I knew and he was petrified with fear. I decided to wait and that waiting was the hardest thing, by far, I've ever done. We finally sailed to St. Kitts which England had just taken from the French. While underway, I killed that worthless shit in my dreams every night. When we were in St. Kitts, I was slipped away and got ashore. I waylaid that murdering raping bastard and carved him into bits and pieces. He died slowly but not slowly enough. I made him confess, then I made him beg. Fuckin' coward, snivellin' cryin' coward. I got my revenge, so waited for them to come for me, knowin' I would hang. What did I have left to live for? But the ship set sail and left me behind. Maybe they were happy to be rid of that bosun, who knows? I aimlessly wandered Nassau for a few days, living off scraps, my mind clouded by fog. A curious seafaring man saw splotches of dried blood all over my clothes. With no Royal Navy ships in port, the cut of my clothes and the blood stains suggested I was probably a deserter with a knack for finding trouble. At any rate, I was a wreck. The big man offered me a drink and escorted me into the nearest tavern. He asked if I'd been injured in some grievous way. When I told him I gutted the man who raped and murdered my wife, he complimented me and bought me another. He asked me more questions and pointed to a vessel in the harbor, saying he had a good captain and they could use a man with my talents. It was not my blood on my clothes and I think the man knew that all along. Next thing you know, I was a pirate."

Valentine said nothing about wedges but I absorbed what he said and felt great sympathy for him. I tried to imagine his pain and his anger and knew I could not.

"I'd like to tell you I sailed with Edward Teach, the great Blackbeard, but friends do not lie to friends. No, my first captain was Charles Vane. I left his crew to join Captain Roberts because Vane was too vicious for yours truly. Roberts was new to the life and I found his temperament more to my liking. Having signed the Articles in New Providence, we left the Bahamas to do what pirates do. The Lords welcomed me and I believed I'd found a home. To me, Roberts, with his magisterial air, for I do not know how else to describe him, was the Lord of Lords. He was wholly unlike Vane and my loyalty to Captain Roberts was, or so I thought, limitless."

I averred that I had heard enough about Charles Vane to understand and softly urged Valentine to continue.

"We were hunting near the coast of South America and came upon a fleet of forty-two Portuguese merchantmen near the Bay of Los Todos Santos. We were to learn that warships were en route to join the fleet and escort it to Lisbon. You can guess what the bold Captain Roberts did. He came right alongside the nearest ship and made it clear to the surprised captain that if his crew made any sign of warning, he and his men would be put to the sword. The trembling captain was brought onto our vessel and interrogated by Roberts, as we Lords in respectful silence watched the master work his magic. The richest prize in the fleet was a huge ship manned by 150 men, carrying forty heavy guns. Roberts was able to determine these important details by his clever questioning of the Portuguese captain. With that talkative fellow as our hostage, we swiftly sailed within shouting distance of the enormous prize. I kept telling myself there is no way any of us will survive this audacious plan. Our hostage called out to his fellow captain, inviting him to come aboard. The latter wisely sensed that something was amiss, ordered his decks cleared and his gun ports flew open. On seeing this, I knew for sure we would die. In a series of maneuvers that would be the envy of any Royal Navy captain, we fired a broadside, came briskly alongside, threw over half a dozen grappling hooks and boarded her, shrieking and cursing and slashing and cutting. Wales and I were among the first to draw blood. The other merchant ships, witnessing our bold attack, attempted to signal the distant warships with cannon fire but after a furious skirmish, the great prize surrendered. We raised our fists and our bloody cutlasses, chanting "Roberts" again and again. I tell you Harry, there are few joys that compare."

Valentine's eyes were shining. He had stopped drinking and was puffing his pipe. I had heard bits and pieces of this tale but never from a participant. He was reliving the event in his mind's eye.

"We sailed away laden with sugar, hides, tobacco, gold chains and jewels. We took 90,000 gold moidores and to top it off, we relieved the King of Portugal of a lavish gift he was never to receive.

A large cross encrusted with diamonds and suspended on a thick chain of solid gold. It was exquisite."

Indeed, it was priceless but worse, it had gone missing. "Forgive me Valentine but Captain Roberts was wearing that cross the day he died. Captain Ogle asked me many questions about it which I could not answer. It seems that no one would admit to seeing it, hiding it or seizing it. I am certain it did not go over the side with the captain's body. But the cross aside, the haul from a prize of this magnitude would've been more than Burgess and Jennings could have carried during their escape. Roberts seized over four hundred ships. By my reckoning, no two men could have left the ship carrying so much treasure."

I was beginning to realize that Wales probably did tell Roberts the true extent of the theft. Burgess and Jennings had carried off the jewels and as much gold and silver as they could carry. What they had to leave behind was significant but the most valuable part of the ship's treasure had been taken and the blame for such a catastrophic loss had to fall on Wales. Wales told me where he thought the loot was buried but when he said it was two bags he was being less than forthright. I thought again of the islanders paid to watch for Burgess and Jennings. They never said a word about *bags* but then why would they? They would not have known what the fleeing pirates carried and if they suspected anything, they would have waited for the men to go inland, ambushed them and taken whatever the bags contained. But Burgess and Jennings, uncharacteristically, had the presence of mind to dig a hole and bury the bags. When they were captured, Wales and Roberts were the only ones who knew the truth.

As I grappled with the enormity of all this, Valentine went on. His thoughts were still on the Portuguese merchant ship.

"Harry, you remember how hard Captain Roberts took it when Seahorse was killed by the French?"

"Of course," I said.

"I know of no sea captain, pirate or otherwise, who could've done what Roberts did that day. Sailing into the very heart of that massive fleet and stealing enough treasure for a lifetime in one brisk and swift action. Even better, the warships who were to be the escorts were just over the horizon. Our vessel was lighter and faster and Roberts knew we could out distance them. Sometimes the truth is so amazing men refuse to believe it. We should have taken that rich and glorious plunder and fled."

Valentine stood up. He was not hesitant to finish his story, he just had to approach it properly. He grabbed a bony elbow in one hand and twisted at the waist, then switched hands and did it a second time.

He slowly shook his head and sat down. "There were two things, I think, that held us there a few minutes more. Roberts was enraged at the captain for not surrendering to us immediately. We lost men, a few, men you never knew. Some of them were good men. More of us were hurt but none mortally. The other thing, and this is just me trying to make sense of it all, the other thing is Roberts and the crew. He was still new. I believe he did what he did to make an impression on the men. Which he did. That much is beyond question Harry. Captain Roberts ordered me and Neptune to bring the Portuguese captain of the massive prize ship up to our quarterdeck. Other men held the rest of our mortified prisoners at bay but all eyes were on us, transfixed. Captain Roberts ordered someone to fetch a deadeye, some small wedges and a mallet. It took no time to procure a deadeye but while someone hunted up the wedges, Roberts began making a speech about defiant captains and boasted about his fearsome crew and his word. When the wedges and a mallet were handed to him, he stopped his lecturing and ordered me to hold the captain's finger in one of the holes of the deadeye."

Knowing where this was going, I told Valentine he could stop.

"No Harry, I could not stop even if I wanted to. Roberts drove in a wedge, pinning the man's finger in the hole. He then shouted, 'what does a smart captain do when he meets Bartholomew Roberts?' The first and second time, I truly think the man was so horrified he could not think. He pissed himself and stared at his bleeding finger and moaned 'sir, I don't know.' Roberts hammered in another wedge, repeating his question. Finally, the answer dawned on the man and he screamed 'surrender'. I lost count of the wedges but for each one used to crush the man's finger, he screamed 'surrender' until he could shout and shriek no more. The crying broken man begged me to bring this madness to a halt. I was still holding him but I did nothing."

Valentine was looking me squarely in the eye but my only discomfort was for him.

"Roberts waved his arms in triumph and bid us throw the crumpled captain into the sea. Without thinking, for that is often how a man responds to commands, we did as we were ordered. I just wanted the torture to stop. We dropped the captain feet first, his mangled finger, reduced to a splintered bone, was still stuck in that damned deadeye. The wood floated momentarily, blood seeping into the water. The man lowered his head, filled his lungs and I watched as he slowly descended until he was out of sight. When I could see him no more, a mass of bubbles broke the surface. I still see that poor chap's twisted face late at night when I wake up, drenched in a cold sweat. Roberts told the dumbfounded Portuguese sailors to carry the word to every port in the old world and the new. Defy Bartholomew Roberts and die. Those were his words, that was his message, his admonition."

I did not know what to say but I had to say something. "So, you avoided Roberts from that day on?"

Valentine looked at me with his watery eyes, his heavy lids drooping, and said matter of factly, "wouldn't you?"

"Yes, I suppose so."

He smiled to tell me it was alright. "After that day, I loyally served the captain but we hardly ever spoke. He knew why. The other Lords did too and that was fine. You see Harry, when a man does things like that, terrible things, his need to do something good becomes an obsession. I'm glad I told you about the wedges. You're a good listener."

He drank and we smoked and we talked. I told him about the dungeon and the trial at the Cape Coast Castle. Mr. Ashplant cried tears of laughter and sadness when I told him about Lord Lutwidge and his performance on the scaffold. I told him what I knew about the last words and deeds of many other men he considered friends. He told me some stories about Papi I'd never heard and we poured a bit of rum and drank a toast to Papi and the musicians.

Valentine was intrigued about my walk in the garden with Captain Ogle and was aware of the knighthood and renown that followed Ogle the rest of his days. He enjoyed hearing about the kind surgeon, John Atkins and we talked a while about the slaves who worked the sugar plantation Wales and Mr. Ashplant owned in Barbados.

We laughed about Wales having trouble burning fishing nets and the book he carefully put in the hole.

There were no recriminations, no regrets, just two men letting go of a few old ghosts. When the sun was peeking up, I insisted Valentine stay and wait for Constance to return. He insisted that I allow him to be on his way. On parting, we held each other like long lost brothers. Which we were, in a way. When he spoke out at my trial and said he loved me, he saved my life. When he left The Prince of Wales and Marblehead for parts unknown, I told him I loved him too.

While our final understanding was unspoken, we knew this was to be our last meeting.

After he left, I sat and enjoyed some much needed coffee. I kept thinking about Wales and the stolen treasure. Wales informed the captain of the magnitude of the theft but failed to tell him the thieves had drunkenly given up directions which might lead to its recovery. To protect Wales from the wrath of the crew, Captain Roberts kept the secret. Wales lied to me about how much was stolen but trusted me enough to give me directions to the treasure in the event he died. When Ogle captured the *Royal Fortune*, all he could find was the Whydah gold and a few silver coins, which explained why he inquired about the grandiose Portuguese cross of diamonds.

During the Battle of Cape Lopez, the conniving Captain Hill and the crew of the *Neptune* stripped the lightly guarded *Little Ranger* of all the sea chests stowed aboard. Everyone, to include grieving pirates and ambitious Royal Navy officers, assumed the bulk of the treasure amassed by Bartholomew Roberts had been stolen by Hill. Not so. The bulk of the treasure had been stolen by Burgess and Jennings and lay nestled in a hole on the island of Hispaniola. When I say 'bulk', I do not mean hundreds of pounds in gold and silver. It would have taken a dozen men to move that much plunder from ship to shore. I mean the most valuable items—ten or twenty pounds of emeralds, fifteen or twenty pounds of diamonds, who knows how many pounds of pearls, and the list goes on—with assorted gold and silver coins for good measure.

One would rightly conclude that Burgess and Jennings were in a hurry when they pillaged the ship's treasure but despite that and their woeful lack of foresight, they knew that a pound of diamonds beats a pound of silver every time. They acted accordingly and when Valentine said Wales left me the crumbs, it was an epiphany.

By keeping the route to the treasure to himself, Wales betrayed his captain. There is no other explanation. As I ponder this business with my eyes wide open, Wales could have avoided taking command of the *Caerphilly Castle* as he was not forced to become its captain. With all due respect to Mr. Ashplant, I believed his story about LaPlaga and the mutiny but Wales was a forceful, brave and intelligent man. Could Wales have stopped the chain of events that took him away from us, leaving Captain Roberts alone to face the Royal Navy? What might have been the fate of the *Swallow* if we had fought with the assistance of Wales, his sleek ship and his additional guns? When Wales was unseated by his unruly men, was he unable to commandeer a longboat which he and Mr. Ashplant could have used to get back to the *Royal Fortune*? I must say, some of these questions had occurred to me before.

I had judged Wales with undue leniency.

But I had also judged Bartholomew Roberts too harshly.

Being young, I lacked experience and perspective. You might allege, after hearing the story of the deadeye and the wedges, that Roberts was brimming over with bloodlust and as ruthless as any so called gentleman rover facing the high gallows and the short leash. All the songs and ditties in the world do not make a murderous pirate someone to view with anything but disdain.

Valentine spoke directly and with admirable verisimilitude such that I doubted not one word of the stories he shared that night at the pub. If he ever had reason to lie or shade the truth, that reason evaporated long ago.

I am in Mr. Ashplant's debt for saving me from execution but I appreciate the troubles he overcame to find me and I absolutely cherish what he told me that night, more than he could possibly know. I witnessed the horrors Roberts was capable of when we took the *Trident*. Whether he was sending a message or avenging the death of Seahorse, it is unlikely if even Roberts knew. As I look back, I know it was impossible for me to be a dispassionate judge of the man who kidnapped me.

When Roberts picked up the gauntlet to challenge the *Swallow* to a duel at sea, it surprised none who knew him. This was how he always met adversity, head on, with alacrity and unrestrained vigor. He did it with the Portuguese merchant fleet, the ships in Newfoundland, he did it when he attacked the *Trident* and in Whydah and these are just a few examples *among many*. His presence of mind, his intellect, his bravery, his ability to think when someone held a knife to his throat, few men like this have ever lived. In my frustration, anger and resentment, I believed Roberts when he told me he'd made his choice. He would never quit. How many times had I heard him say, "a short life but a merry one for me".

I believed he was challenging the *Swallow* solely to chastise his unruly, lazy, and ungrateful crew. I thought he was doing it to teach them a lesson which made sense to me *at the time*. The crew was all that, but even when half of them were drunk, I was still despondent that the ever resilient Roberts, the man they said was *pistol proof*, would figure out a way to win and we would live to fight another day.

But thanks to Valentine Ashplant, this is what I know now.

Captain Roberts had a trusted quartermaster whose primary tasks included keeping the ship's treasure safe and secure. The quartermaster fell short and by his unquestioned failure to take more effective security measures, most of the plunder was stolen by a pair of imbeciles. To protect his quartermaster, Captain Roberts kept the truth from the crew. We can never know if the crew would have tried to harm Wales but one must assume it was likely. One must also recognize that Roberts would forfeit his position as captain if the crew had known the truth and he would never, ever have allowed the crew to kill Wales, whether he was captain or not. The only way to remain as captain and to protect Wales was to get the treasure back or replace the losses with more loot. Wales deviously betrayed the captain by not telling him about the location of the buried treasure and a very serious and unforgivable betrayal it was.

Based on what Roberts knew, that left him one option, replace the lost treasure.

Roberts could not know before the fact that Wales and the *Caerphilly Castle* would vanish, never to be seen again. We all had hopes, which eventually faded, that our beloved Wales might return. Meanwhile, despite the crippling loss of Wales, Captain Roberts still had one clear path. Take more prizes, seize more loot, replace the lost treasure.

I had also discerned a more fundamental truth that had little to do with gold and jewels. Roberts loved being a pirate captain. He relished it for its own sake and cared little about gold and silver.

I believe now that Captain Roberts did what he did, at least in part, for the crew but beyond that, he did it to protect himself and Wales. Roberts would never surrender, it wasn't in him. Moreover, he was not, as I used to believe, simply trying to teach his surly crew a lesson. To a large extent, I was wrong about that and I was wrong about him. His motives were more complex. When all was said and done, Bartholomew Roberts the pirate captain claimed he was free. He was wrong about that too. He only had power as long as the crew kept him as their captain and everything he did was driven by his need to be their unquestioned king. Because Roberts could be deposed on a collective whim, one can argue that Captain Roberts was a prisoner of the crew in everything but name.

There was something else, one more ghost if you will, a ghost of my own that I was sorely tempted to introduce to Mr. Ashplant. As that night wore on and we confided in each other, knowing I would never see Mr. Ashplant again, the desire to make my confession was never stronger. Luckily, I suppose, the strongest thing I drank beside the small glass of rum was a tankard of cider.

My last lingering ghost did not escape.

I told you that there are things that haunt me still.

You will recall that Royal Navy Captain Chaloner Ogle reported the sea battle between the *Swallow* and the *Royal Fortune* occurred in crashing thunder and sheets of lightening with "small tornados". The dispatches written by Ogle and his subordinates would have been sufficiently dramatic without these flourishes and embellishments. I was there. I tell you it was raining, a light rain no less. I doubt if there was enough rain on the deck to fill the scuppers. The only thunder came from the guns and as for sheets of lightening, pure fiction. The *official* reports also said Bartholomew Roberts had his "throat torn out" by grapeshot fired in the *last* volley from the *Swallow's* guns.

Roberts did fall and grapeshot was fired from the British warship but by far, most of the ammunition fired at us was solid shot with sporadic chain shot fired into the rigging. The goal of the Royal Navy was to disable the *Royal Fortune*, not sink it. Ogle wanted an intact ship to sail into port as a valuable prize.

Few shots struck our hull and the primary purpose of grapeshot is to clear the decks of personnel just prior to boarding. There was still considerable distance between the two vessels and we were returning fire. We never had a boarding party assembled on our deck. Consequently, there was never any reason for our foe to fire grapeshot. After Roberts fell, there were more broadsides, so that portion of the report saying it was the *last broadside* is clearly inaccurate, but one must admire the drama in it.

No one from the *Swallow* saw Captain Roberts' body, much less the fatal wound in his neck.

Pirate Stephenson, busy at the helm, saw Roberts fall over a gun carriage and his first impulse was to urge him to stand up and "fight like a man". By implication, Stephenson did not actually see Captain Roberts wounded and he never claimed that he did. When it dawned on Stephenson that Roberts was injured, he stopped berating Roberts for malingering. If our decks were in fact being peppered with grapeshot, the helmsman would likely conclude that Roberts had been hit but as I said, there was *no grapeshot being fired*. Naturally, when he realized his captain lay wounded, Stephenson rushed to Roberts, knelt down, saw the hole and looked up tearfully saying "grapeshot". Men near enough to hear these remarks were stunned by the loss of their captain, as one would expect. They did not question Stephenson about the source of the wound and why would they? We were, after all, under attack from a British man o' war and they had marksmen firing from their rigging using muskets.

The hole in Captain Roberts' neck did not "tear away his throat". That was purely added color flowing from the quills of the imaginative authors of the naval communiqués.

After the governor of Martinique was hanged and as I recoiled in disgust at the bloody carnage involving the French captives, I resolved to escape and find my way to return to Boston, come what may. What I had to do to make good on that resolve was not borne of spite or malice but as the Battle of Cape Lopez ebbed and flowed, Roberts was steadily gaining the upper hand, *as he always did*. The Royal Navy represented my greatest hope of salvation but only if we were defeated. I'd never signed the Articles, carried a weapon or in any way aided the pirates in boarding a vessel or seizing plunder and I was willing to take the chance that an Admiralty court would set me free.

Even if I had shared the truth with the good Captain Ogle, I suspect the authorities would have determined that my actions were justified and thus lawful—but under no circumstances could anyone on the crew of the *Royal Fortune* or any man who had ever served under Roberts know about the decision I made. Pirates and vengeance are inseparable. That is why I could not bring myself to tell Mr. Ashplant. Constance does not know, nor will I tell her. I could not bear the thought of either of these who are so dear to me thinking ill of me for what I did. For what I had to do.

I am nearly eighty. The burden I have carried since February 10, 1722 has grown intolerably heavy. The Royal Navy fell in love with their version of the great triumph too completely to accept something as mundane as the truth and theirs is the tale known to the world.

The legend of Black Bart's glorious death in battle is based on assumptions, exaggerations and outright lies.

Bartholomew Roberts writhed on the deck of the *Royal Fortune*, blood poured from a round hole in his neck as men he had long commanded watched the life flow out of him. As he stood at the rail with his back to me, he had shoved his pistols in the pockets of his long frock coat to keep them dry, as I knew he would as long as the drizzle persisted. While cannons roared and shot tore through the sails and the rigging, I reached into his pocket, withdrew one of his pistols and cocked it. I held it to his neck. He turned his head to see what I was doing. I saw the unmistakable look of resignation in his eyes as the pistol in my shaking hand was leveled, inches away.

He knew he was not pistol proof. So did I.

I squinted, grit my teeth, pulled the trigger, and prayed to almighty God that it would fire despite the rain. One of us had to die.

The Vicar, the day before his murder, had scrawled a Bible verse on a scrap of paper and presented it to me like a proud schoolboy.

He told me it would bring me good fortune one day but only if I believed.

I carried that little bit of scripture in the hold of the *Swallow*, down into the dungeon, and I held it in my pocket and touched it when I strolled through the gardens with Captain Ogle. I kept it on my person during the trial at the Cape Coast Castle and read it over and over again after getting to know John Atkins when we sailed to Port Royal. I still read it long after it was etched in my memory.

When I discovered the treasure on Hispaniola, I carefully put the piece of faded parchment in the bottom of the hole and pushed some dirt on it, saying a quick prayer of thanksgiving and some kind words for the spirit of the peaceful man who had given me so much hope during his short life.

The Vicar's childish scrawl was barely legible.

It read, "He sent from above, he took me, he drew me out of many waters. He delivered me from my strong enemy, and from them which hated me: for they were too strong for me." It may be found in Psalms, Chapter Eighteen.

That piece of paper was in my pocket when I killed Bartholomew Roberts. I shot the pirate who wielded power over me, believing then, as I do now, that it was the only way I could regain my freedom.

What I have told you is the truth and may God forgive me.

The Vicar said if I believed, I would be saved.

I believed.

Acknowledgements

FOR GIVING ME BOOKS AT a young age and the love of what is in them, I thank my mother, Margaret Drescher. Mom, I hope you enjoy this one. I love you.

Thanks to those who read the short story that became *Glasby's Fortune;* Mark Gilroy, Rob Williams, Bethany Sims and Patrick Landrum. To everyone who encouraged me during this adventure, Fred Kane, Sean Martin, Brian Hill, Austin Hough, Jamie Starling, Javier LaFontaine Delgado, Brent Campbell and Kevin Sharp, your support is deeply appreciated. As to those who mumbled at one time or another "whatever you do, don't ask Jay about pirates," you made me laugh and for that I am grateful.

For countless insights and valued friendship, thanks to Clay Stafford and everyone at www.killernashville.com, including Anne Perry, Robert Dugoni, Michael Connelly, Dr. Bill Bass and all the volunteers, attendees and authors who share a passion for great storytelling. It was great fun writing the murder mystery involving the Vicar and the Albino and letting Harry be the sleuth who solves the crime.

Without a navigator, a ship is lost. To my editor, Sidney Frost—you saved me from running aground more than once and your astute suggestions were worth their weight in gold.

To my incredible daughters Taylor and Madeline and my equally incredible son Joe, I hope you know how proud I am to be your father.

For believing in me and giving me the time to do what I want to do instead of what I should be doing, my wife Amy Drescher deserves something far more than thanks. Life is about choices and she is the best choice I ever made.

Historical Note

PIRATE LORE IS A BLEND of fact and fiction. So is this novel.

I came upon Harry Glasby quite by accident; his kidnapping, his bungled escape attempt and the trial where he was saved by a pistol-packing pirate with the tantalizing name of Valentine Ashplant.

Reading on, I wondered why Bartholomew Roberts, a flamboyant brigand who went down in battle, in a raging storm no less, was not among that cadre of infamous pirates known to all.

In the midst of this, I discovered a compelling story. Adventure, conflict, tragedy and redemption. Dramatic trials aboard pirate ships and Admiralty courts, replete with twists, turns, and suspense. Even the mock pirate trial of Chamberpot, the one which resulted in a near riot, comes to us from the historical record.

As a devotee of historical fiction, I saw a cavalcade of larger-than-life characters parade across the stage. On a whim, I penned a short story, which I shared with a few close friends. That tentative effort evolved into this book.

During the process, I resolved to favor real events whenever possible and did my utmost to avoid myths, stereotypes and clichés. There were undoubtedly pirates with wooden legs or those with an eye patch; but when telling a story about pirates, mythology sits on your shoulder like a large parrot. Even if you can keep the parrot quiet, he must be fed from time to time.

The legends that permeate the world of pirates arose long before Bartholomew Roberts was reverently lowered over the gunwale of the *Royal Fortune* into the waters off the Guinea Coast. In fact, Roberts would have known many of these stirring stories as a boy growing up in Wales.

What of real pirates then?

Piracy was and is big business, albeit one with great risks for the participants. Torture, murder and terror have always been crucial components of their *modus operandi.* Contemporary pirates, in addition to seizing ships and cargo, still kidnap passengers and crew, holding them for long periods of time and demanding huge ransom payments as a condition of their release.

We can fairly say when it comes to piracy and modern forms of slavery, there is nothing new under the sun.

As for pirates of the Caribbean in the days of sail, the image of a swashbuckling and quick-witted rogue goes back to the seventeenth century.

Alexander O. Exquemelin sailed with pirates with the intention of reporting his experiences. His book, *History of the Bouccaneers of America,* was first published in Holland in 1678. Due to widespread popularity, it was quickly translated from Dutch into several languages.

A more influential book arrived in 1724, two years after the death of Bartholomew Roberts. *A General History of the Robberies and Murders of the Most Notorious Pyrates,* by Captain Charles Johnson, was in its fourth edition by 1726. There is a lively controversy about the true identity of the author and many contend it was Daniel Dafoe. Whoever he was, the writer had access to a tremendous amount of information about pirates. The illustrated book, consisting of two volumes, did much to create a vivid and familiar image of pirates, an image that embodies their free-wheeling lifestyle, devil-may-care attitude and even their distinctive attire.

The average person in 1724 could neither read nor afford expensive books but books were not the only means of satisfying the public's interest in piracy.

When Captain Chaloner Ogle escorted Harry through the lush gardens outside the Cape Coast Castle, he mentioned a play, *The Successful Pirate*, by Charles Johnson. It was first performed in 1712 on Drury Lane in London. The playwright does not appear to have any connection with the aforementioned Captain Charles Johnson. The play was controversial because it allegedly glamorized the life of pirate Henry Avery. Of course, the controversy increased ticket sales.

Years after the fact, the era of the 'most notorious pyrates' was dubbed The Golden Age of Piracy and many contend it ended with the death of Bartholomew Roberts. Between 1716 and 1726, the authorities hanged between 400 and 600 of the estimated 2,000 pirates who prowled the Caribbean and the Guinea Coast. Yet numerous trials and very public executions made many of these men, and a small number of women, into minor celebrities.

As for Glasby's ordeal, the historical details, in my view, provide the tale with its heart and soul, or, if you prefer, its bones. The following examples are illustrative but by no means exhaustive.

Roberts shot a member of his crew in the face for insulting him. When Jones sought revenge by attacking Roberts, he was tried, found guilty and flogged, receiving two lashes from each member of the crew. Jones deserted along with some of his friends at the first opportunity.

Captain James Skyrm, in command of the *Ranger*, had his lower leg shot off in the battle with *HMS Swallow*. He stubbornly remained at his post, fought on and survived captivity in the ship's crowded and fetid hold and then languished in the fortress dungeon, only to be held upright by two soldiers as he was hanged. In different circumstances, a man with this much fortitude would have been awarded a medal for bravery.

It's hard to imagine a more dramatic scene than the meeting between Roberts and the Governor of Martinique, Florimond Hurault de Montigny. The confrontation took place on a powerful French warship of fifty-two guns. Not only did Roberts hang the Governor, he sun-dried his victim as described. The murder had foreseeable consequences; it increased the zeal of the French Navy and the Royal Navy to bring Roberts to justice.

Allowances and deviations had to be made in order to weave these events into a work of historical fiction.

During his career, Roberts had six different vessels. To streamline the narrative and avoid confusion, the number was reduced. The chronology of events was amended but sparingly.

But back to history.

When Roberts captured the frigate *Onslow*, among the crewmen who volunteered to turn pirate was a seaman Stephenson. Stephenson was at the helm of the *Royal Fortune* during the battle with *HMS Swallow* and it was Stephenson who chastised the wounded Roberts for malingering when Roberts fell. Stephenson was among the fifty-two men hanged at the Cape Coast Castle. You may recall that during the four week trial fifty-four pirates were condemned to death and two of these were reprieved. If you can identify this fortunate pair, please let us know.

Royal Navy deserter Armstrong, who also turned pirate, recognized the *Swallow* and shouted the alarm. He was a real person. Some sources say he was from the *Swallow*, others the *Weymouth*.

As the crew of the latter died of disease, men from the former were transferred to take their place. How Armstrong ended up on the *Royal Fortune* is a mystery. He was hanged from the yardarm of the *Swallow*, the traditional Royal Navy method for executing deserters. He was thirty-four.

Information about Captain Chaloner Ogle, his knighthood and eventual promotion to admiral, among other things, is well-documented. He illicitly kept eighty pounds of gold dust Roberts had taken in the bold raid on Whydah. One surmises Ogle felt confident he could get away with it but his behavior lends credence to my theory that the official reports of his heroics were enhanced and embellished. Sometimes crime does pay.

Roberts' raid on Whydah is based on real events. Captain Fletcher of the *Porcupine* failed to pay the ransom Roberts demanded and disgruntled pirates retaliated by burning his ship, blatantly disobeying Roberts' orders. They killed eighty slaves, most of them trapped below decks and bound in chains.

Not everyone in the book is real and one of the most enjoyable aspects of this adventure was coming up with names. Wales, Cheddar and Captain Ling are to be included in the cast of fictional characters. I admire Constance Sacker and was overjoyed when she and Harry were reunited in the fish market. The Campbell ladies of Boston were very hospitable to Harry but thinking again about their devious servant girl makes me smile.

Many of the characters are named after real men and real pirates. I came across the name Lintorn Highlett, a British veteran of WWII, while reading a book by historian Naill Ferguson. It's a wonderful name and I used it for that reason. Pirate James Starling, the one called Diamond, is fictional but the story of a pirate smashing a huge diamond because his shipmates each received forty-two diamonds from a rich prize is true.

The information pertaining to the significant presence of black pirates is based on the historical record. When the Royal Navy captured the *Ranger* and the *Royal Fortune,* seventy black pirates were sold. I think it very probable that some of these men helped sail the prize ships from Africa to Jamaica.

Hurricanes and earthquakes seem to have it in for Jamaica and the destructive storm that crashed into Jamaica a few days after Glasby departed actually occurred. The hurricane drove the *Royal Fortune* and the other prizes into the rocks, reducing them to splinters. Miraculously, *HMS Swallow* survived.

HMS Weymouth, as it sailed off the disease infested coast of Africa was devastated by deadly diseases, nearly wiping out the crew. Among the victims, famed navigator Alexander Selkirk, the purported model for Robinson Crusoe. Royal Navy surgeon John Atkins survived and lived to write about his experiences. He must have been an extraordinary man.

Valentine Ashplant not only lived but lives on in history. When Harry made his escape attempt, two other men were caught and all stood trial. The jury sentenced the 'deserters' to death. Valentine Ashplant intervened and his words of warning to the crew as well as his stated love and affection for Harry may be found in the written record. How accurate these reports are is unknowable but it is easy to envision Mr. Ashplant slowly drawing his loaded pistols and laying them on the table to insure that his iron will would be obeyed. Valentine Ashplant was among the 'House of Lords' and he was in the first group to be hanged. It pains me greatly to say so. Valentine Ashplant was thirty-two when he was executed and perhaps in another version of reality, Harry interceded and saved him.

Little is known of Harry's personal life but the information about Captain Kidd, colonial witches, the Old Stone Prison, Reverend Cotton Mather and the hanging of pirates in Boston is all true.

As mentioned, I've done my best to portray pirates as accurately as possible. Pirates were virile young men who spent months at sea. The French word *matelot* means seaman or sailor. We know from the Articles that women and boys were banned from Roberts' vessels. However, same sex relationships, strictly taboo in the world at large and punishable by death in the Royal Navy, were common. Pirates had civil unions which they called *matelotage*, another French word. It is said to be the source of the word mate. In the unconventional world of pirates, men formed relationships, exchanged gold rings and married.

Matelotage was so prevalent in 1645 that the French governor of Tortuga, then a thriving pirate haven, requested that the French government ship hundreds of prostitutes to the Caribbean to remedy the problem. I do not know if the request was granted.

During the early eighteenth century, thirty percent of females in London resorted to prostitution at one time or another. Prostitutes favored pirates, not because of their sexual prowess, but due to their generosity. For these desperate women, it was about money, not sex. When Harry had his encounter with prostitutes in New Barcelona, a port city in present day Venezuela, you may recall he drank a 'rattle skull'. A rattle skull is a colonial era drink made with dark porter, rum, lime juice and ground nutmeg. I discovered the recipe on the internet and found a new use for the nutmeg in our pantry.

Jack the cat began life as a yellow calico in homage to his namesake; 'Calico Jack' Rackham. On the eve of making the final edit, our friend Beth Bower told us calico cats are almost exclusively female. Indeed, she is correct. As Harry said after his ill-fated escape attempt, a man cannot know what he does not know. Changing the color of Jack's fur was easy enough but luckily his insouciant attitude was unaffected. The flamboyant Rackham was brilliantly brought to life by actor Toby Schmitz in the STARZ production, *Black Sails*.

The series takes great liberties with history but achieves greatness in storytelling. The team who produced *Black Sails* paid homage to the real world of pirates with admirable attention to detail. *Black Sails* is a treat for anyone who likes pirates. Woodes Rogers is a prominent historical figure and he too is portrayed in *Black Sails*. While doing research on the intrepid Woodes Rogers, I learned the Rogers family motto was *dum spiro spero*. I hope my use of it would not arouse the ire of Captain Rogers or his descendants.

Finally we come to the death of Captain Roberts. While writing the first draft of the story I awoke one morning before sunrise and had an epiphany. I realized in that moment of clarity how Roberts met his end. From then on, everything about the story made sense. Part of me will forever believe there is more truth in *Glasby's Fortune* than the official reports and communiqués sent by Ogle to his superiors at the Admiralty.

Grapeshot? I wonder.

I relished my time with Harry, Captain Roberts, Valentine Ashplant, and Chaloner Ogle.

Thank you for joining us.

About The Author

JAMES 'JAY' DRESCHER GRADUATED FROM the University of Missouri-Columbia School of Law in 1982. He was a member of the Law Review, the Board of Advocates and the Order of the Coif.

As a judge advocate in the United States Marine Corps, he served in Okinawa, Japan; Parris Island, South Carolina and London, England. He has tried over forty jury trials including capital murder and was a member of the National Security Task Force in 1987 investigating and prosecuting cases arising from the Moscow USSR Embassy scandal.

Jay has been a civil litigator and trial attorney in Nashville, Tennessee since 1991. He retired from the Marine Corps Reserve as a Lieutenant Colonel in 2000. His wife, Amy Drescher, is a licensed private investigator and has been featured on local and national television news programs. Jay and Amy have three children and reside in Franklin, Tennessee.

More information is available at www.jaydrescherlaw.com

Made in the USA
Middletown, DE
09 February 2020

84292950R00227